LISBETH

Marina Brown

Published by:
Southern Yellow Pine (SYP) Publishing
4351 Natural Bridge Rd.
Tallahassee, FL 32305

www.syppublishing.com

This is a work of fiction. Names, characters, places, and events that occur either are the products of the author's imagination or are used fictitiously. Any resemblance to actual persons, places, or events is purely coincidental.

The contents and opinions expressed in this book do not necessarily reflect the views and opinions of Southern Yellow Pine Publishing, nor does the mention of brands or trade names constitute endorsement.

ISBN-10: 1-59616-530-8
ISBN-13: 978-1-59616-530-4
ISBN-13: ePub 978-1-59616-031-6
ISBN-13: Adobe eBook 978-1-59616-032-3

Library of Congress Control Number: 2017939589

Printed in the United States of America
First Edition May 2017

Praise for Marina Brown

"Thoroughly captivating and heart-wrenching…as a midlife woman seeks pieces of her own story in the web of relationships woven through the past and present. A brilliant achievement you won't be able to put down."
—Anne Barrett, PhD, Professor of Sociology and Director of the Pepper Institute on Aging and Public Policy, Florida State University.

Royal Palm Literary Awards 2016 - Judge Rubrics

* "…the author's creativity weaving together themes is unique."
* "…the use of language is wonderful and invites readers to take time to enjoy the words."
* "…there is a character here for any reader to identify with—love or hate, but want to know more about."

"A wonderfully-wrought tale of love and yearning, darkness and redemption in which Lisbeth remains an abiding enigma whose secrets ensnare two families long after her passing. Equally gothic and ghost story, but so much more, Lisbeth is a compelling mystery, a love story, and a modern morality tale told in Brown's lyrically beautiful prose."—Claire Matturro, author of the award-winning *Skinny-dipping* and *Sweetheart Deal.*

"The pages seem to turn themselves in this incredibly readable tale of the deep South and its culture. A prodigious and beautifully written accomplishment!"—Henry M. Steele, M. Div, Activist and son of Civil Rights icon, C. K. Steele.

Acknowledgements

The past is never far, especially in the South. Its mysteries have fascinated me since I sped past enclaves of old slave cabins from Mississippi to Florida and peeked through the piney forests of my youth.

My efforts at bringing that past alive have been inspired and helped by many. Some provided the coloration of their dialect; some, the way they wrinkled their nose or used their hands. Others, both real and evoked, shared with me their quests; and still others, whom I never met, left me in admiration of their sense of justice and good.

And to all those who read this manuscript, who kindled my imagination, corrected my grammar, double-checked its accuracy, and laughed at my jokes, I thank you. Michelle Jack, Carol Koutroulis, Claire Matturo, Donna Meredith, and my dear and necessary husband, Doug Kiliman, you have each provided the requisites for creating what I hope is a tale that challenges, tells the truth, and brings a joyful peace.

Other Books by Marina Brown

Land Without Mirrors
Walking Alone Together, An Anthem for Caregivers
Airport Sketches

Before

Tilley, Mississippi
Summer, 1930

Hanny Meyers actually didn't mind the heat, especially if he gunned the accelerator on the Model A to a dangerous twenty-five mph. Dodging the mule-wagons clustered at the courthouse was another thing. Still, the extra turn around the square that reaped a feminine smile or two was worth the shaking fists of locals who still distrusted automobiles, mostly because they didn't have one.

In the nineteen-thirties, Tilley, Mississippi, looked much as it had for the past hundred years. On the elevated knoll in the center of town, city fathers had erected a kind of Victorian Parthenon, a spired, silver-topped paean to government that was the hub of the city's circulation of wagons and sputtering cars. Around it, a leafy park served as a meeting ground for town dwellers or overalled farmers who came to agree or disagree with lawyers in shiny suits. There they paid their taxes and caught up on shreds of gossip that their wives would nag them for when they got home.

But this year, Tilley's June had been stifling. And July was worse. By August, folks were just worn out. Nobody was without a paper fan, and even fashionable women wore little hankies tucked around the insides of their collars. On Jefferson Street, the owner of the men's haberdashery and the fabric store next door had taken to setting out a wash-tub of water along the curb for dogs and horses and right next to it, a table filled with free, cold lemonade for people.

Folks simply didn't have the desire to remain upright into the afternoon. Tradesmen in their undershirts sprawled with hats over their faces in the cool grass of the courthouse lawn, and women at home sometimes just lay flat down on their linoleum floors with their children and pets around them, a fan blowing hot air across the wet cloths draped across their foreheads.

But sixteen-year-old Hanny Meyers was having a fine summer, and an independent and grown-up one too, he reckoned. His father had bought Tilley's small newspaper and in addition was running an up-and-coming supply store on the outskirts of town. For Hanny, the freedom that riding around in his dad's open delivery truck with stacks of seed, nails, tools, and even groceries he'd picked up for farmers from town, made him most definitely a young man due respect. With his straw boater atop his head beneath an awning he'd rigged from old sheets, Hanny happily bounced along Tilley's rutted roads stealing glances at his new muscles as they shone with sweat in the sun.

This last hot day of August was like any other. Hanny had started out late in the afternoon, knowing he wouldn't finish his deliveries until after dark. During the day, the air was humid and the temperature not under ninety-five, but after dark at least, people would be up and stirring. The Cavendishes had needed an axle, and between the old man, his son, and Hanny, they'd actually gotten the thing installed and running without a wheel falling off. That was one of the perks of being a delivery boy— you got to see far-flung school friends when most schoolmates were confined to their farms or neighborhoods.

Night had fallen quickly as Hanny left downtown Tilley. The moon had been slow to rise, and when it did, it hovered at the horizon, fat and orange, too heavy to float free, instead skimming sideways through banks of trees. Hanny Meyers drove slowly, the truck grunting as its tires took each depression in the dirt road. A breeze had picked up bringing to his nostrils forest pine, rotting logs, ginger, and what Hanny laughed was "earth worm sweat." Pulling the knob to switch on the circular head lights, he turned into the gloom at the back of Big Daddy Elliston's property, a sprawling patch of woods, cotton fields, corn, and mowed lawn surrounded by aging iron fencing with no-nonsense points. Charles,

'Big Daddy' Elliston was the town's banker and a Mississippi state senator who from time to time could be found in the capital, Jackson. Hanny thought he'd been the town's mayor once upon a time too. It was said that Big Daddy Elliston ran the courthouse and owned the judges, which seemed like an odd thing to Hanny, since it seemed doubtful you could sell a judge for profit the way you could a socket wrench. But nevertheless, passing the Elliston property always made people slow down and stare.

Hanny wondered to himself if he'd ever heard of anyone going to visit the Elliston's house when suddenly, in the distance, he heard the unmistakable sound of a gun's discharge. Deer season? Not yet. But heck, it didn't matter out here—on your own property you took what you wanted—especially if your name was Elliston.

Hanny looked into the woods to his right, instinctively searching for head lamps, listening for dogs, and slowing the truck to wait for an injured deer to come crashing out of the trees. But there was nothing. Then just as he eased his foot onto the accelerator, she was there.

At first, he didn't know what he was seeing. A woman—dark hair— light clothes that were dirty with something. Blood? And leaves. She was on her knees, pushing herself back up, falling across the ditch beside the road, crying as she struggled toward the truck. "Goddamn him! Goddamn his soul. Let him rot. Crows eat his guts!"

Hanny couldn't move as the woman stumbled first into his headlights and then against the truck. He had come to a stop and now stood up, one hand still on the wheel.

"What's the matter! What's the matter? Are you hurt? Car hit you? Do you need help!" Hanny started to get out of the truck, but now he could hear shouting from the Elliston woods and the sound of dogs.

The woman looked up, directly at Hanny. The headlamps outlined her face; she was a girl, hair cut off squarely at the edges. As if all her features now coalesced into their rightful place, Hanny recognized Lisbeth Elliston, long hair gone, taller, fuller.

"Save me...," she said. "There's killin' goin' on tonight."

A lead dog shot out of the darkness and headed for Lisbeth's bloody legs as she tried to crawl onto the running board. Hanny jumped down

3

and tore the hound away from her, kicking it in the gut and shoving the girl into the cab. Voices and more yaps were close. Throwing himself into the truck, he turned off the headlights, and this time slammed his foot onto the gas pedal.

Hanny didn't slow down until they'd gone over the Wakasau Bridge and were about to drive through the sleeping town. The girl hadn't made a sound. She didn't cry. The cursing was over, but he could see the moon stationary in her eyes—wide and fixed, as if she had stilled the lunar transit and time had stopped on the road in the woods.

"I don't know where we're going," said Hanny. "I don't know where to take you." She didn't move. He let the truck come to a stop in an inky shadow beside the courthouse. He looked around. It seemed as if no one had ever lived here, or their civilization had been dead for centuries.

"Lisbeth, do you know who I am?" There was silence. "Lisbeth, I'm Hanford Meyers... in the class ahead of you. What happened tonight? You said there was... killing going on... who got killed?"

She sat without a word for a long time and then when he was about to turn on the engine, she said, "I think I killed my father..., and my father has certainly killed me."

Chapter 1

Buena Vista, Mississippi
Late spring, 1984

"You can call me Scarlett," Claire said.

Claire Elliston subtly let her shoulders pull back and her stomach tighten. She heard her voice ring a decibel higher and almost involuntarily felt her feet arching like a dancer's as she stepped out of her truck.

She hadn't intended to stare at him, yet with the tanned skin and the golden curls there was a lot to take in. The boy looked like a cherub. A manly cherub. How old was this kid anyway?

The junior college forestry student didn't blink an eye. "Yes, Miss Scarlett. Now see over there.... I been walkin' the property while I was waitin' for you, and I think me and Nathan can take out all them old skinny cypress trees you done tagged. No problem, ma'am." This *was* Mississippi. Even college students spoke through the sweet syrup of the rural South.

She leaned over and batted a mosquito off his shoulder. Startled, the forester jumped away as if a schoolmarm had smacked him with a ruler.

"He was just about to dig into you, Jackson. It is Jackson, right? We can't have those little pesky bugs feastin' on all that good muscle, now can we? Then they'll get big and strong like you, and who knows what they'll do next."

Claire turned slightly away from him and bent over to wipe something off her shoe. Though this young hired-hand seemed as dense as fog, she would magnanimously give him a little wake-up call, even if he'd never heard of Scarlett O'Hara.

"Well that's good, Jackson. You can take out all the old cypress then, but leave every one of the pecan trees, you hear? Clean away the vines and wisteria, and what you're gonna see is the outlines of what used to be here. Like a park. Like a pecan park, they used to say… and with the old house and everything." Jackson nodded politely and fumbled for his knife to begin tidying up his fingernails.

Claire pushed her hair away from her forehead, momentarily wondering if the greys were straying loose. Even now through the trees, sunlight scattered coins of light across the clover she'd planted last winter, little dollops of sunshine in a field of chartreuse. "Come here, Jackson, let me show you something."

He gave her a glance, but let her take his hand and pull him along the road she'd had bulldozed deep into the ten acres. This time she didn't feel coy or flirtatious, but more like an archeologist leading a student with only a dim light bulb over his head.

"When you see the outlines of the old house, you're gonna get a taste of… a taste of… Well, I think it's…"

It's what? It was always like this when, through the trees, she caught sight of the place her mother had lived—this speck of land where her mother had presided until—she didn't anymore. It was the place Lisbeth Elliston had lived as a vanquished exile from the Brick House and Big Daddy Charlie. Claire's own life, this place, it all felt encrusted with the humus of Buena Vista, just waiting for someone to chip it away and reveal the secrets that Claire felt sure slept here. Secrets that lately seemed to be awakening.

"I'm gonna get a taste of what, Miss… Scarlett?"

Claire let her eyes scour the trees. No rows, just rowdy, random saplings growing where they liked. Free. The way she imagined her mother. Strength, too. Yes, that was close. Lisbeth was strong in the way of a willow branch. The way abandoned soil could still make a flower. This fragment of land, Buena Vista—and her mother—wrapped tightly together. A special kind of freedom and strength in them both. There had been joy here, Claire could remember some—but joy rising in the smoke of sadness.

She looked at the youth beside her. "I think this place'll give you a taste of survival, Jackson."

Claire didn't always bring the workmen to this part of the property, and she certainly didn't try to tie her feelings about the ruined house to words for their benefit, but there was something about the stillness this afternoon. With only a drowsy cricket's stir, the warm breeze rose from the field next door and from the forest that extended for a hundred acres in all directions. The stillness cushioned her thoughts, let them recline, and, like indolent cats, roll over and over.

"See that over there? Those bricks are where the front porch used to be. My daddy used to hold me in his lap and swing me back and forth in a wicker swing, right there. And these, these are the old steps going up to the front door, a double door, between two pillars, I believe. And back in there, in that old grove, that's where our maid Gertrude lived. She didn't have her own children, but she treated me like a little princess."

As usual, the remembered house hovered in sepia shadows. Claire imagined Gertrude, milk-chocolate skin, dressed in a blue dress with a long white apron, snapping peas in her lap beside the hydrangeas that circled the porch. She heard the clink of glasses of sweet tea and the spice of ginger cookies and the kitchen mint that was in the air. Even Claire's mother, coming through the screen door half-dressed in a pale, summer frock, combing her hair and twisting it into a proper knot, seemed at ease.

But too often these days, when her mother came through that door, the reveries took another turn. It was on those occasions that Claire would make a hasty exit to reality, hop in her red pickup, lock the gate across the bulldozed road and speed the ten miles back to Doreen's Place, the Bed and Breakfast haven that served as base camp for the homestead restoration Claire had launched a year ago. Better to leave her mother and the outlines of parked Hudsons and Fords and the shadows heading toward the house and push them back among memories where they belonged.

"It's in pretty bad shape, Miss Scarlett," said Jackson, possibly for the second time. "It's like the woods done just ate up the whole house."

He took a step onto the lowest of the three remaining concrete steps, pushing a *"bow-d'arc"* branch out of the way and kicking one of the tree's huge brain-like fruits into a pile of thatch. "You gonna try an' rebuild the house just like it used to be?" He'd taken off his baseball cap and was running his fingers through a mass of hair, lifting the wet curls off his forehead.

"I don't know yet, Jackson," whispered Claire. The sun had run off, hiding behind the trees and anonymous clouds. She watched the boy's ruddy cheeks go grey in the muted light and a shadow of pimples appear along his cheeks. He was right, the place was filled with weeds, broken wires, slumping fences, and the few bricks that scavengers hadn't hauled off over the years. Maybe all the purloined memories she had lifted from collections of her mother's photos and tried to make her own wouldn't suffice. And yet they were more real than most of her own.

"I've got pictures of how it used to look, but I almost don't know where to begin." She turned in a little circle. "That's why I'm tending to the trees and the pond first. You want to see the pond? I put a little fake duck on it, just an old decoy, but I think some dog just comes around and brings it back up here every week or two. We got us a game goin'."

Jackson looked at his watch. "It's gettin' a little late, Miss… Scarlett. I gotta get on back. But I'm thinkin', if you look like you gonna need help with all this, I'd be willin', me and Nathan. I bet we could help you out real good… real good."

She watched him carefully. Only one meaning. Hacking out weeds and chain-sawing trees. "Well, that'd be fine, Jackson. We'll start with the cypress, then." Claire bent over her backpack for the calendar and the schedule they could follow, but when she stood up, Jackson had taken off his shirt.

Under soft brown hair that circled him like moss, his skin glistened over the musculature of a man who lifted and heaved things; whose back could broaden under the weight of hay or beneath that of a metal engine.

Claire forced herself to scratch some dates onto a piece of paper. "There you go. See if those days would work for you and Nathan." She handed him the paper, trying to avert her eyes from his chest as he scanned the little calendar.

8

"Suits me fine, Miss Scarlett." He dug the paper into his back pocket. "I like that, you know, me callin' you, "'Miss Scarlett.'" You didn't teach English, now did ya, ma'am? My big sister had a teacher who taught 'em outta that *Gone With the Wind* book. My sis said it was 'racy.'" Jackson burst into a spasm of giggles that doubled him over and gave Claire a better look at his trapezius muscles. "But, you know, I had to ask my momma what that meant, 'cause at the time… I was only five."

Chapter 2

Doreen McCurdy was having a "sinking spell." The Bed and Breakfast's phone, that hadn't rung much in the last months, was suddenly alive with jingles, each with a desperate woman trying to book into one of the old mansion's six "exceptionally decorated" suites.

All the rooms in Tupelo, forty-five minutes away, were booked and the United Daughters of the Confederacy (U.D.C.) regional convention was now spilling south toward Tilley. A godsend too.

Doreen patted her face, glancing at the wet hankie in annoyance. Nothing much got to Doreen, but years after investing her divorce settlement into the 1830s landmark, she'd expected the B & B to have taken off. Even now, she ploughed most of her monthly alimony into antique bed-skirts, cherry spindle-turned beds, and fringe-trimmed loveseats. Framed photos and paintings of antebellum damsels from thrift stores plastered the walls till they'd begun to lean in.

Swags and crewel rugs, crocheted antimacassars and embroidered throws, tiny ottomans for tiny Confederate feet filled every room. And pillows. Pillows by the scores, in damask, brocade, in silk and linen, round, oblong, trapezoids, and pleated cylinders overwrought with piping and fringe. In other words, the quaintness Doreen had envisioned had turned into a fiscal, and possibly decorative, fiasco.

The windows needed glazing, three stories of turrets and gingerbread needed painting, and the tax man wouldn't wait forever. Even more, when there were guests, she found herself buckling under the physical burden of cleaning and cooking prodigious Southern breakfasts of pancakes, bacon, eggs, fruit, sausage, juice, and biscuits big enough to feed a large dog. Doreen really was sinking.

But maybe the damned Confederate Daughters were a turning point. Maybe Doreen knew something about Southern ladies not everybody knew. And Claire, now pulling a little too fast into the driveway, was just such a Southern lady.

"You look all red-faced and it don't look like just from the sun." Doreen pushed open the screened porch door and held it while Claire grappled with her cooler, hat, and backpack of sunscreen, bug spray, hair brush, and make-up—essentials for a day working in the woods.

Once inside, Claire dumped everything at the foot of the stairs, turned to her friend and leveling her gaze, said, "I am now going to walk up these steps. You will be standing below me as my derriere ascends the stairs. When I arrive at the top, you are to give me an absolutely honest appraisal of what you just saw, you hear? If you say, 'Jiggling and awful,' I will understand that. If you say 'Buy a muumuu,' I will pay my bill and leave. But maybe your absolute honesty will have something polite to say—like that I'm not too old and that somebody will always want to have a look."

With that Claire turned and began to climb the narrow stairs toward the second floor. Doreen shook her head. A kind of waltz, she thought, with that right-left swing of the hips. But then, as long as Doreen had known her, Claire was capable of making men dance to that rhythm. Boyfriends, boyfriends' fathers, supervisors, and their bosses, they all fell under the spell of Claire's particular cadence. And besides her derriere, they seemed to like her for her mind and wit too. Except for Big Daddy Charlie. And as proud as he should have been of his granddaughter, that relationship never took.

"Well?" Claire was out of breath.

Doreen stood with one hand on an ample hip. "What is this all about, Missy? Do you know that I've got pralines just beginnin' to boil, and I do not have time to be assessin' your ass assets!" Doreen laughed her soft, throaty chuckle, dabbing at her hairline. "Your be-hind is just fine, woman. Now get in there an' take your shower and come down to the garden for a glass of fine wine. I got something I want to talk to you about."

The evening breeze was light enough to cause the thick magnolia leaves to shift like so many patent leather shoes on a dance floor, one lifted, one dropped down in a leafy synchrony. The two willows at the foot of the garden simply simpered in confusion.

The garden almost made everything else worth it for Doreen. She'd helped her two black handymen lay each and every one of the bricks that brought four little paths into a circular roundabout. Here she'd placed antique iron chairs and a table and the wicker glider covered in floral chintz. Cabbage roses, snapdragons and summer lilies turned the place, she thought, into a perfect garden of delights. Except that not enough paying customers were there to appreciate it. But maybe she didn't have the right combination of delights.

"Well that's better. Wet hair and all. You look like you might'a left the whole country side a' dirt running down the drain!" Doreen handed up a glass of Chardonnay and on a painted porcelain, Confederate-era plate, some little puff pastries filled with cream.

"You do know how to feed a hungry field-hand." Taking the wine, Claire gazed up at the trees stirring in great swooshes above her head. "The storm, I think, has gone north or somethin'. That's good, 'cause the bulldozer operator's not coming to clean out the pond drain 'till next week. Otherwise, we'd have us a big flood back toward where the old house was." Claire stretched backwards in her chair, rolling her shoulders and neck like a swan or a lioness in the week before she comes into heat.

Doreen believed she read the signs; this was more than just stiffness from the day. Though she rarely thought about men anymore, she knew that Claire did, that women at the beauty parlor did, and the bridge club, and garden club, and the U.D.C. After all, she was a business woman, and despite Claire's ability to hand out micro-loans as the manager of a bank, the stocky innkeeper doubted she'd be the kind of applicant who'd get one. Not with what she had in mind. Still....

"Well, I know it's none of my business, but are you all set with your plans an' all? You got the drawings made and ready to start puttin' up a house yet?" Doreen knew the answer. Knew Claire set aside so much from her salary each month toward the fantasized house, a place that seemed to have become half getaway for retirement, half archeology, maybe wholly obsession. Doreen was never quite sure what the draw was for a sophisticated woman with artistic tastes. Did she really intend to hole up there in the woods in some Depression-era cabin? But that was a never mind for now.

"No, no drawings yet. All I've got are my sketches and the old photos of the house in about 1918. But I'm pushing on. Something tells me this is the time…. The old place even keeps waking me up in the night." Claire laughed, but there was an unsettled edge to it.

"Did I show you the pictures I got from Tilda Murphy's yard sale? I know it's Mama's house. The front pillars show up real well. But there's a man sitting on the front stoop I don't recognize…." Claire's eyes seemed focused inward, and she turned away.

Doreen interrupted. Time for some serious talk about the here and now.

"Like a little more wine?" That's how you started the serious part of the conversation here. And, "…aren't these cream puffs nice?"

Doreen chewed thoughtfully and had another sip of Chardonnay. "How'd you like to speed up those plans, Claire? Ever thought that you might be able to make enough money in, say, six months to get those plans draw'd up and start with the layin' of the bricks?"

Claire was gazing into the ribbons of crimson sky still visible through the trees, her mind momentarily on Jackson's curls, when she realized Doreen was proposing something.

"What are you talkin' about? I'd need more than some part-time job… six months! Besides, I don't have time for another twenty hours of hard labor in my week."

"I don't think it'd be so hard," Doreen said with another cream puff on its way. "But though you don't know it yet, you've got the resources, and I've got the buyers. I do believe I do." She patted her mouth.

"The buyers? What are you sellin'?"

"Well, naturally, darlin', I'm sellin' love."

Doreen pulled the heavy iron chair closer noticing Claire leaned slightly away, but she would be patient.

13

"How many young, strappin' forestry men you got out there? How many dozer operators? How many of them got nice strong friends? Why, I venture the junior colleges and farms around here got plenty of boys like that. All of 'em needin' work. An' all of 'em so tired out from liftin' and hoistin', that a little more enjoyable work they'd take to just fine."

Claire sat with her wine held mid-air.

"And do you know how many lonely women we got us around here? Hundreds! They all are married... over-married! Too married! Done *done* with married! But they're gonna stay married. And between clubs and cotillions and church and the damned beauty parlor, these women need some real lovin'. The old-fashioned kind they used to dream about before their old Bubbas washed it all outta 'em."

Doreen took a breath. "So, Claire, I got the house, with no afternoon guests. And you've got the young studs who'd be happy for a little spendin' money. And we both know just the kind of women who play bridge every day and make that little three PM run to the grocery..., and who would just love a little pick-me-up about mid-week."

Chapter 3

The next morning, a blistering Monday, already had the city's
asphalt-covered brick streets ready to sizzle. In Tupelo, in her
own bathroom, putting on her lipstick, Claire had managed to package
up and put away the image of Jackson Perkins' precocious muscles and
his seemingly unintended swipe at her... goddamn him... advancing
years. Little red-neck. At twenty-something, he probably was a daddy
himself by now. Probably swept some overweight clerk at the Buena
Vista Family Dollar off her feet and now went home to macaroni and
cheese every night. See how long that ripped torso lasted under a nightly
cheddar and white bread regimen. She shouldn't have given him that
little peek at her rear end either. Save that for somebody more
appreciative.

And who would that be? Claire took a final look at herself in the
mirror before heading to the bank. Alright, Cecile had gotten her hair too
dark the last time, but it had a cute swing to it, maybe a little young, but
Buster Brown bangs never went out of style. Her décolleté was smooth
without a trace of crepe, but under the little jackets and gently flaring
skirts, the last few years had laid down new topography in places she
guessed she'd never again let see the light of day.

Okay, maybe, if the occasion should serendipitously arise, with
candles and the discreet drape of rumpled sheets, she might still be able
to pull off one of the kind of nights when she'd known the man she was
with was out of his mind with passion. She had been a "highly charged"
young woman, after all, and some research-based knowledge just didn't
go away. But *if* such an occasion arose, Claire knew she'd be anything
but spontaneous. For her, a love bed would be a stage set with gravity-

defying choreography, plenty of mood lighting, and just enough alcohol involved to keep the man from wanting to explore those flaccid nether regions she couldn't keep tensed forever before he fell asleep.

And then, as it always happened, when it was over, the loneliness would migrate back, like some fragile kitten that crawled along her legs to settle on her chest and steal her breath, leaving her to wonder where along the way the rest of her had been left.

Claire took another look at herself in the mirror, lifting her neck to stretch the skin taut. Was she one of the women Doreen had talked about yesterday? There'd been two fiancés. Three years of bickering with one and six months of money squabbles with the other. This was the decade she would turn fifty, and Claire momentarily wondered if she'd ever be made love to again. Never married and heading for fifty. The odds weren't good, not out here in rural America. Yet, she thought, watching her shadow move along the wall, was that what she wanted? Wasn't it she who had broken off every relationship? Wasn't it she who felt the fear when a man mentioned love?

Still, she'd recognized that special throb when she'd seen the half-naked Jackson. Maybe she wasn't dead yet, by God. So maybe Doreen had something. Claire guessed she wasn't the only one who felt the need to be womanly, but she might be the only one who was so frightened by it.

Suddenly, she felt the light brush against her face. And again. Claire closed her eyes. No, not now, she thought. She needed to get to work. "Mama, please..."

Yet Claire waited for these moments. These whispers that came suddenly in the morning or at a stop light at dusk—with instructions that made no sense. She put the heels of her hands against the bathroom counter and closed her eyes anticipating, like a wave of vertigo, images she wouldn't understand. This was the reason she was rebuilding the old house—a place to let the whispers speak.

What had Momma felt back then? Had she been loved? Her mother hadn't lived to thirty-five. Before the tornado that tore apart Buena Vista, Claire remembered Lisbeth as soft and full-busted, the kind of woman who appealed to Southern men. But there her memories became unstitched. When she reached for their fabric, they floated away in fragments, leaving Claire wondering about the kind of life she'd led at Buena Vista before she was sent away; wondering at the kind of life her mother and Gertrude, their maid, had continued.

Claire opened her eyes and shook her head back and forth. Then she brushed her teeth for the second time just to get her mind back on track. Hell, it was easier just to concentrate on uprooting trees and hauling bricks out at the homestead.

But it was hard forcing herself away. There had been a time when she'd felt herself the youngest member of a marching line of Elliston women who didn't seem to need men in their world. What was it Momma had said? "Men are nice when they visit, and even nicer when they pick up their socks and leave." Claire tried to remember. Momma must have said that after Daddy died, or had he just gone away? There must have been a Daddy. Claire couldn't actually picture his face, but Momma would make herself laugh and give Claire a little hug of womanly knowing saying, "You're just a girl, Clairey. Your big eyes don't need to see everything." But they had seen—if only she could remember what.

Claire glanced at her watch and quickly stuffed her lipstick and comb into her purse. She counted out some change for the parking meter at Rita's Diner, picked up the receipt for stockings she planned to return, and gazed at the wrinkled scrap of paper lying before her on the bathroom counter. She caught her breath—even as she knew what it would say. Always the same. The same reminder. Tiny letters she'd come to recognize.

"*avenge me*" it quietly read. No emotion in the dainty scrawl lightly penciled on a scrap of envelope. No instructions. It sat alone beside a scatter of bobby pins and a single Q-tip. Claire stared at the shred of paper. It could have said, "water the plants" or "do the laundry." She picked it up, examining the furl of the cursive letters, trembling that she hadn't remembered writing them. Then, with a final glance at herself in the mirror, a final search to make sure she was there, Claire brushed the note into a drawer with the others and hurried off to a board meeting before she was late.

Chapter 4

"**M**iz Elliston, morning ma'am. How'd your weekend go? You look like you got a little sunburn on your nose." Starlight Washburn was never out of sorts, never not dressed in the very latest fashion on display at the discount Cato store on Highway 15.

"Oh, it's gonna be a hot one today. I'm just so glad the A.C. been fixed." Starlight's skin-hugging rayon skirt had worked its way around from the back so that the zipper now was a featured aspect of its front, but she was too busy organizing papers along one side of Claire's desk to notice.

"Now, let me see, I think I got everything here. You got two loans to women's co-ops, another one to a youth baseball league for their uniforms, a big one to an organic grower, and this one here, it's a little different. This one requesting a grant. He wants to do some kind of operations on the…" She strained to read the form. "Says here, 'on the African-American and migrant pickers.' Well, I don't know what that's all about."

Claire eased into the cracked leather of the Main Branch Manager's chair. This chair, worn-out since the Seventies, was as much a part of the manager's image as having the engraved metal nameplate front and center on her desk. At the Farmers' and Businessmen's National Bank of Tupelo, everybody took comfort in these touchstones of solidity. From its fluted granite pillars and the gleaming bronze cashier cages perched along thick Alabama-marble counters to the kiosk desks with green-shaded glass lampshades that ran the entire length of its temple-like design, the F & B Bank—established 1920 and unbowed and unchanged to this very day—had been but few changes.

Claire was pleased to have been the catalyst for one.

She had moved her manager's desk into the main gallery, out of the oak-lined hermitage where even the walls had seemed to exhale wisps of the cigar smoke that once circled the heads of decades of bank managers. The black and white photos of those no-nonsense men, partial to revealing their vests and the flash of a gold chain, still lined the hallway to the marble-stalled bathroom. These men had known everybody's secrets, their peccadilloes, their quiet philanthropies, even the payments that were made into unidentified bank accounts drawn upon by young colored women who tried to make ends meet and feed and clothe particularly light-skinned offspring.

Claire knew a few secrets. In the South, everything has a heritage—either good or bad; a connection through family, through schools, or through a hairdresser with authoritative information. But Claire listened to just so much. Instead, as bank manager, she was intent on dragging the F & B into the modern age. Besides, innovation made her feel young.

That's why she had initiated the program whose applicants' forms now covered her desk: Micro-loans. She loved approving the micro-loans to individuals wishing to jump-start their companies or to charitable groups whose members were good at annual fund drives. She especially liked the smart men and women with original ideas.

In retrospect, it was amazing how easy it had been to get the "new-fangled" micro-loan program approved. Most of the Board of Directors still clung to the idea of a tractor or house as collateral, but since the biggest change of all, giving Claire the key to the manager's office—no vest, no gold chain required—the Board seemed to have lost its will to fight. Particularly since Hanford B. Myers, Chairman of the Board Emeritus, and personal friend of bank founder, Big Daddy Charlie Elliston of Tilley, Mississippi, seemed to have taken a liking to her. Claire always wondered if her grandfather were still in charge if she'd be sitting in the old leather chair today. She guessed the answer.

Claire swung the chair around and glanced at the photographs lined up on the credenza behind her. The city fathers, and a few mothers squinted back, holding giant scissors with which they would cut ribbons to some branch opening. The mayor was there, presenting a check to

Claire for the first micro-loan backed by city funds. There were some baseball and basketball team shots, all sponsored by the bank. Finally, there was Hanford B. Myers, his arm around Claire with the expression of a man who had just squeezed a sweet, soft peach—and now intended to eat it.

"Well, you done grow'd up real nice, Miss Claire," he'd said, when she was reintroduced to him five years ago, over thirty years after she first remembered meeting him at Big Daddy Charlie's Brick House. The young pilot's hands had felt like catcher's mitts when she was eight, strong, enveloping, like a fly-catcher plant with a fly inside. She had remembered them because they'd come attached to the biggest set of arms and shoulders she had ever seen. Even in this country of farmers and laborers, Hanny Myers was impressive.

Over three decades later, she had looked him in the eye, sized up the kind of man he was, and instantly known that with only a little effort, this great Mississippi galoot of a gentleman would open just about any door she needed help twisting. It wasn't that she was a conniving "Southern belle," or that he was a fawning pawn, instead, that's how things were done here. A mixture of coquettishness and gallantry, raw power and power powdered and perfumed. When shaken or stirred properly, the cocktail made most everybody feel good and got things done—by the people who should be doing them.

There were rules for this kind of thing, of course, and Claire had not broken a one. They had met out of town, and he remained, "Mr. Meyers." She simply put the little trinkets he bought her in a paper sack stuffed under the hallway stairs and offered up almost manly shakes of his hand in public.

In return, Hanny had sponsored her appointment to manager and locked horns whenever needed with businessmen whose loans she hadn't approved. Quid pro quo. The basic economics she'd learned at college. He'd support her in the Board Room, and in return, she would give him the odd thing he wanted at the US 8 Ramada Inn on Thursday afternoons. Friendly neighbors make for friendly business, a knowledge in the Elliston DNA.

20

***

It was already Thursday, but Starlight Washburn couldn't have told you. Her dark cheeks were burgundy as she blushed under Chauncey Groves' best, "you-is-my-woman" gaze. Every Tuesday and Thursday, Chauncey would saunter into the bank, his Pepsi delivery truck idling in the bank lot, put one of his small, tight buttocks down on her shiny mahogany desk, and fix her like a bug with a pin with his deep brown stare.

"You be early today, Baby," she cooed, her voice reaching the soprano range of a flirtatious eight-year old. "You come to take me out for lunch?"

Chauncey had perfected the gaze; housed it in a square-jawed face under a glistening shaved head. His shoulders stretched the tiny stripes of the Pepsi shirt to bursting, and his thighs threatened to split his denim pants along their straining seams. He really didn't have to say anything. It was better that way, because beneath the sculpted dome of his skull, a great quiet often reigned, so he just slowly dropped his curly eyelashes a notch, let a muscle quiver around one side of his mouth, and got up and left.

Starlight Washburn was definitely in love.

It was only after Chauncey's truck had pulled out of the parking lot that Starlight realized her intercom was frantically blinking on her desk. That was a signal. Miss Claire, twenty steps away, was in the middle of an interview with an applicant for a loan, one of the hat-holding supplicants who, no matter what confident inspiration had led to their seeking money, always found themselves babbling too long and too earnestly for Claire's liking. Thus, the signal.

When Claire unobtrusively tapped her call button, Starlight was to apologetically interrupt the interview with the reminder that Claire had another "extremely important" engagement. Claire said she knew within five minutes of the interview if she were going to make the loan, and the rest was "pure gentility." Well, Claire didn't look so genteel herself right now. The intercom seemed exhausted from flashing.

21

Starlight stumbled out of her chair, twisting at her skirt, and made her way toward her boss who stared straight at her with big, *communicating* eyes, quite separate from the fixed smile she'd planted on her lips for the client's benefit.

"Mr. Norman, excuse me, my secretary has something— What is it Starlight?" Claire raised her eyebrows and poked her head forward with a little nod of innocent curiosity.

"Yes, Miss Claire. I am so sorry to interrupt, but you have another extremely important appoint—" Starlight hadn't even finished before Claire was on her feet and shuffling the applicant's papers together.

"Well, I am sorry, Mr. Norman, but I will review these figures. As you know money is more difficult to come by these days, but I will be back to you with a letter by the end of the week. Thank you so, so much for coming to the F & B Bank first. Thank you." She smiled him right out of his chair and through the front door. Then turned to Starlight.

"Girl, you could a' been all but blinded by that intercom's blink. I almost *heard* it, all the way over here; and if Chauncey had sat any longer on that mahogany desk, he'd a' left his tiny glute imprint embedded in the wax. Now you just have to pay more attention, you hear?"

"Yes, ma'am." Starlight's neck made a little zigzag in the air when Claire turned her back. On Starlight's side of town, people didn't play games or need secret signals to bail them out of situations. If you wanted to finish a conversation, you just said, "Well, this conversation is over." And then you got up and left. Except, of course, if you were in church. Maybe Miss Claire considered the bank her church.

"What day is it, today? I swear Randall Norman just about took my brain away. That man doesn't know the meaning of the word "micro" or even "mini." He wants the big bucks. Well, big don't grow here, does it, Starlight?" Claire's humor was coming back. "We're just the mini-mart money store, around here." She glazed on a little lipstick and swung her Buster Brown bob back and forth.

"Yes, ma'am. And its Thursday, Miss Claire. But you've got one more application to go over. It's that doctor… the one who wants to do something to the migrants. Here's his application. Dr. Gunther… what?

Hoob-shhh? H,U,E,B,S,H. My, oh my, where on earth does he come from?" Claire took the application.

"It's a German name, and I believe he wants to do something *for* the migrant population, not *to* them."

Claire looked up, and at the other end of the bank the revolving door was slowly spinning out several customers. But one of them, a man somewhere in his mid-forties, was coming in. He wasn't wearing jeans or a baseball cap. When he walked, he didn't yaw back and forth like a ship in a swell. Instead, the man coming toward her had on a full grey tweed suit with a knotted tie and buttoned cuffs. His hair was wavy with just enough color left to know that he had once been blonde.

Right away, Claire guessed that this interesting-looking man would not be responsive to anything she'd doled out the day before to the forestry student, Jackson. No little rump peeks. No lingering fingers against a sleeve. Claire knew her way around Southern men—and boys. But a German would be something else.

Only for a second, as she got up from her desk and let her hands smooth her skirt slowly down the front of her thighs, did it cross her mind that she was too old for this… this effort at a conquest. She hadn't liked yesterday's humiliation at Jackson's hands, but then what else did you do with men? Becoming friends wasn't exactly an option, not without a little flirtation, not without a bit of the sticky-sweet fragrance of "sex suggested" that was in the Southern air. Not that everybody *did it*. They just liked to play with the idea.

No, she would review Dr. Gunther… Huebsch's application, and if her drawl thickened a little, if something fell from her hands that caused her to, what the hell, bend over, or if she needed to come sit beside him and lean into that soft tweed suit, well, that was part of being born here in Mississippi. She didn't think Yankees or foreigners had nearly as much fun. And who knew? Maybe he was teachable.

23

Chapter 5

The '79 Lincoln fairly glittered as it slowly rolled into the rear lot of the Ramada Inn, forty miles out on U.S. 8, a place curious Tilleyians or day-trippers from Tupelo weren't likely to visit on a Thursday afternoon.

Hanford B. Meyers liked the slight effort he had to expend in turning the wheel, as if the weight of its 7,000 pounds of steel were exercising the now scrawny deltoids he kept carefully hidden under his fine cotton shirts.

He was early but found his favorite spot where a towering magnolia offered shade, but the car lay outside the drop zone of its juicy blossoms. Hanny wasn't in the mood for scraping crusted flowers off his hood today. He wasn't even sure he was in the mood for—he laughed out loud when he thought the words—*for love. Ramada Inn Love, that is*. The facsimile of love. The something that made him think about what love used to be like.

Hanny ran his fingers along the faux mahogany that made the Lincoln look like the inside of a fancy cigar box—thick, polished, masculine. He'd gotten used to going first class. That was part of keeping your place in society when underneath there might be all hell going on. But, he had to admit it, he'd hate to give up the perks the bank had brought.

He reached inside the glove compartment, a deep receptacle stacked with forgotten warranties and old maps, and pulled out a silver flask over half-full with caramel-colored bourbon. Hanny took a slow swig, washing the liquor around his lips, feeling the slight numbness he always got with the first taste, then letting his eyes close with the swallow.

It was warm inside the car, and as it always did, the liquor slowed his breathing, letting him inhale memories that seemed on deposit somewhere around the aging Ramada. Hanny's head nodded forward. His kind didn't *"mess with her kind,"* his teen-age friends had told him.

"D'you forget where you come from... where you wanna be?" his dead buddy Jack had said later. *"This is the South, you ass! You gotta think who you bang, brother!"* For Hanny, it had never been about that. He had never touched her. At least not then. Although when he thought of her now....

"Mr. Meyers." Hanny sat up, blinking at the auburn-haired woman tapping on his window.

"Goddamn, girl, you scared me! I was near asleep!"

Claire smiled that combination business meeting smile and gentle come-on he'd seen her execute on bankers and lawyers before. He rolled the window down and smiled back at her. "You go on up, honey, I'll be right behind you... appreciatin' all the way."

Claire nodded. Anyone watching them would have assumed a chance meeting between colleagues—banking after all, takes planning meetings and plenty of oversight. Hanny wasn't actually worried they'd be seen, after all these years of dispensing a kind of Solomon-like benevolence across both the black and white communities, he had arrived at a place where he could do practically anything and get away with it. There were just some things he didn't want to do. Particularly what Big Daddy Charlie Elliston had begun to demand—to have Hanny use his influence to have Charlie's daughter's grave moved to the "nigger side" of Laurel Rest Cemetery.

Chapter 6

Doreen could hear the trills from the front porch. There were titters, soprano runs, ululations, and an occasional avian squawk. The first thing that came to her mind was—parakeets—the pesky kind that flew up from Florida; the noisy packs that made her want to get her daddy's shotgun out. Then when the giggles and the high-heeled stomping across the front porch started up, "Christ-a'mighty," she realized, "the U.D.C.ers are back!"

Doreen had been up since four. Between her and Esperanza, her on-call assistant, they'd rolled and baked biscuits for hours before breakfast. They'd fussed with a table set with both the pink table cloth and its lacy overlay. The flowers were in matching crystal vases. Each antimacassar was starched and all the orientals' fringes were straight.

For the ladies' lunch, she'd made plates of varicolored petit-fours with crisp cucumbers, picked crab, and shrimp remoulade from her great aunt's cook book. And like the fudge she would soon swirl onto tiny éclairs for afternoon tea, she could feel the United Daughters of the Confederacy beginning to melt into her hands, spongy and soft, relaxing into the sensual mood that chocolate, and later, champagne could bring to middle-aged women.

"Doreen... oh, Doreen!" A tall woman with white hair swirled into an ice cream confection atop her head, poked her head through the swinging door of the kitchen. "I cannot say, I absolutely cannot express to you how much each... one... of... us... *loves*... our room! I mean, really, we just did... not... *know*... that such a priceless gem existed down here! If we did, Doreen, and I really mean this..., we would have been coming down here a lot more! I mean what a perfect little B and B!

A perfect getaway…, a little hideaway! Why, nobody we know in Tupelo would even know we're here! It is so pretty it just makes you just feel naughty! We are just enjoying ourselves so much!"

Doreen stood looking at her, sweat seeming to bubble up in polka dots across her forehead and lip. "Well, you are so welcome!"

Damn, she'd get this woman to write an infomercial. She glanced quickly at the woman's left hand. Married. Good. The statuesque ice cream cone still had a nice figure, expensive clothes, and a certain forwardness that in Doreen's experience, often meant she was good at flirting. If the kind of discreet occasion arose that Doreen had in mind, this social leader may be very helpful.

"Let me bring out an afternoon pick-me up, Georgina. You all just go sit down and look gorgeous. Why, I am so happy to have you all here." Doreen turned around as the door swung shut, shoved a newly arrived property tax bill under the crystal cake stand, and yelled, "Esperanza, make up some iced pink squirrels! Double strength."

Chapter 7

He didn't know how it'd begun—the Ramada Inn Thursdays. Half of it was little more than an old habit, the favor received for the favor done that Hanny Meyers had practiced for so many years. With men like him, such favors would often be a little something extra tucked in with the bottle of Jack Daniels or a backstrap of cured venison that his associates exchanged over the holidays. Depending on the woman, it might have been little more than being allowed to undo a few buttons at a Christmas party or discreetly cup a breast. Hanny had never been greedy nor overt. But Claire had been something different, and strangely, it had never been physical.

He glanced over at her now, rolled on her side on the edge of the geometric motel room quilt. Her torso softly rose and fell, occasionally giving off little breaths as if a tiny teapot were cooling down.

He had never asked her to take off her clothes; had never touched what he suspected was pale white skin with sporadic galaxies of little brown moles scattered across the soft expanses. In truth, he didn't want to know.

No, it was Claire's voice, Claire's soft brown eyes, the way cloth draped across the small of her back that aroused memory. Another voice, another time. But Claire, or some essence which she carried, still brought on a manly response that in his seventies, Hanny Meyers could look down upon with pride and not a little surprise.

Seated in the Naugahyde chair next to the bed, he studied her hips. Ignoring the shuttle of sound and mildew being emitted from the room's air conditioner, Hanny knew that for Claire, Thursdays were more about an office respite and the nap she would catch than any affection she held for him. For Hanny, the Ramada was a kind of no-man's land, an anonymous launch site for excursions into a past where now few could go. Claire was the necessary catalyst, and closing his eyes, Hanny found himself drifting there in spite of himself.

The summer of 1930 was stifling. Even men carried paper fans and people slept on their front porches rather than go inside at night. In the woods, fireflies appeared and disappeared in drifting squadrons while wet air carried frog calls from a pond a mile away.

The moon had been slow to rise that night as Hanny finished delivery rounds for his father's sundries business, and tired and sleepy, he proudly pictured how his friends would gawk in the fall when they saw how much he'd grown.

He turned the open truck toward the back of Big Daddy Charlie Elliston's property, bouncing along the dirt road next to Elliston's woods and cotton fields, holding the wheel steady while he tried to peek through the trees toward the biggest house in town. Hanny's father had told him that the banker and senator was a powerful man who didn't mind stomping on anyone in his way and who had dirty secrets on everybody from here to Jackson. Still, or maybe because of it, passing the Elliston property always made people slow down and stare.

Hanny was wondering if he'd ever heard of anyone going to visit the Elliston's house when in the distance, he heard the sound of a gun.

He looked into the woods searching for head lamps, listening for dogs, and slowing the truck to wait for an injured deer to come crashing out of the trees. There was nothing. Until she was there.

A woman. Dark hair. Light clothes that were dirty with something— was crying as she struggled toward the truck. "Goddamn him! Goddamn his soul. Let him rot...; crows eat his guts!"

The woman stumbled first into his headlights and then against the truck. He had come to a stop and now stood up.

"What's the matter? What's the matter? Are you hurt? Car hit you? Do you need help?" Hanny started to get out of the truck, but he could hear shouting from the Elliston woods and the sound of dogs.

The woman looked up, directly at Hanny. The headlamps outlined her face. It was a girl. Hanny recognized Lisbeth Elliston, long hair gone, taller, fuller.

"Save me." she said. "There's killin' goin' on tonight."

A lead dog shot out of the darkness and headed for Lisbeth's bloody legs as she tried to crawl onto the running board. Hanny jumped down and tore the hound away from her, kicking it in the gut and shoving the girl into the cab. Voices and more yaps were close. Throwing himself into the truck, he turned off the headlights, and this time slammed his foot onto the pedal.

The girl hadn't made a sound as he drove. She didn't cry, but only stared at a fragment of moon as he headed into Tilley. Her cursing was over as he pulled to a stop beside the shadowy Courthouse Square.

"I don't know where we're going," said Hanny. "I don't know where to take you."

"Lisbeth, do you know who I am?" There was silence. "Lisbeth, I'm Hanford Meyers... in the class ahead of you. What happened tonight? You said there was... killing going on. Who got killed?"

She sat without a word for a long time and then when he was about to turn on the engine, she said, "I think I killed my father. And my father has certainly killed me."

***

Claire was awakened by two things at once—the quiet rumble of occluded mucous membranes coming from Hanny Meyer's nose where it had planted itself against the Ramada Inn recliner and her pager's more insistent vibrations.

Hanny was sprawled in the chair, his shirt half unbuttoned and his belt undone, but it seemed he had either lost interest as he attempted the zipper, or simply been overcome by the sleep that Claire knew often swept over her elderly admirer. She gratefully rolled back toward the wall, reaching for her purse and the tantruming pager.

"What is it, Starlight?" It was the first time Claire had made a call from the hotel phone, and she wondered if a record were being made.

"I am *not* whispering," Claire whispered. "Now what did you page me about?" Hanny shifted his weight and pawed at his nose but went on sleeping.

"Call him? Well I already told him I'd have to look over his documents, but alright, what's the number?" Claire wrote down Gunther Huebsch's number feeling a little thrill run down her arms and warmth across her cheeks. She knew that feeling by heart; had come to think of it in the same way she did the glow she felt when she'd won the Miss Fulton County beauty contest, or a teenage modeling gig at Hurley's department store, or when two men had asked her to be their wife. It was an affirmation. In this case one that seemed to say her shelf life was being extended. A little victory over those extra pounds and the deepening shadows that were attempting to eliminate her from the "running." Of course, she'd give him a call, just to see how long they'd talk about documents, before she would feel the conversation shift—or her reticence return.

"Thank you, Starlight. I'll return his call tomorrow and be back in the office in an hour. You better be busy when I get back, now, young lady. Have all that paperwork laid out and don't be talking on the phone with any Chaunceys when I walk in." Claire was giggling now, enough for Hanny to wake and wonder why.

With her back to him, Claire stretched, extending her arms and letting her head and its soft swing of dark hair slowly circle back and forth. She guessed Hanny might be awake now, but she was already in a kind of mental dress rehearsal for what might interest a tweedy German. Claire stood and turned toward the man in the chair—the elderly banker who asked nothing but that she be present in the room. "Present" was only relative though, wasn't it?

In the strips of light slipping between the venetian blinds, Hanford B. Meyer's eyes were open. He smiled at her, then pulled from his pocket a hankie and patted his forehead. "Well, it's always a pleasure being with you, Miss Claire, you drivin' all the way out here… takin' the time outta your busy day. But why don't you just go on ahead, honey… and you be careful on that drive back." Hanny stood up and gently took her hand in

31

the genteel way of a Southern gentleman. "I'll just bet I can carry this vision with me all week long."

Claire headed back to Tupelo as puzzled as she always was on late Thursday afternoons—a puzzlement tinged with pity. But in minutes she found herself not thinking of the Ramada, but of what she could recall about Germany, and for any German words she knew besides *gesundheit*.

Chapter 8

Claire wished the calendar already showed the end of May. It had been stifling on her front porch, in the bank, and here on the outside restaurant's patio. It was as if liquid heat poured along the fronts of Tupelo's brick buildings, and the steam rising from the sidewalk was enough to boil peanuts. But until Memorial Day, convention required her to keep to her close-toed shoes, three-quarter length sleeves, and even a proper jacket in meetings.

Just a weekend to go, she thought, and stretched her arms out like spreaders from a mast. But the slight jiggle inside her sleeves made her quickly pull them back in again with the discomfiting thought that maybe this year would be the last time she would wear sleeveless dresses. One more reminder of passing seasons, disappearing years, and along with them, plenty of collagen. Well, you've got to accommodate, she sighed.

Claire shifted on the metal chair and silently practiced quieting the upper arm wobble by clutching her ribcage with her elbows, hands demurely folded in her the lap. An added benefit, she decided, might be the chance that with a little extra arm-pinch, her cleavage would deepen and her bosom swell upward or—oh God—she'd just create a scratchpad of chest wrinkles where all eyes would be focused. Claire was staring down into her blouse when Doreen puffed up to the outdoor table.

"There you are! Why you look all pink and moist around the edges, don't you? What *are* you lookin' at down there, girl? Missin' a button? But, my goodness, you also look cleaner than I think I've seen you in two years, I do believe it...."

Doreen had driven all the way from Tilley to Tupelo, having announced that she finally had a business plan to discuss and that the future was "looking bright, very bright indeed."

Claire hugged her friend, and they both found angles under the umbrella that kept their skin from the direct sun. Claire knew that Doreen would choose pasta. That woman's alert for rivals to her own cooking kept her on a near straight diet of cheesy sauces and variations on roux. Claire might have ordered the same thing, but today when she looked at her, Doreen's body was reminding her of an Anjou pear, and Claire decided to just keep to a bed of spinach.

"Claire, you are seein' a fully formed, risen, and baked happy woman!" Doreen's halo of slightly raspberry hair had collapsed on one side and now stuck to her scalp. "I am very, very fortunate to have so many women who are, well, advanced in their thinking in my own circle of friends. I never would'a thought they would just see the beauty and the ease of it. I really would not."

Doreen's skin drifted to crustacean pink in hot weather or when biscuits were in the oven, and today Claire thought she looked like she'd cooked a whole hog.

"But you know, I think there are just some things that women don't know, or don't think they know, or just keep a fibbin' to themselves about, until all at once they say, 'Well, if not now, when? What are all these white gloves and facial rubdowns and pecan pralines and canasta parties doin' for me? And then, we are just smarter these days, aren't we? We know how to put things together... all by ourselves."

Claire glanced at her watch. It was one thing to talk like the old men in front of Tilley's Court House, chairs propped against a retaining wall under the oak with the histrionic branches, whiling away the afternoon the way she herself did at Doreen's B & B. But it was another to swelter with her friend over mediocre food on the bank's busy day-before-Memorial Day.

"Doreen, why don't you just lay out what you want a loan for exactly. If it's to use on the mortgage or the roof, well I'm not sure I'm the one you're going to need. But I can arrange a meeting with...."

"Well, hell, no. I told you back a month ago, Claire. I'm startin' a little business on the side. I guess you'd say a subsidiary or spin-off of the B & B. Remember, it's sort of a service industry. It's gonna be called the Excelsior Ladies' Afternoon Spa Retreat. We'll offer relaxation and some very, very needed… uh, feminine exercise. A kind of spiritual and physical rebirthing. And like all good treatments, provided in total discretion," she nodded confidentially.

Claire looked carefully at Doreen, trying to decide where the joke was. Then decided her friend's seriousness meant she really had lost her mind.

"Wait a minute, Doreen. Are you telling me you want me to place a micro-loan, *through the bank*, into a ladies'…, well… *brothel*? Are you nuts?" Claire glanced at the one other table with several women leaning in to its center, laughing at something that seemed to make them all blush. Claire expected she was too.

"Claire, I want to guarantee you something." Doreen pulled her doughy middle upward into a kind of puffed chest look that suggested religious indignation.

"If there's one thing I know better than cooking, it is the nature of the feminine mind. Oh, don't roll your eyes. Yes, you are a woman… well, you *seem* to be of that persuasion, but I see you out there in the woods, all determined with your tractor and your backhoe and your topo map and house plans. Why, hell, girl, you could just about dry up out there in them blue jeans and mud boots the way you're hidin' your inclinations. Oh, I don't say you're not havin' them, but let me see, you would be… well, crossed over the wrong side of forty if I am not mistaken, and there are certain things, like the sweet pies in my kitchen, my dear, that just do not keep."

Doreen took a breath, her cheeks dotted with perspiration. "And that is what I aim to provide, Claire—a buffet. A place where women like you and me and the others who've forgotten that they don't come with shelf life preservatives, can sample some tidbits of love in a place that won't judge them, but will spill them out to their husbands as better women and more whole."

35

Claire's bite of spinach sat perched on her fork, her mouth ready to receive it. She had never heard Doreen give a speech, much less a manifesto—some soulful insight into the female psyche—as if Doreen were a seer or a shrink.

Damn! So, was she sitting on a shelf, done with affection? Is that how she seemed to Doreen and to others? A functionary? A competent goal setter with no longings except for doling out money to the underserved or recreating a past, that she had to admit, was only marginally her own.

Well, there had to be something left. What about that surge of libido for the forestry student, Jackson ? He had taken off his shirt for her to gaze at all that muscular bounty. Had he been offering some up? What if she had touched him? Would he have touched her back? Why had she stopped with only a thought?

Because she was a lady, that's why. Probably even daring Scarlett O'Hara wouldn't have done any touching in her own mother's woods.

A lady. Alright, she was ladylike, but what about Hanny? What was the actual point of being an old man's muse, his little springboard to a distant memory? She knew she'd carried gratitude too far, and it bored her. Was being a lady part of that? What stopped her from just checking out of the Ramada Thursdays? How far was compassion supposed to go?

But the German—that was something else. She had returned his call, feeling herself unable to add syrup to her accent or drop a coquettish innuendo. Instead she realized, as he requested a dinner meeting to elaborate on his interest in some blanket medical testing, that she felt comfortably anonymous behind a business-crisp listing of all the paperwork he should bring. Like a youngster at a first dance, Claire was happy to be chaperoned by the specter of her role as bank manager. Yes, she was every inch the lady, skirt-wearing, but probably sexless to him. Could it be that she, like the women Doreen was describing, needed to be made into a "woman more whole"? Was the damned universe giving her permission to find out?

"Claire, I want you to meet someone I asked to join us." Doreen was standing up to greet another woman coming toward their table. "I believe you know her... she even lives here in Tupelo... just so we could talk."

Claire turned to see a tall, straight-backed woman with tight grey curls surrounding a dust bowl face, but she was smiling and holding her hand out to Claire.

"We do know each other. But not really socially, Ms. Elliston." Claire thought she caught a peculiar flash in the woman's eye as the word "Elliston" came out in little spikes. "You know my husband, I believe."

As they sat down, a sense of panic poured through Claire's chest. "Of course, Mrs. Meyers," said Claire. "I sometimes do work with your husband. Hanford B. Meyers is someone I met when I was just a little girl."

Alma Meyers patted Claire's hand. "That's right. That's about when Hanny was working for your grandfather, I believe. How is Senator Elliston, now? He must get weary of living in that big house all by himself in Tilley with you up here in Tupelo. You drop in on him, I bet, every chance you get, now don't you."

"Every chance," said Claire, who hadn't seen Charlie in years. Had been told to keep away just the way he had told his own daughter.

"Claire, Alma here is gonna help me run the Ladies Spa," said Doreen, flicking her eyes proudly back and forth between the two women. "She just gets the whole concept, and she knows at least a dozen... patrons... already willing to sign on too. You just wouldn't believe who they are, who their husbands are. Even I don't know all of them. The membership chairwoman is going to be Alma, and she's got lists!"

"Really?" Claire eyed Alma. Could this woman sue her as "correspondent" in some front-page divorce scandal? Could this librarian of a tweed-suited woman want to roll in the hay with a forester too? Jesus Christ.

"That's right, dear," said Alma. Then turning to Claire, "Now all we need is a small loan to buy a van for transportation, another bit of money to put in some bidets—which we think would be a very nice touch—and uh..., well, Doreen said you were well-equipped for this next part... for you to bring us the men."

"I wasn't sure how many we'd need at first," said Doreen, shyly holding some papers out to Claire. "But I did a little spread sheet on my computer, and given that your foresters are all in their early twenties, I think a one to three ratio might work."

Chapter 9

"Pretty hot for late May in Tilley, Mississippi. Temperature's tippin' ninety-six today." The radio voice sounded bedraggled even at seven AM.

The old man switched off the machine and shoved himself off the pillow better to hear the kids hollering in the backyard and down the linoleum-floored hall, arguing about the bathroom, starting to throw a ball against the listing garage, clamoring like fledglings for some item of food they knew wouldn't have been purchased in this household. The usual cacophony of too many people in a too small space. He smiled. Just the way he liked it.

Eustus Pitts moved his long legs in measured increments across sheets as flowered as a daisy patch and finally placed one dry, flaking foot against the coolness of the floor. The rest of him he pried up with a yardstick arm.

He sat there a moment before feeling for the Bible that would begin his day and the plastic spectacles that connected him to the world. In fact, Eustus didn't need the glasses for his Bible; its messages and cadences were simply a part of everything he said and did anyway. No, eyeglasses were for the ancillary parts of life. What mattered, he carried in his head and in his pacemakered heart.

"Granpap! Granpap! Granpap!" The small fist of Lionel, the youngest in the household, was beating against the bedroom's blue door. A chip of paint skittered away and onto the floor.

"You get yourself away from Granpap's room, you hear! What you think you doin'! Now go and sit down by Anthony outside that bathroom door, and you wait your turn, young man!" Eustus could hear Lionel's feet being marched away in a series of little stomps and Starlight's voice calling to another child to bring in the picnic hamper from the garage.

The old man bent over chuckling as quietly as he could. Eustus didn't care if it hit 100, this was the best day of the year. Decoration Day, he still called it. Memorial Day to the rest of the country, it was the day when he too felt like a boy again; when the cemeteries would open and scattered families would reunite to clean the tombstones' weeds away, whitewash the ones that had gone moldy, arrange flowers, and spread big picnic cloths under the live oaks where the old folks could recline and the children play tag among the monuments. Eustus felt sure it wasn't disrespectful. He was so close to that underground time himself that he was pretty certain he'd be tapping an embalmed foot to the sounds of some childish rhyme in the turf above him when his time came. The very thought made him slap his leg in merriment. Decoration Day was a time to feel young, to tell stories, and remember the old folks, some not so old..., but the ones who remained connected to you by blood or something just as deep. It was a time to pass on what was important about their lives; a time, each year, to share another secret.

"Grandad? You up now, Grandad?" This time it was Starlight tapping on his door. "You need any help in there? I got your coffee going in the kitchen, now."

He heard her precise little steps heading onto the back porch where he knew she'd have her girlie pinks and whites hung out on a line. Half her paycheck he reckoned, but then, he was proud of this girl. She liked the finer things alright, but she worked for them, and found enough extra to help out her mother and sisters and auntie to boot.

Eustus pulled his cane from its perch on his iron headboard and inserted his feet into the big brogans he wore every day. At seventy, he was still tall, still able to square broad shoulders, and lift his head high and his voice higher still when called upon to deliver a sermon at the church he'd led for over forty years.

He looked, as he always did, in the small tilting mirror atop the oak bureau. In another time, Peony, his wife of fifty years would have already been up, oiling her hair into place, and taking the time to come over and in that tiny mirror, smooth his out as well. That woman knew about night rags and how they preserved and conditioned the hairdos so popular in the fifties, but Peony hadn't cared about "beautifyin'." She just pulled her long, springy hair into a braid and laid down her head. Peony believed in her family and her church, and that was just about it. Eustus thought for a moment as he looked at the creases dividing his dark face into fjords and canyons, at the white stubble and the yellow teeth, the eyes whose jet pupils were curtained with cataract blue, and thought that he had loved Peony above all others. All others, but for one.

And he would go to see them both this very day.

Chapter 10

By one o'clock, cars were beginning to turn at regular intervals into Laurel Rest Cemetery. Like a city-wide cortege, they followed one another at discreet distances. Somber passengers sitting straight up, smaller cars sporting hoes and clippers from their trunks, they flowed in isolated cadence into the winding lanes of the cemetery.

Occasionally a car doubled back as if lost. Sometimes one would pause at a rise where an elderly historian would struggle out, scan the horizon, then gesture toward one of hundreds of tombstones. The car would then readjust and make its way through the cemetery toward the resting place of family or kin who waited patiently every year until the end of May.

The layout of Laurel Rest and its "black sister," Heaven Land, was as if two siblings lay back to back, forever connected, but refusing to acknowledge the other's presence. Laurel Rest was sprawled over a softly-mounded hill, shaded by Victorian-era live oaks, and dotted with obelisks and mausoleums, stone benches, and pointed iron enclosures. Here, generations of Tilley's humble and elevated citizens were laid to rest. Soldiers, farmers, tradesmen, landowners, and share croppers. The churched and sinners alike slumbered and snuggled in Laurel Rest's consecrated ground. Ground meant for all—as long as they were white.

Heaven Land, separated from its high-ground white sibling by a meandering drive, reached down to a dry pond bed, but here only three oaks survived, albeit to mammoth proportions. On this steeper downward slope, headstones were small, old, and even toppled. Places to sit and meditate and exclusive family plots were absent. The black cemetery contained the remains of families who had been born on the plantations and farms that stretched across this part of Mississippi.

Some had started life as slaves and ended as free men. Others were born free, but whose lives remained as conscribed by convention and practice as if their white bosses had simply lost the ownership deeds. They were maids and chauffeurs, fieldworkers, and laundresses. They minded white families' children and shoed white men's horses, and when a white girl needed a friend in time of need, it was a black woman lying here who would have known what to do.

The U. S. Supreme Court had officially ordered integration in 1954, though thirty years later you'd never know it looking at Mississippi's schools and universities. But at Laurel Rest, run by what most locals thought was a spineless administrator with no stomach for Federal authorities forcing him to integrate this burial soil, the cemetery had officially merged the two expanses of holy ground the year following the court order. Now an occasional black family could be seen silently hacking away at weeds around a small headstone in Laurel Rest, the "white" side of the cemetery, but one well away from families of prominence. No white families had ever opted to have their loved one buried on the other side.

Claire came alone this year as she'd done since she'd moved back to Mississippi. She'd made no calls to Big Daddy Charlie in order to stand on decorum, to stiffly act the part of a dutiful granddaughter helping an old man shuffle through spring flowers fertilized by his long dead friends. Her grandfather had hired the sullen-faced niece of the gas station owner to do his laundry, make his lunches, and haul him to his numerous doctors' appointments. She would bring him here too, if he so decided. No need now for Claire to keep even the pretense of a relationship. He didn't. Today, all she needed was to steer clear of his muscular green Oldsmobile, find her mother's grave, and leave.

"S'Ultana, do *not* put that quilt down there, girl! Don't you see that ant hill? Why, it's as tall as a laundry basket!" Starlight was directing four teenage girls as they struggled with blankets and sheets toward the biggest oak in Heaven Land.

43

Five or six cars had backed up with trunks open toward the tombstones as if a tailgate party were revving up, and the graves might open up so their occupants could join in.

"Alright, Dalwynn, gather those kids away from that tree! There's no climbing trees in the cemetery, you hear. Go get the hampers and the lemonade. Tawn-ee, you and Sylvester please take the rakes and bags over to Great Granma's grave. Go on, you can find it. Just read! Don't be stupid!"

Starlight always emerged as the crew boss on Decoration Day. Her sisters were the cooks, her brothers-in-law the brawn, and her nephews and nieces the jostling, scrambling lackeys. Outlying family members and church friends would join them soon, but Starlight liked to get to Heaven Land early to pick the best spot under the big tree for her grandfather to preside.

"Where's Aunt Gertrude's chair?" puffed Dalwynn, the lanky teen who sometimes acted as go-between between Starlight and Chauncey.

"Well, I'm surprised you didn't hit it with your nose, Dal. It's strapped to the top of the car. You better get some glasses, boy!" He had already positioned the old man's cushioned rocking chair on a hard, flat spot at the base of the oak and now would put one for Aunt Gertrude next to it.

It didn't take long for the long table to be opened and draped with a table cloth. Only then would the warm barbeque be piled next to potato salad, collards in bacon fat set out, three-inch biscuits, slaw swimming in vinegar cream, and jugs of sweet tea spread across the table to fill each available inch. Red velvet cake and sweet potato pies next to pecan tarts and pralines would be loaded onto the big table and two card tables besides.

The cars kept coming. They clogged the lane in front of the big oak and the shady trees beyond where other families united and set up their "eatin' out" supplies. Men in rolled up shirt-sleeves and straw hats wandered next to women carrying umbrellas against the sun, their hats adorned with flowers and twisted ribbon, all of them, heads down, reading gravestones, stopping to tell a story or a joke, and to relate the powerful thread of family connections.

Eustus Pitts loved Decoration Day, and despite the heat, everything was just as it should be. Church elders sauntered over and took the empty chair next to Eustus for just enough time to inquire after his health and his family and then move on and let another man or woman respectfully sit down.

His granddaughters brought him his iced tea and cake, and he knew when he stood up, his sons-in-law and their children would pick up the tools and head out to pull the weeds from the graves and put down the flamboyantly colored plastic flowers that would be biodegraded grey by September.

It would only be after the graves were adorned, and when the harmonicas, the banjo, and guitars had come out and when people rested against the tree or curled up to nap on a blanket, that Eustus would slip away, first to his wife's grave and then, carefully, to the one on the hill.

He stared up toward it, to the place under an oak just like the lowland one here, tidily fenced, but he knew, rarely visited. A figure knelt in the grass, pulling at weeds and from time to time, stopping to press a handkerchief to her eyes. From behind the rise, another figure, different, yet somehow the same, appeared to hesitate. The first one rose, and the two women faced each other for a long time. Eustus felt he could see the air around them heat, the space between them vibrate. He rubbed his eyes, and when he raised them, the two silhouettes had merged, holding each other momentarily, one black form against the fading lavender sky.

Eustus took a step back. Behind him, Sylvester had begun a slow gospel tune, the one that Gertrude, with her low contralto could make come the spirit of God to any man's side. He waited in the falling light to hear her first throaty notes, but they didn't come. His family swayed gently around him, humming softly, but Gertrude wasn't there.

***

The Tilley residents, who that morning Gunther Huebsch had seen spilling out of the Piggly Wiggly and the Dollar Store, arms filled with artificial flowers and even a resin statue or two, had all moved off toward the graveyard that he could see on the hill in the distance. He noted a few

45

carrying new rakes and trowels and wondered what was going on at the cemetery.

Feeling as if Tilley had been evacuated, he walked slowly around the courthouse. Claire Elliston had agreed to have lunch with him, but she was late. No, be honest, he told himself, he was early.

He glanced at his watch again, then loosened his tie. The temperature felt more like Africa than a continent the same general latitude as Bavaria. Yet, despite the heat and the enclaves of obvious poverty, the American South had a charm he had not expected. A charm and a sense of style!

He looked up at the courthouse. He'd circled the leafy block set squarely in the middle of Tilley several times now and tried to picture the people who'd conceived this building. A sense of style, maybe, but these nineteenth century Southerners seemed not to have been able to say "no" when it came to architecture.

Still, the yellow brick of the gaudy courthouse mesmerized him. An amalgam of French Empire élan and Confederate decadence, it was an overstuffed confection of oval windows, two foot moldings, turrets, a scalloped slate roof, and more Corinthian columns than Gunther could count. He knew the city residents swelled with pride when they gazed up at the design cataclysm, and it made him shake his head. Mad King Ludwig's Neuschwanstein was a fantastic caprice, but he could forgive the Black Forest fantasy castle and its eccentric builder because no one ever took it seriously. But these Southerners simply loved their overwrought courthouse. It was something that intrigued him about the South. The people here lived in everything from crumbling trailers to sprawling mansions, yet every one of them had a pride and confidence that was never seen in European peasants and was suppressed in its elite. Threadbare overalls or vested suits, there was a sense of being right that Gunther had yet to figure out.

And yet he liked them. He'd met Americans from the North, but it was only in these Southerners that he found the kind of continuity with the past that he felt in his own homeland. In Germany, he lived in the house his great-grandfather had built and slept in his bed. In the South, he saw the same kind of reluctance to leave the past. Was it that peculiar

46

quality of the people, their chin-jutting pride and a feisty resiliency that made an old German soldier weep with longing thirty-five years after his return home?

Gunther remembered the night he had watched slow tears fall from his father's eyes onto a handful of tiny photos taken in Tilley when his father was a young man. He had known his father as a physician and scientist, a philanthropist who had opened his heart to the poor, an entrepreneur who had built his reputation and gained great wealth in post-war Germany, but slowly, Gunther was learning, he was also a man who had lived with secrets. Ones that had perhaps kept him alive.

Gunther looked around. A few more people seemed to come down from the cemetery. The lady banker surely wouldn't be long. He sat down heavily on the balustrade surrounding what looked like it was meant to be the courthouse moat and pulled the letter from his pocket. The folds had begun to separate, and the typing even now was turning from black to a weary sepia. This was a legend, he thought, a key, a kind of map of his father's life that would lead him to the treasure the old man thought had been lost. Though his father was gone now, some of his secrets spilled out of these very pages. Gunther had decided he had the means to discover the last and most important one. And to right the wrong the old man had lived with until his death.

Gunther looked at his watch then up at the courthouse clock. Fifteen minutes before the appointment with the attractive Tupelo banker who seemed to know this area well and whose small loan could justify his being in tiny Tilley at all.

He hadn't met many of the locals—someone from the department of health, a country doctor or two, a city father called Hanford Meyers —all of them warm in the way of these Southern small town people. But this woman Claire had a kind of audacious femininity that he sensed she'd kept yoked under a business suit and reading glasses when she'd interviewed him at the bank in Tupelo. She was smart, and he guessed that once resolved to something, this woman could do the most terrifying things with the toss of her head—or the thrust of her hips.

Gunther quickly took out a cigarette, as if by inhaling the smoke, he could then exhale some of his thoughts. No, Tilley was about his father.

There would be no absurd involvements here. Plenty of those left behind in Frankfurt. He was a medical doctor here to conduct science, and if he were lucky, peer back into history. He reopened the letter and for the hundredth time read the last pages of his father's meditational will:

> *I cannot say that I am proud of the decision, my son, but if I had not taken it... I doubt very much you would be reading these words today. My uncles in Frankfort had already been taken. Your grandparents had fled to Bremen where they later were exposed. Your aunt Katerina, who had married a goy, had been discovered and sent to a camp in the east. What chance did I think that I had, a poor medical student with a Jewish identity card? Except that by some miracle, I, as you are as well, had been born blonde and blue-eyed, as if we had come into the world in masquerade.*
>
> *Military police swept through neighborhoods as the war news turned desperate..., dragging off straggling Jews and making on the spot conscriptions of cowardly Germans. One of these, a man named Helmut Gruber, decided he would rather die in Germany by his own hand than be shot in Russia or die at sea. It was I who found Gruber's body.*
>
> *What I would do came to me quickly. It was sudden and surprising. I went through his pockets and, being blonde like him—a haircut, a certain sidelong grimace he had—and within hours, I became Helmut Gruber. I volunteered for the Wehrmacht infantry immediately, I didn't care where they sent me. It was an easy choice between that and Dachau. And two weeks later, I was fighting in Dresden, a soldier on the side of killers and fiends. Two months later Americans found me in a burnt-out cellar—and I let Helmut Gruber get back on his journey to the beyond.*

48

Gunther stood up, shoving the rest of the testament into his pocket. He surveyed the leafy square, the innocence on the faces of elderly women doing their errands, the old men who shook their heads over the price of hog feed or the latest political imbecile, and wondered how all of these people had struck his father when he arrived in Tilley as a German prisoner of war. They might have been his father's age. Perhaps one or two of them had met him and the other prisoners on the surrounding farms to which the captured German soldiers had been sent in a kind of indentured servitude. Maybe some of them were privy to what went on here.

Gunther took a breath. Now Claire Elliston was late. That wouldn't have happened in Germany, but he knew the United States South preferred a different gait. That, and that this woman might just as likely set her own pace. Somehow that aroused him slightly.

Gunther lit another cigarette and for the third time pulled out his father's letter.

> *...and so if I tell you about the war and my part in it, the men I killed, the women too, perhaps, I would be telling you a story many men bring back. But I wish to tell you of something strange and beautiful in a land lifted from another planet.*
>
> *When I was taken prisoner, the Americans shipped me to their country. There were so many of us. What else was there to do? More than 40,000 of us Germans were scattered onto the farms and villages of America. My destination was a place with an Indian name, Mississippi. Exotic I thought at first, but when I arrived, I found it to be an idyllic place of pastures and forests and rolling farmland. It was like Germany before the war. That place, as I left its cinders, had simply ceased to exist.*
>
> *We were divided into "squadrons"—small groups; divided so that we could not reunite and cause trouble. Some of us were set to work as colliers, if we could, or plowmen, or simply handymen who hauled water and*

*built fences for the local farmers. At first, we spoke no
English and stayed to ourselves. Only once every two
days did a warden drive out to check on us. Where would
we run? We had only our prison clothes, no money, and
what they called, "Kraut accents." We were prisoners in
a prison the size of a nation. Besides, they fed us well!*

*But not every American was forgiving. After about
six months on a farm in Waynesboro, the family's son
came home. He had fought in North Africa. He was
missing a leg and an eye. And perhaps he was missing
what humanity he had left with. At night, he would come
into our bunk house with his dogs and a shovel, perhaps
a hoe. Sometimes he simply took shots at us while we
tended his farm. That is when I decided to leave. I would
find another prison.*

"Mr. Huebsch?" The woman standing before him laughed as if
something had just tickled her. "Don't you recognize me? Well, that's
not much of an impression we here in Mississippi make, now is it?"

Gunther looked up, but the sun blazed just behind her head, and he
only saw the soft dark features of a woman in shadow and felt the river
of sound that floated on her long vowels. He stood up with a start, a tilt
to his head and a formal bow as he tucked away his letter.

"Please forgive me, I did not see you. I am so sorry." And again, as
it had in the bank, as it had in their brief conversation by phone, Gunther
felt a recognition, the awkward feeling of coming home—to a place he'd
never been.

"You have come such a long way to tour this little area, Mr.
Huebsch, I do hope it is going to be worth your while. I can point out
some empty store fronts where you might set up your... your clinic, but
beyond this six-block square, all you're going to find is pastureland and
forest."

The woman still wore a business persona that fluctuated like a
weather vane, tight and fact-filled one minute, soft and teasing the next.
Yet something had changed. She seemed tense, preoccupied.

"I see that you are not wearing your bank attire today," smiled Gunther, hoping to relax her into conversation. "You are doing your gardening duties?"

Claire glanced at him, unsmiling. They walked slowly toward a row of turn-of-the-century storefronts. "I have been to the cemetery this morning. It is something we do here once a year, tidying the graves, paying respects."

"Ah... yes, this is something I know of as well. Sometimes I think that Germany is one big cemetery." He stopped, not knowing if she, like many others, would still think of Germans as a land of brutal Nazis. "Good people as well as bad die in wars; do they not?"

Claire wasn't paying attention. She glanced up at the hill where cars were slowly making their way down.

"Is your family buried in the cemetery?" asked Gunther.

Claire gazed back at him. Though she met his eyes, Gunther recognized the look of someone whose mind, in its wayward fashion, had carried her off. He thought she heard his voice, but her look suggested she was waiting for answers to different questions.

"Come, Ms. Elliston," he said, the professional healer coming to her rescue. "We shall get some tea, some coffee, perhaps, here in Tilley. Can you take us to such a shop? And then I will describe to you my research in detail and explain why this German wishes to become a Southern vampire!"

Chapter 11

Hanford B. Meyers had on his Sunday suit, even though it was Tuesday. It was oppressive in the humidity that had descended on Tilley by the second week of June. Damn, he hadn't even moved the rake from the trunk after tidying his parents' graves a couple of weeks before. He stretched his neck out of the absurdly starched collar and smoothed down the ruff of hair that still tended toward curls in the heat.

These command appearances, these visits to an aging "pontiff" filled Hanny with self-disgust. Every few months his secretary would delicately lay a note on his desk as if it were written on vellum or parchment. As if a request from Charlie Elliston was still something approaching a dictate. As if Big Daddy Elliston still ran this part of Mississippi. And every few months Hanny made the pilgrimage.

He turned the Lincoln from the highway onto what had been the main street in old Tilley, the one he ran the delivery truck up and down as a boy. And then he took a smaller road into a subdivision of post-World War II cracker boxes, a little burb that had risen out of the woods that once surrounded the old Elliston place.

Charlie's big brick Southern colonial now sat on a grassless plot of land surrounded by what had been a Gothic-inspired, Victorian iron fence. Two metal sheds had been deposited in the back near the summer kitchen, and the century oaks in the front yard seemed to be bowing under the weight of relentless Spanish moss.

Christ, the next time I come here the whole damned chimney is gonna a' come down too, thought Hanny. He remembered how he had brought his deliveries to the front door on purpose just to admire the white molding and pillars that gleamed under dozens of coats of paint.

He laughed out loud thinking of how Charlie's exasperated maid, Sarah, had practically semaphored him to the back door so as to keep him out of trouble. Now the paint was grey and appeared only in patches against the raw weathered wood, and Hanny knew there was no maid.

As he expected, he'd had to wait in the heat on the front porch for the door to open. Whether it was on purpose now, Hanny doubted, but in another time, he knew old Charlie Elliston had instructed the maid not to answer a bell's ring for a full minute before opening the door. Humbling a visitor was part of the elaborate layering, the drama with which the old man manipulated those around him. Hanny wasn't sure why he kept playing his part. The play was well past its run.

There was shuffling behind the door before it slowly swung open. A very dry set of fingers curled around its edge. Hanny knew Charlie was just inside, that the old man had on a wrinkled shirt, a tie, pleated trousers held high on his abdomen by sprung suspenders—just as he always had. He knew the folds of Charlie's face, the winnowed-out hollows at his temples, the high, intelligent forehead that took in a man and his weaknesses at first sight. And he knew the low rumble of Charlie's voice—thick molasses mixed with the growl of a gator in a swamp thicket.

"Come in, Hanford." Hanny was a delivery boy again. Plugged into his role, taking orders, executing them, not questioning.

"Good afternoon, Mr. Elliston." The room was dark and belching with mildew, yet Hanny knew where each piece of furniture was, where it had always been. He knew the old rugs, frayed into "dog run" patterns where feet had shuffled to and fro through the years. He knew the books yellowing behind glass doors, the fireplace whose cinders were hardened to lava, a spinet piano that was bought as a badge of culture but whose keys now slumped flat and untouched.

"I believe you will not need any refreshment, it being so soon after lunch time." Charlie never offered a guest anything. Hanny wondered if the old boy ordered pizza or Chinese every day, since he refused any domestic help after Sarah died. Most people thought Charlie would die too after the family's "retainer" departed, but Charlie didn't seem to agree.

Hanny took the seat he knew he would be offered, the velvet bench six inches lower than Charlie's large leather armchair. Hanny could practically see the spores rise as he sat down.

"I think you have an understanding as to why I am desirous of meeting with you again, Hanford," began Charlie. In the old days, Charlie would have wrapped any bricks in layers of charm. But along with the Big House's paint, even pseudo-hospitality seemed to have worn thin.

"We, of course, do not need to review your position. We've talked of it before…, the one that became possible as a result of certain doors being opened for you. I, in fact, believe that all in all, you took a good deal of advantage, excellent advantage of what was made possible for you back then. Many a young man might not have been so smart. But you, even at a young age, saw which way the water ran, and you chose to climb in the boat goin' downstream. It would have been hard on you if you'd done otherwise." Charlie folded his hands across his gut.

It was stifling in the living room, filled with dusk at midday. Hanny didn't need the preamble, each time, the build-up, the pats on the back praising the fact that at seventeen he'd left the beginnings of a moral life behind. Hanny knew the old man would go on like this for a while and that just for a few minutes he could close his mind off and search in the shadows for his past. It didn't take long for his eyes to find it—in the picture frame, now with a faded painting of an Italian meadow, the one that used to hold a photo of Charlie's daughter, Lisbeth.

"What do you mean your father has killed you?" Lisbeth *Elliston sat quietly in the car beside the courthouse. Then slowly, she began to daub at her legs with her skirt.*

"I'm still bleeding. I don't know how long that goes on…." Her hair hung across her face in a latticed tangle. "I think I need to clean myself." Lisbeth's voice sounded as if she were speaking from inside a dream, emotionless, observant, but detached.

"I'm taking you to a hospital, or a doctor's, Lisbeth. Something happened that I don't understand, but you need a doctor." Hanny turned on the car.

"The deed's been done, don't you understand?" Lisbeth turned to him, beginning to shake. The town had gone to sleep, but the traffic light still played red and green against her face.

"He thought he was the only one who laid a hand on me, but once a garden's plowed, seeds from other fields can sprout." Lisbeth gave something that might have been a laugh and ran her fingers through her hair, wet from tears or sweat.

"Do you understand, Hanny Meyers. The high, the almighty Charles Rutherford Elliston didn't like what was growin' in his property, and with some rope to hold me down, a knitting needle and the kitchen tongs...." Her face was beaded with sweat now and the words were interrupted by racking shudders.

"I think I might 'a killed him, Hanny. I fought him back, tried to fight him off. His neck was cut all around. Bleedin' on my hands, bleedin' down my legs. Important Mr. Charles Elliston on his hands and knees squirting blood all over the barn floor...." Lisbeth's whisper was full of disbelief.

"And now, Hanny," she said quietly, "If it is your desire to see me lying on a morgue table, you will take me to a hospital. Because if he lives this night, Senator Charles Elliston will see that my story ends right there in such a place."

Tears fell along Hanny's cheeks. "What should I do? Then where should I take you...?" He wanted to sob, to be someplace else.

Lisbeth gripped Hanny's arm and looked at him with eyes that bored through the dark. "Take me to Sarah's house in the woods," she said. "It's her son who's got to grieve too."

"So again, Hanford..., you may not have heard me..., but I remain pleased with the way the Bank's Board has kept on the tight and narrow." Hanny started, wondering if Charlie's cloudy blue eyes had seen through to his thoughts. Of course, Charlie would never show that he knew and continued on with the flattering section of his speech.

"Some of these other Mississippi and Alabama banks are making loans that just about ask for defaultin'. I believe that you have put in place the practices that I consider prudent for makin' money and for helpin' people when they should be helped. Of course, we all know that not everybody falls into that category, don't we?" Charlie chuckled with the camaraderie he exuded when he was about to rifle your pockets or put on the squeeze.

Hanny shifted on the bench. Sometimes he thought he felt Lisbeth in this room, sometimes it was just her absence. Today she was somewhere else.

His neck was aching from sitting like a school boy, and he knew the top of his collar was spongy with sweat. Thank God, the meeting would end soon, as soon as Charlie made his demand.

"So young man..., well, not so young, anymore, are we? There is this issue that I feel most strongly about putting to rest. Some things, as you know, are best handled discreetly. Not everybody needs to see how things work, do they, boy? And yet the natural order of things... well, someone needs to uphold nature's rules and to have the strength to live by those. You and I, Hanford, as you've shown me all these years, are the people who must do that. And it's time you got to it."

Hanny shifted on the bench. Here it came.

"You made a very bad choice over fifty years ago, didn't you, Hanford? You took my sinful daughter to an old, uneducated woman to try and hide her sin. I acknowledge that you may have thought you were performing an act of mercy, but there had been an *abomination*, a mating of bodies that God has commanded be kept apart. And the result was a *pestilence* that lived and grew." Charlie rarely mentioned the details, but the old man seemed animated by disgust today.

"Born black as night from that girl's white body..., we now have a proclamation of her spitefulness that walks our streets to this very day." In his rewriting of history, Charlie's face had taken on the ruddiness of the hypocrite.

"The product of such an unsanctified union is not to be blamed, though it would have been merciful for it to have died before a first breath. However, I, as a *believer*, can only pity that aberration of nature, but it is the sinner who should pay for her insult to God's Holy plan." He wiped his face back and forth with a large, yellowed handkerchief.

56

"And so I say, let her no longer lie with God-fearing people!" Charlie slammed his palms onto the armrests with a smack. Hanny had seen him determined before but never like this.

"While my wife lived, I gave in to too much! 'Forgive her. Bring her back.' That woman sniveled until the very end of her life. What'd she want me to do? Did she want us to live with that girl's little black bitch right here in this house? Have it sit on my lap and me make funny faces to keep it happy? No sir! This is a Godly-man's house. And that was not about to be!" Charlie was pacing in front of the spinet.

"By all that breathes, I did right by giving that girl a place out in the country to stay. I could have shipped her North... or worse. But she abided by stayin' put out there, and I abided by not ever seeing or hearin' from her again. And you, Hanford Meyers, abided by keeping your mouth shut for these years..., and you've been paid rightly for it. Hell, runnin' a whole bank ain't nothin'. Now it's time to get her ass out of the white cemetery where I'm gonna lie and over to the nigger side where it belongs!"

Hanny stood up, jolted awake it seemed for the first time. He was seventy-one years old. He knew sinners, and he had sinned himself, but watching the bent frame of this ancient wraith, watching the seething hatred Charlie stoked even as he teetered toward eternity, whose very life had been built on manipulation and hate—Hanny Meyers decided it was time to stop.

The doorbell jangled just as Hanny took in the breath that would put an end to what he suddenly saw as his subservient complicity and pathetic patriotism to a way of life that had ended long ago. Why had it taken so long to find his own heroism... to grow a set of balls?

Without Charlie Elliston answering it, the door swung open, and a woman's silhouette appeared. With a lightness of step that was somehow familiar, Hanny watched the woman come toward them, swing around and sidle up to the old man. She gave him a "magnolia kiss," the kind Southern women reserve for other ladies and elderly gentlemen. Then she primly sat down on the musty sofa, patting it for Hanny to sit beside her.

It was Alma, his wife, gaunt and unappealing in her toothy smile. "Well, Hanny, how is the conversation going? Has Mr. Elliston gotten to the good part?"

"Well, if you don't look like a spring willow... just fresh and full of sunshine," oozed Charlie. "No, Honey, we was just about gettin' there."

"Getting where?" asked Hanny, suddenly disoriented. He felt as if a trap were about to be sprung.

"Why, getting to the part where I tell you that Mr. Elliston and me done made a little plan." Alma's gums looked inflamed when she smiled. "We decided that you're gonna do what he wants 'bout puttin' that floozy on the nigger side, and you're gonna do what I want with a nice big monetary... we'll say... 'surprise' birthday present." She tilted her head and clasped her hands under her prominent chin. Alma was suddenly the quarterback on the winning team.

"'Cause, Hanny, if you have any second thoughts, why, Honey, I'm gonna make it known from the halls of heaven to the gates of hell, that every Thursday in a Ramada Inn, you been fuckin' the *bejeezus* out of... you hear me now, your own goddamned daughter!"

Chapter 12

"Two this week! And one don't even need to be repaid? Well, you done loosened the purse strings, for sure, Ms. Elliston." Starlight had been on a buying spree and now was poured into a pink pants suit that she'd coupled with red platform shoes.

"Starlight, one of the agreements is for a loan; the other is being made as a grant. The bank has always had provisions for giving money without strings for causes deemed worthy to a community." Claire wasn't in the mood for justifying herself to her assistant this morning. "You just get all those little blanks filled in on the forms and bring me the cut checks so I can sign them. And, Starlight, the bank examiners are here today. Do not be bending over to file things while they are in the office, you hear?"

Starlight didn't hear. She was leaning over the thick book open on Claire's desk. "Are you sick, Miss Claire?" Starlight looked up, her forehead corrugated in concern. "You look okay, but you can tell me if something's wrong."

The page Starlight was focused on was pasted with sticky notes defining various medical terms, and the smell of the Tupelo Library's basement floated around its age-stiffened pages. There were illustrations of distended abdomens and swollen joints and a notebook on top where Claire had been taking meticulous notes.

"You go an' get on with your business, girl. Thank you for your concern. I am fine. You are fine. Go see if Chauncey is making a delivery today or something." Claire closed the book and turned toward her typewriter. "Just make sure that one check reads to: The Excelsior

Ladies' Afternoon Spa Retreat," she called over her shoulder. *A porcelain bidet? What am I getting into?*

But it was the grant she'd decided to give to the German doctor that fascinated her. Claire looked out the bank window. She couldn't identify what kept the rumpled doctor's image dancing before her. Thick blond eyebrows over eyes that weren't communicating what his lips were saying and a funny way he had of tipping forward when he addressed her, like an insecure shoe salesman who'd told her oxfords accentuated her arch. And yet when the German did it, he didn't seem insecure at all.

Claire absently thumbed through the medical book, smiling to think that he probably knew everything inside. Why it gave her a little thrill she couldn't say, but the doctor had impressed her. He said he was repaying a debt to America for the kindnesses his father had been shown when he'd visited this part of the American South as a young man. Now Gunther, yes, she thought she could call him, Gunther—somehow a reassuring name—was going to offer free blood screenings to each and every person in the area around Tilley where his father had been welcomed. He'd explained that it was perfectly legal. He had trained in the U.S. and been licensed here before returning to Germany. He simply wanted to return the kindness extended to his father.

Claire glanced towards Starlight's desk, then put on her glasses and reopened the thick medical index. She was halfway through the list of nasty illnesses Gunther said he'd be testing for. She wanted to know what each one was in case the board questioned her sudden fiscal benevolence. *Thrombocytopenic purpura, Wilson's disease, Crohn's disease, celiac disease, HIV, Sickle Cell Anemia, and Gaucher's disease.* Gunther said that each could be diagnosed by a simple blood test. Lord knew this part of Mississippi had its share of diseases. Some Claire guessed were caused by diet, others perhaps from the tendency of people never to move away and to marry within their own counties. She wondered if people used to living with a certain level of illness would be willing to come forward.

Gunther's plan was to open a small storefront clinic incentivized by gifts of dinners at the Apple Pandowdy, a bag of groceries at Piggly Wiggly, or half the cost of a hunting license. "Even in health-conscious

Europe you sometimes need to bait a trap with sugars and fats to lure people into clinics," he'd told her.

Claire took a sip of sweet tea. She'd noted down the copper overload of Wilson's disease and the gastric disturbances of Crohn's. She'd heard all too much about the devastation HIV and AIDs were wreaking across the country. Thrombocytopenia had to do with platelets in the blood, though she wasn't sure what those were, and celiac disease was about not being able to absorb nutrients. Gaucher's disease, however, wasn't in the library book. She would ask Gunther about that one the next time they got together. The next time? Was she expecting to see him again?

Involuntarily, Claire scanned her appointment book: bank meetings, city council, audit review, but there would definitely be room for a dinner or a lunch. Perhaps even something home-cooked. A foreigner might like that. Then she saw the Saturday entry she'd scratched in red. "Interview candidates" it said. Below it was Jackson's familiar number.

"Miss Claire," sang Starlight from her office chair. The red shoes were obviously hurting enough to prevent Starlight from sashaying the fifteen feet to Claire's desk.

"It's that Mr. Hoob-ster on the phone for you. The one with the accent who's gonna do things to us."

Claire sent a visual missile toward her nubile secretary and picked up the phone, checking to see that Starlight had replaced her receiver. "Well, good morning, Mr. Huebsch. How are you this lovely day?"

Gunther was doing well, he said, and hoped that she would again address him by his given name, especially in that he was inquiring if she would care to dine with him in the small carriage house he had rented just outside of Tilley, and where he would prepare a German dish if she didn't mind.

"How very kind you are. And what a special experience that would be. Why, I'd be delighted," said Claire. Starlight was a little out of control now, watching Claire and pinching her own cheeks to tell her boss she saw her blushing.

Claire noted Gunther's address and time they'd meet, then hung up and without a smile, snapped toward her secretary, "I need the Hampton files and the Public Service compliance forms and the Jacobs foreclosure

61

on my desk now." In a series of wave-like undulations, Starlight managed to rise from her desk and wobble towards the file room, leaving a V-trail of Pink Jasmine floating behind her.

Claire closed her eyes and waved a Kleenex in little circles to disperse the bank of cheap cologne that was settling on her clothes. Gunther Huebsch. Who was this man? Surely something in her experience would give her an answer. He was making dinner for her? That alone was eccentric enough, but the kind of concern he expressed for people far removed from his own world and in gratitude for long-ago kindnesses, these were far from anything she had known from a man.

If she were honest, her experience with men had been confusing at best. Like puzzle pieces, both of her fiancés had simply fit into spaces that needed filling at the time. They'd been templates, prescribed models that might have been picked from a catalog and C.O.D.ed right to her door. But, she smiled to herself, somebody had forgotten to glue down the cutouts. A storm, a breeze, a passing cloud—it hadn't taken much. First one, then the other, had lifted off, a tiny tissue paper image of what she thought she'd wanted. Drifted away, not so much as leaving a pleasant memory behind. Experienced? Hotel rooms for weekend getaways with salesmen, the manager of a bar at a New Orleans convention, a first-year professor at the junior college who'd said he wanted to marry her and introduce her to his mother because they'd have so much in common. None of those liaisons, and certainly not what she provided for Hanny Meyers' inspiration, would qualify as experience for understanding who Gunther Huebsch might be.

"Well, I do not think you are gonna get all that done this week... or next," Starlight gasped as she arrived back with an armload of manila folders. Demonstrating the weight of the files by dropping them with a thud onto Claire's desk, she limped across to her own desk, one hand pressed heavily into her flank.

"Oh, and Miss Claire, you got another couple of calls to make this morning. I just been stackin' them up as they come in." Starlight crossed her legs and leaned back into her chair, waving a wad of little pink notes in the air. "Let's see here, there's a Tommy Lee Hancock, and a Jack Culmer, and a Nathan Grubs, and a Sammy Pratt. Oh, and here's that

Jackson fella. Sounds young. He done called three times." Starlight paused, batted her Dollar Store eyelashes in a tiny feathery flurry, then, with executive secretarial authority, turned back to her work.

Chapter 13

Claire hadn't checked into Doreen's B & B yet. She knew that Saturday mornings would bring the usual whirlwind of culinary tension as Esperanza and Doreen hauled in bags of groceries, shouted orders at each other to "chop the onions finer" or to "get me more cleanser," and whimpered with angst over flowers that had begun to wilt before Monday. On Saturdays, ladies scheduled showers for pregnant friends, or for the soon-to-be-marrieds. Saturdays were for anniversaries and for old-marrieds trying to reignite an ember with the subliminal naughtiness supplied by "going out of town." Saturdays were days when you dressed up, whispered about your friends, and silently praised Jesus that you didn't have to bear the burden of being them.

Saturdays for Claire had been the absence of all of that. The B & B was simply a pretty staging ground on her way to her mother's land. Someday, she thought she wouldn't go to Doreen's place at all. Some future day, she would lie on a little metal cot at Buena Vista, looking out a window at the view she had had when she was a child. She would hang clothes on a line near the grape arbor she remembered as a toddler. She would carry ashes in a bucket from the brick fireplace that would be positioned just as it was when she was small, and she would scatter the charred wood and dust on a garden like the one she and Gertrude had tended.

She would build the house just as it had been and make it—*force it*— to reveal her past. The script was there, she knew, someplace on this land, written in vines that wrapped themselves like snakes around innocent saplings and amongst the bricks that once were home. Claire guessed that where others had brilliant Technicolor memories, her own were blanched and filled with erasures. This is where her morning whispers came from. From the ghosts who kept evaporating, who walked back and forth on the old porch, who sat beside her on a wicker swing never showing more than their torsos, hiding their faces like criminals, but ghosts like a home just as much as anybody else. And Claire figured the house she planned to build on the old property would give her a chance to meet a few—to understand the meaning of the notes in her drawer.

Claire had driven straight past the B & B today, and now she sighed into the quietness of the morning air as she arrived at Buena Vista. It was a verdant calendar photo. She arranged a lawn chair under a wild fig, the "panorama chair" she liked to call it, and gazed at both the crumbling pilings from Gertrude's cottage and those of the main house. She could catch the glint of sunlight on the pond and see the big gate leading from the main road. A little rush of melatonin and hazy, happy fantasies of how the finished houses would look must have allowed an hour to pass, but Claire knew she'd need to be awake soon. Doreen had plans.

And now, from the road, a caravan of big-wheeled pickups growled and sputtered into her property. She hoped to God Doreen wouldn't be late.

Lining their trucks up like ponies at the gate as they parked, the young men inside began piling out. Red-faced, thick-necked, a few with guts that strained their shirts, others wearing sleeveless shirts that exposed tattooed flags and a dagger or two, the men gingerly eased out of their cabs as if sore from heavy lifting. Their baseball caps and Jackson's new signature hat, a weathered Stetson, were taken off, punched, slapped against thighs, and replaced amidst much spitting and hauling up of jeans.

Claire could feel the air change in the glade, now seeming heavy with testosterone and the light fragrance of chewing tobacco. But, she had to admit, the line-up of candidates was superb.

"Morning, ma'am…, Miss Scarlett." Jackson walked with the swagger of the trail boss now, the subordinate supervisor who could speak to the natives. "Well, I done what you said, Ma'am, an' rounded up all the strongest boys I could find. I would be pleased to say that they are some of the best workers in this part of the county. Some is just outta high school, some just farm workers, but all is honest and needin' the pay." He clearly wanted to spit after combining three sentences in a row, but forced himself to swallow the brown liquid.

"Well, they do look strong, Jackson. How many did you bring?" Claire was eyeing the road and thought she heard the downshifting clank of Doreen's old jeep.

"There is nine here today, but depending on the work we got to do, I can get another three."

"Uh-huh… well, good. Yes, that is excellent, Jackson. Why don't you have the boys come over here into the shade, and… well, they can sit down here in my new rye grass, and I— Oh, wait just a minute, Jackson. Have them sit down, then I want you all to meet the person who'll actually be paying you." Eyes wide with relief, Claire sprinted toward Doreen's belching four-speed as it bounced up the rutted drive and clanged to a halt.

"I got here just as soon as I could," wheezed Doreen, pulling her dress down from her thighs. "The cake done collapsed and lemonade got spilled all over that Queen Anne loveseat—"

"Doreen!" Claire jutted her neck toward her friend. "I may have set this up for you in a manner that neither I, nor potentially the bank, is very proud of havin' done, but one thing that is my bottom line… you are the owner, manager, responsible person, *and* personnel director of this little spa operation! Now get on over there and pick out your *pulchritudinous* studs, if you can convince 'em of the oddities involved. Then let me get all that manliness off my land. Makes me nervous."

"Well, that's just what they're supposed to do, now, don't ya see? That's how it works. First comes that little fluttery feelin', then a little curiosity, then somebody gives somebody a look, and well, the rest is Biblical. It just is… Biblical, an' pure sexual science."

"Cut it out and get over there."

Doreen took her time, but finally settled into the lawn chair, the men in a scattered circle before her. She took out her glasses, cleaned them, arranged them on her nose and surveyed the sprawled litter of bodies.

"How many a' you is married?" she asked. Two hands went up. She politely asked if they would move to the right. "How many engaged or is currently shacked up?" The men began to exchange glances. Two more hands slowly rose. Doreen asked them to join the marrieds. "Now, ain't none of you is gay, am I right? An' none of you is a deacon or an elder somewhere." The men were starting to squirm and arms were folding across muscular chests.

"Well, alright! This is good!" Doreen clapped her hands together. "Now I'm going to tell the group on the right that we appreciate your comin' out, but that I am going to spend my time talkin' to the group that is left. An' if we see that we are in desperate need of more manpower, I may yet come callin' on you. But for now, you all can go on home."

The men on the right spit their streams of disgust into the rye and with muttered curses shoved themselves toward their trucks.

Doreen shrugged at their wasted time. "Now, you boys," she smiled toward the five remaining men, "are goin' like what you hear."

For the next half hour, Doreen called each man up beside her, where they sat or squatted as she explained the basics of her spa: one afternoon of work a week which would be comprised of not more than two "appointments" lasting about forty minutes. She was sure any one of those boys could handle four or five appointments, but she smiled that she knew they probably had appointments of their own.

Doreen would pay two hundred dollars per month. Yes, that was for less than an hour and a half once a week. She'd pack them a nice lunch to take home afterward. And best of all, if they stayed on and worked for a whole year, they would each receive a five-hundred-dollar bonus.

As each man rose from beside Doreen's knee and marched back into the little circle, he eyed the others, shaking his head, rubbing his hair back and forth, noisily cracking his neck. Some put their heads on their knees, deep in thought. Others threw themselves backward in the grass. Two of them exchanged glances, covertly smiled, and gave embarrassed thumbs up.

"Now that you know the nature of the operation," Doreen said to the five young men, "I will tell you that nobody will know what goes on there. The ladies will be fine, upstanding citizens from another city. The neighbors will understand that I am having an extensive basement renovation done, and you will be entering through my back door to

67

conduct that work. The one requirement, besides taking a good soap shower, is that you talk about this only to each other. Nobody else. If I need more help, I'll ask you to send me a candidate. For if this becomes known to everybody, well, then there goes your income and your bonuses and your reputation, don't it boys? So be good, and let's see a show of hands!"

For the whole time Doreen was talking, Claire had been propped against a tree, her back to the interviews behind her. She couldn't hear Doreen's spiel nor see the faces of the young recruits, but instead found herself wondering about the women who would be coming once a week to "relax" in the arms of boys the ages of their children. Claire wandered closer to the old homestead. Perhaps the women coming up from Mobile or down from Memphis were like her, as emotionally untouched as virgins. In her case, Claire wondered if you could technically revert to physical "virgin status" after five years without a man. In either situation, the memory of intimacy lingered, a tiny lit candle that flickered in the darkness. She wondered if she would ever know it again, and if she did, would it burn her.

Claire wandered away from Doreen, whose motherly drone was beginning to make her sleepy, toward the remains of the old house. There she stood staring into an old bed of rhododendron near the crumbled foundation, when her eye caught the glint of something half-buried in the soil. She was always finding bits of metal: a crank handle, a water spigot, random forks and spoons, and even a five-gallon container with something wrapped up inside that Claire guessed was a rusted gun from when some good-ole-boys had target-practiced back near the pond. She'd simply covered the dented can with dirt and would dispose of it and the other fragments when the metal pile had grown. Still, each new "find" delighted her as much as if she'd found an Egyptian artifact. Now, looking down, she readjusted her eyes to the glint near the brick pier, separated the leaves with her toe, and reached down to extract whatever was there. Then she heard herself gasp with pleased surprise.

Digging with her fingers, Claire pulled out first a blackened chain and then a tiny orb fastened at its end. Sunlight still sparkled off the dirt-covered glass front of the little disc, while the back, Claire guessed, had turned from gold to green and now a pewter black. Yet it was the delicate flower still pristine inside its glass that Claire turned back and forth to see better. On a background of what might be blue velvet, the white blossom seemed freshly picked. Could this have been her mother's? Or dropped by a high school girl with a suitor on the abandoned property long after her mother had died? Claire turned it back and forth trying to imagine it around her mother's neck, but like her father and other people who came and went in her childhood, each drifted off into the watery vista of the past, identities and provenance unknown.

"Well, the deed is done!" Doreen stepped through the stands of purple iris that had spontaneously appeared around the yard. She was dusting her hands back and forth as if she'd just hog-tied a calf. "There is five young and healthy employees hired and agreed to!"

Claire turned around, the dirty chain dangling from her palm. "That didn't take long. Well, were they all eager to have a go at... spa delivery services?" Claire laughed in spite of herself. "Did you get Jackson too? He was looking pretty proud of himself in the beginning... before he knew what he'd be having to do."

"Oh honey, Jackson just about bolted, I'll tell you. I had to take him aside an' tell him I'd make sure he never was with anybody over forty-five. He said he had principles, you see..., an' I asked him which one, Miss Pervis at School 82 or Mrs. Jeffers at Oak Forest?" Doreen doubled over laughing. Then she caught sight of the little necklace.

"Well, what you got there? Ain't that pretty! Even though it's nasty and black. That come outta the dirt here?" Doreen reached over and delicately took the necklace from Claire's hand. "My, my, if it ain't an edelweiss. You don't see that too much. Pretty."

"Edelweiss?"

"Yes, honey," said Doreen, dropping the necklace back into Claire's palm. "There's a song about it..., a little German flower, I believe. Austrian or German. Yes, I do believe, German."

Chapter 14

Hanny had never cancelled a Thursday at the Ramada, not in the three years since Claire had been named bank manager. Now he knew he would never resume. There had only been a slight hesitation on the other side of the line when he'd begged off. Claire, resolutely professional, seemed to have quickly buried any questions she might have had.

But he kept the appointment anyway. Claire was only the catalyst, a kind of effigy, the medium for transport. And though Alma's opinion didn't matter to him, he would be discreet.

Imagining he was being watched, Hanny made sure to look confident as he strode up to Room 219, carrying his briefcase, his tie straight, casting a harried glance at his watch. It would be obvious to anyone that Hanny Meyers, retired banker, was on business.

And in a way, he was. For wasn't the past the business of the old? Hanny loosened his tie and stretched out on the bed. Like possessions he no longer wanted to accumulate, Hanny didn't want to make more memories, didn't want to sift them, prioritize them, shove aside old ones that had become friends for new memories that would be only acquaintances.

Hanny slipped his arms behind his head and surveyed the grey corners of the ceiling and the shadowy contours of the drapes. Anonymous. A planet removed. This dingy room was a place he could safely go.

Whether Claire were present for his rendezvous with the past or not, the hot stale air of the Ramada acted on him like truth-telling serum, a place where the people of his youth got together, rehearsed their lines, and acted out Hanny's life before his eyes.

He hadn't been sure which house it was. It had been dark when he'd brought Lisbeth there ten days before. Besides, each of what had been old slave cabins was just like its neighbor, unpainted wood, a rotting shake roof that sloped down to a shallow covered porch, and one or two primitive wooden chairs created from clapboard that had been part of some abandoned house that was now simply a scavenged skeleton. Hanny thought he was likely on Charlie Elliston's property, an outlying part of one of the adjacent plantations the old man had slowly piled up as he foreclosed on one farm after another. But Hanny guessed Elliston didn't come here; at best, he would send an overseer. At worst, a contingent of white-robed citizens—upright churchgoers whose fathers and grandfathers had told them how much they'd lost during Reconstruction, and how there was only one way to gather it back.

"Do your daddy know you here?" Sarah didn't open the screen door of the little house. She stood inside the darkened living room where all Hanny could see through the barrier was a flowered dress, rolled down stockings topping dark black shoes, and Sarah's chocolate hand holding the door shut as if he might have thought to rip it off the hinges.

"He does not know, Miss Sarah. But I am on deliveries, and I wanted to see how Lisbeth was doing... if there's anything I can do... anything she wants."

Sarah hesitated. She didn't seem used to turning white men or boys away from doing what they wanted. "I don't think it's a good thing for you to be payin' visits to Miss Lisbeth at this time...." Sarah's flowered cotton receded into the dark.

"Look, I brought her here. I know things is bad with her. But she may be dying. She may be... already dead." Hanny had seen how his father treated blacks, kindly at times, polite as required, but as he'd told his son, "never let'm gain the upper hand." Hanny shifted himself upward and took a breath. "Sarah, you let me in, now. If you know what's good for you, I will see Lisbeth Elliston."

Slowly, the little hook holding the door was lifted and fell, and Hanny stepped inside. The only other time he had been in Red Mouth Hollow was when he had carried Lisbeth onto the front porch nearly two weeks before. Then Sarah and one or two women wearing bandanas around their heads had rushed out and whisked the moaning girl inside. All Hanny remembered now was Sarah's long look that without words said just what Lisbeth had, "Keep your mouth shut, or we're all in for hell."

And now he was inside the wooden cabin, as foreign to him as would have been Big Daddy Charlie's front parlor.

Hanny looked around as his eyes accustomed themselves to the dusk that seemed a permanent feature of the room. A wide brick fireplace took up one wall filling the room with the smoked smell he was used to getting from ham. On the other wall was a homebuilt table with a washtub upside down drying from use, and a metal corrugated washboard leaning against it. Glass jars with rubber gaskets sat along crude shelves behind the table and a pie-keep was to the left. A low cushioned bench and a rocking chair in front of the hearth were the only pieces of furniture. Sarah had disappeared.

"Who's there?" A fragile voice came from not far away. "Tell me your name and who you came with."

Hanny looked toward the back wall. The voice came from inside a low doorway that led into a still darker room. "Hanny Meyers," he said. "I ain't got nobody with me." There was a long pause, possibly the sound of another voice.

"Well, come back then," Lisbeth said. And there was the scrape of a chair and a door closing hard as if somebody who was leaving was not pleased.

After that Hanny had come every week, sometimes two times, sometimes three. His father had given him more responsibility, and as long as the boy could show him some good school marks from Miss Higgs, the storekeeper let Hanny take over all the deliveries.

Sarah never wavered from her aloof politeness, the kind of demeanor that in another time and place would have gotten her cuffed for her unspoken "cheeky thoughts." But as the fall wore on, the gifts of small bars of perfumed hand soap, a ruffled apron, and packages of chewing tobacco that Hanny had seen Sarah stuffing in her lip, seemed to bring a change. Now when Lisbeth and Hanny sat on the front stoop, glasses of lemonade would be waiting alongside the porch steps. And as the fall turned the leaves to shimmering Medusas of red and yellow, Hanny would sometimes find a jar of Sarah's hot pickles sitting on the fender of the truck.

But it was Lisbeth who was changing the most. The high-spirited girl, a kind of daredevil whom the other girls had both wished to be like and hated, had slowly been replaced by one who would stare into the stands of oaks and low palmetto hedges at what she called, "vines like Hindu snakes that dance to the songs of birds." Hanny had never heard anyone talk like that. She told him that the gloomy trails they walked were "spotted like Dalmatians with daubs of purple shadow" and that "oak leaves were falling so fast they thought they were raindrops."

She also told him how Sarah had given her tonics and potions that were known only to the midwives of Red Mouth Hollow and the other black settlements nearby; how the old woman had taken a sewing needle and boiled thread and "sewed" Lisbeth up tight. So tight, said the girl, that Sarah promised that as her belly swelled, what the old man had tried to remove was only going to come out of Lisbeth when it was a fine, big baby.

"What happened to... the father?" Hanny had wanted to know. He didn't like using that term, "father." When he'd said it, it implied a bond, an act of adult intimacy from which he was totally barred.

Lisbeth's form had changed by then, her skinny arms and legs having taken on a womanly contour. They'd walked around the house as the sun heated up the creaking veranda, searching for the coolness beneath the big willow. Already the stalks of corn were high, their tassels beginning to brown at the tips and the afternoon insects frenzied in their quest for autumn nectar.

"Did you tell him? What's gonna happen if anybody... when... people find out, Lisbeth?"

"Why, ain't you never heard of a secret, boy?" Hanny jumped up to find Sarah coming out of a row of corn in the garden behind the tree.

"See this here willow? You cut the thing open, and you gonna find circles and circles of things you never would'a guessed was there. That's the kind of secret I'm talkin' about—the kind where life just grows over and around it. You can shimmy up it, and listen at it, and even cut it good and deep, and they is certain secrets down inside that it just ain't gonna give up."

"But Sarah, everybody's gonna know when the baby comes. I mean it's already gonna be hell for Lisbeth that she's got a child... but a black..."

Sarah slowly crossed her arms and shook her head, looking at Hanny as if she were searching for the intelligence that had enabled him to tie his shoes.

"Well, they is two kinds of hell, ain't they. They is the hell that Miss Lisbeth might have when no white somebody will say her name, and her baby will be no better than like that little mongrel pup over yonder. And they is the kind of hell that will run you down with huntin' dogs and will beat you with a club. The kind that might burn you while you still livin' and while you is torched, run you up a tree and holler when they see you swingin'. That is the hell in store for my boy. Two folks a' done wrong, that I say. But only one is set to be a shadow hangin' limp in the wind."

Hanny looked at her; dark leather wrinkles furrowing her cheeks and neck; greying twists of hair circling her head like a nest of thorns. Sarah's son had stepped across the line that divided their worlds; had, in a moment sealed his fate. Hanny wondered what it would have been like, if it had been he who had kissed Lisbeth in some glade and in a thrill of discovery made a creature that neither of them wanted. He knew he wouldn't be hunted down or on the run. Sarah sighed and pulled Lisbeth to her feet.

"Time you go in now, Missy." *She dusted Lisbeth's dress like she would a child's and followed her toward the house.*

"Sarah," *said Hanny, turning her towards him.* *"There are two things I want to know. The first is what's gonna happen to your son. And the other is, why did you sew her up... when you know how to... take it out?"*

74

Sarah glanced at Lisbeth's silhouette against the setting sun pushing herself up the steps to the house. She was quiet for a long time. Then, "My son, Eustus, is long gone from here by now. We done sent him away, away from everything he'd know'd. But my boy is gonna live. He didn't wanna go, and he wanted to take Miss Lisbeth along with him, if he had to leave. But with prayer and every penny we could gather, that boy will have a life that makes us proud..., all of us here in Red Mouth Hollow."

Sarah turned to leave. "And why did you want to save the baby, Sarah? Without it only old Charlie would have known, and he wouldn't have told anybody."

"Why, because it was made by love, son." Sarah looked surprised he would ask. "Love don't wait around till you're twenty-one, and love don't take no note of what color you're wrapped in. It just wants to multiply itself. And that's how this little baby happened. It's arithmetic, don't you see? One lovin' girl, one lovin' boy—why that's a multiplyin' for one little baby."

Sarah smiled at him for the first time and with a flick of her hand shooed him home. It occurred to Hanny as he worked some tins of biscuits into Sarah's mailbox, why Lisbeth had chosen this little cabin over the great brick plantation house. He doubted seriously if the word "love" was ever said at the Elliston's, much less doled out.

Chapter 15

Claire left the bank early, went to the beauty shop, then slipped home to change from her suit and white blouse into a soft blue crepe with pale yellow flowers that she hoped said "It's Spring and time to be light-hearted and young" and not, "you are an aging, unmarried woman and look like you're dressing for a Baptist funeral."

She kept the air conditioning on high for the drive down to Tilley, taking the convertible she'd bought last year on a whim and not her usual weekend-at-Buena Vista pickup. She swept the fullness of her dress's skirt up and into her lap so that her girdle sat directly on the leather seat, assuring herself that when she stepped out of the car at the address Gunther had given her, she would appear as fresh and wrinkleless as someone who had not driven forty-five miles in scorching summer heat.

She'd even brought a kind of housewarming or office-warming gift for him, a small, discreet philodendron that carried no message. Conveyed practically nothing at all. Which is what Claire needed for it to say. She wasn't sure if Gunther's preparation of dinner were the kind of old-world invitation that she understood Europeans doled out— gracious, but arms-length, a kind of waist-bow for a service rendered— or perhaps something more. Still, she found herself fighting off the fantasy that somewhere in the evening her hand might be bent over and kissed, or that he might offer his arm on the way to the table.

It was in the middle of wondering if Gunther would wear tweed on such a warm night that she realized his directions had brought her into Tilley on the far side of town. The side she had entered when she used to come back to visit her grandmother and Big Daddy Charlie so long ago. A route she carefully avoided ever since the old woman died.

Ruta Lee Elliston was like no one Claire had known before or since. Small-boned with a wide jaw, small eyes, and a high-voice that twanged when she sat on the side verandah plucking at a guitar her mountain-born father had made her as a girl. Granny Ruta kept her dark hair and wiry build until the day she died and with it a devotion that simply crawled up and over adversity. "You make you a bridge or build you a fence—that's how you handle gettin' things the way they should be," she'd told Claire.

The old woman had never learned to drive, but somehow Claire remembered her pulling up onto the dirt road at Buena Vista in a battered sedan. There might have been a black man at the wheel, she thought. Claire's mother and Granny Ruta would spend time on the front porch, sometimes laughing like girls, sometimes with Ruta's arm around Lisbeth, or smoothing her hair when she laid her head in Ruta's lap. That was when Claire would run off to sit with Gertrude in her house or quietly go off to where the chickens were. It was embarrassing and disturbing to see her mother behave that way. Sometimes she wished Granny wouldn't come, but there was always the sense of power around her. As if a granite stone had shown up and if you anchored yourself to it, nothing really bad could happen.

Claire remembered that it was sometime before she went to school that the man who brought milk to Buena Vista had asked her if she "was gonna be for sale when she grew up." Later when the coal man had wanted to know "if a Daddy lived in their house too," he'd said he could be her weekend Daddy. But it was sometime before her sixth birthday that Granny Ruta had taken charge. It was a Saturday when the old woman had come for her.

"I don't wanna go!" Even now Claire could feel the words choking in her throat.

"You gonna take me from Mama! Oh no, oh no, you ain't! I'm not going nowhere but here. You can't make me go! You can't make me go nowhere!" With that, Claire had run off the porch, twisting her skinny arm loose from Ruta's equally skinny vice hold. Ignoring the gum tree bristle balls that tore into her feet, Claire ran back toward the pond, headed for the woods, ran from Grandma Ruta, and Mama who sometimes seemed like one of the wild does that grazed near their house—soft, beautiful, and unwilling to run. *Resigned to being shot,* Claire had thought angrily.

Claire spent that whole afternoon in the woods. She sang a song she had heard on her mother's phonograph, she almost got a squirrel to come inspect the acorn she held in her hand, and she plucked stickers out of her feet, but Claire couldn't stop thinking about why they'd come for her. If grown-ups could somehow read your thoughts. If Granny Ruta knew that deep in her heart Claire wanted to get away from Buena Vista. There were some things you couldn't tell Mama, but Granny hadn't batted an eye. Not when Claire had drawn her a scary picture of something a big man, one of Mama's visitors, had held in his hand. He'd told Claire it was like a corn dog... like the kind at the fair... that she should take a bite. And then he had tried to make her eat it... but it wasn't the kind at the fair at all.

"Why, darlin', you are way, way better than eatin' old hot dogs at all. You done right to shove that nasty thing away and git. You are gonna be beautiful when you grow up, and the world is gonna be all yours. We just gotta decide *which* world. Oh, yes, there are a many to choose from. My, my...." She held up her fingers. "You can live in the woods..., out there in Buena Vista, where your friends are sheep and a once-in-a-while horse. Yes, and Gertrude too. Or you could come out of the woods and go to a fine school, with pretty clothes, and nice little girls who might invite you home to play with them on holidays."

"But would Mama come too... and Gertrude?"

"No, no..., I think they really want to stay out there by themselves. I think the woods suits 'um. But I don't think it suits you; does it now, Baby?"

"I don't know," said Claire. Granny Ruta had fixed her with a look that meant that Claire should be packing her bags, a way the old woman had of sending love with her eyes and absolute dictatorship with the set of her jaw. It was two weeks to the day after Claire had come sullenly walking back from the woods to Ruta that she had left her Buena Vista home forever.

For the next fifteen years, as an itinerant student, progressing from one boarding school to another, she rarely visited Mississippi. Granny

Ruta managed to visit on the holidays and arrange trips for them both, once to Paris and once to London—even a couple of skiing trips in Vail for Claire and a friend. Later, at university, Claire had enough of her own friends to make the semester breaks fun. And along with those of her peers, the bindings of home slowly dropped away, each young person stretching toward careers and their own lives.

Except for the rare appearances at the Big House in Tilley, Claire almost stopped thinking about the woods and its pond, about Gertrude, about the swing where her mother hummed to herself, or to the visitors who came at dark. Not until much later—after the storm. After the end of Buena Vista and the death of Granny Ruta in a sanitarium outside Atlanta. But now, the fragments of those days had reappeared—sunlight bending as it fell through trees, freshly crushed clover, the shape of a man's shoulder, and whispers whose words lay just beyond sense. Sometimes the memories didn't even seem her own, and Claire wondered more than once if alongside her own, another life were being lived.

***

Gunther Huebsch was standing beside one of the great oaks that stretched across the lawn in a kind of woody hysteria, its massive limbs gnarling in every direction as if attempting to throw off the bushels of grey moss that draped themselves along its branches. One hand was in his pocket, and the other busy bringing a cigarette to and from his mouth.

Claire pulled onto the gravel lane, and Gunther gestured her to follow. The drive wound past the sprawling Victorian main house that served as an insurance company and law office and back to the carriage house where Gunther lived. She could see him jogging heavily behind her in the rearview mirror and couldn't keep from smiling.

"Ah, you have found your way! I am delighted! You are very brave to take directions from a foreigner in your own city." Claire kept the door shut at first, while she distracted him with laughter and worked feverishly to get her dress back under her. It didn't seem to matter since

Gunther was still attempting to catch his breath, but when they both were ready, he opened the door with a flourish and extended his hand.

Would this be how it was done, she wondered. He held her hand in his large palm. She felt the crevices of it, its coarseness and a pounding warmth; and with her fingertips sensed the soft hairs curling toward his knuckles. If his hand pulled hers to his mouth to kiss, what would it signal? Was this how meaning was communicated, secret European signs forecasting romance? Perhaps a passion that could roll down an arm and pass discreetly with a neuron's discharge into the fingertip of another?

Then Gunther began to cough. Wrenching his hand away, he bent over double with a handkerchief pressed to his mouth. Gasping between hacks, he leaned over the trunk of the car in a spasm of lost air and managed, "Asthma!" while he frantically fumbled for an inhaler. Embarrassed for him, Claire sat back down in the car, covertly watching Gunther wheeze and pant, gently pounding the car until he forcibly slowed his breathing. Sponging sweat from his brow and still visibly heaving, he managed to indicate that they should head toward his apartment. She twisted out of her seat and taking Gunther's elbow, slowly walked him toward the carriage house, aware not of tingling neurons, but of a middle-aged man's rattling phlegm.

***

"Well, nothing happened!" Claire sat at her desk arranging for her regular room at Doreen's B &B. "After his asthma attack, he was too weak to lift the pot roast which I ended up taking out of the oven and covering with foil to shove in the fridge. And the poor man couldn't talk. Just a little wheezy croak that he'd shut off with a blast from his... well, whatever that little squirt thing is. I mean, Doreen, it was a strange evening. Hmm? Yes, I said we could try again. What could I say? It wasn't his fault. It's just that sometimes when the stars don't line up right... well, you shouldn't try to push them."

80

Chapter 16

S aturday had started hot, and by mid-morning temperatures kept everyone but the red-faced little children and lodge keepers consigned to their porch swings or beside an oscillating fan.

"Oh, the things we do outta curiosity!" Doreen had perched herself on one of the Queen Anne side chairs in the B & B's Jeff Davis dining room. Her ankles were swelling from the early heat, and she'd pulled on some flesh-colored support stockings while she hauled in fresh fruit from the car.

"I will tell you, Claire Elliston, that if I didn't have a feelin' about people and think I know how to read what's goin' on in their snaky little minds, I would not have done this for you." Doreen rubbed the crook of her elbow where a puffy cotton ball seemed intent on freeing itself from beneath a strip of tape.

"Done what for me? You just wanted to see him for yourself. You and everybody else in town, I might add."

"Well, that is right. It's not every day that a—should I call him 'handsome'—*handsome* European bachelor comes to town. Him with that rigid, poking implement of his."

"It's a lab needle, Doreen! And he's doing experiments and... and a service. It's all very scientific." Claire shook a newspaper loose and stared at a half-dozen ads for local churches. "By the way, have the bidets come?"

"Come and in! Lordy, I even tried one out! You know the old Confederate fountain in the park down on Duval... the one with the new high-powered jets, or like the spray hose when you clean the mildew off your driveway. Well, just imagine hiking your skirts and—"

"Doreen, I got it. Sounds dangerous to me. Hope the ladies like it, though." Claire stood up. "I hate to ask, but when do you actually start with the... appointments?"

"Well, that would be tomorrow at three PM. The boys will come at two, go to their rooms, and just relax. They can listen to their little headsets, or whatever boys of that age do, until their *guests* come. I think *guests* sounds like a nice relationship word, don't you? I'm putting scones and organic Lord Elgin tea in each room."

"OK, I'm not an expert on this kind of thing. But I'd suggest losing the tea bags and opting for something a little more suited to...Well, just keep the lights down, the shades pulled, and give 'um some alcohol for heaven's sake."

"Oh, I wish you'd come up and have a look, Claire. I know what I want, but my only recent experience has been with ol' Harold Dawkins."

"At Persimmon's Nursery! The gardener? The one with the..., what is that thing... a... goiter?"

Doreen jammed her fists into her hips and locked eyes with Claire. "It is a benign growth he's had since childhood, I'll have you know. And it is very, very sensitive. Sometimes I could get it to swell up when I'd—

"Shut up! Shut up!" Claire ran out of the room laughing as Doreen lumbered after her holding a virtual watermelon. "Just show me your best room," giggled Claire, "And I'll give you my most bodice-ripped opinion of what else you need to do in your new 'Middle-Aged Land O' Sluts'!"

They started up the stairs, but Doreen stopped to pull a tiny card out of her pocket. "Oh, I almost forgot. This is for you. I made an appointment with the good doctor for you to give a little sample too. He had a nice warm touch, and it's the least you could do... helpin' him with his work. But you know he does ask a lot of questions for just a tired blood test. He asks about your liver and weak joints, and he asks if you have any Jewish blood. Now I thought that was real strange."

***

82

Claire had had no intention of keeping the appointment Doreen had made for her at Gunther's clinic. Her blood was perfectly fine, and she wasn't about to sit in a waiting room for a glimpse of anybody. Instead, this morning she would do as she always did, make her way to Buena Vista where time waited, holding its breath, playing hide and seek with her memories, and very occasionally producing a tangible clue as to who her mother really was and why knowing felt like the most important thing in Claire's life.

With a clawfoot rake bouncing in the back of her truck and the tiny necklace with its *edelweiss* in her pocket, she intended to explore the perimeter of the two houses, looking for more lightly buried reminders of the days when her mother…

Suddenly Claire put on the brakes. Quickly looking for cars, she pulled to the side of the road, punched at the radio knob, then punched it off again. It was as if an orchestra had burst to life in the car. She could hear the instruments blending, riffing, trying out little solos, coming together in codas, and she could hear the scratchiness of the record that was producing the music. She punched the car's button off again. Yet the beat had turned snappy. This was—what did they call it? Big Band music… saxophones, clarinets, and *swing*. Claire twisted around in the car looking for a house with an old phonograph on the porch. Yet it was only the lush sway of greening fields she saw. She felt a shudder go along her shoulders. It wasn't the first time she had heard Benny Goodman or Vaughn Monroe swelling from the background when she was alone.

She closed her eyes, and the music seemed to grow louder and with it, muffled background noises. People were laughing; someone was trying to sing to the beat. Slowly the music in Claire's ears dimmed, and she felt the seat beside her sag slightly, as if someone very light had opened a door, then closed it and now sat beside her. She kept her eyes shut, sensing the air shift in the car, parting itself for someone else.

"Now, don't be frettin', Claire Belle. Stop those tears, or you won't have any left for tomorrow." Her mother's voice was wispy and warm, as if blown from the old wire fan on the porch. "What you see… well,

your big eyes, they just might sometimes tell you fibs, you know that, Honey?"

Claire touched her hair. She was sure someone had just stroked it. *"It don't hurt none. He was just playin' and I was playin' too. See all my parts is workin', Baby. Don't you worry about Mama at all…"*

The voice was saying more, but the music had gotten loud again, and there was another voice, a rough one. Then the seat beside Claire readjusted, and all she heard was the sound of a strident horn, its Doppler effect telling her that her car was parked too near the side of the road.

Claire opened her eyes. She shakily gripped the little edelweiss in her pocket and was desperate for a breath of air. Stepping out of the car, another car horn practically pushed her back inside, but this car pulled over ahead of hers and came to a stop. She could see its driver looking in the rearview mirror.

Slowly its door opened, and Gunther Huebsch stepped out. "My dear Ms. Elliston, it is me, Gunther! Are you alright?" He came back toward her with the assessing eye of the physician.

"Oh, Dr. Huebsch… Gunther, what are you doing out here on a country road?" Claire felt her bangs wet with sweat and was trying hard to focus. "I was just… looking for something in my purse. Now I'm headed out to my property down the road… just a little place." She continued to rifle through her pocket book trying to discover something to say. "It's called Buena Vista."

Gunther stopped as if a bar had fallen before him. "To Buena Vista? This would be a small community with several little farms and houses? Along… Route 3?" He pulled out and searched for the road on a crumpled piece of paper with a hand drawn map.

"Yes, it is. It goes back generations. My mother used to live there."

Gunther's eyes had grown wide under the golden brows. "I have finished my day at the clinic, Ms. Elliston," he said, drawing his heels together. "And although it is presumptuous, I should like to be so forward as to inquire if I might come to Buena Vista along with you? You remember that my father had traveled in this area? Yes? Well, he

84

recommended me to visit a place called Buena Vista. Yes, yes, I believe he had some friends there once."

Gunther had the look of a child asking Santa for a special gift—unsure, expectant, charming. Claire ran her hand along the back of her neck, still wet from the moments before, and with her eyes closed, flipped her hair away with a short wag of her head. If she had been a lioness, she might have swatted Gunther's nose with her tail. The little thrill she'd felt on her way to the carriage house had returned. And without meaning to, she noted that Gunther's breathing today sounded healthy and deep.

"Oh, really? Friends in Buena Vista? The coincidences that do come along." For a moment, Claire thought she heard the low, throaty sound of a clarinet somewhere across the fields, then the breeze seemed to push it away. "Why, of course, Mr. Huebsch, Gunther, if you're feeling better than you were the other evening, you are more than welcome. You don't mind if I drive do you? I know these roads and their curves." Claire smoothed the fabric along her thighs.

"Maybe if you like, we can pick up some lunch… and do you know what else? I just happen to have a bottle of wine in the back of my truck. Forgive me for being an independent Southern lady." Claire caught sight of her rake and the shovel tossed behind the cab and casually shoved them out of sight. A time for everything, she impulsively decided, and excavating might have to wait.

Chapter 17

Hanny Meyers had arrived early, he thought. The drive from outside Tupelo to the little church just north of Tilley should take only thirty minutes on most mornings, but today he had allowed plenty of time. On Sunday mornings, he knew the rural road would be packed with people headed for services in every direction. It didn't matter if they'd worked all week in the fields or had logged stands of pine, if they were domestics or their employers, were drinkers or teetotalers, they would all be up on Sunday "representin' and testifyin'" and making it known that the "Lord was at their church this holy day."

Hanny pulled his car into the grassy lot among twenty or thirty others; each one old but each having had its weekly wash so that, just like its owner, the cars would be proud to be seen.

Hanford B. Meyers immediately felt himself out of his depth, at least out of his own world. In many ways, he felt like he shouldn't be here at all—at a *peelin'-paint* clapboard church in the country—at a "negro church" without a white person in sight. He knew that the Zion Top Baptist Church had been a hotbed of seething emotion in the Sixties when the Jim Crow laws had essentially reestablished segregation. He also knew that Zion Top had buried at least one lynched activist from these very steps. Yet Hanny also knew that the old man who presided over that service was the only one who would have the incentive to help him.

Hanny sat for a moment in the car. Instead of the low medieval drone the Episcopal pipe organ in Tupelo would be starting about now, he heard the rhythmic thump of a drum set coming from inside the church.

Above the "one-and a-two" of the drums, a marginally-tuned piano was beginning a gospel song Hanny thought he'd heard on his car radio.

"Hello, Brother." Two men approached Hanny's Lincoln as he twisted up and out of its leather seat.

"Good morning to you." They stood at a distance, greying heads held high, lips tight together, hands clasped together in front over black suits of a cut Hanny couldn't identify.

"Good morning, gentlemen." Hanny could see several other men standing in small groups talking under the trees with ladies whose flowered dresses fluttered in the morning air, each man keeping an eye on Hanny and the Lincoln.

Hanny smiled, gazed at the ground, nodding as if agreeing to some unspoken question while he tried to figure out what to say. The two men gave him no help.

"It's a beautiful day to have such a good turnout, isn't it?" Hanny decided nobody could get agitated over such a bland statement.

"Yes, sir. We have this many every Sunday." The man's voice was husky, polite, waiting.

Hanny looked about him. Some of the younger people were entering the church, while the older ones were now frankly fixed on Hanny and his "greeters."

"Well, I just thought I'd come out and attend a service, if I might. Thought the Lord might be visitin' here too. Are you, by chance, the elders of the congregation?"

"We are."

The taller man's pupils had little blue circles of cataracts around them, the result of fifty years of field work without protection; yet, Hanny felt the scrutiny of each of his own white pores and the man's burrowing into the motivations of Hanny's white brain.

There was a long silence; for each of the three men, a calculus of risk versus the teachings they all had heard every Sunday of their lives was going on.

"Sir, we don't often have guests. But... you are welcome to join us in our worship." The tall man moved aside with a sweep of his arm toward the church. "We are pleased that you would come pray with us."

Involuntarily, Hanny felt himself sway with relief. The smaller man escorted Hanny up the wooden steps as ladies with large platters of covered food stopped on their way to an eating shed to unabashedly stare.

The church was already crowded, and pleated paper fans shaped like insect wings shoved the humidity back and forth. The shorter elder led Hanny to a seat on the aisle halfway back, centrally installed with parishioners on all four sides. Some of them met his eyes with a nod; others kept their eyes on the worn hymnals; still others pulled their children into their seats whispering instructions with glances in Hanny's direction. Yet a new face, even a white one, would become no competition for what was to follow. The elderly, possibly confused, white man was soon forgotten in Zion Top's weekly emotional purge.

The drum's relaxed throb had now picked up pace, and the sound of clapped hands and sheer joy began to pour down the aisle as the choir in red gowns swayed toward the altar. Hanny noticed older women in white dresses, stockings, and shoes, each with a nurse's cap on her head, marching behind the choir. Then came the somber assembly of elders, straight as pines and as animated, and finally, supported by two younger men, the man Hanny had come to see, Eustus Pitts.

Eustus looked much the same as he had the last time Hanny saw him. Besides some particularly dry winter seeming to have ravaged the lanky form, dusting the preacher's hair white, and replacing the supple molasses of his skin with a layer of aged parchment, fifty-odd years had left him alone.

Hanny watched as the ladies in their massive hats, heavy with ribbon and unnaturally colored flowers, reached out to touch or pat Eustus as he progressed down the aisle. It was as if their prophet spent his days in the desert, and each Sunday they welcomed him home.

The choir had arranged themselves in the front of the church now, ranked with the men on stands behind the full-bodied women. They clapped in unison, but each singer had their own conversation going with the Lord. Some bent forward swinging their heads; others tilted their chins toward heaven. As one hymn rocked into another with barely a change in the beat, one or two of the congregation seemed to come loose from their places. An older man in an ochre suit suddenly spun into the aisle, head down, snapping his fingers, knees nearly touched his bobbing head. Then to Hanny's left, a woman threw her arms upward, her eyes rolling toward the rafters until her companion seated her carefully back in the pew. A woman in her fifties danced up the aisle, clapping at her thighs and shaking her fingers in the air as if warding away a too-big dose of the Holy Spirit. And then, it stopped. With some key chords on the piano, the congregation seemed to take a breath and collectively return to their seats, smiling and pleased with their opening foray into worship.

Eustus' two young attendants turned out to be co-preachers of some sort and read the Gospel and the Scriptures from opposite sides of the altar in overly-exhortative cadence. During particularly elaborate passages, the congregation dug into their Bibles with the concentration of accountants Hanny had seen scan suspicious sets of books.

Then, the music began again. This time, the drums were joined by a saxophone and an electric guitar, and no one attempted to contain themselves. The "nurses" moved up and down the aisles fanning women who were swooning in ecclesiastical ecstasy, helping them to lie down on a pew, pouring them sips of water from little paper cups. Hanny wasn't sure this kind of excess was healthy, yet as they dripped perspiration, shed jackets, and even shoes, the congregation seemed in the throes of the purest emotional abandon he had ever witnessed, and he briefly wondered what would happen if the Zion Top "band" ever played at St. Peter's Episcopal Church on Walnut Street.

"Come to the Lord now, Children! Come to Jesus, You Who Are Called." Eustus had risen from a simple wooden chair and was standing alone at the center of the altar, his voice having parted the music like a shimmering current.

"Turn your faces to God and your hearts to each other ... and come. Let us embrace another Child of Heaven!" Eustus looked directly at Hanny.

"When we was lost, a Samaritan came. When we needed water, a vessel appeared. When the lions encroached, the gate was opened. And though on this here earth, the Devil walks in broad daylight, they is some who will still his approach at night." The congregation was responding with "Amens" and "Praise Jesus's."

Eustus closed his eyes and laid his hand on a Bible beside him. "When a man crawled alone in a shed, beaten and cut... when that man a' had his manhood done twisted and burst... when that man was a' finally wearin' his collar of rope that they done drug him around with like a dog from a cart... that moment..., Brothers and Sisters, a Samaritan came. An unexpected hand reached out and made a promise and saved another man so he could be given to God."

The congregation was turning to each other with questioning looks, as Eustus began to make his way down the aisle toward Hanny. The old cleric stopped just in front of him and reaching his bony hands down to audaciously hold Hanny's face, Eustus spoke directly and so quietly that only the nearest-by heard him.

"I never had the chance to tell you; it always be too dangerous. But after all these years, we two old, old men... we pretty much the same now. We both lived over lots of sorrow; we both talked one way and walked another for a time; but you did do the right thing, man. Don't let nobody tell you you didn't. You was brave. Yes, yes you was. You was the bravest man I ever saw. And I have tried to live the life you gave me back as close to God as I was that very night. And I thank you."

Tears streamed down Hanny's cheeks, his face crumpled, and his eyes shut tight. He grasped Eustus' hands with his own, afraid his legs would not hold him.

Eustus turned to the congregation and raised his voice. "This here man... this here righteous man... anyone here should be proud to shake his hand. And anything I can do to repay him for a kindness in my hour of darkness..., that I will gladly do." Eustus turned back toward the altar as the "band" began to play.

Hanny slumped into the pew, black hands laying along his shoulders and reaching out to stroke his back. They swayed him to and fro, and he felt something like water flooding him with—perhaps love. And as the crowd sang around him, Hanny remembered the night he had saved Eustus's life and in the doing, sent his own in a direction from which he would never return.

It hadn't seemed like an unusual day. As he had every afternoon for the past two months, Hanny made sure his deliveries would take him near to Red Mouth Hollow. Close enough that his father wouldn't wonder at any extra mileage on the old truck.

Seeing her every day, Hanny hadn't noticed if Lisbeth's form had begun to change, but somehow to him her breasts looked rounder, and her skin seemed to have a soft cushion forming along her shoulders and arms.

Lisbeth didn't leave the inside of Sarah's cabin except when Hanny came by. Then they would wander into the pine forest behind the settlement, occasionally spying a wayward cow grazing on the scrub it discovered through a broken fence or wild turkeys pecking at acorns in a clearing. It was during those late summer afternoons, sprawled on an old quilt against a log, that Lisbeth's voice would waver from high and optimistic, sure that Sarah's skills had preserved something precious, to a bitter fury that retribution against her father would never come.

"There's lots of things that go on in rich houses you don't know, Hanny." Lisbeth's eyes were closed, though her head was tilted up toward the spangle of chartreuse leaves nodding overhead. Then she whispered, "You ever hear about Alma?"

Hanny quickly ran through the roster of girls in the social strata Lisbeth belonged to. He didn't know many. The funeral home director had a daughter. The pharmacist, he thought had one.

Lisbeth sat up and looked at Hanny. "Alma, she's Doctor Edward's girl. I know you've seen her. Tall, lots a' teeth..." Lisbeth closed her eyes again. "Well, she was another one almost got ole Charlie ruined. I guess what they did still could, but sweet ole papa Charlie ain't about to let that happen."

"I don't know what you're talking about. If what he's done to you doesn't get him in trouble..."

Lisbeth laughed out loud. "You don't get it, Hanny. I'm his property, kin, daughter. I got no voice. Not until I would'a got me a husband. Well, in this town... not my word, not even a husband of mine could pit his testimony against ole Charlie's. But Alma is a different case."

91

Without knowing that he wanted to touch her, Hanny pulled a stray hair from Lisbeth's forehead and suddenly was submerged in a wave of tenderness that for a moment made him want to run from the glade.

"Charlie did to Alma what he did to me, Hanny. From the time she was about twelve. But there was a difference; She liked it." Lisbeth now stared straight at him. "You want to know the truth? The real truth about what goes on in big houses with rich people... them who's got power just wrapped tight around them like walking fortresses... while others got nothing... nothing. We just got... invisibility."

Hanny hadn't seen Lisbeth like this before. She felt dangerous, but she was not to be stopped.

"Ole Charlie would start it. He would ask Doc Edwards if Alma could stay overnight. 'Little sleepin' parties' he called 'um. Doc must'a thought me and Alma was real good friends. In fact, I hated her. Then she'd come over and after we'd played Monopoly or something, Charlie would say he'd want to come 'join our party.' Mama was so often off with her TB treatments that those little parties got real regular. He'd make us lemonade or sweet tea with some cake Sarah had for us. But it wasn't just lemonade and tea. There was bourbon in there or somethin' else outta his locked cabinet. And then when we was half drunk, he'd say he wanted us to show him our 'pretty parts.'"

Hanny knew that though Lisbeth's eyes were on him, she now only saw the inside of the old brick Big House. Her voice dropped to a hoarse whisper, as if of its own volition her story wanted to remain secret.

"Later, later he would make me do things to him while Alma watched. And then he'd do things to her, and if I tried to get away, the both of them would tie me... tie me sittin' up on the bed so I could see just what they was doin'. Didn't do no good hollerin' and there wasn't nobody to tell." Lisbeth was crying soundlessly, still looking at Hanny, but trapped somewhere else. He took her hand.

"You're not there now, Lisbeth. Things is different now."

"And then ole Doc Edwards found out!" Lisbeth suddenly doubled over laughing, wiping at tears, and shoving her hair back; and Hanny wasn't sure if this is what someone losing their mind looked like.

"No, he did, Hanny! Doc found some drawing Alma had made of what Charlie's private part looked like, with a title! 'Charlie's Big Pink Cock.' Yes, he really did! And Doc come over to the house with a gun and he drew the line for Charlie. Well, I think some money changed hands and promises got made, and ole Doc Edwards kept his mouth shut so that he'd have some hopes of marryin' his slut-daughter off to somebody someday."

Lisbeth's mood shifted again and after a period of silence, she said, "But they never stopped. They both like it. That's what Alma told me. And Alma's afraid that if she marries, she'll have to go away and leave him. Fancy that. And all I've ever wanted to do is leave."

Twilight was all about them by the time Hanny and Lisbeth walked slowly back to the cabin. This time Lisbeth slipped her arm through his and from time to time Hanny felt her weight lean into him, and he hoped he was strong against the path's pebbles and twists to catch her if she stumbled.

"Hurry! Hurry on back here!" Coming from between the cabins, a silhouette was running toward the couple, apron flying like a banner against her thighs. "We need you help! Oh, do get on up here!"

Several other people were running between cabins and the whole settlement seemed to have been ignited with some kind of slow burn.

"What's the matter, Sarah?" Lisbeth broke ahead and ran to the black woman.

"Come here! You too, Mr. Hanny." Sarah's perspiration had turned her face into a watercolor of umber and purple shadows. "Someone done found Eustus! Found out where he hiding!" She pulled them down onto crude wooden benches outside her door.

"Eustus didn't make it North yet. He been stayin' in the woods out by Parker's in some old hay barn, sneakin' in to steal somethin' to eat, I guess. An' somebody... somebody told Mr. Elliston 'bout the 'nigger stealin' food.' Well, it didn't take no nothing for the boss to figure out who that be."

Lisbeth looked at Hanny and wrapped her arm around Sarah.

"An' that ain't all. Before I left today, I heard the Mr. roundin' up his Klan. They gonna go after Eustus. They don't know he be my boy, but *they gonna find him and they gonna hang him!" A crowd of black faces had circled around behind Sarah, murmuring and shifting back and forth. For them, it was as if a young deer had been singled out of their herd. Though filled with consternation and panic, there was also a familiar numbing impotency.*

"Oh, Hanny..." Lisbeth was holding Sarah against her chest, with her other hand involuntarily on her belly. "Hanny what can we do? What... can you do?"

"I can try to find him first." It seemed matter of fact. "I'll try to find him first."

It was dark as Hanny Meyers pulled out of the little community, its oil lamps flickering on checker-clothed tables inside the cabins. He'd have to explain engine trouble to his father, but for now, as it had been two months before, Hanny seemed to have been given an assignment he truly didn't understand, but from which it was impossible to turn away.

Chapter 18

Doreen had just changed into her blue polyester dress, the damned one with static that clung to everything. Now it was hell-bent on climbing up her thighs. But there was no time to change.

The men were arriving in pairs and singly, each carrying a bag of tools or dangling a hammer or drill from a belt around his waist. A passerby might think the old grey Bed & Breakfast was about to undergo one of its occasional facelifts, but note would have been made of the physiques of the "carpenters and plumbers" who trudged toward the Victorian backdoor, perhaps provoking a curiosity as to why they were arriving on a Sunday and why they looked as nervous as cattle going up a ramp.

"Jackson! Well there you are, aren't you! And look how you got everybody here at once!" Doreen led the troupe through the laundry porch and kitchen and toward the back stairway that was a narrow as the men's shoulders.

"I am just so glad you are here. But before we go up, fellas, and I show you all your rooms, I do want to tell you how proud I am to have you and me workin' together now. This really is America, is it not? You find you a job. You work real hard at it. You *rise up* in your job...."

Doreen stopped with a twinkle in her eye, glancing at the young men's faces, then finding nothing, went on. "You make yourself some money, then get that education *under your belt*..., way under your belt...," Still nothing. "Get that *good hard* education *under your belt*, as I was saying, and go on then to be successful in the career that you choose to do. And I am just so proud of you good ole American boys." With that

Doreen hauled herself up the stairs, followed by the tight-jeaned gaggle who stared wide-eyed at the lacy fans mounted along the wall.

"Beau, you're gonna be in here. This here may look like a small room, and it is, but we gonna switch you boys around from time to time. Look at here, I put some little cookies in this bowl, and on this doily is some crème filled scones, but I do believe that should be for afterward. Beforehand, I just think sharin' a little glass of sherry might be nice. I'm not a woman of the stronger spirits myself, so you just tell me later if the ladies feel relaxed with that or somethin' else is better."

They moved from room to room, dropping off a muscular youth in each suite where he sat quietly on the bed as if waiting for a doctor to arrive and start an exam.

"This room is for you, Jackson. You was the first one hired, so I'm given you the big room. Now please, be careful with this piece of furniture; it's from the early 1800s and only got slats across its bottom. I see you brought your carpenter tools, so if you go and break that bed, I'm gonna keep you here till you fix it! Here, maybe there is a few too many pillows—"

Downstairs the trill of the doorbell stopped them all—men sniffing their armpits and smoothing their hair, and Doreen, arms full of pillows and an out-of-place afghan—each aware they were heading down a new road without a map.

"Well, here we go, boys! Make sure the ladies have fun…, and do not think of them as your mother's friends!" She hesitated on the stairs, "Or maybe… *do!*"

On the other side of the double glass doors five women had congregated on the porch, dressed as if they'd just come from church, which two of them had. Three had fibbed to their families, saying they were attending an outreach program north of Tupelo. Then they'd headed south. *Membership chairperson* Alma Meyers seemed to have told the giddy women something hilarious, and a few now stood doubled over, their gloved hands covering their mouths.

"Why, look at all of you beauties!" Doreen opened the door and stared at them with blue-eyed admiration. "I never saw such an attractive bevy on a Sunday afternoon!"

"Doreen, let me introduce you to some of our Spa guests," said Alma nudging the women into the tiny reception room off the hall foyer. "Now you all sit down anywhere. I know you're gonna want to look at Doreen's pretty antiques before you go on to your rooms." The women perched on crewel-stitched ladies' chairs and wedged onto a tiny camelback settee covered in splashy red roses.

"Now, this little enterprise, which I do believe is the first of its kind in our area, is just so excitin' to me and to Doreen here. And we want you all to know that though it's exciting, it is also very, very private." Alma looked around the room. There were platinum heads and deep brown heads, with not a grey hair in sight, though most of the women were in their late fifties. She guessed one or two of the blondest were well into their sixties.

"This is gonna be the most relaxin' afternoon and the most satisfyin' that you will have had in a long, long time," beamed Doreen. The ladies tittered and began to remove their gloves, punching at the bubble hair styles they hadn't changed in thirty years.

"I put special soaps and gently heated lotions in each room. A little something for refreshment, and something very, *very* warm should you get cold. Oh! What I meant is I put out a little robe for you all!" The ladies giggled, began to stretch their legs and toss their heads. Anxious laughter turned to glances toward the stairwell, and it seemed that the hens had become ready for the nervous roosters waiting upstairs.

Chapter 19

Claire pulled into "*Long's Groc. Store. Since 1939 in Same Locashun.*" The Longs and their sundry relatives had run the store ever since she could remember, catering to blacks and whites alike, something Claire remembered her grandmother commenting on at the time. It was a mile down the road from Buena Vista and a convenient place to pick up forgotten Kleenex or motor oil, or in this case something for sandwiches. Gunther dutifully pulled in behind.

Sully Long was sitting on the front porch—American Gothic after a lifetime of fast food. All of the Longs looked the same: overweight, pale skin, scant yellow hair that disappeared altogether after thirty-five. All of them habitually garbed in overalls.

"Afternoon, Miss Claire," drawled Sully, after she had said hello. She knew that was the end of the social conversation. Claire made a distinction between the sweet nectar and flirtatious courtesies of Southern city men and the monosyllabic, slightly suspicious utterings of those from the country. She had known Sully since she and her mother had walked to his store and she bought penny candies from behind his nose-high glass cases. But Claire learned that "the Ellistons" were "city folk," though they were only ten miles outside Tilley, and Sully and his relatives always watched them with vague alarm.

"Afternoon, Mr. Long." Claire walked toward Gunther's car even as she shot a smile at Sully. She knew Gunther would be the talk of Long's Groc., and she wanted to shepherd him carefully through the stares.

"Why, my friend and I just thought we'd stop by here and get some of your very best lunch meat, if you have any, Mr. Long." Sully looked like he was committing every inch of Gunther's appearance to memory in case he'd have to testify somewhere.

"All've got is head cheese." He didn't budge from the kitchen chair he was crushing into the porch floor.

"Well, that'd be alright, Mr. Long. It tastes like braunschweiger, I do believe." Claire announced that for Gunther's benefit, but Sully didn't like the sound of it.

"It's made from hogs we done shot and boiled ourselves. Don't care what you call it, but I'd call it good. I'd say it's real good." He archly hoisted several of his chins out of his collar.

"Well, so would I! And we're going to need enough for two big sandwiches, Mr. Long!"

Sully reluctantly countered gravity and shoved himself up and through the store's screen door. There, crowded between Little Debbies, cold sore remedies, bottles of Dr Pepper, and for some reason, twenty dusty glass punch bowls and their cups, sat the rest of the Longs. Lined up one after another like a linear row from an airplane, four greasy recliners faced a television mounted near the ceiling.

"Afternoon, Ms. Long. Afternoon. Afternoon." Claire nodded to each of the Longs as they slumbered or stared vacantly at the commercial above them. The slightest of nods welcomed her greeting.

Gunther wore a fixed smile that must have immediately marked him as an outlander even before he opened his mouth, but while they waited, he followed Claire in the tiny circle in which the shelving permitted them to move. Like Claire, he pretended to evaluate the qualities of fluoridated versus non-fluoridated toothpaste and the fascinating list of ingredients in a box of Post Toasties.

Sully slathered mayonnaise onto the white bread, looking up only to ask, "You want some extra jelly with that head cheese?" And from time to time he glanced toward the door checking for who had entered. Teenagers in shorts and sleeveless shirts, old men with baseball caps and suspenders, a thin young mother with two babies and possibly a nasty habit, came and went. Then a very old black woman slowly tugged at the door and shuffled inside.

99

She was the only person Sully addressed first. "Afternoon, Miss Floene." The old woman's eyes seemed to follow her feet, making sure they were doing what she wanted them to, but she made her way toward Sully's counter as if she were in her own kitchen. "How you doin' today Miss Flo?"

"I been good. I'm eatin', an' that ain't just nothin'." Sully nodded and handed her a tiny package from the upright refrigerator.

"I made you a cheese sandwich today, Miss Flo. You gotta be careful with your old skillet now. When you done with flamin' this thing up, you make sure and turn off your gas. Now don't forget."

But Floene wasn't paying attention. She was staring at Gunther, and then she made her way toward him, squinting and opening her eyes again and again.

"I think we done met us before, I believe." Floene had on the little white straw hat she must have planned to wear to church that evening. A blue dress with small white flowers and a large patent leather purse made her look almost sophisticated in the tiny store.

"Good afternoon," bowed Gunther, startled. "I do not think I have had the privilege." Sully had stopped making the sandwich, and the other Longs seemed to have jerked their heads in unison toward Gunther.

"Yes, sir, I believe I met you out on the property yonder. You stayed with them two. Big secret, it was. What was it, 'bout three year?" Floene pulled her lips back over several remaining teeth, laughing silently. "How you do it? You must'a hid from them guards or somethin'. You been lucky, I'd say." Sully had come around from the counter.

"You better be gettin' on back now, Miss Flo. Sun gettin' hot and that's a long walk you got."

Floene tapped Gunther's arm. "D'you ever know 'bout that little surprise?"

"Toby, you get up and walk Miss Flo here back home now; she lookin' real tired." Sully seemed like he could be fast if ever riled. One of the Longs got up, took Floene's arm and with no conversation, moved her to the door.

"All I can say, is you and her done made one pretty little baby," muttered Floene as she was made to disappear out the door.

Sully shook his head. "She gone daft. That's all. Just a daft ole lady."

Chapter 20

Eustus took off his hat and looked squarely at Hanny Meyers. Just as Hanny had sized him up after nearly fifty years, Eustus took stock of what the years had done to the man who had saved his life.

They were sitting on a listing wooden bench in the little graveyard behind the Zion Top Church. The parishioners had taken leave of Hanny as if he were an old friend, and now the only sound was of bees buzzing some post-liturgical tune as they skimmed the ground between the stones.

Hanny had been tall once, remembered Eustus. And strong. He'd had a quiet, earnest look, and Eustus knew Hanny's father worked him as hard in his own way as Eustus himself worked in the fields. In fact, he remembered Hanny once stopping that old delivery truck and coming out into the cotton to pull a heat-crazy dog off one of Eustus' sisters. Not every white boy would do such a thing.

And now the white man, shorter than before and thicker, and the black man, gnarled and sinewy as a spider sat holding old hands beneath a still beech tree, regarding each other through filmy eyes and thinking variations of the same thoughts.

That night, Hanny had put his hand on Sarah's trembling shoulder and looked at Lisbeth. Both he and Lisbeth had been to Klan rallies. When there was a lynching you didn't stay home. Hanny's father, covering the "event" for his newspaper, had taken the boy to one when he was ten explaining that in the South the races simply do not mix. To do so was "like breaking a Commandment," he'd said. And then, "You wouldn't have a baboon makin' babies with a bunny, now would you? No, son, God and Nature do not allow it."

The night of that lynching, holding his father's hand, all Hanny could recall was the fear on the face of the young man as he was led by torch toward the tree, a white rope already forced around his neck. The Klansmen had crowded into a large circle, jeering and yelling. Hanny remembered the smell of sweat that welled up from beneath the dirty white robes and that he thought he recognized a classmate's father, Mr. Stanley, and Chief Hobbs, the policeman who went to his church.

Hanny's father had covered the child's eyes when the Imperial Wizard kicked the chair from under the feet of the black boy. But afterwards, with his neck arched oddly back and to the side, the youth swayed gently from the tree, looking like an unwanted rag doll caught on a thorn or the limp puppets that swung in the art closet at school.

Now, with Sarah's nodding head pleading for him to change the course of a river of history, Hanny wondered if Eustus would end the same way. Lisbeth's tear-washed face was still dancing before him as Hanny got back in his truck. It hadn't been hard to figure out where the boy was hiding. Word was out that the "Klan had collared a coon" and that there was likely to be a hanging. Already, lights of cars could be seen snaking down the dark, dusty roads that east of Buena Vista, led out toward the Redmond farm. Hanny made deliveries there from time to time and knew the back of the barn backed up to a thick forest. He guessed old man Redmond's hunting dogs had located a "quarry" in the woods that had taken refuge someplace in the farm's outbuildings. Now, Hanny's adolescent bravado would take him there, to something he only vaguely understood and to events that as far as he knew, like that river, could not be dammed.

In half an hour, when the delivery truck turned down Redmond's rutted drive, Hanny wasn't sure what he was seeing in front of him. The trees in a clearing near the barn were illuminated from below with car lights that danced malevolent shadows skyward. Here and there torches sent smudges of black into the Spanish moss, while the smell of barbeque hung in the air. Some of the Redmond clan had decided to make a party of the occasion, and silhouetted figures handed out buns filled with dripping meat. And slowly, around and around in a kind of witches' circle before the barn, an old truck pulled something behind it—a trussed and wailing young man, unrecognizable now beneath the crusted blood and dirt.

Hanny didn't really know Eustus, just another black field hand breaking his back beside his fellows—hired out like a mule at picking time, likely cheated of wages when his boss could, and like the others, an animal to be kept corralled especially when white womenfolk came into heat. At least that's what Hanny had been schooled to believe.

But somehow this was a boy whom Lisbeth loved. This boy had a mother who, at her own risk, saved babies and didn't murder them before they'd taken a breath. And Hanny guessed this was the time when he would see if he would be a part of a white-draped crowd crowing for a killing, or somehow try to save a life damned for loving a white girl back.

Odds were, by daylight, he could be swinging in a tree too.

Hanny pulled his father's truck behind the thirty or so others that were scattered among the trees. He didn't want the "Meyers Sundries" and the "Chickasaw Gazette" signs on its sides drawing attention. A few horses and a wagon were hitched to trunks nearby, and he could hear the horses nervously calling to each other.

The old Plymouth that circled the yard had now begun to sporadically rev its engine. Speeding up then slowing down, it caused Eustus' battered head to bounce under the rear bumper, then be jerked out, sometimes face up, sometimes not. Each time the engine noise increased, so would the thrill for the crowd. And Hanny noticed that at the circle's perimeter, men were dragging dry wood into a pile. It looked like they didn't intend to barbeque just a hog.

Hanny stood behind men with white shirt sleeves rolled up and women in pretty summer frocks. Children stood alongside them, holding their parents' hands, startled to be pulled from their beds to see a man beaten and hanged. At one end of the yard, near the barn's open door, the Klansmen had congregated, jostling each other from time to time, yet maintaining an ecclesiastical decorum. Flags and crosses on sticks poked up in their midst. Their masked leader, girdled with a brilliant red sash, stepped forward; two "acolytes" holding a Confederate flag and an American flag stood beside him. He was helped onto a stump used for axing chickens and now raised his arms above his head in a kind of bishop's pose. And the old Plymouth slowed to a halt.

"With the blessing of God Almighty! With the might of the Knights of the Ku Klux Klan, who fight for liberty and freedom of the good people of our state. Who stand for the Sacred Nature of the Races' Divide. Who will not tolerate its womenfolk to be abused. To be downgraded. To be humiliated at the hands of inferior vermin, those who are mere scabs on the butt of humanity.... We who have pledged an oath to abide by all duties related to the Elevated Cause of the South, who march in step with what God has proclaimed to be his Holy Order, find it our Justified Duty to, this night, in this place, with the Lord as our witness and our Guide, Order the Extermination of this bundle of filth for infractions to the laws of both man and beast!"

The Imperial Wizard remained with his arms above his head, while the flags were pumped up and down and the crowd roared their agreement, putting tikes onto their shoulders for what was likely going to be the child's first lynching. Now the Klansmen opened their circle and ignited the bonfire. A woman near the house hollered that cold lemonade could be had for fifteen cents.

It was then that Hanny saw someone he hadn't expected, but who, perhaps in some impossible way, could help. The very person who had begun tonight's process toward murder. Hanny had no weapon, couldn't yet grow a beard, had no way to assess the power the man in the shadows stored in his back pocket. Yet he felt himself a champion of right on this night—oblivious of the next minute's consequences. Audacious he was: Daniel in the den of the lion.

"Good evening, Mr. Elliston." Charlie Elliston sat in the rear passenger seat of a dark sedan; a white-robed driver staring raptly out the window. Elliston wore the black business suit he appeared in on political posters and the gold chain and fob he wore only at his banks.

"Yes?" Elliston barely shifted his eyes from the churning crowd.

Teenaged Hanny was as excited as the dancing spectators, who were now running up to Eustus' moaning body with spit and kicks and

105

handfuls of sand; yet, he spoke quietly, in the way in which he had heard men approach his father with secret news they wanted made public.

Leaning close in toward the window, Hanny said, "I believe I know of a very good reason to stop this here hangin', Mr. Elliston."

Elliston may have blinked, but he didn't look at Hanny. "Oh, really." There was a long pause and Hanny felt himself close to fainting. "And what might that be?" the banker said with a bored sigh.

Hanny moved a little closer. "Because, Sir, I know what you done to your daughter over all these years. And I know what you done to her one awful night. And more 'n that, I know what you done to another one too. An' still doin' it."

Hanny saw the muscles of Elliston's face tighten as his teeth ground back and forth, and eyes dancing with flames, fix on the boy as if down a rifle's sight. The man slowly opened the door and stood up. Hanny was surprised that Elliston was of only medium height and that though the man outweighed him, Hanny towered over the elegant politician. It gave him hope.

"You don't know shit, boy. I don't know who you are, or what Goddamned crazy bug done crawled up your ass, but you done pretty well cooked it, 'cause nobody talks to Charlie Elliston like that. You hear me? Now get away from here before you be number two!"

Hanny could see sweat oozing from the gaping pores on Elliston's face. He saw veins pounding across his forehead and how the banker's chin was forced unnaturally forward. Hanny recognized these as signs of desperation—the same things he saw when dogs or wild wood boars faced off.

"I'm Hanford Meyers, Mr. Elliston. And my father, I believe you know him, editor of the Chickasaw County Gazette, he knows everything I know," he lied. "And I can tell you, Sir..., he is just itchin' for a scoop."

The blow knocked Hanny onto the running board of the car. He guessed his nose was bleeding, but he was aware only of the last card he had to play. He pushed himself up, hoping the driver was too distracted by the rowdy carnival in the yard to notice.

Elliston's breath was dry and foul. "You little bastard, I could turn this crowd on you in a flick of my eyelash? An' you know, that no one...

no one... would believe you anyway. I suggest that you get your wormy ass out of this county an' don't let even your soft-bellied papa see you goin'. You understand me?"

"Well, that wouldn't do you no good, Mr. Elliston. 'Cause I'm here not just for you to stop this here hanging, but to offer you somethin' real, real good, too. Somethin' that you can have, and you can hold for as long as you want. Let's say it's just a real nice insurance policy for the future."

There were little quotation marks of spittle at the edges of Elliston's lips, and in the instant he wiped them away, Hanny caught the fear and curiosity in his eyes.

"I propose you a deal, Mr. Elliston. I will marry somebody you know quite well. Oh, why is that important to you? Well, because I will marry... Alma... the young thing you like to play house with. Oh, secrets are hard to keep, ain't they? And in return for this here bloodied-up nigger, I will give her to you. Her father lets her stay in town as a upstandin' married lady, and you and her get to continue those little "unusual habits" you both like so well. See, Mr. Elliston, you get a win-win."

Hanny was sure no one had seen Charlie Elliston dumbstruck before, but Hanny felt the banker, for this instant, was incapable of speech. Perhaps though the calculus added up, the pros and cons silently shifting on some balance scale of graft and coercion that Elliston used every day. And then the banker was pounding on the top of the sedan.

"Get Clarence over here right now!" The white-robed figure lumbered toward the Grand Dragon who was trying to fit a rope over the head of the nearly inert Eustus. "I tell you this, Hanford Meyers, is that your blasted name? I am holdin' you to this. You and your father. You will be a married man in one month. I will arrange it with the Doctor, and you will keep your mouth shut from this day forward. Or so help me, I will put you deep into Hickfield Lake myself... and your daddy too."

The Imperial Wizard came alongside Elliston and turned toward him with a sidelong glance at Hanny. "I want that nigger first," said Elliston.

"You what? These people done ready for a hangin'!" protested Clarence. "I'm hangin' somethin' tonight, Mr. Elliston."

"Yes, you are. But I need my prerogative satisfied before they get theirs. Now go get him, wrap him in that blanket, an' put him in the barn. I only need a couple minutes, now, Clarence."

Eustus was half carried across the yard, his bare feet stumbling against rocks and gravel, his face unrecognizable. The Klansmen held him away from them like a stinking fish, furious that his blood was soiling their robes. Clarence returned to the mob and began a chorus of Onward Christian Soldiers, after assuring them they'd get their lynching but needed a better rope and a hotter fire. The crowd erupted in cheers, and their anthem swelled.

Once in the barn, Elliston made use of the moments they had. "There's a curin' house behind this here barn. Redmond just slaughtered him a sheep. Go get it," he told Hanny. With that the banker pulled the checkered blanket off Eustus, untied him, and knocked him to the ground. "You son of a bitch, you should be dyin' in hell this here minute. An' I hope you do!"

Hanny threw the sheep carcass down on the dirt floor beside Eustus, and the two men wrapped it from head to hoof in the blanket and trussed it tightly, leaving a rope lead which they pulled toward the big sliding barn door.

"Now you take your prize nigger outta here. You get rid of him. You get him as far from this county so as I can never know he lives. Hope he dies. Hope to God he dies. I rightly hope he does." With that he kicked Eustus into the shadows, opened the door, and called for Clarence.

The next day photos of a burning body, wrapped in a blanket were published in the Chickasaw Gazette. "Hanging Unsuccessful due to Poor Quality Rope. Body Cremated Instead." "Justice served," says Klan Wizard, Clarence Hopkins."

Another notice in a different section was published one month later. "Hanford B. Meyers and Alma Edwards celebrate nuptials at the Good Savior Episcopal Church in Tilley. Happy couple to live in Tupelo where Mr. Meyers has accepted a position at a bank owned by State Senator Charles B. Elliston."

Chapter 21

Gunther had climbed in beside Claire for the short ride to the Buena Vista property. Neither of them had known what to say after Floene was whisked from the roadside grocery by a husky Long nephew. Whether the old woman was delusional, half-blind, or harboring a memory of someone else was unclear; yet, Claire and Gunther separately wished they could have drawn her aside to find out.

"How old would you estimate that elderly black woman to be?" ventured Gunther staring straight ahead.

"Well, I should think she's in her eighties maybe.... People live a long time down here. I think all the greens and field vegetables keep 'um young." Claire laughed, but she also wanted to know more about Floene. She would have known her mother and Gertrude as well. Most particularly, nobody had ever mentioned a baby. Wasn't Claire the only child who had lived at Buena Vista?

Claire pulled her car near the swinging gate, unlocked it, and drove Gunther down the winding drive that seemed to wait for each of her visits in a kind of leafy doze. The pecan trees had filled in in the last weeks, reaching up branches that seemed to hold hands somewhere near a blue-drenched sky, and her spindly grape vines now clung to their support wires like inexperienced tightrope walkers fearful of a fall.

"It is beautiful," said Gunther. He barely waited for Claire to bring the car to a stop under some dusky cedar trees. He jumped out, inhaling and exhaling, looking in every direction, grinning with palms up, and his head shaking in delight.

"I had not imagined such tranquility, Claire. I can smell, is it cedar? In Germany, we make little boxes that produce such a lovely aroma. Ah, yes, look! Look here. We have the tracks of deer. And here something very ambitious was digging. And these, these you call... I don't know..., they are orange lilies, but I don't know their name."

"We call them day lilies," Claire laughed. She had not seen him this animated, like a boy set free from school at the end of the year.

"How fortunate you are, Claire. You are making something lovely, I am sure. You can sense it in the air. Your Buena Vista is happy you are here." He turned to her beaming, genuinely joyful at being in this place. She had never seen anyone else with that expression.

"Would you like to eat first, or should we walk around? Down to the pond, by the two ruins, into the woods?"

"Yes, let us walk first, and you will tell me more about this place? There is a familiarity here. Perhaps I read about it in a book. Perhaps I always wished to find a peaceful spot such as this." Gunther shrugged his shoulders, looking about with a great exhalation. "I have been in mountains in Switzerland and at sea for long spells, even in Amazonian... glades... I think you say. But there is something different here, just as quiet, but more desiring." He looked at Claire who stood staring at his outpouring.

"Forgive me, Claire. Perhaps this place has a special private significance for you, and I am intruding. Forgive me. I simply was struck by..." Gunther laughed again, his cheeks flushing. "Maybe there are hospitable ghosts nearby."

"Come with me," said Claire, reaching her arm through his. She walked him through a field of shade violets, little purple faces subtly shifting to gaze toward the sun, to the old wooden fence, greyed and deeply grained, where the two of them leaned, feeling the warmth that wafted in from the grassy field beyond, and finally to the pond, where it seemed its heart beat from beneath the surface as tiny wigglers struggled to become frogs.

Gunther had been silent as Claire told him about the Buena Vista of her mother's time, of the front porch swing, of the maid's house, of secrets that she felt hid within the trees. She was amazed that he had a sensation of the same things.

"How can one be nostalgic for things he has not known?" Gunther stooped to join Claire on a mossy crown between some jagged stones. "I sometimes am not sure whose memories cross my mind, mine or my father's." He looked to make sure Claire was not frightened by such thoughts. "Do you believe that memories are locked somehow into genes, Claire? That you pass desire and longing on to your children?" Gunther laughed softly, staring into the black pond where the forest and sky danced on its surface.

"That is why I needed to come here to this place, this Mississippi, this Buena Vista. The questions began in the soul of my father, I think, and now they reside in me. I think a whisper of an answer has been with me since I have arrived. I just need to find its source... and to listen."

Claire let her eyes follow the contours of his neck and jaw, the sandy spill of his hair. Perhaps that was what ran through her—a genetic echo of Lisbeth and the things a mother could not say to her child. Yet when the child became woman, the conversation had begun. Perhaps Lisbeth's unfinished business was hers now, tying her to this land until she understood.

Claire turned from watching clusters of purple wisteria draw circles along the surface of the pond to Gunther, whom she found gazing back at her, a smile in his eyes. "Have you found answers, here, Claire?" he asked, touching her hand.

She had taken his arm earlier, a friendly, camaraderie-filled gesture, but his fingertips on her hand brought tears to her eyes. Answers? Answers were hard to come by. Was there a father who had held her on his knee, floating her back and forth on a porch swing? Who were the other faces, some smiling, some angry; men who seemed to have resided in her house, but whose images were soon pushed out by another.

Claire closed her eyes and felt her other hand being taken into Gunther's. His lips followed, soft, cool, waiting, trying to discern their welcome.

"Is it too soon?" he asked putting his forehead against her cheek.

"No," said Claire. And then Gertrude's voice whispered, "*But it'd be wrong to be seen.*"

Gunther pulled back, looking at Claire quizzically. "Is there someone here?" He looked into the trees and the field that swayed empty behind them.

Claire was just as puzzled. "I... I'm not sure what you mean." She too wondered why she'd added that they might be seen. There was no one within miles. "It is not too soon," she said. "It is a compliment that you pay me." She smiled at Gunther and let her hand run along his cheek.

Gunther slipped his arm around Claire's waist, pulling her closer and this time gently opening her lips. A feeling of warmth spread along her shoulders, as if a protective shawl had enveloped her. There was no power, no force, no agenda here. Just a kind of gratitude that seemed to arc between them, his tenderness touching that in her.

"This could bring you into trouble, sir. You sure to be found out." Gertrude sounded slightly panicky.

Claire pulled away from Gunther, surprised and frowning. "I don't think I'm feeling myself. I..." She put her hands on Gunther's shoulders, closing her eyes and letting her head drop.

"Ah, yes, you must eat something. But..." He took her hands and helped her to stand. "I will not be in trouble. I am already in trouble!" Gunther laughed and put his arm around Claire. "I hope I have not stepped beyond my bounds. You are a person demanding respect, and I offer it to you and perhaps more, a beautiful woman... in a magical place."

Claire and Gunther walked back toward the brick pile of her mother's house, arm in arm, laughing as they pointed with admiration at the wrist-sized vines that climbed trees like ladders and the armies of bumble bees that hovered Harrier-like while they drank their sugary draughts.

Claire arranged their blanket in the middle of the clover, and the headcheese sandwiches and wine were settled into the soft folds. She didn't feel like a lioness, simply filled with a happy innocence that comforted rather than prodded.

"Oh, Gunther, I forgot to show you this," she said. "Someone told me it may have something to do with Germany. I don't know if someone may have dropped it. A lot of young lovers used to find the privacy they wanted in these woods, I understand. But I think it's lovely." Claire pulled the little edelweiss out of her pocket where she'd taken to keeping it as a talisman. She opened Gunther's hand and dropped it in.

He didn't move. Staring into his hand, she began to wonder if another attack was about to overcome him. "What is it?"

Gunther picked the worn chain up with his other hand, letting the little globe dangle in front of him. "I have seen one like this before," he said.

"Really? Were they quite common in Germany then?" Claire began to uncork the wine and get the glasses ready.

"My mother wore one." he said. "I believe... I believe that it is the mate to this one." Gunther's eyes rose to meet Claire's. "I do not think it was dropped recently. It is very old..., perhaps over fifty years." Gunther turned the edelweiss over and over in his hand.

"My father, before he left for the War had given a necklace like this to my mother. Another one he wore around his own neck or in his pocket. When he returned, she told me they planned to exchange them, to meld all that had gone before, and then he was captured." Gunther looked at Claire.

"May I ask, where did you find it?"

Claire was trying to hear him over the voices clambering for attention in her head. *"There's going to be trouble." "Don't leave me now." "He didn't mean it."*

"I found it among the bricks and wood of my mother's house," she said over the roar.

Gunther stared at her for a moment, then dropped his head. "Claire, my father was not a tourist visiting in Mississippi. Not a mere visitor. He was a German prisoner of war, a man put to work by the military authorities who had no place else to house thousands of German prisoners. They were scattered all over this state. And here in Buena Vista, while he was a prisoner, he fathered a child. It was here also, Claire, that he wrote to me that he had found the one great love of his life. That is why I am here... to find the child of that union."

Claire could hardly take in what he was saying, yet, she was the manager of a bank. She thought in numbers. "What year would that have been?" she asked barely above a whisper.

"I know that he came here in nineteen forty-two," said Gunther.

Claire drew her breath in. "How interesting..." She stopped for a moment to listen to the cajoling voices in her head. *"Don't nobody gonna know" "Well, what'd you expect goin' on out in them woods." "No use bein' sorry now... but you'll be sorry later..."*

"That's interesting. When were you born, Gunther?"

"In December of nineteen forty-six. After my father came back to Germany."

Claire looked at the trees. There was no color there now. "I was born right here on this land," she said. "It was nineteen forty-three. Could have been the year your father put this necklace around my mother's neck, couldn't it." Claire closed her eyes and silently let the tears come.

"Well, well," she said. "Well, well. I guess having a brother, even a half-brother is something I'd never have imagined. Something I'd never even have wished for."

Chapter 22

Claire let June slither by without going to Tilley or Buena Vista. Doreen had called her to let her know that cyclists from the Natchez Trace had begun to book rooms and combined with her new "Reserved Days for Spa clients," it was going to be hard to guarantee Claire a place.

Gunther called too. Claire wasn't sure why he continued, since she didn't pick up the phone, but if the German thought she wanted to become involved in some quasi-incestuous romp, he was sorely mistaken. Misleading is what he had been. All the talk of nature, of genetic memory... his wonderful kiss. No. Absolutely no thinking about his lips.

She wasn't sure what Gunther had suspected about his father's dalliance at Buena Vista, or if he had known of Claire's attachment to the place when he'd come to ask for a loan, but to think about his lips for even one second, would leave her vulnerable to playing a part in a third-rate Italian opera.

In fact, as she had calculated the dates of their birth and the time his father had stayed at Buena Vista, Claire had mentally changed Gunther. A pheromone fog had lifted and instead of gentle wrinkles and rugged comfort, she had tried to transform him into an overweight kraut with a beer gut and straggling eyebrows. It made it better. Her "Do Not Disturb" sign firmly in place, she could now safely observe what misery feelings brought to others. Or, with her bank manager's visage firmly settled, simply turn away, opaque and empty.

Claire tugged at her suit jacket and repositioned her reading glasses. Starlight was out again; stomach flu that just wouldn't let go. Claire would have to call Doreen herself. She'd already cancelled the last month's Thursdays with Hanny, feeling surprised and a little hurt that he didn't seem to mind but had simply offered up his gentlemanly wishes for her "sniffles" to be better. Yet there had been something else in his voice. Something assertive and preoccupied. Traits that her fiancés had complained of in her. She rather liked them in Hanny's tone. It made him sound younger. Like he was nobody's fool. And she wouldn't be either.

"Hello, Doreen? I'm comin' for the whole week. Give me the Lee Room, if you can... I feel like spreadin' out!" Nobody was going to keep her from Buena Vista. Not the proximity of Gunther and his probing into his father's past nor the voices that had started to be disruptive even in meetings at the bank. Trustworthy voices or ones that were trying to trick her? Suddenly Gunther's questions and her own were the same, though she prayed for different answers.

***

"Long's Groc." looked even more forlorn beneath a scowling July scud of grey. As if a dirty wash had been brushed over one of dozens of the same print, Sully sat just as he always did on the front porch, in sun or fog or twilight, his dog snoring at his feet.

"Good afternoon, Mr. Long." Coming straight from Tupelo so as to get a leap on clearing a second flat building site behind her mother's house, Claire hadn't bothered to change from her bank clothes.

"Afternoon, Miss Claire. You're either a whole lot early or comin' in late."

"Well, I'm going to need a few things that you might have so I can start doing some proper cleanup out there bright and early this weekend." Claire flashed her crinkle-nose smile and topped it with a blink that she knew made her dark eyes flash, something she felt sure would make old man Sully get up out of his chair. His dog would have complained if he'd cared that much, but Sully shuffled through the screen door, dragging at his overalls where they'd crept too high in the crotch, pausing only for a long stream of tobacco juice just outside the door.

"Whatcha need?"

Claire needed another chain for the saw. She needed a roll of plastic bags. She wanted a backup padlock for her storage shed and tape to mark the trees that she wanted Jackson and his crew to keep and not cut. That was something she wanted to talk with Doreen about. Was Jackson now "off the market" as far as hired labor was concerned? He may be a stud over at Doreen's B & B, but he also knew a lot about heavy equipment and land clearing. Claire hadn't intended to totally hand him over to Doreen where no doubt the "hourly" wages were better, and the work barely made it to that definition.

"That 'bout all?" Sully was worn out from having to stand upright for ten minutes.

No, it wasn't, Claire told him. "I'd like a little information, while you're at it, Mr. Long."

Sully's eyes lit up momentarily. Folks who asked for information were immediately suspect. If you needed to ask, you weren't from around here; if you needed to ask, you probably didn't need to know; if you were asking the grocery owner and not a private source, you were definitely from not from around here, and very definitely were not going to get even a tidbit of information that you thought you wanted.

"What can I do to he'p you, Miss Claire?"

"You know several weeks ago, when I came through with that... foreign friend?" Sully was back in his blue, inside recliner, staring at dry fingernail beds laced across his belly.

"We had head cheese sandwiches," offered Claire.

"Well, yes, I think I do remember that," nodded Sully.

"There was an elderly lady who came in. Very old, possibly a bit confused, but she seemed to think she might have remembered my friend..., my German friend. Course that would be impossible, but I'll bet she could know something about my land down the road... what it was like when she was a girl."

"Well, she won't tell you nothin', I'll guarantee you that."

"Oh, I know, Mr. Long, you said she was mentally... handicapped. But she seemed to like you, and I thought that if you made the introduction, even if I could pay you for your time for being a kind of go-between, it might work for both of us?"

"Won't do it. Won't work out." Sully nodded his head sideways in a kind of a Wobble-doll figure eight.

"It wouldn't work out? She wouldn't do it? Not even a little conversation?" Claire felt herself loathing the unctuous sloth who obviously delighted in his "fix-it-man" role.

"Well, it'd be hard to do at this time, Miss Claire. Ole Floene done died yesterday night." Then he brought his hand down on the blue corduroy with a smelly bang and a toothless snort. "'Course, you can go talk her up all day tomorrow. She'll be laid out at the A.M.E... just waitin' and wantin' to be polite."

***

"I could have smacked his beefy old jowl," Claire told Doreen after she'd settled into the Lee room, "But I didn't want to get those thorny whiskers pokin' out of my hand!"

"I don't wonder that you might!" Doreen laughed, swirling her Chardonnay into a whirlpool. She seemed to have Kewpie doll curls pasted to her forehead and cheeks, the result of a hot flash colliding with three fast trips up the narrow stairs to make sure the Spa Rooms were ready.

"Claire, I would just love to hear some more about what is goin' on out at Long's and all, but I have got to mix and cool those julips, or there is gonna be a whole Sunday School of longin' ladies mad at me." Claire followed her out to the kitchen.

"That many?" she laughed. "Really? I just hadn't thought about how things were going. I mean, it's such an 'undercover' kind of business, if you know what I mean...."

"I know what you think you mean. But I tell you, when these women think they hit on a good thing, they talk about it with their friends. They swear each other to silence, then they tell everybody they know... well, know, and I guess trust. All I can say is I have had to tell the bike riders I am full up. I have had Jackson recruit three other... handymen, and I am makin' a fortune! And so are you!"

118

"What?" giggled Claire. "Do not tell me I am makin' anything! I'm not gonna be a Madam, thank you. You just plough those profits back to pay off your "construction" loan as soon as you can. That's all I want!"

"Claire," Doreen stopped and looked at her with a flushed face full of concern. "You deny yourself too much. I heard through the grapevine that that nice German doctor been askin' a little about you. Everybody likes him here. He's just turned into a practicin' doctor not just an experimenter. And I understand he makes house calls."

"Stop it. Enough of the good German doctor. Besides, this stuff is just not in my DNA, alright? I'm not like other women. I've tried to get married, tried what you're talking about with all kinds of beaus. Tried. But my opinion? I'm missing something important. Or maybe I've got it—the "Can't Love" gene. I've gotten used to it. No, just let me go on out to the land, do my clearing and building, and I'll be happy there. Look! I'm happy now!"

Claire swirled around the kitchen, tossing back the last of her wine, and grabbing the bottle to take up to her room. She was tipsy and didn't care. Through the corner of her eye she saw three middle-aged women on their way up the walk and was suddenly aware that there were six large pickups behind the house. Were the men already upstairs? Already the house felt tawdry. Was that the word? She was having a little trouble putting thoughts together. Tawdry, must be it… or was it "exciting"?

When she woke up in the Lee Room, most of the music that had quietly vibrated through the house timbers seemed to have stopped. Now only something down the hall, something with a slow bossa nova beat was discernable. In the darkened room, thick in blue twilight, anything other than Stephen Foster would have seemed wrong.

Claire stretched on the bed. She'd cast off her blouse and skirt when she'd come in; she couldn't remember more. Now she simply welcomed the cool air that came from someplace overhead, swirling along her legs and across her breasts. For a moment, she found herself smiling as she tried to keep track of a certain paddle on the overhead fan, wondering if it were turning to the bossa nova's gentle throb. Inevitably, her eyes would lose track, and with relief, she simply closed them and found herself near the pond at Buena Vista.

How old was she? Nine? Ten? Had she been there like this before? Had Granny Ruta brought her here when school was out? Or was it before she'd been taken away from Buena Vista for good? Claire could remember lilacs, cones of blossoms that spilled like confetti onto her nose and into the crevices of her shoulders. And warmth. So warm that like today, she had taken off all her clothes and pretended to be an animal, wondering how fawns felt not having to put on shoes or undergarments, able to lay their bodies against the bodies of little insects, or rough roots, or against grass that you could sleep on or eat.

There had been music then, too. Bird voices that stopped mid-call or sang elaborate cantatas, and like deep celli, cicadas that droned their melodies together. She saw a baby mantis that afternoon, so light that it had walked across her body anonymous, unseen, until it stopped and seemed to touch the tip of Claire's upturned breast with one tiny foot. And she had wondered if it had been sent to awaken her.

She too had then touched her breast... so alien and unexamined. Like the rest of her body, a living stranger she covered in modesty, but in that moment, a friend she wanted to know.

Claire let her hand circle her breast's pointed tip, a tan dome atop a tiny swelling colline of flesh, and with the heel of her hand she moved herself back and forth watching the little peak harden and subside, rise to make a valley with its sister. She let her other hand trail lower, curious and frightened of knowing what lay there.

She sensed a wash of cedar in the air, heavy and somehow masculine, a fragrance that with its inhalation made her stretch wide her legs, clover embracing her buttocks like lace. Claire had never touched herself, feeling only shyly perplexed by the soft bower of hair, but today she stroked her thighs, made strong from days' running in Buena Vista's fields, discovering between them a shallow cavern, a haven as smooth and moist as the sweet interior of a daffodil. Her other fingers joined the first, venturing further and further inside, exploring, circling, widening the opening for... Claire couldn't know what. And then as if God had been scandalized, He struck deep within her with a lightning bolt. Electricity coursed down her legs and arms, making her scream out and

120

grasp her hand with her knees, rolling herself small, wishing to be a pebble and not an animal with the power to incinerate itself.

A cloud had drifted over the pond, and as if a candle dimmed, the warmth of the air turned cold. The voices of the birds and the gentle clicks of insects had stopped, and above them all had come another voice, laughing and hard. And soon a second, blurred with tears.

"Well, ain't that there a show. Now I do believe I'm gonna just take some of that for myself. I do believe I will. Better n' what I just got, I'll reckon."

"Stay back. She don't belong to you. You didn't pay for nothin' here!"

There were more noises, sad noises, noises that got hollered out and then got broken off, thoughts that got stuffed down and suffocated, feelings that got broken and that didn't heal. And even the insects fled.

In her room, Claire watched the fan circle for a long time, looking for its patterns, losing, then finding them again. And finally, relinquishing the desire to see, she closed her eyes and lay still, listening for the music, a thread to hold onto, and only then discovered the bossa nova had stopped.

Chapter 23

"Well, why don't you just go on out an' visit?" Eustus sat in his old brocade easy chair facing Gertrude, who stood with her back to him staring out the window.

"She said it would be fine, didn't she? I saw you two, up there on the hill, Decoration Day at the cemetery. You two was huggin' each other. I don't think she'd ask, if she didn't mean it."

"Pappy, she thinks I was their maid. Miss Claire's got no remembrance of nothin' else, I don't think. It's like she remembers the trees and the houses, but all the people who done come and gone there, what happened in that house, and all the sadness ... well, none of that lingered with her; and, sure enough, that's a good thing."

Gertrude walked over to the old man and sat on the little footstool beside him. "Even you don't know 'bout all the badness of that place, Pappy. You was away... learnin' things, findin' out about the Lord." Gertrude grew quiet, her eyes moving back and forth as she counted the ghosts entering from the wings of her memory.

"I'll tell you now, if that's what you want, Pap. But it's a long time ago. No use secrets bein' all stored in some root cellar for safe keepin', I guess. All that time ago..."

Eustus looked at his daughter. He doubted her secrets were dead. He knew such things had a way of resurrecting.

"Tell me what you remember, girl," he said. "Tell me everything."

Gertrude closed her eyes, and watched them stroll in. Thirty, thirty-five years, their figures were as lively now as they'd been in life.

"Hey, Nigger! Pour me some more lightnin' into this here flask before I go." The drunken farmer was one of the worst. He'd already laid his horse whip across Gertrude's back once when she'd been too small to hold his animal still while he climbed into the wagon.

"You make me tell you again, an' I'll give you a hard workin' over!" She still had the scar from the empty tin can he'd hurled her way.

Elder Watkins had been another visitor. A big brown hat that smelled like sweat when he handed it to her to hold. And shiny shoes that Gertrude fancied she could see her face in. But he was noisy. And when he and Lisbeth disappeared into the house, his fat hand already clutching her mother's behind, Gertrude knew that roars and hollers would soon follow. She'd thought it was funny and wondered where Elder Watkins learned to make so many animal calls from the jungle.

There were lots of visitors when she'd been a child, when she'd slept in her mother's house in a tiny room off the kitchen, warm from the cook stove and far enough from Lisbeth's room for the child to stay asleep even with all the moaning and caterwauling. It was only later that another little house got built so that, Lisbeth had said, Gertrude could have her own place... like a real grown up. But through the trees, there were nights when the sound of blows and shrieks of pain weren't stopped by the little house's walls. And even a sugar bowl newly stuffed with green bills the next morning didn't seem worth Lisbeth's bruised and swollen face.

There had been one man she'd liked. She thought he came all the way from Tupelo. A tall, lanky young man, always wearing a proper suit, with his hair cropped short and parted in the middle. A young man who came so often, she watched him grow a mustache and get taller before her very eyes. He would never rush Lisbeth into the house, but linger with her on the porch, swinging back and forth, laughing at something Lisbeth said, bringing her wild flowers in the spring. Gertrude remembered he had once made her a dandelion crown. She thought her mother looked at him the way she sometimes did at Gertrude's dark face, when Lisbeth would say, *"You look like somebody I love..., but I won't tell you who!"* Gertrude always wondered, but could never guess it out. And her mother, laughing, would never tell.

And then one day when Gertrude was twelve, the world shifted.

"Yes, ma'am, he is yours to work as you see fit. He is our prisoner, but the U.S. government is handed 'um out to our locals to help with whatever chores or field work you may devise. No use just us keepin' 'um in jail cells all day. These is big strong fellers... an' you can use 'um like a hired man."

The official had arrived in a small bus, painted orange as if it were driving white children to school. There were other men slumped inside, but the one he was holding by the arm was taller than he was and stood quietly looking at his shoes.

"We will check on this man... this here Dieter Huebsch... on a weekly timetable, seein' if he is doin' right by you. He done run away once, but we deemed he almost had a right. So once we caught up with him, we think he knows which way our Mississippi wind blows. We gonna give you a small compensation for his feed and shelter. But I do rightly believe that he will help you enough here to make it worth your while, ma'am." And with that the officer handed Lisbeth an envelope with what Gertrude thought to be money, threw down a small duffle bag and crawled back up into the school bus. "Don't you worry none, ma'am. These prisoners is all docile and will not disturb your peace." And the bus lumbered out of the drive. That was the day Gertrude fell in love.

Lisbeth had had the man Gertrude came to call "Dee Dee" build a small lean-to room on the porch of Gertrude's little house. That would give everybody their privacy, she'd said. Gertrude now knew that meant that Lisbeth needed her own place set aside for the money-makin' part of their lives. Throughout the spring and summer, Deiter had worked hard during the day, felling trees and chopping them up for fencing and fuel, and digging out the pond, lining it with stones he collected from the field beyond. At night beside a small oil lamp, he studied a booklet the U.S. government officer had tossed through the window on his way down the drive: "English for German Speakers." He was quiet and polite, and unlike the other men who came and went, he never went into the house where Lisbeth lived.

As fall arrived, Dieter had come to be a kind of odd family member, poking coons out of the fireplace, building a kitchen table for Lisbeth, even cooking rabbit stews and boiled cabbage that made Gertrude wish she knew where Germany was.

Christmastime had come, and for the first time the little house seemed to have joined the rest of the community with garlands strung along its rafters, a tree Deiter had hauled in from the woods, and presents that the three of them had made from pine cones and paint. It didn't seem odd that the German lived among them any longer. Just as long as he stayed out of sight when the locals came and when Lisbeth would disappear.

The months had rolled by. Then a year. And another. And while the war raged in Europe and now the Pacific, one evening, as Gertrude sat knitting and Deiter sat whittling on their front porch, he had paused his knife and stared down into his hands.

"I see you every day, Gerta. When I do work, I think of you. When I rest, I think of you. I see that you are schoen, *even the kittens love to curl near you." His accent was heavy, but Gertrude saw that his lips were trembling and that his eyes, when he lifted them, were round with yearning.*

"I watch you. I watch your beauty grow more each day. From a child to a maiden. When your hair falls onto your shoulders, I would like to touch it, have it touch me, to place my face in its... curls." His head had dropped and he ran his fingers across his forehead. "Forgive me, for my rough language, dear Gerta. I have not much more."

Gertrude sat beside him, her eyes widening in disbelief. She didn't know what to do. She was vaguely aware of what went on in the house through the trees where Lisbeth made men wail with feeling. But this was different. It felt safe, a protection offered. Yet though she was frightened, not of his words, but of the realization that they came from a grown man, Gertrude felt herself... ready. For something. Letting herself down to the step beside him, she slowly let her head rest against Deiter's shoulder. And on that night, the pale young man and the dark girl held each other's hands until the moon swam upward through the trees, lingered, and slid back down again. Neither of them would ever love so deeply again.

Gertrude was well over fifty, but she never tired of the way Eustus babied her. Now he rocked her against his thin chest, murmuring understanding. She had had a mother and a father, but never at the same time, and even at this late date, she drank in Eustus' affection.

"I been far away, Pappy. Thank you for comin' with me." She looked at him, this living oak, strong, bending, ever-growing over obstacles, spreading his shelter to families and anyone whose troubles doubled them over. Eustus always headed for the sunlight or somehow out-maneuvered the vines of life that pulled others down. And no matter what he did, he checked it out first with the Lord.

He reached out one of his hands, the cuff pulling high along his wrist. Veins like snakes wound beneath the skin, trapped there in bas relief. "Don't you worry none now, girl. I can handle the bad things you might a' seen and heard. You wanna tell me somethin', I can know it and my love won't be diminished none. You know I done seen some bad a' my own."

It was odd how little they'd told each other over the decades. Only recently had Gertrude, along with the rest of the congregation, learned something about the circumstances under which the teenaged Eustus had fled Tilley. She would be grateful to Hanny Meyers for the rest of her life. Beyond that, Eustus had never said who had ordered the lynching. But she could guess.

"Pap, I do want to tell you somethin'." Gertrude drew the old sweater a little tighter around her shoulders and shifted on the stool to face him.

"Things happen, don't they? Feelin's arise, and we know that most folk would say they is wicked thoughts or that Heaven would not be smilin' on such and such." Gertrude felt her legs itch to move, and she shifted back and forth on the stool.

"Stay still girl," said Eustus. "You is wigglin' like you was nine. Now just say what's in the front of your mind."

She drew in a breath. "Pappy, just like you and my mother had me and trouble came down on everybody… well," she looked into the ball of her fingers. "Well, I had me a baby too." Gertrude wagged her head back and forth; she couldn't have said if it were in remorse or shame.

"It was him. It was the white man, Dieter, from across the ocean."
She looked carefully into Eustus' rheumy eyes. "He was a good man,
Pappy. He'd place his hand on my big belly and sing to our little
somethin' and tell me that he didn't never want to go home again to his
old country. Said I was all he'd want."

Eustus stroked her hand, watching his elderly daughter turn into a
child again. Watching as the room faded from her eyes and Gertrude was
back again in Buena Vista.

*Lisbeth held fifteen-month-old Willy in the crook of one arm, and
Gertrude massaged his legs. The little boy struggled and screamed
against the strokes, as if each caress along his knees or feet were a blow.*

*"Ma, something is wrong. This ain't right..., I feel it. Look, he's got
him bruises all along everywhere." Lisbeth rocked back and forth,
crooning to the child, telling him to look up toward the fluttering trees
and the butterflies that lingered in the summer air, cursing to herself that
she and her daughter lived in this rural captivity. This place where
shame and poverty kept them prisoners.*

*The child had been fine in the beginning. Gertrude had thrived in
her pregnancy, and when baby Wilhem came, it was Lisbeth and Sarah,
who had come to help, who felt the slippery little life shove into their
hands. But as the months wore on, Willy seemed to find everything
painful, and now even his little belly was as big as a melon.*

*"Mama, what can you do to help him? This can't go on like this."
Gertrude kissed her child's forehead and felt it hot and wet.*

*"Well, I'm gonna get him a doctor. I'm gonna call somebody on the
telephone to get him a doctor," said Lisbeth. "I don't care what I've got
to promise."*

*Lisbeth handed the screaming child to Gertrude and put on her
straw hat. The walk into Sully's store was three miles away, but they
would give you credit, and they had a party-line phone.*

*Several hours later, she peeled the limp hat from her sweat-soaked
head. "My Ma is gonna come and get him. She won't tell a soul," said
Lisbeth falling into the chair next to the still crying Willy. "Or she'll say
he is the child of one of her maids."*

"I wonder what Dee Dee would say to do," said Gertrude into the baby's ear.

Lisbeth forced herself up and put her arms around Gertrude. The girl grew more beautiful month by month. "Your Deiter would have been a good father to this here baby," she said. "He'd have thought of something." Lisbeth let her fingers pull at the curls that coiled in little helixes and circled Gertrude's face like an ebony halo.

"Well, he didn't think of nothing to keep hisself here when they come to ship him back to Germany," countered Gertrude. "All I got is my baby and a locket with a little flower."

"You've got the love of a good man," said Lisbeth, unsure if it were true. "And when a man truly is in love, it can last for a hundred years." Of this last, she knew herself right. And she was lucky to have two men who loved her just so.

Willy had cried and refused food for most of two days. Gertrude and Lisbeth took turns squeezing drops of water from a rag into the corners of his mouth. But he was pale, and now even his cries were soft and pathetic. And then Gertrude had heard the sound of a motor vehicle coming up the drive... a big one. Odd in the middle of the day.

"Christ Almighty." Lisbeth was already on the porch, staring with a set jaw at the large, black Packard that ground to a stop. "Ma done got found out."

Ruta Elliston sat in the passenger seat staring straight ahead. She only turned toward the house when Charlie Elliston had gotten out and was heading toward the porch. But she seemed too distressed to make a sign toward her daughter.

"Where is this child?" said Charlie. He'd never been to Buena Vista's little house before, but now he came all the way onto the porch, no perfunctory hesitation at the steps. He knew he owned this property, and it seemed that he assumed everything on it was his.

Lisbeth was pale, swallowing again and again, as if she might be sick. "Why is it you want to know?" she said, taking a step back.

Charlie smiled. The smile he used on posters and at rallies, the one he wore when passing favors back and forth. "Why, Ma said there was an ailing child here that needed a doctor. And I believe I do have the means to take him there." Charlie gestured toward the idling car. There was to be no social aspect to his arrival, simply a pickup of a package.

Lisbeth looked at her mother, noncommittal and frightened. And then from inside, Willy had mustered whatever strength he had and burst forth with screams that seemed to disconcert even the portly politician standing cross-armed on the porch.

"You can take him. Just make him better." Gertrude came from the shadows inside the house, banging the screen door behind her, and holding the feverish child out to Charlie.

At the appearance of the boy, Ruta Elliston got out of the car, and without looking at Charlie, walked straight up the steps and took the child. She stood looking at Lisbeth and then at Gertrude for a moment. "My children..." she whispered with her back to Charlie. Then she turned and carried the whimpering child back into the car.

Charlie followed her without a word, shoved the Packard into gear, and disappeared with it and Gertrude's child down the dusty drive.

***

The days had passed with an Indian summer wallop that left corn harvesters cursing each moment of sunlight, though they knew they were damned lucky it wasn't rain. And yet Lisbeth and Gertrude had heard nothing from Mrs. Elliston or anyone else, and Willy's condition was unknown.

Lisbeth had walked up to Sully's twice, but her calls to her mother went unanswered, the phone jangling in her ear as she heard six or seven of the party line phones being quietly lifted up to get the lowdown on whatever would be said.

Gertrude was up before daylight each day, washing clothes in the grey galvanized tub and hanging the bleached linen on the line, or donning her straw hat and hacking at their little garden with a hoe. Yet the empty time she would have spent with Willy now poked and ached like a thorny bush in which she was trapped.

And then in the afternoon of the fourth day, she heard the sound of a truck bucking its way down the road running along the front end of the property. It wasn't one of the corn wagons running up and down. This one was coming too fast. Gertrude ran toward the end of the drive. The truck was red, a kind of burgundy under layers of dust. And as it came toward her, it increased its speed.

"Get outta the way, nigger!" somebody inside yelled. "Y'all look out!" And then a package flew out of the passenger window, tumbling in the air, its flying fabric turning it into a blue robin or a butterfly soaring on a thermal wind. The package turned end over end, unwrapping in the air, catching the sunlight, the flowered blanket filling in little sails. And then it fell. And the blanket spilled its contents into the dirt of Buena Vista.

Lisbeth had dug the hole herself. She told Gertrude that Willy had probably died peacefully at a hospital several days before, the something the doctor couldn't cure had been the reason he had died. Yet the blue color that stretched from his purple lids to his fingers and toes suggested to her that he had somehow... somehow... not gotten enough oxygen. As if that oxygen had been taken away. Over time, Gertrude came to understand who had probably withheld it.

They had wrapped the baby in the sheet that covered his bed, tightly like a little swaddling blanket; and in a tiny metal box used for aspirin, Gertrude had placed the one photo she had of Willy, stating his name and his age, and put it in his little hand. "This is so Heaven will know who's comin' to visit," she had said. "This is to identify you, since you ain't old enough to talk." Then they'd lined the grave with field stones and an old rubber raincoat, and on top of some boards, laid more stones, covered with soil. No bobcats nor dogs were going to dislocate her boy, she'd told him. And only Lisbeth and Gertrude would know where Willy slept.

Eustus said nothing. Silent as the old house, he seemed to listen to the brush of leaves against the window and the tick of the bedroom clock. His eyes were closed, or so Gertrude guessed, but his breathing was coming quick and angry. Something she had never heard.

Eustus readjusted himself in the chair, his old knees cracking, and she heard him rumble something from deep within his throat.

"Seems to me we've got a visit we need to make," he said at last. Eustus, pulled Gertrude's chin up toward the window's light, looking at her, evaluating her, and within her, the woman with whom she'd been created... and now the child he would never meet. And he seemed to make a decision.

Chapter 24

Mrs. Hanny Meyers still didn't like going out without a hat. It had been one of Alma's first teenage memories, wearing a flower-covered hat with a pretty blue eye-veil. She'd thought it made her look like Lauren Bacall, not Ida Lupino, as her mother so-mistakenly had suggested. But now people didn't wear hats anymore. Gloves were out the window, though Alma still wore them to church. And you couldn't buy a decent girdle. No, people had just turned slovenly. As for her, she'd be goddamned if she'd give up on stockings, silk ones, by the way.

And that went double if she were having lunch with Millie Sue Stanton. Millie Sue was one of the first people who'd welcomed Alma and Hanny when they'd moved to Tupelo decades ago. She was two or three years older than Alma and had married a prominent widowed attorney nearly the age of her own father. That coup had bestowed an early gravitas on anything Millie Sue thought or did. Her imprimatur was the seal of approval Alma had needed as she began to work her way into Tupelo society.

Millie Sue's elderly husband was, ironically, Charlie Elliston's longtime friend and attorney, something that as the years had deepened her friendship with Millie Sue had given Alma a kind of insider's view of the political machinations of wheeler-dealers like Big Daddy Charlie.

"Oh, I almost had to put on my sunglasses! You were just shinin' over here in this corner. Lookin' like a sunbeam, you are, Millie Sue." Alma wagged her head in amazement as Millie Sue half-stood, shoved her abundant girth over the top of the table, and extended flabby arms for a hug.

"And you, I do not know how you do it. You never put on a pound, Alma Meyers. I swear you could be one of them high-gloss fashion models, or whatever they call 'em."

The women bounced their chairs back and forth and into table position on The Viewtop's thick carpet. They fidgeted with their purses and cast side-long glances at whom else of note might be nearby.

"Well, I was gonna wear white the way this heat is disorganizin' the calendar," said Alma. "I wouldn't say this to everyone, but I swear I was so heat-swayed this mornin', I had to stop an' uncork some lavender to smell. It took me about ten minutes just layin' there on the sofa before I began to feel like a real person again."

Millie Sue had pulled a large biscuit from the basket of baked goods the waitress carefully set on the table and was slathering an entire melon-balled sphere onto the flaky wad of risen dough.

"Whatever happened to when Indian summer came and went in a couple of weeks," is what Alma thought Millie said through her masticating of the bread. Alma broke off a little crust just to be sociable. They were longtime friends, but despite Millie Sue's occasional visits to Doreen's "spa" enterprise, Millie Sue would always be the alpha dog, and it paid to mirror her here and there.

The women ordered and chatted, dipped carrots into Roquefort sauce, and decided to be daring and order wine. After the second glass, it had the stage set for exactly what Millie Sue seemed to want to share.

"Did I tell you, you look exceptional today?" Millie Sue tossed back a particularly large swallow. Alma looked up with a hint of alarm. Too many compliments meant something unpleasant might be on its way. Millie Sue shifted toward Alma and put her pudgy hand over Alma's corded one, her tone now serious, the tilt of her head the angle of a mourner at a funeral. Alma crammed a fork of fluffy greens into her mouth and grabbed for the last of the wine to wash them down.

Millie Sue wouldn't let go of Alma's right hand, and her polished nails sank into the crevices between Alma's veins. "You know that thing I done told you about… what your… your admirer gonna do for you? You know what I'm talkin' about? Long time ago? You know. That over-the-top generous thing?"

Alma thought Millie was oddly nervous. Of course, she knew the "thing." *The thing.* Oh sure, it was squeezing ethics a little for the wife of Charlie's attorney to have shared private legal matters she'd learned from her husband about the contents of his client's will. But pillow talk has always had a way of going public. Alma thought nothing of it. Did Mille Sue's husband actually think she'd keep "the thing" to herself? "Of course, I remember, Millie. And I have always been grateful. And yes, a little taken aback that such a fine man as Charlie Elliston had somehow singled me out—little backwoods me—to be the recipient of his generosity." She tried hard not to sound disingenuous.

Alma rolled her eyes toward the carved flowers on the ceiling. "It must have been some favor my father did for Senator Elliston. It certainly has nothing to do with me. I mean, how does it read? 'I bequeath all of my fortune, both real and monetary, to Alma Edwards Meyers...' Well, of course, when the time does come, I will be donatin' most of it to charity."

"Well, honey, I think he done beat you to it." Millie Sue withdrew her hand and knocked back the last of her third glass of Chardonnay.

Alma didn't move. She didn't understand one bit of what Millie Sue was saying. "What do you mean?" She had no intention of understanding. No intention of losing out on any portion of Charlie's windfall. "What do you mean, Millie Sue?"

Millie Sue shook her head, her eyes closed in sympathy. "Just like him. That's all I have to say. I've seen Charlie Elliston do this a hundred times. Promise one thing, do another. It's in his nature. String you along; that's his game. Oh, I imagine in your case, Alma, it's been a long string he used. But somethin' gets in his craw, and Bam! Charlie jerks the line, and you get cast off. Don't matter what people done for him or for how long."

Alma's hands were frozen in her lap, her eyes stationary on Millie Sue as if she'd turned into a photograph of herself.

"Alma. Alma..., don't you worry. You'll still have Hanny's money. Alma?"

Suddenly Alma couldn't turn off the newsreel that had begun to run in her mind. In something like the faded colors of a Kodachrome home movie, she saw herself in grade school, half-smiling at her own birthday party, but knowing that afterwards, Charlie would take her to the outside gazebo where he would run his hand beneath her panties. Now she was carrying her trumpet home from school, when Charlie invited her into his car and had her perform, "*just the way you blow on that golden horn, honey.*" Later she saw herself obediently letting Charlie tie her to some ancient bed when she'd overnighted with Lisbeth; the green ribbon he used around her wrists made her hands tingle even in thought. She hadn't fought it; sometimes she liked it. Most of the time, yes, she had liked it. But goddamn it, it was worth something. He'd had her most of her life. Had her in every way he could. And goddamn him, she was worth something. Yeah, she was worth his fortune… "both real and monetary."

"What does the new will say?" Alma formed the words from cotton.

"It says that a few hundred thousand are gonna go to his last remaining blood relative and after that, everything goes to a foundation he's set up for victims of sexual abuse."

Millie Sue rubbed Alma's shoulder. "I don't know, sweetie, I think it had somethin' to do with the little enterprise at Doreen's B & B in Tilley. Remember, Charlie was an old-fashioned man. I think he'd heard some rumors that made him, pardon me for sayin' it, just old-fashioned jealous."

Chapter 25

The old air conditioner, jammed into a window and rimmed with foam strips to keep the late summer heat from canceling its feeble efforts, had sputtered to yet another halt. Dr. Gunther Huebsch inched his swivel chair toward it, and with a practiced slam, made it, like a dutiful patient, cough to his will. The ancient machine protested but eventually resumed its musty responsibilities.

He looked around the rented office. Linoleum squares in maroon and grey, a desk from Goodwill, glaring florescent lights under which sat a table salvaged from a defunct massage parlor.

Everything about the little medical office said "temporary," "impermanent," and "don't get your hopes up that this will last." Yet, surprising to the doctor, patients had begun to roll in.

The little incentives, lunches and a free "real glass thermometer," had started it. But judging by the swell of local citizens from Tilley, rural farmers, migrants, and whole congregations from the black population who were making appointments, Dr. Gunther Huebsch had made a favorable impression.

"It's a mix of your knowledge and the way you seem to walk with the Lord as you care for these people that makes 'em come," one old preacher had told him. Though Gunther had diligently cultivated no direct relationship with the Lord, he found himself caring about the poor and undereducated of Tilley. When dealing with the upper classes, however, he often thought of himself as doing pure anthropology, probing into a society as alien to his own as the Incas'. But he liked it. Rich or poor, he had to admit that he was falling in love with Tilley, Mississippi.

Yet the reason he had set up this clinic hadn't shown itself. Despite having taken samples of blood or saliva from every one of his new patients to send to Atlanta for assay, none had come back with reduced levels of the enzyme glucocerebrosidase. No one he had seen in the clinic had shown the symptoms of the genetically passed Gaucher's disease that in later life had caused the death of his father. The trail to find his missing sibling remained cold. Cold—that was the lie he tried telling himself. The trail in fact, was not cold at all. It pointed in only one direction. Until recently, Gunther had satisfied himself with the expectation of testing hundreds of people. Now, with trepidation, he guessed there might be only one sample he needed to know the truth. Like Claire, he could do the math.

He rubbed his eyes. Gunther could hear the afternoon's patients starting to arrive in the tiny waiting room. Diabetes, congestive heart failure, arthritis, dementias—all of the normal crumbling away of health provoked by too much butter, sweet tea, bacon fat, and television. Patients with sickle cell disease, undiagnosed cancers, low-grade depression, as well as his own illness, asthma, comprised other challenging echelons. No, Gunther smiled as he opened the door to call in the first patient, he was tired, tired every day, but this was much more rewarding than the barren life of a university professor. He could get used to this.

The afternoon's first three patients had all eaten at Pedro's, a new Mexican restaurant at the edge of town, and each now was swilling Gatorade after days-long bouts of diarrhea. Gunther scribbled out prescriptions and shared recipes for German potato pancakes that would help riled guts settle down.

His next patient was a thirteen-year-old girl whose mother insisted the child was sexually active. The girl tearfully denied it, and they all eventually settled on some birth control pills that Gunther carefully explained were not used to cause abortions nor promiscuity. The "deal" was made sweeter when Gunther thoughtfully included an extra prescription for the mother whose six other children were causing havoc in the waiting room.

Throughout the afternoon, back-to-school physicals, boils, head lice, stoved toes, infected cuts, and a blushing sixty-something asking for something for his erectile dysfunction came and went. Over the months, Gunther hadn't realized he had begun to collect patients on their way home from work as well, but when he did, he stayed to see them too.

It was after eight, dark now as he shoved his empty lunch sack into his briefcase and turned off the grumbling air conditioner, when he heard the jangle of the bell attached to the glass front door. Left over from the storefront's days as an antique showroom, Gunther had grown fond of the door's little tinkle.

He opened the door slightly and peered out into the empty street. But not quite empty. Stretching his neck forward, he thought he saw Claire's car slowly turning the corner—as if she'd stopped but had decided to move on.

"I'm sorry to be comin' so late, sir." The woman's voice came from the shadows beside the Victorian entry, startling Gunther. "I was just wondering, if you'd have time to answer me a question or two. I don't think it'd take any of your time to speak of." Disembodied and emotionless, it wasn't until she was inside that Gunther could see the owner of the voice beneath the florescent glare.

She was an older black woman of indeterminate age, Gunther noted, who wore her hair oddly straight, not braiding it nor hiding it under a wig. Tall and thin, she carried herself with a kind of dignity that made Gunther put his briefcase down and flick back on the shuddering air conditioner.

"Yes, of course, if I can be of help. Please sit down, and tell me what it is you need."

She seated herself on an armless plastic chair, while Gunther perched on the examining table. The woman kept her head down, perhaps embarrassed, humiliated by some malady she wished not to speak of?

"I know it may seem strange, sir, but I been thinking about this for a long, long time."

Suddenly, as she lifted her gaze to his face, she stopped, mouth ajar, white teeth catching the fluorescent's blue. The woman seemed to have lost all concentration, and Gunther's medical mind started checking off diagnoses: epilepsy, a cardiac event in progress, or perhaps it was simply the first time the woman had been in the presence of a white doctor? And then she was fighting back tears. Without looking up, but darting glances from side to side as if she wished to flee but could find no way, she said, "Excuse me. I... I didn't expect you would look like... I didn't expect you.... Not tonight. Everything was so long ago...."

Gunther didn't believe that laying hands on patients was particularly necessary in medicine. Some liberal types did it, rubbing shoulders and even giving hugs. That wasn't for him. But this tall woman with the bowed head and heaving sighs somehow touched him. This wasn't epilepsy or a stroke. It was a call for compassion. He reached out his hand and took her gnarled one with its maroon veins twisting along her wrists. "Please feel that you are safe here, Madam," he said. "Tell me what I can do to help you." The woman looked at Gunther's hand. He could feel hers trembling inside his grasp. "Are you ill?"

She didn't speak until the overhead light began a quiet buzz. Then removing her hand from his, she wiped her face and with eyes still shut, turned to Gunther.

"I hear that you are a good doctor, sir, and that you don't judge nobody." The woman had turned a mental page and was trying to move on with the reason she had come. "So... I decided that I would come here to see if you could tell me... if there is a way you could tell me... why my baby died. What happened to him all those years back when I was young?" She dropped her head as if the memory of those youthful years filled her with sorrow.

Gunther suppressed an urge to sigh at her naiveté, but took her hand again and pulled a chair near her. "It may be very hard to do that, my lady. At best, we might only guess. But I see such a question has troubled you for many years. Don't worry, we will see. We will see. Perhaps I can offer you a guess that will help you. But it would be only a guess."

The woman moved as if to pull her hand away, and then let it settle into Gunther's large one. She felt her fingers relax into something like a caress. She nodded. "I know it would be but supposition. I do know that. But he was just so young... helpless he was."

139

"How old was your little child? Can you tell me how he died, the circumstances?"

She closed her eyes again as she began. "Well, he was born in the country. Only my mother there to help me when he come. But he seemed so healthy. He was beautiful from the start. Very light he was, light skinned. He almost never cried... in the beginning. But then around three months or so, I noticed he had these little yellow spots in his eyes, and sometimes he moved his eyes real strange. And then came the bruises. I told you he was light skinned. Well, I never dropped him, and nobody never hit him, I tell you that. But he just started to have these big bruises all over his little pale legs and arms... and on his midsection. It looked really big there, all swelled up... even though he was startin' to not want nothing to eat. Sometimes he had blood comin' out of his nose too. But I swear to you that nobody never hurt my little boy..., never."

Gunther involuntarily sat up straight. "How old was he when he died?" he asked.

"Under two year," the woman said. "His pappy never even got to hold him." He could feel her eyes wander across his features as if looking for landmarks.

Gunther crossed to a tiny bookcase and pulled out a thick green leather-bound book, but didn't open it. "Did your boy ever try to walk?"

"No, sir. He would cry, if you tried to put him down on his little legs... like they hurt him. But even holdin' him sometimes I couldn't give him no relief. He just seemed tired... like he just wanted to sleep and get him some strength. But then pretty quick, he sickened more and... and he passed on. And nobody could do nothin' for him."

"Where did you live back then?" asked Gunther, holding his breath.

"Oh, just a little place out in the country from here," the woman said. "A place called, Buena Vista."

It was quiet in the office now, except for the sound of an old woman's muffled sobs and an ambulance someplace in town. Gunther picked up the book and thumbed through the pages. Clinical photos of infants and children showed swollen abdomens and bluish blotches along their arms and legs. One photo showed a child in the midst of an epileptic episode. The devastation of Gaucher's disease took its toll early in some cases and in others allowed its sufferers to live long, painful lives. Another curse upon the Jews thought Gunther, another genetic anomaly that like Tay-Sachs, Canavan disease, Nieman-Pick, and Fanconi anemia was passed on by Ashkenazi Jewish carriers.

He looked carefully at the woman, wondering what she must have looked like when she was young. She would have been tall, perhaps strong, athletic from work. Her skin was still supple, a light mocha, and her eyes remained almonds above a narrow, carefully turned nose. And he noted in passing that her hair had not been chemically changed after all, but was softly wavy and fine, like a Caucasian's.

There had been a "beautiful baby" at Buena Vista. The old woman at the grocery store had said so. And there had been someone there who looked very much like Gunther himself. He felt his head spinning and his heart pounding unnaturally.

"Excuse me, Madam, but may I ask about the… about the baby's… father?"

The woman looked up, her eyes wide and frightened. Even as the tears shone along her cheeks, her demeanor changed.

"Well, it was a long, long time ago. A lot of life got lived in between then and now." She began stuffing tissues into her purse. "I forgot that I got to catch a bus right about this minute. Sorry I took up your time, Doctor. I guess some things just ain't to be know'd… " She was on her feet.

"Please wait just a moment," he said. "Would you happen to have some small memorial of your child…, a lock of his hair perhaps? It is something that perhaps would help me understand more what happened to him and then just a few more questions. Perhaps we can discover—"

Suddenly there was a loud knocking on the glass storefront door setting the little bell into a spasm.

"Anybody in there! Doctor. Doctor! We need you. There's an emergency! Doctor!"

Gunther pulled the door open to find a flashing blue light circling behind a red-faced deputy sheriff. Another policeman ran into the street to flag down a second siren-blaring car.

"What is it?" Gunther could see the panic in their eyes and motions.

"The regular doc ain't here, and there's no time for the ambulance from Tupelo to get here! Grab your bag, Doc. There's a shooting. A big-time shooting!"

Gunther turned to see the black woman he'd been talking to easing out of the clinic door and down the street. "What you waitin' for Doc! I said to hurry!" The sheriff was bearing down now, as if he would go in to find the medical bag himself.

Within minutes, Gunther found himself in the back seat of the squad car, which with a pulsing scream, carved its way through town to the home of Charlie Elliston, still regal in his black suit and golden watch chain. Who, with a look of peevish surprise, was currently dying on the steps of his elegant front porch.

Chapter 26

Chauncey had been arrested the day after Senator Charles Elliston's funeral.

"I do not understand any of this," said Doreen. "Well, alright, maybe over the, what is it...? Hundred years of his wheelin' and dealin' your grandfather was not all that loved, I guess. In public life, enemies do get made. But my goodness gracious, all that black boy a'have to a'done was waited a little. What was that old man really, ninety-two or somethin'?"

Doreen had yet to put her black lace mourning dress back in its plastic bag. It had served her since her first husband's funeral right up through today at wakes, New Year's get-togethers, and even a party in Birmingham when she went overdressed to what turned out to be an oyster-shuck.

"Nobody understands it, Doreen," said Claire. "Nothing taken. No note. No demand. And as far as I can see, no motive for Chauncey. I wouldn't have thought he even knew who Charlie Elliston was. Nothing makes sense."

Doreen eased a little brandy into some afternoon tea. "I'm havin' a little pick-me-up, want any?"

Claire shrugged away the offer. "All I know is that sitting in that front pew with Hanford Meyers beside me sitting stiff as a corpse himself and Alma blubbering next to him—like she'd lost her own daddy—made me want to run."

"Well, Mr. Meyers said some good things about his old mentor, I reckon. Talkin' about all his philanthropy. All that money for the library, and money for the new sheriff car, *and* money for that Confederate monument next to the courthouse. But honestly, I thought he'd be more broken up, workin' in Elliston banks for so many years. Why, I don't think old Hanny Meyers seemed that upset at all."

"Yes... I haven't seen Mr. Meyers lately." Claire paused, briefly wondering what had interrupted Hanny's weekly calls to the Ramada. "He'd seemed... preoccupied, like his mind was somewhere else, when I last spoke to him on the phone. Hope the nice old guy's not going senile. He has always treated me well." Claire glanced at Doreen. If Doreen knew anything, so far, she was keeping it to herself.

"Frankly, I'm sorry he's burdened with Alma. I know you like her, Doreen, but..." Claire poured herself another coffee and let her mind wander. "But why would Chauncey, a delivery truck driver, shoot an elderly senator? He's the boyfriend of my secretary you know. Nothing makes sense."

Claire finished her coffee and decided to head out to Buena Vista, although it was late in the day. She wasn't sad Charlie was gone. It really made no difference to her. Yet shards of an old poem kept running through her head as she drove by fields that were starting to bend in the late autumn heat.

> I didn't realize he had left.
> I wasn't watching.
> I didn't see him go.
> And yet the world has changed.
> The air has shifted,
> The space that was his slowly filling.
> This man I didn't know, nor whom I cared about
> Whose passing has moved the universe.

She sensed somehow a difference in the mesh of her own life. As if something she had been pushing against was removed, and now she found herself flailing against empty air. There was always a trace of Charlie on the property at Buena Vista, although Claire was sure he never visited. Yet he seemed part of something that constrained its very boundaries. She wondered momentarily what Charlie's last thoughts had been... of his wife, of his daughter, Lisbeth..., certainly not of Claire.

And though she didn't care, she wished she knew. Wished she knew why Buena Vista had been made to exist at all.

When she arrived, she saw the gate to the property was unlocked, and somewhere near the pond she could hear a chain saw being yanked in frustration. She had given Jackson a key to the lock so that he could begin the clean out of summer vines grown fat in the heat and rain. Mostly, she was glad he had the energy to come to Buena Vista when his other activities seemed to be so much in demand.

Claire waved to him as she strode knee-deep in ferns to his growing pile of wrist-size kindling. "Jackson! You are here so late! Didn't you hear the whistle, boy? Work day is over!" He was just as beautiful as the first day she saw him, perhaps a bit more brawny from a summer of cross-training at Buena Vista and at Doreen's Spa.

"Afternoon, ma'am." Jackson hauled the saw out of a crevice in a thick stump. "Thought I'd work a little more till I have to go... uh... to my second job." He blushed under a glaze of sweat and the setting sun. "After all, I sorta owe you that. You were the one who got me hired for that second line of work, and I aim to show some gratitude." Jackson dropped his head, shaking it and laughing out loud. "It been workin' out real well, ma'am... real well."

Claire stood staring at him. He was still reticent but seemed to know his own value in a market he hadn't been aware of before. "Well, that's good, I guess, Jackson. So two jobs. How's that degree coming? You've got what, another year before you're a full-fledged forester?"

Jackson dug his hand in his pocket and looked across his shoulder into the trees. "Well, I kind of put that on hold for a little bit, Miss..., I'm gonna still call you Miss Scarlett," he giggled. Claire put her hands on her hips and cocked her head.

"Yes, ma'am, I done opened another place. Just like Miss Doreen's, but up in Lafayette County. Got me a..., a friend..., well, a cousin, we'll say. Up there with a little house out on a lake... with four bedrooms. She runs a beauty parlor or somethin' she says, and that's how she signs up the ladies who want to come to the lake. Me and some of my experienced helpers takes care of the rest."

"Oh God," Claire murmured under her breath. Well, she'd certainly done her part for advancing education in Mississippi. She briefly wondered if Doreen had heard there was competition coming from the other side of the state.

"Alright, Jackson. Well, I can't say everybody would approve of your chosen profession, but you'll probably make a million dollars. So before you drive off in your new gold Ferrari with its platinum spokes, what more needs to be done here to clean up this goldurn pond?"

Jackson laughed like a boy relieved to have not taken a willow branch across his behind. "Not much, Miss Scarlett, pretty much cleaned out. But before I forget it, there was some folks out here wantin' to look around a few weeks ago. Slipped my mind to tell you. Kind'a strange too."

Claire stopped and turned around. "They was both blacks," he said. "An older woman and a still older man. Didn't look like no trash, exactly. He in a suit and she wearing a hat. Like they be out doin' church work or somethin'."

Claire was perplexed. "Did they give their names?"

"I didn't think to ask that," said Jackson.

"Well, did they say what they wanted?"

"They said that something here was buried that they wanted to look for. They said it was from a long time ago, and that it don't hold no value for nobody but them."

Chapter 27

Chauncey's dark chocolate skin, usually tinged with burgundy from the sun, seemed grey. The uniform he'd been poured into two weeks before—an oddly festive set of pajamas in red and white stripes to indicate his high level of security risk—now seemed to hang against muscles he no longer bothered to flex.

With Hanford B. Meyers' word to the Sheriff, Starlight Washburn and her boss were being ushered into a small room with both a wall of bars and bulletproof glass separating them from a shackled Chauncey, who now stood before them flanked by armed guards.

Claire at first wasn't sure it was wise for Starlight to slither into a blouse and skirt that seemed two sizes too small when visiting a man who could very likely end up on death row. Wouldn't that simply throw him into some subbasement of depression? But Starlight seemed to know her man, and when he saw her swelling breasts bulging together against the light orchid silk, he straightened up, seemed to expand his chest, and let the slightest of smiles crease his cheeks.

"Hi, Baby boy." She didn't cry, and she didn't let worry creep into her voice.

"You are lookin' fine… fine and handsome. Ooooh… and I can see they is treatin' you right, by the looks of your big shoulders… which I'm gonna be layin' my head against sooner than you think!" Starlight rubbed her own shoulders with fingers sparkling with polish. It looked as if Chauncey and she were sharing a vision of what that would be like, but Claire knew their visit was for fifteen minutes, and she had to interrupt their mental coupling.

"Chauncey, Starlight says you don't have a lawyer, so I and some people I know are going to get you one. Now understand, I am not a legal person, but I want to ask you a couple of questions so we can get this thing started, alright?"

Chauncey and Starlight seemed to be communicating telepathically. Claire couldn't imagine what odd language that might sound like. "Chauncey, did you hear me?"

His eyes, which seemed to be all pupil, turned toward Claire. "Yes, ma'am, I heard you. Ask me what you want."

"Baby, you is so brave. So brave, I want to just give you everything I have... all of it..., right now."

"Starlight. Just give me a minute or two, here." Claire worked hard to keep from rolling her eyes. She'd never been in a jail and was trying to hold herself together and act as if she knew what she was doing.

"Chauncey, can you tell me exactly what happened that caused the police to arrest you?"

"They say I shot Mr. Charlie Elliston, State Senator, retired," said Chauncey, as if reading from the charge sheet.

"Well, how do the police connect you with Mr. Elliston? Did you know him?"

"No, ma'am, I did not know the retired State Senator. But they say I shot him just the same."

"Okay, Chauncey. Did they present some evidence of that? Is there anything they say connects you with his being shot on the steps of his house?"

Starlight straightened her skirt, bending over slightly to wiggle it lower on her hips. Chauncey momentarily seemed to flow out through the bars.

"Chauncey, what do they say connected you to the scene of the shooting?"

He refocused his eyes on Claire. "Well, ma'am, because I was driving a car."

Claire took a breath. "Chauncey, that does not make you a suspect. Where were you coming from? Were you anywhere near Senator Elliston's house?"

Chauncey sat up a notch taller, causing the guards to glance down to make sure the cuffs and shackles would hold if he tried anything. "I was coming from out by Miss Starlight's house, yonder," he said. "An' I guess I was goin' back there too."

Then more quietly, with a depth of thought Claire hadn't expected, "I didn't do the shooting. But I couldn't just let the shooter walk home alone, could I?"

***

Alma hadn't come out of her room in days since Charlie's funeral. Not that Hanny minded. Rancor, spackled with hard silence, punctuated by raw vitriol was a way of life in the sprawling brick colonial in the best section of hilly Tupelo.

No, this was better, he thought. Silent in her room. Maybe she'd taken a page out of a novel he'd read in high school—Jane Eyre—where the demented chatelaine was kept in solitary, muttering to herself and out of everybody's hair.

Yet when she did come out, Hanny had never seen her this distraught. He was pretty sure she didn't actually love the old man, who had long since ceased treating her to what Alma described as his special modalities—humiliations that she had once or twice tried, fruitlessly, to entice Hanny to engage in. Instead, there was some other linkage, part father fixation, part triumph over the one she considered the rival for his affection, the long-dead Lisbeth. Even now, when Alma would occasionally appear in his study, it was to breathe hatred of Lisbeth.

"What was she like to fuck? Huh, Hanny? All of you... everybody wanted to fuck Lisbeth! And everybody did!" she would cackle. "Even me! Do you hear that? Do you hear that!"

And then her rants would taper into self-pity and paranoia. "No one would believe what you do to Claire at the Ramada, would they? Lisbeth, the whore, and Claire, her saccharine-sweet daughter. Oh, the Paragon of the Good, the upright Banker, the front-pew Elder Meyers. But we know, don't we, Hanny. Well, the only one who cared for me at all was Charlie. He cared for me. He loved me. He was gonna give me everything… Gonna give me everything when he died…" Then Alma would rock herself back and forth, glancing into the corners for corroboration.

"Maybe you're the one who killed him. Hmmm, Hanny? Could have been you. Maybe the police need to know how you hated Charlie. God knows you hated him. You hated us. All the things I let him do… And you too good for any of that."

Then she would wander back into her room leaving Hanny thinking thoughts he'd never had before.

Chapter 28

In the twilight of his leaf-strewn garden, Gunther Huebsch pulled the old shawl around his shoulders. He guessed the strapping... alright, fat... men he saw as patients, at the barber shop, and following their wives up and down the aisles of the Piggly Wiggly would laugh at him for cuddling up in a shawl as the evening cooled. Yet, he had learned that if you pounded such men on the shoulders and punched them lightly on the bicep, they were good-natured and just as needy of female warmth, or a shawl in its stead, as any other man.

Just now, Gunther could dispense with a shawl. He wanted a woman. Alright, he wanted Claire. But following their afternoon at Buena Vista, she had declined to take his phone calls and hadn't answered the notes he had posted to her bank. All he had was the tiny edelweiss locket that his father, or the someone he had given it to, had dropped at Buena Vista. After showing it to him, Claire had refused to take it back.

His head reeled when he thought of Claire now. If they were related... well, he was an adult. That's what he'd come to find out, wasn't it? But another woman had appeared in his office, her child dead as an infant with symptoms that he felt certain were Gaucher's. And that woman too had lived at Buena Vista. The answer, he thought, was close. He got up and began to walk the perimeter of his little back yard, the threads of understanding waving in the wind like a spider's guy wires that had broken free. Grab one, and everything else could be tied down.

Yet tonight he only wanted Claire's advice. She was smart, and she knew this community. She probably also knew something about Mississippi law. Gunther knew he was out of his depth on that subject, but guessed that the night of Charlie Elliston's murder he had probably done something very, very wrong. Now he wondered what the repercussions might be.

He gazed up into the trees. The sky had turned a velvety sapphire, like a tufted robe pierced with tiny diadems, almost pretentiously beautiful, he thought. We're in farming country. What is a sky doing looking so royal? For a moment, he thought of his father, wondering if on a night like this he had scanned the sky with a woman from Buena Vista. If they had thought of diamonds and crystal stars. If they had realized that together, they were making something just as miraculous.

A car turned into a driveway a few houses away, causing an arc of high beam light to suddenly track across Gunther as he moved toward the garden chair, and for a moment he was back at Charlie Elliston's house, surrounded by a half dozen police cars pulsing red and blue in a kind of cacophonous light show.

"Hurry up, Doc!" the cop had said. "We haven't moved him, 'cause we know'd we could mess things up. But hurry on now. This here is bad!" Police were standing around Charlie like a painting of Roman senators at the killing of Caesar—posed with one foot on a step or with arms draped on each other's shoulders.

Gunther had had no idea who was the man face down before him. Only that he lived in the largest house he had seen around Tilley and that his obviously precarious condition was scaring the police half to death.

Charlie was sprawled head down across three sets of concrete steps. The front door was wide open, as if he'd just stepped out to speak with someone. With flashlights playing across the well-worn back of the old man's pinstripe suit, Gunther could see that blood was coming from a scalp wound that itself would profusely bleed, and that on the steps, hidden from view, probably fatal amounts of blood had already accumulated.

Gunther pulled on rubber gloves. "Help me turn him over very carefully. But first, do you have a backboard, a stretcher of some kind?" Gunther pulled out his stethoscope as the police churned about looking for something flat. Putting the head of the scope on the old man's neck, Gunther listened for the sound of blood being pumped from the heart to the aging brain. And heard nothing. Then he lifted the old man's jacket and placed the scope against his back, listening for breath sounds. And as he expected, nothing again.

"Here you go, Doc. We knocked the legs off a table. Will that do?" The police were out of breath and in full ingenuity-mode. Whatever it took.

"Alright, fine. We will be careful, no? Place the table here. We turn him in one straight piece..., no twisting." Gunther knew the old man was dead, but the excitement in the officials' eyes told him to keep pretending.

As Gunther pushed his hands under Charlie's chest and head, he bumped first into the gold watch chain, then the watch. There was a wallet and a small packet of pills that fell out onto the steps. One-a-Days, Gunther guessed. Then there was something stuck in blood to the old man's face. Gunther peeled off the sticky square as he and the policemen gently laid the body onto the table. The note-size paper was stuck to Gunther's glove and he jammed it into his own pocket to free his hand.

The front of Charlie's chest was nearly black with blood, deoxygenated and drying over the nearly hour he lay on the steps. Already he had assumed the waxy whiteness of death. There was no need to point all of that out to the police. They had all seen death—hunting accidents, farm impalings, simple bathroom calamities. Gunther simply said, "There is no pulse. Do you have a morgue? A funeral home?" And the police looked at each other with wide eyes, each recalling a payoff or a fix they heard Senator Charles Elliston had pulled off. Each wondering who would have decided to execute their own justice before Death did it for them.

It wasn't until Gunther had returned home that he remembered the sticky piece of paper now attached with fibers to the inside of his pocket. Carefully, he worked it out and holding it up, realized it was a photograph, spattered with blood on the front and covered with it on the back. Gunther guessed that as in Germany, the tiny scallops around the edges of the picture would peg it as taken in the late forties or early fifties. His mother had pasted many such photos into albums of him and his sisters.

Gunther took the photo to the light and readjusted his glasses. It was of a baby—maybe a year old, sitting up and holding a fat rattle. The slight sepia tone of the black and white photo suggested it had faded from age, and now the browns of dried blood gave it an almost artistic look.

Gunther turned it over. The age of the child was written in careful, primary school print: *Age: 13 months B: Jan. 3, 1946.* Above it, the last name seemed legible: *P-I-T-T-S.* The first name was smudged. Yet the letters... *W-I-L* ...and the last letter... *M* were visible. *William Pitts.* Gunther turned it over again. This time he noticed writing along the very bottom of the photo. Something written in haste in a different handwriting as the back. Two words: *To Grandpa* and an angry exclamation mark that had nearly torn through the paper. Gunther turned the photo over a third time, and with his finger nail, scraped at the blood covering the first name. Here was an *"H,"* then an *"E,"* and finally an *"L."* And Gunther closed his eyes, dizzy, as he attempted to pull fragments of knowledge together.

This baby, little *Wilhelm* Pitts, a child whom Gunther could now see was both white and black, had a German first name, and he had died a little over a year after his own father had been a prisoner at Buena Vista.

Gunther closed his eyes. Claire would have to help him. Help him know why Senator Charles Elliston, both respected and feared, was grandfather to this little half-black, dead baby boy.

Chapter 29

It had been a long time since Claire had gone to church. St. Peter's Episcopal Church in Tupelo was her spiritual home. That's what the rector always said to his parishioners. A home for the spirit—where it could rest.

There was no doubt that the exposed walnut rafters against that robin's egg blue ceiling, the softly worn velvet of the pew cushions, the fragrance of years of "incensed" Sundays all conspired to make one feel homey. Claire knew she wasn't the only one who felt so at home there that she and many of the devoted regularly fell asleep.

Of course, there had been other reasons Claire went to church each Sunday. The widowed president of the Tupelo Chamber of Commerce was one. The retired Army Brigadier was another. The genteel evenings with a businessman, sipping port while listening to a Vivaldi recording. Or sometimes in sunglasses and headscarf, walking with the General out to a skeet shoot on someone's plantation were what every woman her age would want. Yes, St. Peter's Episcopal Church in Tupelo provided exactly the right venue to meet someone who suited her to a tee. And to praise the Lord, of course.

Yet, seated now beside Starlight Washburn at the Zion Top Baptist Church eight miles outside of Tilley, listening to an upright spinet being meticulously hammered by an elderly woman in a pink dress, it was as moved as Claire had felt in years. Nobody was caring what she wore or whether she'd put on a few pounds like they would have at the blue-ceilinged church. No one noticed if a good Episcopal husband's eyes had wandered along Claire's neck and shoulders. Here she was a white woman in a black church, but she was as anonymous and free as if she were running in the woods. Claire leaned in to Starlight. "Thank you for inviting me here. I like it."

Starlight smiled back. "Wait till you hear my granddaddy preach," she whispered. She shoved at a lacquered wave that swept down over one eye. "And I believe, if you're able, he might have an invitation for you too." Starlight adjusted one of her breasts with the inside of her arm. "You know we all appreciate what you and Mr. Meyers is doin' for Chauncey. We really do."

Then the clapping had begun and arms were raised. The heavy florals of men's aftershave and women's autumn scents began to rise on the heat of bodies that let themselves perspire for the Lord. With heads thrown back or wagging from side to side, eyes closed as they pictured Jerusalem, the congregation called and worried, cried out and went weak, spending itself in praise and an afternoon of choral Amens.

Eustus' sermon had mesmerized Claire. The thin man appeared like a lightning rod, powerfully invoking heaven to strike him with the Holy Spirit in order that he may send it forth to the people who wept and prayed before him. Claire wondered if like a light bulb with too much current, the Power might overwhelm him, and he could evaporate before her. Yet he glowed with strength, kindness... and something more. Something familiar.

"Well, ain't that there a show. And now I do believe I will take some of that for myself. I do believe I will. Better n' what I just got, I'll reckon—"

"Stay back. She don't belong to you. You didn't pay for nothin' here!"

The voices were coming from the woods behind Buena Vista, one voice, deep and confident, the other frightened, as if risking everything.

Claire grabbed frantically for her clothes, scattered like petals around her. She didn't want to stand, but only to disappear into the grass—a grub, a mite, a speck of pollen. But ducking as she did, she could hear the man's legs thrashing through the high weeds toward her.

"Well, ain't that nice... a little hide n' seek, is we? Now don't you be frightened. Ain't nothin' goin' happen to you that ain't already happened to your mama."

Claire couldn't see her, but Lisbeth's feet were pounding toward her, and her screams echoed off the trees. "Get away from her! You get back away! She ain't yours! Get ba—" Claire heard the sound of flesh colliding with bone and heard her mother drop to the ground. And then moans of pain.

"Well, we don't want none of that goin' on, do we? No interference with what I'm bound to do." The man was on his feet and pushing at the high weeds like a tracking dog. Claire slithered as best she could, staying low, sharp thorns tearing against her stomach and chest, her clothes clenched tightly at her throat.

"You know what's good for you, you're gonna stand up and let me find you, you little tease. Hey... I'll give you a quarter... ha ha... How 'bout I put it in your slimy little slit!" The man roared with laughter as he careened through the undergrowth.

There was the sound of dogs barking somewhere in the distance, and her mother's moans, and then the pain of the man's shoe as he found Claire's curled body and kicked the boot into her ribs. Her head spinning, she immediately began to retch. He reached down and pulled her to her knees by the hair.

"Aw... that's not nice. You better not be a barfer." He threw her down backwards into the grass and shoved his boot hard against her stomach as he unbuttoned his pants.

"Clairie..., Clairie!" Lisbeth's voice sounded sleepy, far away, as if only her voice could move. "Help..., somebody help us!"

"Shud up..., cow.... Gonna get me some young calf over here." The man laughed, but sounded out of breath, his breathing coming fast in pants as if he'd been running. He took his boot off Claire's middle, and with his other foot kicked her legs apart, pinning them open, standing over her in the wide stance of a soldier at ease.

She opened her eyes for a moment and saw that his pants were around his knees and that something protruded from a mass of hair between his legs.

"You ain't never had this happen before have you, Honey. I'm gonna be the first. I ain't never been the first before. Always had ole used

cunts. So you an' me both are gonna be real proud when I'm done with you."

The man dropped down and forced her arms out into a kind of crucifix. She heard her mother crying. She heard dogs barking. And she heard a crack. And the weight of a dead man fell heavily across her chest.

It all might have been a dream, except for a long time she kept the shirt of the one who had covered her naked body and helped her back to her mother. It belonged to someone with a thin dark face, someone whose kindliness she hadn't seen again... until today.

When at last the singing recessional had carried the worshippers out of the tiny church, Starlight turned to Claire with magenta lips pulled into a brilliant smile. "So this is my church, and that was my grandfather, and you are welcome to be my guest at any time at all."

Claire gave Starlight a hug. "I would like to come again."

"And we would be happy to have you be a regular." Claire looked up to find Rev. Eustus Pitts opening his arms toward her. The old man still had tiny globes of perspiration near his cropped white hair. "The gap is not so wide as we have pretended it to be," he said with the nod of a man who knew the gap to be a chasm.

"Your preaching was remarkable, Reverend Pitts. Very moving. You are all so generous to have me visit." She looked hard into his face, forcing herself into the small talk of polite churchgoers everywhere. Yet there was no mistaking it. The eyes of Eustus Pitts, their blanched brown now surrounded with milky blue, were the same she had seen that day at Buena Vista, filled with mercy and the capacity for holy retribution.

Eustus took her hand and led her toward a side door and out into a tiny yard where under a live oak, a picnic table had been set up. Someone had put fall leaves into a No. 10 peach can for a centerpiece, and an old woman with her back turned was unpacking casseroles. "Be our guest for lunch," he said. "Others you might know will be coming too."

Chapter 30

"Miss Doreen," said Jackson, "this meetin' is not what I want to do, ma'am. But the boys here are just... well, they say things seem to be gettin' a little out of hand."

From the tiny Victorian footrests to the hand-painted wallpaper, even Doreen's parlor looked uncomfortable—as if so many tall, muscular men standing under its crystal chandelier would make it swoon. If Doreen had had a fan, she would have flapped it back and forth with a fury. As it was, she daubed and patted and tried to perch herself on the armrest of the flowered camelback sofa nearest the door.

"I swear I do not know what can be the matter, Jackson. You and these boys are being paid like bandits, the women are happy, or so I understand, and well, I hear things, Jackson... that you're so good at this that you're branching out."

Jackson glanced at the other men standing in a ragged circle in the parlor. Most of them didn't know about his new out-of-town operation. "Yes, ma'am. But this..., this problem... is something about here. About some of the... well, of the things the boys don't like bein' asked to do." He shifted his weight from one slight high heel to the other of his new boots.

"Well, that sounds odd. Seems to me there's one thing and one thing only that goes on up there. That's what you're bein' paid for." Doreen's tone made Jackson look up. "Just what and just who are you gettin' ready to complain about?" Doreen hadn't handled disgruntled employees over the years without knowing when to turn tough guy.

"Ma'am, it started with one askin' for things, then it seemed like it done spread to the others. And the boys done brought evidence too."

Doreen looked from one sunburnt face to another. "Evidence? Are you sayin' this... whatever... is going to go to a court of law? Are you just now gettin' ready to bite the hand that's feedin' you? To bite off your nose to spite your own face?"

The men were silent, grasping their wrists and shooting sidelong glances back and forth.

"Well, why don't you do one of two things... or both, I don't care. One, you can tell me exactly what you are having a hard time with. Like the ladies are not givin' you big enough tips, or you have to go out and buy new underwear 'cause the clients don't like dirty grey?" She was turning it on. "Or, two, you can lay your "evidence" right down here in front of me. What? Did one of the ladies get a crush on you and write a love letter?" A dose of humiliation should work. "Or you boys can hightail it outta here and be happy as corn-fed beef that you are makin' money the way you are makin' it!"

The men didn't move. Then a teenaged blonde at the back of the room cleared his throat, reached into a paper grocery sack, and pulled out what appeared to be a delicate set of jumper cables. Next, he drew out what Doreen thought were four pink dog collars, except that there were pieces of cord attached to each. And finally, he threw a handful of Polaroid snaps onto the beveled marble topped table in front of her.

"This here's our evidence, ma'am," said the blond boy, drenched in embarrassed sweat. And looking from one to the other of the blushing men, "An' it's Miss Alma an' a couple of the others who makes us do it." Jackson was staring intently into the border of the carpet.

Doreen's lips didn't seem to want to move. She didn't know what the items in the grocery sack were for, but she could see that the photos were filled with poses more suited to torture than the kind of afternoon bliss she'd presumed was taking place above her head.

She felt her heartbeat filling the room. "I understand," she said finally. And again, "I understand." Doreen walked slowly to the door, reaching out to steady herself against its jamb. "Take those things away

from here. Burn them. Don't worry about coming back until I call you...,
if I do."

Doreen turned back and looked at this cream of rural Tilley's crop.
Young men who were willing to take a few risks for money and what
Doreen had thought of as mildly humorous—and lucrative fun. Who did
she think she was? She didn't have any children, but one of these could
have been hers.

"Jackson, you pick up their money tomorrow." He nodded, not
looking up. Then she added, "I'm sorry. Sorry. Maybe I had a very bad
idea, didn't I? Now you boys promise me, promise me that you're gonna
all go to church as soon as you can and ask forgiveness for me and for
yourself. And that whatever happened up there, that you will never,
never do none of that with nobody again. Not with your girlfriends and
not with your wives. You hear?"

The men shuffled out, hands in pockets, heading toward their
pickups. It was left to Jackson to pick up the upstairs implements and
photos and shove them back into the brown paper sack. He dumped them
into his new pickup and felt in his pocket for Alma's number.

Then he headed north toward Oxford, sure he could double the fees
with the competition out of the way.

Chapter 31

It had taken Gunther longer than he'd thought to find the woman who'd come to his office the night Senator Elliston was shot. Tilley was a small town, but the surrounding county was peppered with small enclaves of blacks and whites who lived in almost tribal insularity. Buena Vista was such a place. But the Piggly Wiggly and Dollar store were magnets for country people who couldn't resist bouquets of fluorescent flowers manufactured in China or gigantic boxes of cereal coated with chocolate and cream. Like a deer hunter, it was there that Gunther eventually thought he would net his quarry "nosing for corn"— or corn chips.

"No, sir, I don't know who you is lookin' for. 'An older black woman' is not much of a description." Gunther had started out feebly. The cashiers lifted their shoulders and scratched under their wigs, but nobody could think of "an older black woman" as anybody in particular.

It was only after he added that this woman "stands very tall and straight and has hair that is as fine as... that blonde's in the corner," that looks of recognition crossed their faces. "Why you must mean Miss Gertrude," they would smile. "She was my Sunday School teacher," said one. "She done watched over my sister's baby," said another. Gunther learned that Gertrude came on Thursday mornings to the grocery, and when that day arrived, he positioned himself as far from the overflowing storefront ashtray as he could and sat down to wait for a "tall, regal woman" who might have loved his father.

***

"We have heard about you from various parts of town," said Eustus. He wore black trousers, probably salvaged from a suit that had grown too threadbare to wear, and a dark cardigan against the September chill running through the clapboard shotgun house.

"But it'd never occurred that we'd have the privilege of entertaining you in our home." Eustus took the tray of warm biscuits from Gertrude and bent down to offer one to Gunther.

Gunther had been surprised at the Piggly Wiggly a week before when Gertrude, accompanied by this elderly man, had greeted him not only politely, but even with some warmth. She'd apologized for "leaving without a proper good-bye" from the clinic, her long neck bowed, but her lips carrying a smile. Then the Reverend had followed up with an invitation for a visit, which Gunther now knew to be a rare event in the rural South.

"It was my good fortune to have found your... to have found Miss Gertrude just coming into the Piggly Wiggly," said Gunther, pretending a serendipitous meeting and still not understanding the relationship between these two. "But our conversation some weeks before had left me wishing to speak with her again." He wondered if he were being too forthright. If what he wished to ask of Gertrude was something this dignified old man knew about. "I am somewhat surprised and am very honored that you and she have invited me here today."

Eustus took his time, setting the tray down and slowly lifting a glass of sweet tea to his lips. Gertrude had been standing somewhere near the long open hallway but now seemed to gain confidence and came in and sat down.

Gunther looked at her carefully as she smoothed her dress along her lap. With her long neck, only occasionally-creased, smooth skin that lay tightly against her cheeks, and fine, slightly wavy hair; she could have been a gypsy or of Egyptian lineage, he thought. Yet more than what had obviously been her beauty, there was a quiet strength that floated around Gertrude like an aura.

Eustus had quietly set the old rocker he was in moving in slow arcs, as if to set the pace at which he wished the conversation to proceed. He asked if Gunther had settled into his home in Tilley and if he liked it. He asked about the physical health of the population of town. He wanted to know if Gunther had seen any of the countryside and if he had made any friends. All perfunctory questions that allowed each man to take the measure of the other. And each of them seemed pleased with what they found.

"I would imagine," said Eustus finally, "that in your country, a place where innocents suffered much during the war, there are many things that happened... inadvertently, surprisingly perhaps. Things, shall we say, that would or could not have happened at any other time."

Gunther glanced at Gertrude, wondering if Eustus were offering an invitation to continue the conversation he had had in the clinic with the now quiet, but very engaged woman beside him.

"That is true. During times of upheaval many things happen that are out of the ordinary."

Eustus leaned forward and looked carefully at Gunther. "You had asked to take something from my daughter." Gunther eyes involuntarily widened. Daughter? Had he understood? Gertrude was Eustus' daughter? The height. Yes, he could see the resemblance.

"Yes, I am taking samples from each patient." Gunther began his blanket explanation for why he was taking blood—general good health required a screening; sickle cell disease may be lurking—but he could quickly see that Eustus wanted a more frank explanation for why Gunther had so intently wanted something else. Something of her dead child. A lock of his hair.

Gunther cleared his throat. What came next would determine if the patrician old man would escort him to the door or not. "I had asked your daughter if she had something of the boy who died. With something, a bit of hair for instance, we could examine it deeply for evidence of an illness that may have caused his death. We might find an answer as to why her son died."

"But you didn't only ask about the child," said Eustus.

"No," said Gunther. He looked out the window across the golden fields, paler now that the sun had settled behind the trees. "I also asked about the father." And though fifty years had passed, Gunther sensed the

164

room grow thick with fear, as if it flowed from the walls where the ghosts of Sarah and others long gone kept it hidden.

Gunther closed his eyes. "I asked about the father of the child because I believe that he was my father too. My father, a German prisoner, who carried a hidden disease that was passed on to the child whom your daughter bore."

Gertrude's lowered head slowly raised, proud now and with a smile. Tears streamed along the ruddiness of her cheeks, but she shifted in her chair and nodded gently toward Gunther.

"I knew him, your father, before you did, then didn't I? And you... had a little brother." Gertrude was stifling a laugh, as if she were opening revelations like Christmas gifts. "I saw something, you know, doctor, sir. I saw something that night at your office. I saw my Dee Dee standing there talking to me again, and I had me a hard time to concentrate on what you was saying. So much had happened that night...." She stopped, closed her eyes, and for a moment when she opened them, Gunther thought he saw not joy there, but death.

Chapter 32

Doreen had let three months go by in a kind of dream state, avoiding the hairdresser, and ignoring the growing basket of bills piling up next to the refrigerator. She now sat at the kitchen table of the B & B picking up each statement, carefully removing its envelope, and writing down the deficit tally it made in her monthly income.

The weather had turned cool before she'd even flipped the page of the calendar hanging next to the window. Her lacy curtains rose and fell with a light breeze and the waft of smoke in the air. A perfect time for guests, she thought. If there were any.

With blue-bound ledgers spread across the table, a calculator, pencil, and requisite glass of wine beside them, Doreen had placed the basket of bills smack in the middle. The figures were not cooperating. Ten in the morning or not, she was going to need that glass of last year's Beaujolais.

She shoved her chair away from the table with a glance at the final tallies of the last few months' expenses and the amazing income that had flowed in from the Excelsior Ladies' Day Spa. All she had to do was look down where she'd written those wonderfully swelling balances in a thick black marker and know it had been a damned good idea. Three months of profit, three months of delighted ladies—even a growing out-of-town clientele, and then—Alma.

Alma, the "membership chairman," with her twisted predilections. Despite what Doreen knew to be her own "advanced" points of view, there were certain peccadillos where she drew the line. Hell, a little swat on the fanny, some love nips maybe. She'd been "experimental" when she was young too. But that bag of... of... implements she'd sent Jackson packing with... Well, no siree. Not in her house. Not in her likely to be foreclosed-upon house.

If only she hadn't notified her original clients, the cyclists who plied the Natchez Trace, and who begged her for rooms after a twelve-hour ride on their week-long treks. She'd rather proudly told them she'd be full-up for the next few seasons. Now she reckoned that though they hadn't paid all the bills, they had kept the lights on. Worse, she'd have to let the ladies of the UDC know the Spa was permanently shut. A hell of a price to pay for having morals, she laughed. Doreen took a swig of Beaujolais. Then another. What the heck, it was going on eleven— maybe she'd put another bottle in the cooler. She tilted her chair back and gazed at the ceiling. Needed painting. Shoot, the whole place did.

"Well, damn," she said out loud, after washing a buttermilk biscuit down with another jolt of wine. She slammed the top of the table feeling like Eisenhower making a decision to invade. "The only one who shouldn't be in church is Alma! What am I doin' shuttin' down a goin' business?"

She wasn't sure why, but an old philosophy professor's words suddenly danced in her head. "The greatest good for the greatest number," he'd intoned. "Always measure a decision by that yardstick." Well, thirty-one ladies, ten young men, versus Alma and her handcuffs. And she hadn't even counted in herself! Yes, reopening the Spa would be a very great good for Doreen McCurdy whose windows all needed glazing. Who needed Alma? Membership Chair, indeed! Doreen had a list of all the clients she needed. What would take some doing was getting back the "servicing agents."

Doreen put in a call to Jackson, who since the Spa had opened had served as a kind of go-between with his lady boss and the other men. Doreen had told them to not come back. Now rounding them up from their diaspora, she'd need Jackson's buy-in to start rescheduling, but no one was answering.

In a way, Doreen was more worried about the skittishness of the ladies. Habits can be easy to break, even naughty ones, when you start thinking too long and hard in the middle of the night. But running a B & B was all about making pretty promises—drawing a fantasy with a doily and some fringe. Doreen knew how to do that. Surely she could keep these ladies interested with a little sweet talk about the benefits of "exercise."

After seven phone calls, it was clear that two of the ladies had begun to have second thoughts as they'd bounced some grandchild on their knee. Several realized they'd gone down a road with Alma that had frightened them. Another's husband was surprised and suspicious of her newfound willingness. But by a dozen calls, Doreen felt she had a whole lot of Tupelo and beyond still interested in the relaxing entertainment at the Excelsior Spa.

This time when she called the number Jackson had given her, the phone picked up. "Why, hello, Jackson. You'll never guess who this is. Well, yes, it is. It's Miss Doreen, for sure."

"You are where? You're outside a' Oxford! Well, well. Just outside a' Oxford. Long way off, isn't it?" Doreen topped off her glass from the new bottle. "And you done what? Well, what about school, Jackson... all that forest stuff you love so much?" She began to perspire despite September's cool spell while she listened to Jackson. Jackson, the newborn entrepreneur. What the....

"You're now runnin' a what? A franchise? How many? No, you're not! Hattiesburg? Gulfport, too? Well, I don't know whether to say I'm mad at you or I'm proud. And you say business is... That good. Well, my, oh, my. They do say imitation is the sincerest form... What? Say that again, Jackson, 'cause I don't think the connection is about right. You are proposin' what!"

Doreen stopped her pacing and sat down hard on a tiny Federalist ottoman she knew she'd pay hell to get up from, but she feared her knees were ready to give out. "You want to Buy Me Out and make my B & B a what! A *branch* of your... your... Well, I'm gonna just say it, your 'brothel business?' Is that what you are sayin'?" Mother of God. Doreen wanted a little outrage to come through her voice, but instead she could feel the smile creep all over her body.

"My goodness, Jackson. That is just something. Something I never would'a thought about. Well, yes, I know it was my idea. You're right, you likely would have never found such an opportunity without me.

168

Hmmm? How much? Oh, really? We could bring in that much? And, uh, what would my percentage be then... although understand, I am not all that certain this is something I want to be doing... full-time." She'd pulled a pencil out of her pocket and was already figuring percentages on the inside cover of a 1903 copy of *Peter Rabbit*.

"Hmmm... well, you know what, Jackson, I always liked you. I think we done real well together here in Tilley. Now as long as we don't get into any of that... that kinky stuff... I'm a willin'. Yes, I think I am. And honestly, I think we could just open up here again in about a week. Is that too soon? No? Well, I'll plan on it, if you can get me some nice strong employees." Doreen didn't care if she sounded eager now. She was. Better strike now or all her ladies would begin to focus on their arthritis or some damn fool vacation to Biloxi their husbands wanted to take.

"Oh, and out of curiosity, Jackson, I'd just love to come on over to Oxford to see what your place looks like. See how it compares an' all. See if I can learn somethin'" She was ready to be deferential to a partner who in two months was bringing in twice the clients she'd worked hard at cultivating over half a year.

"It's on a lake. Oh, that's nice! That many rooms? Sounds fancy! And it's whose place you say? What? I think our connection dropped again, Jackson. Your other partner? *She's* your other partner! You say that Alma Meyers—from Tupelo—is in this here franchise business too?"

Chapter 33

August had been wet and steamy across all of Mississippi.
Storms seemed to crack nightly until the first week of
September, and the mighty river to the west was still swollen at the delta
where it spilled into the Gulf of Mexico. Since then, the sun had turned
bright; the sky that particular powder-blue that left people at bus stops
and while pumping gas gazing heavenward, trapped in reveries they
couldn't quite define.

Claire blinked into just such a sky as she stepped out of the interior
of Zion Top Baptist Church and was led by Eustus and Starlight toward
a picnic bench covered in a fluttering flowered cloth.

"When I told Granddaddy that my boss... and you know I talk about
you in the highest glowing terms you can imagine... was willing to come
on a Sunday with me to church, well, we was all just about undone! You
are helping us all, like the good Christian that you are, Miss Claire. And
you know I'm talkin' about Chauncey. You know too what that means
to me in my heart. So, this is just the nicest thing, Miss Claire. I am
tickled pink. I am blessed by the Lord Jesus Christ!"

Starlight's bosom was weighted down today beneath an ornate
necklace that seemed to be made of chainmail, while sunlight bounced
in little starbursts off her canary-yellow dress.

In fact, Claire had the feeling that sunlight was pervading everything
in the meadow behind the church. Even where the oak dripped its purple
shadows, the air seemed bright.

"We are indeed blessed, Miss Elliston, and we ask you now to join
us for some autumn bounty." Eustus held up a pumpkin pie that had been
unpacked and gestured toward a casserole of baked apples that was being

uncovered. Church men were setting up card tables in another part of the glade, and the women were organizing the silver.

"But while all of this gets arranged," said the preacher, "I thought you might like to have a little chat with someone... somebody you might not have expected to find here." Eustus pointed toward a little arbor some distance from the church. It was settled into a shallow ravine, secluded, where clusters of grapes were beginning to fatten and bulge among its leaves. A man in a suit stood in the arbor, his hands clasped before him, waving now when he saw Claire turn.

She looked hard. Hanny? A flush of embarrassment swept over Claire. What on earth was Hanny Meyers doing here from Tupelo? She tried to fit him into any of several scenarios. Something from the business community, loans to the church, more about Chauncey, an impulsive Ramada Inn confession? She didn't want to have a conversation with Hanny Meyers right now. She was actually savoring the fellowship she felt with these upright and generous churchgoers and the simple luxury of a September picnic. Whatever Hanny had to say, it would be complicated.

"Go on down, Miss Elliston. We ain't eatin' for a bit."

Claire carefully picked her way down the hewn stones, pausing to check her balance after each of several steps. Then Hanny's big hand was there to guide her the rest of the way.

"Well, ain't this an unusual place to meet?" Hanny could never keep his natural chivalry from turning even a simple sentence into a lullaby. But this time it rang hollow, as by omission, he seemed to allude to the other place they met.

"It was a beautiful service, was it not? In fact, I've made an effort to come here more recently, though it's a haul from Tupelo." Then he lowered his voice as he sat down beside Claire. "I must apologize for having to cancel several of our meetings. You know, they have long been a source of comfort to me." Claire adjusted herself, moving decorously away from Hanny on a bench that had lost its paint. He sounded nostalgic, perhaps confessional, she wasn't sure. They both sat uncomfortably for a moment, searching for the right thing to say.

"Well, I was hoping there was nothing wrong, nothing medical," she said. Even this felt unseemly in the shadow of the little church. She thought Hanny had aged in just the weeks since she'd seen him. But perhaps she never had looked during the Ramada interludes. So much about those rendezvous was simply shutting off her mind and continuing her thank-you to a kindly old gentleman. She wondered briefly where Hanny mentally went when they were together. She knew he used their meetings as a kind of jumping off place to somewhere else.

The little hollow was cold now. The sun still glittered overhead, but Claire found herself shivering.

"Ah, Gertrude. Come sit down." Hanny stood, offering Gertrude a place. Claire looked from one to the other, unsure of how these two would have met.

Gertrude, dressed in a shiny black suit silently joined them, her eyes riveted on Claire and a delicate smile across her lips.

"Pleased to," she said.

Claire looked at each of them, feeling the leaves begin to move in and out as if they were breathing. Gertrude smiled at her and moved something into her lap... a bowl of snap beans? Why would she be doing kitchen work here?

"Gertrude... Why, I am so happy to see you so soon again. I didn't know you attended this church. I had this nice invitation from my secretary, Starlight Washburn, to come visit, and I've just had a wonderful morning."

Claire glanced up to see if Starlight was near and would join the little group. She wanted her secretary's bling nearby for its attachment to the office, the bank, and a certain reality—which all had somehow loosened in the little glade. And Hanny seemed to have disappeared.

Claire turned to look for him, when Gertrude reached out and smoothed down Claire's skirt. "*Got to send nice messages now, Honey.*"

Claire stared at her. Had Gertrude changed her clothes? Pulled off the black jacket to reveal the blue cotton work dress beneath? As if it were the most natural thing in the world, Claire reached over to help her snap the beans she held in her lap.

172

"I can snap faster than you can, Gertrude. Faster than Mama. Faster than anybody. Just watch!" Claire's painted fingernails flew through the pile of green pods, whipping off pointed tips and stubby ends. "Look a' here... I got me... got me thirty!"

Gertrude was looking up, over the top of Claire's head at something that had nothing to do with snap beans. She suddenly put her own bowl down and reached down for Claire's hand.

"You promised it, Rainey, you promised it before you come." Claire didn't turn her head. Gertrude was holding her tight against her apron. And behind Claire, Lisbeth's voice was high, light, yet sweet with hoarseness as if she'd been singing. "You don't come here for free, Rainey... It's money or a sack of food provisions."

"Who give you those snap beans you nigger's cleanin' yonder? I did! I done give you beans and more. What you call that sack a' flour? What you call that cane syrup? Woman, I ain't no goddamn grocery store. My mind..., it's you owin' me. And I gonna take back some too! You better be ready.... I gonna take it!"

Suddenly, beans were everywhere. Beans on the porch. Beans in the grass. Thirty beans flying from Claire's lap. "What's he gonna take, Gertrude?" Claire asked as she picked them from the grass. "What's he gonna take?"

"Miss Claire, did you drop something? My, you are huntin' like it's something real important." Starlight, who sounded perplexed, was bending down where Claire had dropped to her knees in the grass. Hanny was reaching down to help her up, but Gertrude was gone. And the beans were nowhere to be found.

"We're gettin' ready to eat now, Ms. Elliston," someone said. "Come on over and join our lunch."

***

Hanny had fled the church social. Instead, he shoved his polyester jacket into the back seat of the Lincoln and began to drive. It had all been a bad idea trying to explore what Claire Elliston knew about her own

173

parentage. Who did he think he was, some high-priced-therapist? No, better to let sleeping dogs lie for now... until he knew how badly they could bite.

Instead, Hanny rolled down the windows and focused on the smell of the fields and their airborne-dirt. Tilley's roads hadn't changed much since he'd covered every last one in his father's delivery truck over fifty years before. The trees still swept up and over what was now oily asphalt, and fallow fields or a few with bulging pods of cotton still waited like living room paintings, silent and unpeopled.

Hanny wasn't due to be anywhere. Alma had moved several suitcases of clothes and lots of her best china to the lake house near Oxford. Hanny guessed her daddy had given it to her because he'd thought that sooner or later Hanny would throw her out. But he never had. Too much trouble. Too much "repressed" to feel much of anything. Odd, somehow, now that she was far away, thoughts he must have packaged in cardboard and stored in a mental attic were overwhelming him. Charlie. Eustus. And, as always, Lisbeth.

He switched on the air conditioner. Then turned it off and reopened the windows for the September air, fresh, but oddly heavy and warm. The sky was brilliant blue with a band of muscular looking cirrus clouds low in the sky. He let the wind race around him, swirling from front seat to back, lifting his tie, pulling his hair in tufts and spikes. Remembering again the way the bees had buzzed in his dad's garden before the old man had bulldozed it to put up an aluminum shed, the way old Jack had barked at squirrels, and Hanny had shot his first one, straight through the tail... and he began to relax.

And weren't those two days in the woods with his buddy, Tommy, the best he'd ever had? And wasn't the water from his grandma's well the coolest and cleanest he'd ever tasted? Hanny wanted to close his eyes, but his home country was just too beautiful. Too much time in Tupelo, he thought, not enough time smelling the grass and pastures of Tilley.

He glanced up. The clouds were building with an energy that was unusual, darkening part of the sky as if a curtain were being lowered. Yet the sun still bathed the little town in a nostalgic wash. He passed a wooden church that needed painting and thought of the upright in the sweltering hall his parents had attended. The holy ground where grown men sang hymns with tears running down their cheeks while the flyer for the Klan rally they would attend that same Sunday was stuffed in their inside pockets.

Hanny had seen just such a flyer today pasted on a light pole near the courthouse park. He knew from a front-page story picked up by the Tupelo Register that a "known criminal from Chickasaw County had been caught by the Klan" and recently hanged. Certain things didn't change in Mississippi.

Even so, today he had come under Eustus' spell. Eustus, who had lived and learned and come back to Tilley. Hanny still didn't understand why, though parts of the story had come through.

For people whose reading and writing skills were never developed, news came mostly by word of mouth. Over the years, Sarah had told him that Eustus had found his way up north, then later that he was "getting schooled." Later still, that he had taken a wife. She said her son was going to be a preacher someday. Well, some things, some dreams, do come true. Not all....

Hanny remembered the dreams he had spun along these dusty roads. Remembered hopes he couldn't collate, now flying in a messy conflagration of mental snapshots. Which year had he first heard the word "war"? Which year had he seen a woman's breasts? Which year had he sold himself into servitude to Charlie? Long ago. All of it long, long ago.

He had been on this very road. The newspaper beside him was filled with news of Europe and Germany. Germany again, the troublemaker country that a few years before had left him with a crippled father who screamed out in the night. That first time—was it 1916?—when Hanny was four or five, many women, including his mother, were left struggling to run the farms and stores left unmanned by husbands off fighting the Germans in the First World War. He remembered that everybody had hunkered down to save food, to buy War Bonds, to send every last bale of cotton to the troops for uniforms and bandages. Well, the Yanks had won the War to End All Wars, and his father had come home.

Then only ten years later, the Great Depression. Hanny, along with half the country, remembered eating nothing but potatoes twice a day and being damned grateful for it. Scared men had walked the streets, and in tiny Tilley, beggars had lined the church steps. But somehow his family had survived, and his father, ever the optimist, had started a little newspaper that would eventually grow to the fourth largest in the state. Then, before Hanny felt he'd reached his full manhood, everything had started over, just the way it had for his father.

The newspapers were reporting that a new European threat, some kraut called Hitler, was claiming he could raise Germany back to power from the beating it had taken in the First War. But as the Tilley Register had warned, the newly-appointed Chancellor Hitler was already too powerful, rounding up people he didn't like, and moving them somewhere. Nobody knew where they were being sent, but Hanny would find out, wouldn't he?

The sky was flint now, streaked with clouds raked by high altitude winds that left the landscape uniformly grey. Grey, the way it was that day so many years ago. Hanny directed the Lincoln to the side of the road, pulled out a cigarette, and gazed at the distant fields. He loved how they shifted colors in the wind, moved in sections, like a chorus giving sopranos and altos their moments until the baritones and basses roared in. Yeah, that day had felt just like this one.

Jesus Christ. Wallowing in reveries, that's what he was doing. Just like an old man. But hell, why shouldn't he? He was old. He could do what he wanted. Besides Alma was gone, wouldn't smell the smoke inside the car and launch into one of her harangues. Hanny pulled off his tie and exhaled smoke against the upholstery. Then he let his eyes close in the heat and in the fragrance of grass drying on its stalks, and he stretched into the memory of a cotton skirt ruffling in the wind on a long-ago September day when the wind blew....

Hanny knew the blue Nash would draw stares; though, now you could see a few new Fords on the dirt roads of Tilley after the old ones had been handed over to the bank in the Depression. But now, ten years later in hamlets like Buena Vista, where war rumors had only recently begun to tamp down excitement over the higher price of cotton, a flashy Nash convertible could draw stares. The four "klieg-like" head lamps, a three-foot-high grill of solid chrome, and a cavalier whitewall spare tire mounted on its running board had the old-timers stopping, spitting, and shoving their hands deeper in their pockets with rural disdain. Hard times or not, if you had it, you didn't show it.

Yeah, Hanny knew these people. Knew the rough scrabble of all their lives, blacks and whites alike. Guessed if they knew he'd got him "a catch of a wife" and a big job in Tupelo, they'd resent him even more. He understood. Still, Hanny straightened his tie and glanced at the packages he'd stacked on the front seat and the floor boards. Made him feel good. Well, now maybe with the pretty things in the bundles, they would look at Lisbeth and envy her too. And that was alright. Maybe one day—maybe one day people in Tupelo or someplace on up North—maybe they could just take their sweet time and envy the hell out of the both of them. Age twenty-seven and sitting in his own shiny car made him feel that way.

Just then, the wind that had been rising since last night slammed against the Nash and took the steering wheel momentarily out of Hanny's hands. Reports were coming from the Gulf Coast that a big storm was on its way. September always brought them in. Hell, every year hurricanes were crashing into Cuba, Florida, Texas, and right up along the Mississippi Delta leaving thousands dead and wrecked economies in their wake. Hanny saw that at the bank. Even a young loan officer like him felt moved by the stories of people applying for loans to cover their catastrophic losses. He hoped this one would hold off or move, say, a little west toward Galveston. Let Texas pick up the tabs.

No, what Hanny really wanted, was not to be worrying about hurricanes or threats of war; but instead, with Alma and her father off visiting in Georgia, to be spending a weekend with Lisbeth, and yes, young Gertrude too. It was rare that Lisbeth would let him come; their chaste meetings and the letters that passed between them over the years he'd been married to Alma had somehow carried him through

But something had to change. Over ten years living the devil's bargain hadn't been as easy as Hanny had thought. Now, he figured he *had done his duty—or as much of it as he intended. He'd saved a boy's life, and he'd given cover to things he'd probably go to hell for just knowing about, but did that consign him to a living hell with Alma? What could Senator Elliston do anyway? Fire him from the bank? He'd find another job. Maybe not in banking—the recent Depression had nearly toppled even Charlie Elliston's money cow. But somewhere. For now, it was a matter of seeing if Lisbeth would have him.*

He passed Long's Groc. Same Locashun Since 1920. Looked like they'd added a single gas pump what with more automobiles turning up on the roads. Tall, thin, white on top, and red at the bottom. It looked like a little lead soldier, Hanny thought. Then he turned onto the freshly tarred road leading to the property where Charlie had installed—or more rightly, banished—Lisbeth.

Beside the road, rows of cotton covered with road dirt whipped back and forth. He could see clusters of black cotton pickers further in the fields, their backs to the rising wind, some bent like pipe cleaners rapidly stuffing ripe cotton into the enormous bags they dragged along behind them. Others struggled back and forth with their heavy burdens, cotton jammed into ten-foot tubes, staggering under the weight of the overstuffed sacks. Nearer the road, wagons sat half-full, packed with flattened cotton bolls from the pickers emptied pouches, as overseers covered what they could with flapping oil cloth ahead of the rain. With the steadily rising wind stealing their voices as they yelled at the pickers, the bosses were hell-bent to harvest as much of Tilley's money crop as they could before the rain and wind turned the fluffy bolls into sodden knots.

The clouds had darkened now and seemed to bear down just above the trees, while the wind lengthened into sustained gusts. Hanny couldn't guess its velocity, but by the time he'd turned the Nash onto the rutted lane leading to Lisbeth's house, branches were scattered across the path and pines were singing in an odd soprano overhead. Best put the car under a tree, he thought, not out in the middle of her front clover field where something flying could hit it. Best keep it out of sight of anybody driving down the road, even in this weather.

178

Hanny gathered the brown-wrapped parcels into his arms, juggling a ball for Gertrude and some flowers from Mazie's Floral for Lisbeth, then he looked toward the house. Squinting into the wind, he suddenly wondered if he'd made a mistake. The unpainted clapboard house was dark. No lights. No one on the porch to meet him. The front door firmly shut. Had he misunderstood?

Then from behind a wooden pillar, the flap of a little blue skirt wacked back and forth in the wind. Hanny could see caramel fingers wrapped around the side of a scuffed pillar, and when a bare foot inched out, along came a pink bow tied into a set of braids arching across the girl's head.

"Is that Gertrude?" called Hanny over the wind. "Well, I hope it is, 'cause I've got presents for Gertrude!" He regathered his parcels and started along the raked path, stepping over a bunch of grapes that had been wrenched loose from the arbor. "I hope Gertrude's got a mama someplace around here..., 'cause I've got presents for Gertrude's mama too!"

As Hanny stepped onto the front porch, the girl sidled to the far side of the pillar, still keeping one eye on the man with the light hair and blue eyes whose arms were filled with something likely to be wonderful. And then the door slammed shut. And reopened—Lisbeth pulling it against the suction of the wind.

"Oh Hanny! There you are! I wasn't sure you were comin'!" Lisbeth threw her arms open, and as the ball tumbled onto the floor, she took his face in both her hands and laughed out loud. "I was hopin' we'd made it certain, but you just never know! I am so happy to see you! So happy." She didn't take her eyes off his face. "Well, never mind, you are here! Gertrude, Uncle Hanny is here to see us!"

Lisbeth put her arm around his waist and led him into the dusk of the house. "The electricity's gone and cut out," she said, grabbing Gertrude's hand and pulling her inside. "I just hope it'll stop right here, not go no further and rile us up a hurricane." She sounded giddy in spite of the heat inside. "But storm or high water, Hanny, I am glad you are here!"

179

How many times had he seen her in the last ten years? Ten? Twelve? Small towns don't make such things easy. But thanks to Sarah, letters got through.

Still, they met, and each time he saw Lisbeth, she was different. When he'd come to see her when Gertrude was born, she'd been quiet, unsure. She'd sat in a corner of Sarah's house as Sarah and her friend Floene had rocked the baby, cooed fragments of song, and encouraged Lisbeth to feed the child the "newfangled" way, from a bottle.

Later, when she'd gone to stay at Buena Vista, Lisbeth seemed to have taken to the child, and while Floene sat rocking on the porch, Hanny and Lisbeth and little Gertrude had made dandelion crowns on a blanket in the green-clovered yard.

Hanny had watched Gertrude learn to toddle, grow a set of tiny white teeth, and to sing with her mother nursery rhymes from books he'd never read. Looking at Lisbeth, by then toned and tanned, her silky hair auburn from the sun, Hanny thought she might actually be happy. Until, it seemed, the money ran out.

Hanny learned that Lisbeth's mother had provided Buena Vista and funds for her daughter's support with her own money. But the Depression had wiped that little cache away, and Charlie's fist wasn't opening. With only the little help Floene and Sarah—and when he could, Hanny himself— could provide, Lisbeth was on her own.

The men of Tilley and its surroundings took notice.

"I don't want you worrying about me, Hanny," Lisbeth had said when Gertrude was three. "See that there myrtle... all covered in little blooms. You break off some of its flowers, and it grows new ones. You cut it down to the ground, and it sprouts back up again. It don't feel nothin'. It puts its little flower mind upon the sunshine and lays it down inside a cloud, then it concentrates on growin' more flowers. It's its nature, I guess. It can't stop but havin' hope." Then she'd added, "But you bring the water to nurture me, Hanny. You didn't let me be cut down and pulled loose."

Last spring, Lisbeth's face was covered in bruises, and she only sat on the porch near a cane she'd had to use. There was no talk of flowers or clouds, and Lisbeth wouldn't explain what had happened. That was when Hanny had begun to plan the changes he would execute today.

The little house was plainly furnished, not much above the raw interior of Sarah's house with its walls covered in newspaper against the heat and cold. There was an old sofa with faded green velour in one corner—perhaps something Ruta Elliston had secreted to her daughter—and dark shelves along one wall where Lisbeth had made a little natural history collection of paper wasp nests, a deer skull, a shed snake-skin, and a bowl of little dried lizards she'd arranged as if they were at a dance. And there was a dog-eared encyclopedia and a book of poems.

She came from the kitchen carrying lemonade in a frosted pink pitcher, serving it to Hanny and Gertrude in old coffee cups as if she were the Queen of England. Lisbeth was glowing today, Hanny thought, her hair bobbed stylishly short with little bangs she shoved to the side and her freckled arms ruddy from the sun or the heat, which despite the wind, was now oppressive.

"What do you think, Hanny, we gonna have us a big one? I think I feel the shingles lifted up already. Scares me, 'cause all the dogs started hollerin' yesterday night... like they knew something bad was gonna happen." She sat down beside him on the sofa, while Gertrude played with a set of little wooden people that had come inside Hanny's present of a wooden house.

"Uncle Hanny, can we make dandelion crowns tomorrow?"

"Why Gertie, that was years ago. I'm surprised you remember. How can you keep that and more all stored inside that pretty little head?" Hanny pulled her up and sat her on his knee.

The child suddenly sat very still and looked at him, surveying the color of his eyes, the lay of his nose, the fullness of his lips. Without embarrassment, she said, "Are you my Daddy?" Gertrude's dark eyes were wide and curious.

"Oh, honey...." Lisbeth reached over and shifted the child to her own knee. "Course he's not your Daddy. This is Uncle Hanny, remember?"

181

"Well, I had two big men done told me they was my Daddy," said Gertrude, authoritatively. "But I didn't like none of ' um. I like this one." And she jumped down to her spot on the hardwood floor, rolled onto her stomach, and began to create the perfect family with her new wooden friends.

Hanny looked at Lisbeth, whose face was crimson, even freckles seeming to blush. "Hanny, I don't know what to say." Her head dropped and shook slightly back and forth.

"Let's go outside and have a look at the weather," he said, taking her hand. "Sit with me in the swing, and we can watch the clouds."

The rush settee, suspended from a rafter, didn't need help moving. Only their weight kept it from swinging forty-five degrees. "Are we safe out here?" asked Lisbeth, watching skittering branches peel away from their trees. Hanny looked at the sky, now a dirty cobalt from the south, and listened to the pitch of the wind's wail. "Lisbeth, we are safe enough right now, and I have something I have to ask you."

"No, Hanny Meyers" Her face looked suddenly stricken, as if a sucker punch were coming from somewhere. "Something you have to ask me? Wait. Wait just now. Not from you, Hanny. Don't ask me what you don't want to know." She put her feet on the porch floor and stopped the swinging motion.

"You have stood with me all these years. You knew me from where there was no comin' back from. But for you..., I would have gone to that far place for sure. I was more n' halfway there." Her voice was rising over the wind and she stood up and backed away from him, her throat stretched and her eyes wide.

"And from then and even now, you come visited me. You held my child, been my friend. And Hanny, you have not ever asked me a question. You have not ever asked how I maintain to live. You have not ever brought me low with inquiries about what it takes to make a joyful life alone in the middle of a woods with a young child that most the world wishes were a little ghost. Wishes she were just blowed away in... in a wind like this."

Lisbeth stood facing him, a solitary survivor watching a lifeboat leave, when a powerful gust threw open the door and Gertrude screamed

182

from inside. "Don't worry, Baby girl, just oleman Blow. He blew a big puff our way, didn't he?" Yet she seemed paralyzed with grief.

Hanny went inside, picked up Gertrude, and came out to Lisbeth. "I wasn't gonna ask you a thing about... about any others, Lisbeth." He put his arm around her waist. "I was gonna ask you if when I get myself undone from this powerful mess I've been livin' in for the last ten years... if you would be willing to leave the "loveliness" of Buena Vista... and come with me? Come with me..., and be my wife?" He was laughing between his words and shouting them above the forest din. Buena Vista's loveliness looked like it was about to fly right by the door. But Lisbeth heard him well.

She stood still as the porch swing bucked and her dress yanked along her legs, and her eyes widened in disbelief. "Say it again, Hanny. I heard your words, but I think I heard them with my heart, not my ears. You better be sure I understood..., 'cause this here forest can play some awful tricks." She was looking at him, her face upturned as the first drops of rain began to pummel the ground and wet her forehead and lips.

"I am asking you to marry me, Lisbeth Elliston, mother of Gertrude, and strong lioness of Buena Vista." He smiled at her while Gertrude's arms reached around his shoulders. "Tell me if your ears are in on this too... or it's just a conversation between our two hearts?" Hanny was laughing out loud as Lisbeth laid her head against his chest, the three of them thrilling to the sting of the rain.

Later that night, with Gertrude wrapped in a sheet on the couch, Hanny laid Lisbeth down on the iron bed in the tiny bedroom. It didn't matter that the storm would howl for hours. Its center had passed, and in its silence, in the stillness and crystal clarity of a night filled with stars, Hanny loved Lisbeth with a tenderness so powerful they both wept. That bodies could produce emotion was for them new. That a turquoise profile in the moonlight would leave the other speechless, or that the graze of lips upon another's eyes could engender devotion that would last a lifetime was for each of them, an amazing surprise. But their pact was sealed. Lisbeth would become Hanny's wife—when Alma had stopped.

Chapter 34

Claire stood in the women's dressing room of Bigelow's Department Store gazing at the dresses she'd pulled from the sale rack. End of season bargains they were too—fifty to sixty percent off. Perfect for one of the still hot days of early September. Perfect for the Restaurant Montmartre in downtown Tupelo, the place where tonight she intended to sweep a rumpled doctor from her mind for good. A woman has to do what she has to do.

Claire peeled off her bank attire, jacket and brown shirtwaist, avoiding looking where the fluorescent lights tended to cast shadows along her arms and neck. Damn, does a woman have to lift weights or something? She ill-advisedly pictured Jackson's muscles as he lifted tree trunks in the woods, then concentrated on the dress hanging limply before her. Keep your mind on business, she instructed herself. That's what you did. That's what she guessed all Elliston women did. Focus. Close off what's not going to help. Don't think about what can hurt you. Don't listen to ghosts.

Claire stepped into a green crepe shift, pulling it over the slip she'd tucked between her legs and the powerful girdle beneath. No sense romanticizing anything. These dresses were meant as sexual enticements. They were not about romance, love, even happiness. They were tools you used to get through to the next day or year—and to tell yourself stories that proved you had worth. Stories that would pile up. Stories that would become a collection. Stories that you could tell to yourself, when you sat alone and doubts came calling.

The fluorescence danced off the sheen of tight green crepe across her stomach. It seemed determined to catch the light even before her bust line would be noticed. The side view wasn't hopeful either. Claire wrenched the thing down over her hips, threw it on a bench, and with a shrug watched it slither onto the floor.

The second dress was a two-piece floral. Alright, a little late for flowers in September, but they were deep orange—so—call them leaves. Claire pulled the dress over her head, winched on the zipper, and slipped into the jacket. At least she could sit down in the dress, she thought, squatting against one wall. But the jacket collar didn't allow any peeks at décolletage at all. Hell, what's the use of looking like a giant bouquet, if there's no skin to make Bob Cutwright want to smell the flowers?

Bob Cutwright, the Alabama CPA who from time to time led the F.D.I.C auditing team. Bob was in town once every two months, occasionally more often. He probably had a wife. Claire wouldn't inquire too closely. She'd learned how to step over awkward pieces of information at such rendezvous. She would counter any attempt to share wallet size photos of adorable little people and instead would turn the conversation to things that might arouse men like Bob—fishing, hunting, tracking dogs—and perhaps later, whether he'd like to come by her house for a nightcap of really fine port.

Claire looked down at the red wool dress she'd pulled on. This was sexy. She had to admit it. Against her pale skin and dark hair, her body was a series of warm curves in a soft wrapper. Any man would like what he saw. Hell, she liked what she saw.

She wore the dress right out of the store and headed toward the Montmartre. This is how you did it. This is how you turned approving masculine heads your way. This is how you become bank manager. It's all about confidence, she thought. Believing that you're "desirable." This is how you needed to feel if you were going to clear a forest, build a house, and poke around in places that scared you.

Claire pulled into the empty parking lot of the Baptist Church, next to Tupelo's only French restaurant. The Montmartre was expensive, but she figured Cutwright was on an expense account and could afford to pay for her half of the dinner with his own money. For an 1870s' building, the restaurant's restoration had been exceptional. Tiny topiaries stood out front beneath a scalloped awning twinkling with tiny lights, while inside, the brick walls and iron tables felt most definitely Left Bank—wherever that was.

Claire stood momentarily at the maître d's podium, gazing casually into the dining room. She was only "slightly late," as was appropriate for a lady, and with a satisfied glow she could feel herself being appraised by the suits at the bar—some of whom she might know, but whose gaze she wouldn't acknowledge. Yet she couldn't just stand there forever.

Claire took her jacket off. Then put it on again. She made a decorous visit to the ladies' room. She read the menu and appeared fascinated by a shiny fake palm. Eventually she pretended interest deep inside her purse while surreptitiously looking at her watch. Bob was twenty-five minutes late. Had she been stood up? That had never happened before. At thirty-five minutes, it was pretty clear she had.

Claire looked up to see the maître d' smiling at her with his eyebrows raised. "Hungry, Miss? Table for... one?" He was enjoying this. She suddenly wished she weren't wearing red, at the same time fighting down the desire to flatten the little maggot gripping his desk like a cheap politician. Claire needed to get out of the stifling foyer with its ridiculous posters of the Moulin Rouge.

"Oh, this is embarrassing," said Claire, throwing her head back and allowing her teeth to show how amused she was. "We weren't to meet here. I am so silly. It's the Silverton Hotel Restaurant." She picked the most expensive eatery in town. "I'd ask you to phone over there to let him know I'm on my way, but it's so close…" Claire tossed her hair and turned to flee.

"Oh, I'd be more than happy to telephone there," he smirked. "But I'll wager you don't know the gentleman's name?" The maître d' looked her steadily in the eye. The son-of-a-bitch thought she was a prostitute being stood up by an AWOL john! Claire could read his mind. She was either for sale, or she was some desperate divorcee waiting for her young toy.

Claire wasn't aware of her arm raising and barely aware when it swept across the supercilious little runt's desk. Later she thought she heard a voice she knew from the bank yell over the maître d's squeals something like, "one bitchin' broad." It was the only victory of the evening.

Claire marched to her car, realizing that three-inch heels were not made to withstand the adrenaline flooding her legs.

"There she is! That's her car!" A knot of angry Baptists with Bibles in their hands had gathered around Claire's car in the now-crowded parking lot.

"Well, some people got no respect for churchgoin' folk!" An older woman came nose to nose with Claire. "Oh, you must think Wednesdays are for eatin' out. We know, 'cause people like you do this all the time." She gestured angrily at Claire's car. "But some folks believe Wednesdays are God's days. And we give to the Lord our singing and our study and our praise." "Yeah," someone else shouted from the back, "An' red-dressed women are not welcome in God's house or in His parking spaces!"

The next day Claire called in sick then returned the new dress to Bigelow's. What the hell. She'd only had it on half an hour. Alright, a little more. The dress was supposed to have given her confidence, but its magic hadn't worked.

Then she got into her car and headed for the one place that sometimes did feel like magic—the quiet kind that didn't ask any questions—but might still be willing to give her answers.

***

Buena Vista looked like it was dressing for a party—despite the straight-laced pine trees standing decorously green and not joining in the changing of colors that made the rest of the woods dance. Maples were swimming in magenta against oaks dolled up in high-falutin' gold. Already in Tilley, fall had turned late-blooming rhododendrons a flamboyant pink. Next to them a few orange blossoms of a hardy trumpet vine clashed unashamedly, draping themselves along the tarp-covered lumber that would soon become Claire's house.

She hadn't come in three weeks. Now she wished she hadn't missed the slow "burn" that had turned the quiet forest into this riotous palette.

187

The warmth of the colors and the freshness of the air were like walking into a properly maintained museum—beauty on display—and the comfort to enjoy it.

Looking around, Claire wasn't sure now why she'd fallen into such a torpor. The architectural plans had been drawn and sealed and lay in a tube in Tupelo. She had purchased the lumber the builder said would be needed. It was time to move on now. Wasn't it? Time to bring something new to Buena Vista. Time to honor the past, yet move away from it?

Yet she knew why she wasn't ready. Claire kicked at one of the footers that had supported the old front porch and halfheartedly pulled at a blackened piece of chain under a prattle of vines. All of these artifacts meant something. Each had had its place when she lived here.

She walked to the small repository of items she'd collected from all over the property. The empty tins of food, the bicycle rim, a piece of pipe, a sliver of a mirror, and threw the hank of chain on top. That chain, the rusted whisper it used to make supporting a swing that yawed gently back and forth—she could almost hear it now. Claire's eyes widened. For a moment, she thought she saw his face. She looked toward where the house had been. She imagined the swing where she'd sat with a man. He was tall. His hands were strong. And Gertrude—Gertrude was pushing the swing and laughing. Does Gertrude know who he is? Claire needed to sit down. She felt a rush of excitement.

And then she thought of another discarded piece of metal. The one she'd been afraid to examine and had simply put back where she'd found it.

Claire walked to the back of the property to a small rise beside the pond. There may have been only a few trees when her mother lived here; now it was covered with mature maples and water oak. When she'd wandered there before, Claire had come upon three or four small sticks embedded in the soil where they had essentially rotted into mulch. Two of them had had a second stick, forming a little cross. In the back of her mind, she somehow thought of it as a graveyard—for pets, for discovered prey taken down in the woods, for little skeletons that she herself might have buried. It was also where she'd found the gun.

The soil was soft and loamy from the heavy rains, and Claire's thick soles were soon covered with mud. But she remembered that the five-gallon tin in which the gun had been wrapped and placed inside, had been half uncovered from erosion beside an outcrop of Mississippi's ubiquitous limestone. Claire headed directly for the rock at the top of the rise.

She looked where she thought it had been—and beside it and behind. She dug at the earth with a stick, shoving layers of leaves aside. But the can and what was inside were gone. Claire got down on her knees in the wet dirt, shoving some vegetation away from the area directly in front of the limestone. She could now see where a spade had made clear lines into the hole where she'd reburied the container. This wasn't erosion, and the can wasn't at the bottom of the rise. Someone had carefully come and gotten the gun.

She stood up, suddenly frightened. Why would a presumably unworkable gun be valuable to anyone? Who had known it existed? And then she remembered what Jackson had said. That two people had come to Buena Vista saying they needed to get something—something of no value to anyone else. Two elderly people. Two black people—a man and a woman.

Chapter 35

Gunther Huebsch shook his head, delighting in the fact that he was living in a day and age when technology could potentially solve a crime *and* ease a human heart.

Yet for all 1984's cutting edge advances, the investigation into the murder of the venerable Senator Charles Elliston was stuck. And the local Tilley police department wasn't exactly thrilled to have detectives from the state capital in Jackson roaming around butting their noses into their investigation.

Gunther's medical expertise had helped the forensic detectives home in on an approximate time of the old man's death. That, coupled with the fact that Charlie's circulatory system was collapsed and the oxygen concentration of his tissues essentially nil, had led the doctor performing the autopsy to concur with Gunther, writing that the Senator Charles Elliston must have bled out an hour or more before he was found sprawled across his own front steps.

But other evidence was missing. No bullets lodged anywhere but in Charlie. No tire tracks. No witnesses except a ten-year-old boy out calling for his cat, but who'd changed his story a dozen times as the police tried to coach him into remembering the license plate of a car he swore he'd never seen. And then there was the matter of no murder weapon. The police had been unable to find the gun that sent two .45 caliber bullets into Charlie. At this point, all they could say for sure was that the weapon had been fired at close range—once into the old man's sparsely-haired head and once into his heart.

As for the sole suspect, Chauncey Groves, who'd been picked up heading back into Tilley from his girlfriend's house several miles south, local police were being put on the spot.

Of course, no white man was likely to have been picked up for questioning. But when no other blacks were out on the streets of Tilley the night of the murder, Chauncey in his car was the best they could do. Maybe the little kid would remember more after a few more trips to the ice cream parlor. But for now, even after the police had lifted fingerprints from the Senator's door handle, front door bell, even from the face of Charlie Elliston's watch, Chauncey's prints or other evidence that he had been there was nowhere to be found. That wouldn't necessarily have mattered, but with the state detectives watching over their shoulders, despite the Tilley police's eagerness to show off a taciturn, powerfully-built black man who might have gotten crosswise with Charlie for some perceived insult, the only thing on Chauncey Grove's lily-white record was a run-in with a neighbor for reporting the weekly dog fights held in Chauncey's backyard. But even that complaint had gone nowhere once police realized half the force had been there too.

Gunther pushed the wobbly brown chair back from the desk. The desk, a Goodwill find after its salvage from a car dealership down the street, threatened to buckle beneath manila folders. Filled with patients' ailments and treatments and medical books that Gunther always forgot to put back on their shelves, it now swayed under the batch of laboratory reports just back from Jackson. And of course, the special one he'd sent to Atlanta.

"Why wait?" he muttered, ripping into the envelope containing the report on the little sample he'd sent to the University of Georgia. It was the only place in the Southern U.S. able to do DNA testing on human tissue and on hair. In this case, a small lock of curly black hair given to him by Gertrude.

"Well, let's see," he smiled, "let's see if I had a little brother." Gunther couldn't help but shiver. He had looked at the blood-stained photo of a small child named Wilhelm as often as he had his father's letters. Yet though the photo was of her child, Gunther hesitated to show the soiled snapshot to Gertrude. If she had grieved all these years, seeing a blood-stained photo of her baby was not going to help. Gunther had also not shown it to the police, but he wasn't sure why. Need to talk with Claire, he thought for the hundredth time, and he wasn't sure why that was, either.

Gunther drew the chair closer to the light and took a breath as he peeked inside his drawer where he'd taken to keeping the little photo for easy access. Aside from a cherubic smile, he could in truth only guess if the baby in the photo would grow to look like Gertrude, his own father, or perhaps some other man who had also keenly admired a tall dark girl from Buena Vista. For now, though, he felt very close to kin.

Careful as always, Gunther readjusted his glasses and slowly slipped a pocketknife along the envelope's crease. The flimsy copy of the original typed report was difficult to read, but below the lines of what had been received and what tests had been performed, Gunther read, "The GBA gene is expressed positively for Gaucher's disease in the hair sample received September 19, 1984"

Gunther closed his eyes. And there it was. He had had a brother— once. A preceding soul, linked to his own. But now, there was no young man he would embrace as kin. No one in whose eyes he might reunite with a father whose capacity for love had included not only the wife to whom he had been devoted but another who had touched his soul. No big brother. No sibling to care for as they grew old, or to reassure that his father had indeed loved him till the end.

Gunther walked to the window. The little photo had been a curiosity until now—an important clue—but was now imbued with overwhelming sadness. Would they have been friends? Would Willy—yes, now he would call him Willy—would he have been proud of Gunther? Envious? Ashamed? Gunther gazed at the stark diagnosis. Would Willy have even survived a painful and sad childhood? The evidence suggested no. And yet, a brother had existed. A little life that somehow made Gunther feel complete. The complicated threads of a life, he thought—unwoven, but whose threads always retain the pattern of the cloth.

Gunther wasn't sure how to tell Gertrude and her father, but he was sure that the inheritance that would have been Willy's would help them both as they entered their old age. In an odd way, Willy would be looking out for his mother even if he wasn't there to do it personally.

Gunther slipped the report into its own manila folder and turned out the light. He needed to get outside. To walk. To examine what he might do now. He may have answered a question for himself and for Gertrude about identity and why the child died so young, but he needed to massage the feeling of dread that was slowly settling over him. How did the photo of his tiny brother, this long-dead, half-black baby, end up stuck to the blood-soaked face of an aged senator? He doubted that any answer would let him sleep tonight.

Chapter 36

Hanny's brick house barely protruded through live oaks that had been planted when the house was new. Now they simply kept the old Tupelo Victorian in a state of permanent gloom. Hanny reached up and adjusted the light. His eyes were aching and switching glasses hadn't made a difference seeing the filmy letters that floated across the pages he held. It seemed as if an early winter had descended as another storm snuffed away the long twilight. In its darkness, the tiny bulb over Hanny's shoulder illuminated only his spotted hands and the odd sheaf of notes.

He took a long swig of bourbon. He could read Alma's large swirled script almost without glasses. They'd taught them that way years ago. Taught little girls to read poetry and to recite sonnets at school convocations. Taught them to cook and how to set a nice table. Taught them to be ladies. At least on the surface. That was important in the South. The surface was what counted. For the rest, let 'um draw their own conclusions. Your reputation rested on what you presented and if you went to church. His wife had mastered her cursive in all its swirling artifice, and she'd also led the life she wanted. All it took was keeping that surface smooth.

The box that now lay open beside him had apparently been in the back of Alma's closet for years, judging by the drying tape that had allowed the cardboard sides to splay apart. Alma had left in a hurry, leaving behind a few pieces of luggage he hadn't seen in years. Now, unwanted shoes were scattered across the room: hats, boxes of gloves, the costume jewelry she had to match every outfit. Half of the closet seemed to have been making a run for the exit before Alma got away.

It was only when Hanny caught his foot on the brown cardboard box under an old tennis racket and wad of winter jackets, that he saw that Alma had apparently kept journals. Dozens of them—some from before he had married her. Each of them dated with the month and year. Each of them a delicate testament to a proper upbringing for a doctor's daughter and a banker's wife.

He pulled the little porcelain shepherdess beneath the lampshade closer and angled the light onto the first of the journals, one dated 1923. Alma would have been ten. Hanny felt no embarrassment or impropriety reading his wife's diaries. Hell, he was overcome with curiosity. Curious if there had ever been a time when Alma was gentle, when she had been sweet, a time before she had been corrupted. And mercifully, he smiled, he was reading them with the harridan out of the house.

He picked up the first of the little clothbound books. Frayed blue linen on its cover and yellowed, lined paper inside. It smelled like papyrus from a pyramid, he thought. How old is that woman anyway? Hanny knew he was making light of going through Alma's journals— knew it was because he was somehow terrified of what he might read.

Dear Diary, My puppy has made Daddy mad again today. Why can't she go in the backyard near the outhouse like she's supposed to? I'm not sure what will happen to her, if she goes on the big rug again. Mama says it was woven in a country where they cut men's heads off for mistakes. I hope my pup doesn't get into such trouble.

Dear Diary, Franklin Houser has big ears. I don't see how boys with ears like that hope to get married. Why just dancing around the room to a phonograph record would probably hurt those ears to where they'd make big fools of themselves. The ears I mean!! Tee Hee. Maybe Franklin Houser wears earmuffs when he goes dancing!

Hanny put down the 1923 log. For Christ's sake, she was naïve once. She'd even had a sense of humor. It surprised him. He tried to remember

195

what Lisbeth had told him. When was it Charlie Elliston's and Doc Edwards' girls had been friends? When had everything changed?

He picked up 1925. Alma was twelve. Printing had given way to what would become her mature flourish. The content and tone had changed as well.

> Dear Diary, Guess what I did today? I shaved my legs! Mama says it's not necessary, but I want to. Tansy Bollinger does 'cause she'd be a gorilla if she didn't. I used Daddy's razor... and a skeptic... septic... something pencil 'cause I nicked myself. (This is my fourth time to get my period. Oh my, how my bosoms got big this time!)

Then, six months later:

> "Dear Diary, Party at Florence Talbot's. My blue dress got stained when Bobby Rogers knocked over his red punch. I hate boys like that. Stupid. He tried to rub off the mess. He doesn't even know how to do it to make a girl feel good. I'll have to tell that to Mr. C. Tee Hee."

Hanny put down the journal, feeling sick. So it had begun... sometime right around twelve. He didn't want to read more, yet with a rage swinging between his contempt for Alma and fury at Charlie Elliston, he did, picking up 1927.

> "Dear Diary, Daddy says I need more friends and that we're going to the lakes in North Wakeenina for the summer where I will make me some. But I am not going! I am not!! C. cares more about me than anybody, and he says that parents only do things to please themselves. Well, that's what Daddy's doing. If only C. and me could be the ones going to North Wakeenina without stupid Lisbeth. Oh Diary, he done something to me... real grownup he said. I didn't want to at first and it hurt, it

196

really, really hurt, and I cried at first, but he said if I want to show him I love him and if I want to be like a real grown woman... then I'll just take it. And I did. And afterwards, he held me and told me I made him feel like he never done in his whole life and that it's only me who lets him have his way, and that's why he loves me. Says he'll show me more things too... that I got a lot to learn. But I'm going to do it..., 'cause I love C... more than anything."

Hanny saw something hit the page then spread across the blue scrawl and realized he was weeping. He had hated Alma for... how long? Over fifty years? Yet there was once a child who had loved puppies. Once a little girl in a blue dress. But one who before she went to high school had become the willing victim to Senator Charles Elliston, the manipulative predator of not only his own daughter but the young Alma as well. Hanny took off his glasses and finished the glass of the bourbon.

He should have killed Charlie years ago. He could have at least tried. But even though he'd come back what they called a military hero, Hanny knew he could have never pulled the trigger. He was glad somebody had.

He put the diaries back in the beaten-up cardboard box and shoved them with his foot toward the chaos at the rear of Alma's closet, then padded down the hall and slumped onto a settee in a guest bedroom he'd made his own. This time he carried the Maker's Mark with him. Facing the street on the old horsehair antique, he sometimes felt like he was in a hotel—an anonymous place apart from the remnants trailing from every part of his life. It was a place Hanny could think. Most often a place for visiting old regrets.

"Mr. Elliston, I have been turning this over in my mind for many months now, and I believe that we have both completed our parts of the agreement into which we entered several years ago." Hanny had dressed in the dark suit and wide tie that he wore daily to his job as loan officer at Charles Elliston's Farmers' and Businessmen's Bank in Tupelo. He thought it made him look at least thirty, the age at which Hanny believed

people would take the smooth-faced youth seriously. In fact, he knew his immediate supervisors were impressed with his diligence and long hours at the bank, despite his oddly abrupt appointment by the bank's owner himself.

Hanny had arranged to meet with Elliston in his Senate offices, where Hanny hoped decorum would trump any emotional responses from the older man. Still, this was Charlie's territory. Hell, every place was.

Yet, determined to take hold of the meeting, Hanny sat down in the chair in front of Charlie's desk without asking, took a breath, and began the lines he'd rehearsed for the last week:

"Mr. Elliston, I believe that the time has come for Alma and me... to divorce." There was an echo in the high-ceilinged chamber, and it seemed his words were taunting him like children across a fence. "I have completed the terms of the agreement you and I entered into to the tee— for the last ten years. Alma is a respected young woman in the community now. She is already a provisional member of the Daughters of the Confederacy and the Junior League. We go to church regularly, and she is well-accepted into society here. I would say, Mr. Elliston, that her position is secure... no matter what happens."

Charlie said nothing, and Hanny shifted from his left to his right buttock. "I appreciate the opportunity at the bank, Mr. Elliston and that my father's paper has been able to write most of the breaking news from your legislative committees, but a lot of time has passed... and..."

Charlie was silent, rocking slowly back and forth in a massive upholstered chair, never making eye contact, but alternately attending to the ceiling's molding and to the contour of the window drapes. When Hanny had sputtered to a finish, Charlie gently angled the chair around like a cannon calculating distance.

"Well, well. I see that you have done some thinking on this issue. Tired of our arrangement... which we done arrived at with careful consideration. Feel like you done paid any debt for what you got... some worthless piece a' black rabble. Now I presume you got other plans, Hanford? Other plans for employment, I'd reckon?"

198

"No, sir, no direct plans for another job. But I figure that a hardworking man can get some. Lots of places hiring now."

"Any other plans? Young buck plans? You know what I mean... Why I wager you already got you a little harem someplace, don't you Hanford? I'd expect that. One situation don't work out, cast around for another with just the right fit. Something with a real tight fit, I advise!" Charlie's smile was smothered in the folds of his face. *"I know Alma ain't had nothin' to do with you since you married her. I'd know, wouldn't I. She keeps me real close. So I figure you already got you a little pet pussy somewhere. Nice tits. Plenty of ass..."* Hanny felt a wave of revulsion slide over him. Charlie wanted them to talk dirty together.

"I am only here to let you know, Mr. Elliston, that from this time forward, I wish to consider our agreement complete. There is no need for the... relationship... that you and Alma have to include me."

"Well, that's not as simple as you think, Hanford B. Meyers," said Charlie. *"You don't think I'm blind as a bat do you?"* The older man shifted his own buttocks. *"You think I don't know what you do and who you write to—a bitch out in the woods? A whore who screws niggers? Hell, I done got my hands on enough of those sappy letters you write to know you're in so deep you got something crazy in mind."*

Hanny stood up. *"Not crazy, Mr. Elliston. No, not crazy, but clean and prope..."* Hanny's tongue was refusing to work.

Charlie burst out laughing. *"You're full of shit! What you proposin'? That you just go out an' take as a blushin' bride the Whore of Chickasaw County? Oh, I can hear that now. "Charlie Elliston's slut daughter marries* boss's ex-protégé from *the F and B Bank." Well, sure. How about we get us a wedding party of your nigger friend who done run away up North? Oh, and my, my..., I just remembered, he'd be the one who screwed her first and give her a bastard. Yes, sir, just what I've been wantin'."*

Charlie's face was magenta where it touched the soggy collar. This time he made direct eye contact. *"My answer to you, Meyers, is this: No. Ten years ago, you done bought yourself a coon back on a farm under some trees. And I done bought one too. Your nigger got away. But mine, he better still be workin' for me just the way we set it, or this is what'll happen to that uppity son-of-a-bitch.... His little honey gonna disappear. That's right. The 'woman I want to marry' gonna end up gutted and trussed and in a deep woods where she can do a little something for the animal population. You hear me?"*

Charlie got up and walked around to the front of the desk, resting his backside along its polished edge. "Now this is what you will do, Hanford Meyers. There's a little something stirrin' in Germany these days... something far away... a good place for my nigger right now. And that's where you gonna go. Why, yes you are! You gonna be a patriot. You gonna join the goddamned Army, Navy, the Marines, or shit, go fly somethin'. That is what you will do... or so help me God, your little cunt Lisbeth gonna end up a pile of meat 'side the pond at Buena Vista."

Hanny turned off the overhead and gazed into trees dappling the sidewalk with a streetlight's yellow daubs. For a moment, he found himself picturing the moment when Charlie had been gunned down. The crumbling old house, the abandoned out buildings. The old man coming out onto the stoop to meet someone. Making his armed visitor wait humbly on the porch—negotiating with them, threatening them, before the fatal bullets were squeezed off into the corrupt old body. Hanny smiled. You can never bully a bully—unless, perhaps, if you have a gun.

Chapter 37

"Yes, of course, I am happy to test your blood…, Mrs.… My flyers have brought many people here for that very reason. Stretch out your arm a bit. Anything else that brings you here?" Gunther barely looked at the rounded woman who sat down in the patient chair.

Gunther had lost weight over the last month. He was tired. Tired, and if he were honest, aimless. He had called the airlines checking flights back to Germany, then hung up when he realized it wasn't there he really wanted to go. Perhaps he would go to the western part of the United States for a while. The Grand Canyon, the Golden Gate Bridge. Maybe a stay in Canada. He had a colleague there, yet he'd come each day to the clinic, empathizing with Latinos, who though they worked side by side with black pickers and farmers, had assumed the bottom rung of the American dream and sympathized with black field hands and the occasional tradesman who marched in place, careful to not step over the dozens of lines drawn by white culture. He had grown to love these people—and with an outsider's distance—even the people who drew the lines.

Doreen burst out laughing. "Doctor, doctor…, why, I do believe you have forgotten me." Gunther looked up, unsure of what she was getting at. "I done had my blood tested months ago…, healthy as a horse it come back. But yes, there is something you can do for me. After somethin' I do for you. There is something I have been remiss in doing for a long while," said Doreen. "When a new somebody comes to town, it is a polite thing to have them over for dinner. That's what we do here in Mississippi. Well, I have not done that, Dr. Huebsch, and I want to rectify it right now. I am invitin' you for a real home-cooked meal this Thursday. I hope you can come."

And as if a ritual had been established in the space of a breath, Gunther began to eat at Doreen's Thursday and Sunday nights. Fridays and Saturdays being booked for "party events."

***

On the Monday after the debacle at the Montmartre Restaurant, Claire had gone to see Dr. Acker at the Tupelo Women's Clinic. As if reporting on an anonymous patient, she described to him what she called a couple of "episodes of not feeling myself"—the afternoon at Eustus' church, the mysterious music in her car, and with Gunther at Buena Vista. There had been the other times and the note-scattered drawer that she left out, glibly joking she thought she was simply losing her mind. But surely, she said, it was only a temporary loss of sanity. Shaking her bob to demonstrate that she really was "all there," Claire laughed that lots of people probably felt this way; but coupled with the discovery of the missing gun, which she also hadn't mentioned, she told him she thought she needed a little something for anxiety. That she just needed a pill to get back to being herself.

"Too much work." "Spreading yourself too thin." Ackers had agreed. "Maybe a little too much dwelling in the past. Sometimes happens with menopausal women other side of forty," he'd added.

Claire didn't like the sound of that. Reminded her of the Freudians who ascribed "hysterias" to problems with women's uteruses. But Ackers had at least prescribed her some Librium, which he told her would put everything in perspective. Unfortunately, the "new perspective" had turned into sleep. She wasn't sure which was worse, dragging herself through the day with anxiety or doing it in a drowsy fog.

"I know just what is wrong with you," Doreen had said two weeks later over the phone. "Now cut out them poison pills and get on over here sometime before the weekend. I ain't seen you in a month or more! What'd you do..., go out an' get fat and don't wanna show me?"

Claire had packed up her weekend bag and thrown it in the back of the car. This time, for once, she wouldn't go to Buena Vista. Didn't feel like it. No, a little wine with Doreen—a change of scenery in Tilley—couldn't do any harm.

Claire almost passed Doreen's B & B as she sailed down Main Street, even though the creaky Victorian pile stood where it had always stood. Twisting her neck, Claire now saw that it glowed unrecognizable in the afternoon sun. The old dowager was as yellow as an egg yolk.

"What on earth do you call this color?" Claire gazed from sparkling turret to freshly whitened fretwork. There was still the smell of fresh oil based pigment, if you got close.

"Honey and Cream," said Doreen. "But privately, I call it Sunstroke. It's not exactly what I'd planned... but then plans do change, do they not!" Doreen was in full hostess mode, ebullient and popping with one-liners. "But y'all come inside now, Miss Claire Elliston, and let me show you a few more things you ain't expected."

Doreen poured Claire some sweet tea and settled her onto the swing on the glassed-in porch. Claire thought the new red-striped cushions were a little too barbershop, but she had to admit they beat the flowered chintz.

"You heard about our little... hiatus... didn't you? No? Well, you been too busy up there in Tupelo to pay attention, girl. Don't matter now, but after a little shut down, kind of a management shift, this here establishment is off and runnin' again. And I do mean makin' money!" Doreen patted her lap and rubbed her chubby hands together.

"I'm callin' the place an 'event venue' now. Though, confidentially, we're offering the same kind of entertainment." She sipped her tea and savored its sticky mint. "The way we're doin' it, I put on parties—events—but only for people from out of town. Then the people from here, they go to our other establishment in Oxford to enjoy their own events. Keeps everything real discreet. And I tell you, Claire, business is sailin' through the roof."

For the hundredth time, it crossed Claire's mind whether this whole thing were legal. "And what else has turned out real nice," Doreen went on, "is that we even got the law assistin' us. The off-duty boys from

203

Oxford come over to keep an eye on things here, and the ones from here go there... to keep out pryin' eyes, you see. All private, very private. Though between you and me, this whole operation is just too good to be a real secret." Somehow, Doreen had struck business gold.

"Whew, I had no idea," said Claire. "Who would have thought there was such a demand for…."

"For sexual fulfillment?" Doreen shrugged. "I been tellin' you all along it's what women need. It brings its own relief, Claire. You told me you were under stress. Well, this here is where the stress gets boiled off. This is where you clear your mind and refresh your soul."

She got up, leaving Claire swaying back and forth on the wicker swing. "I'm gonna go fix you a little something stronger to drink. Then I am going to walk you upstairs to a newly redecorated room. And then, I am going to flip a little "thinking switch" off. And you are going to just relax, Miss Banker Lady, and feel like these other upstandin' women let themselves do. Womanly, Claire. Know what it's like to feel like a woman? Before in that blink of an eye... you turn into an old lady!"

***

Gunther had had to stay late at the clinic. Chicken pox should have been eradicated in the United States by now, but there were still pockets in rural communities where too few children had been immunized and little outbreaks occurred. Gunther patiently prescribed cooling lotions and techniques of fever control. He hoped he made headway in health education, but at least he was comforting worried parents and itchy boys and girls. It made him happy. Now, though it was late, he would gratefully drive over to Doreen's B & B, which she now called "Event Central," for his Thursday feast. It was one of the two good meals he ate each week.

Listening to Doreen's banter as she weaved in and out of the kitchen, serving him three-course meals that she seemed to make just for fun, was like an anthropology lesson for Gunther. He found Doreen a fascinating example of the *Southern type*—bawdy, warm, tough, manipulatively charming. He thought maybe one day he would write a paper about this particular personality type. But for him personally, the good meals, and every so often the offer he couldn't refuse to just bed down in one of her new rooms rather than his spare lodgings, made him grateful to have a friend.

***

Claire stood in the middle of the room, turning in circles, surveying Doreen's new creation. She was right, the room was beautiful. Gone were the bushels of pillows and the extravagant fringed antiques, now replaced with smooth grey silks and soft creamy rugs. There was even a rheostat—a clever device which let you lower the lights to set the place glowing as if lit by a single taper. Best of all, Doreen had turned a fragile, nailed-shut balcony into an intimate porch, that with the double screened doors open wide felt like a bower in the trees.

The wine had begun to unwind her, and maybe a second Librium would help her relax before dinner, Claire thought. Thankfully, the house would be quiet tonight, "a Thursday... nothing special going on." And frankly, she smiled to herself, she wouldn't mind skipping dinner altogether and just sipping wine in some dream state on the little leafy porch all by herself.

Claire drew a hot bath, gingerly tested the water, then settled herself into the scented foam. Leaning her head back on a towel, she watched the gold of the wine sparkle in her glass as its level dropped, happy to be thinking of nothing at all. Able to think that she *wasn't* thinking of guns or buildings or men who wouldn't love her.

She may have drifted into something like sleep, when slowly she became aware that the air had changed; a cooling rush that had come and then gone had awakened her. Wrapped in a light robe, she noticed that the balcony door had opened and that the curtains were lifting and falling like graceful gauze apparitions, and she lowered the lights even more to watch them dance as the moon rose in the trees.

Outside everything had turned to silver. Claire touched the curtains wondering if they would be cold as metal or splinter into crystal shards beneath her fingers. Instead they undulated like strands of hair, silky and

205

pliant. Even the shadows in the room seemed to move of their own volition. She let her robe fall open and almost laughed as the cloth grazed her breasts and fell across her hips. She wondered if her cells were made of nerves, had their own little brains, each one teasing and playing, titillating her, begging to be touched.

She turned the lights out and stood naked before the wide doors. She could feel the night air in sensuous eddies along her body, stroking her from without and within, though her breath seemed suspended. And then Claire felt herself relax into his arms. With one arm around her waist, his hand moved along her back, feeling her skin, spreading it and grasping it, his breathing growing warm against it. Soon his other hand found her breasts, lifting them and pressing them, and she sensed he was barely under control.

When had he entered? Was he allowed? Claire's eyes closed as she found his scent. Each man different, this one green, moss. She let her head drop back to his shoulder, while with the night air he traced her abdomen and her thighs. And found her moist and willing.

***

"Why, where'd you come from, you rascally demon?" Doreen was finishing washing the last of the dishes herself. There weren't many. Gunther always liked everything piled on to one plate. Esperanza had taken to teaching salsa at some community center on Thursdays and Fridays and absolutely could not be counted on as before. Doreen shoved the big plates onto the lower shelf and mopped at her forehead despite the cool night air waffling the kitchen curtains.

Jackson just laughed. "Never know where the devil'll show up!" Doreen thought he'd actually grown since she'd first hired him months ago in the woods at Buena Vista. He'd certainly packed on some muscle, though she didn't exactly know how.

One thing for certain, was that their roles had shifted 180 degrees. Jackson, the entrepreneur, the "co-director" of the Oxford headquarters was now the bankroller; and she had to hand it to him, he was damned good. Even so, young men with money in their pockets and looks on their side could be annoying.

"You over here from Oxford for any good reason?" she asked, dishing him up a piece of red velvet cake. "Or are you just checking up if I'm doin' some side business upstairs?" Doreen patted his back as she poured him a glass of milk.

"No ma'am, Miss Doreen. Just wantin' to see if I could talk you into lettin' me have one of your upstairs rooms for... uh... my own use some night." He took a gulp of milk. "Wouldn't be business exactly. Just a little entertainin' of a friend."

Doreen poured herself a glass of wine. This could have been a son of her own, and wouldn't his real mother think she was somethin'. But she'd learned a lot about human nature lately, more than she'd even suspected. Hell, his mother may be a customer at Oxford for all she knew. "Sure, why not," she shrugged. "But I'd better show you the rooms. You haven't seen the one I just redone... with the new balcony and all."

Jackson finished the last of the cake, scraping off the icing around the rim of the plate. "That's OK, Miss Doreen. I already done seen it."

Chapter 38

Hanny tried one more time to drag the metal off his finger. He'd done it every morning for as long as he could remember. He figured that between his arthritis, some extra weight, and the previous self-brutalizing efforts to remove the symbol of marital fidelity from his hand, the knuckle was a ruined barricade he couldn't breach. He'd have to have the thing cut off one of these days. It embarrassed him to have worn it all these years—a ring that branded him a hypocrite. Unlike other things, this one was clearly visible. It had been, he sighed, like the rest of his life, a sham.

Hanny shoved the old-fashioned bureau shut with his shoulder and adjusted his tie. Maybe that's why it pleased him so much to meet with Eustus. Eustus was a tie with a past when Hanny took risks. Christ, heroic risks. His missing fingers, his ruined back—the Japanese had made him a hero just by surviving what the POW camp had handed out.

He gazed at himself in the mirror of the dresser. The overhead light shown down on his pink scalp, casting shadows into the embankments along his nose and mouth, his abdomen a soft sack. Was it true we end up looking like the decisions we've made? Well, in that case he deserved the image in the mirror. Hanny tilted his reflection slightly. He'd been admirable once, hadn't he? Even noble. He'd stood up when others hadn't. He'd shot men; he'd killed two with his bare hands. He'd done it honorably. They'd even called him "hero." Now, ironically, he wondered if the young man would recognize the old. Pretty much a lifetime shot to hell, he thought. A good beginning and now, little to show—about the things that counted anyway.

He picked up the morning paper he'd brought upstairs to read on the toilet. These days it was one of his few joys. And as he always did, pulled out advertisements and coupons bound for the trash. Oh, he might save that one for Wild Turkey, a case of it on sale. Who knows, thought Hanny, maybe he'd never need to buy another one. You never know. You just never know. Then he glanced at the headlines for anything pertaining to the bank, and did a kind of double take. This morning the letters were bold-faced and two inches tall. Hanny sat down hard on the bed and stared at the thick black statement scrawled above the fold. ELLISTON MURDER WEAPON RECOVERED. And below it: Deputies Uncover World War II Gun Believed to Have Killed Senator Charles Elliston.

Hanny threw the other sections onto the bed and turned on the nightstand light with the 100-watt bulb. The story described two hikers coming across a .45 caliber Colt military pistol apparently dumped in the woods on the outskirts of Tilley. The Federal investigators had completed forensic tests on the bullet markings which apparently were a perfect match with the two fired into Charlie Elliston. There were also full and partial prints that they hoped could lead to a suspect and an arrest. Getting his own two cents in, a side article quoted Tilley Chief of Police Grady Sanders as saying that local police would continue their questioning to determine if someone had seen Chauncey Groves' car along that wooded section of road around the time of the Elliston shooting.

Hanny knew that weapon. At least he knew the Colt M1911, the ".45." He had had one—and he'd given it away.

"Get away from here! I don't want that, and I don't want you!" Lisbeth's face had glistened in a sweat of rage. She screamed at him, hit him, ran from him as far into the woods as the cattle fence would let her go, and now she stood staring at Hanny, as broken as she'd seemed years before when Charlie's dogs had caught the scent of her blood.

"What you gone and done, Hanny?" she whispered at last. "Suited up like a hero... runnin' outta this here place? Runnin' out on me? You gonna go fight somebody? Gonna kill somebody?" She sank into a squat

against the fence post, trembling the way he'd seen rabbits do after they were shot.

"Lisbeth, I swear it's the only thing I can do to save you... to save us." Hanny pulled the khaki pants of his uniform up and sat down beside her. "Listen to me again, I told him... yes, I did. Outright. I said I'd served my time with Alma, and I told him that it was over." Hanny took her hand and spoke slowly, leaving spaces between his words. "He knew it was you and me, Lisbeth. You that I wanted all along. He knew it from our letters he'd got hold of. And like some snake lying quiet in the bushes, he was waiting to strike. He is dangerous. You know that. He wouldn't even take promises from me to stay away from you." Hanny pulled her hand, wet with loam and tears, to his lips.

"And he didn't give me no choice. If I divorce Alma, he won't hurt me, Lisbeth; he's gonna kill you. He's got the power. He's got the hate. I never seen a man hate like that."

She turned her head away. "Charlie..., Eustus.... Men with no faces I can recall. Now you, Hanny. Each one hurtin' me in his own way, I guess...." Lisbeth's eyes looked beyond him. She seemed to be in another place now, a place of white noise, white feelings—the inside of an empty jar. He buried his head on her shoulder, remembering the smell of her skin and how joyously she had held him on a night filled with wild winds and rain. And now he, like the others, brought her pain.

"I want you to keep this, Lisbeth. I don't know what that old man could do. All I care about is you're safe. If you use the gun, you'd be doin' God a service. But I pray to... I pray to whoever looks out for the likes of you and me... that you never have to touch it."

He pulled her to her feet and kissed her, trying to see and smell all that made up the simple country girl, Lisbeth and, with despair, feeling terrified he would forget.

"Wrap it up, put it in a metal can." Hanny finally called as he ran to the waiting car of the other anxious Air Corps recruit. "Bury it and keep it for when you might need it! I love you, Lisbeth.... Don't forget me."

Hanny had nearly been thrown in the brig for reporting his weapon lost. But they would issue him another. And another when that one was blown up in Burma..., and a third when he'd lost not only his sidearm, but in a fight with a Japanese, three fingers from the left hand he didn't need to pull a trigger.

***

It was noon when Hanny parked his Lincoln in the spot under the century oak near Reverend Eustus Pitts' rusty cistern. Lately, once a week, Hanny would drive to Eustus' wood frame house where Gertrude turned her garden's crop into salty delicacies and buttery fried treats. Later she would send him home with another entire dinner wrapped tightly in the morning's paper. She knew Hanny's wife was out of town and that you couldn't leave a man on his own without good food. "You might die a' hunger before we see you next," she'd laughed. She clearly loved Hanny's new visits and babied him if she could.

After lunch, which today had been served picnic-style in the backyard, Hanny lit up a cigar, though he wasn't sure Eustus approved. Then he'd pulled a weathered wooden chair up to a wicker table he guessed Gertrude had inherited from some white woman on Avon Street.

"Lay 'um out Eustus," said Hanny, upending the box of checkers. "I got a feelin' Lady Luck is with me this afternoon."

Eustus chuckled and shook his head. "OOO..., nooo.... You just think she be there waitin' for you. But she gonna look over your shoulder and send me signals as to what you have in mind." His laugh was high-pitched at first, rumbling into a New Orleans-style growl. "Yes, sir, an' you better play fast too, 'cause it look like we gonna have us another late summer storm, you ask me."

"No, heard on the radio it's not just a summer storm, but another gosh-darn hurricane a' brewin'. My, my they are botherin' us this year." Hanny looked up as bullying black clouds forced the cumulous billows to flee.

The two men carefully arranged the little round discs across the board, flicking with their long nails at disarranged pieces. Today Eustus

211

had chosen red. They were both quiet for minutes while they mentally played through their opening moves, remembering the other's tactics from games before.

"D'you see the morning headlines? See that news about the gun? It was a Colt... a military weapon. A .45." Hanny took his first tentative moves toward Eustus' front row.

"Yes, sir, I did. That's right; they think it's an old military gun or somethin'? They found it in the woods not far from here."

"You think it might actually a' killed Charlie?" Hanny wondered out loud. "I mean could a gun that old still work?" He, like every other man around here had shot his share of doves and ducks, and yes, in his case, Japanese soldiers too. But he wasn't sure that a forty-year-old gun not regularly maintained could even fire.

"You know," he said casually, "I used to own a weapon like that...." He paused for a moment, glancing up at Eustus. Eustus was staring back at him.

They both knew that many people in Tilley and beyond had reason to have had both murderous thoughts and Charlie Elliston's name mixing it up inside their heads. And Hanny could read Eustus' question even as the old preacher's rheumy eyes flickered back to the checkered board.

"No, my friend, I didn't do it, but a gun of that very make has laid buried there on Lisbeth's property since before I left for the War. I was afraid Charlie was gonna do her in one way or another. And I had her bury the thing up on that hill above the pond."

There was a hesitation. "You been out there lately, Hanny? Gun still there?" Eustus took a swig of tea. "Anything else dug up around that hill you notice?"

A shiver went down Hanny's back. The wind had picked up with that faint heaviness, the weight of moisture that could easily spin.

What was Eustus getting at? The only time Hanny remembered Eustus being on Lisbeth's land was the last time. When another hurricane, the big one, had changed everything. "Why, I don't know..., I haven't been out there lately. You?"

The two men sat staring at the checkers board, black and red pieces held between their fingers, the ties that bound them shifting as each strained to test their strength.

Eustus seemed to decide to toss another line in case the first should fail. "I remember bein' at Buena Vista in '48."

And Hanny did too.

He hadn't gotten back to Mississippi until 1948. The war had officially finished a couple of years before, but what the Japanese prisoner of war camp had done to Hanny had taken a year of surgeries and months of rehabilitation before he could hobble back to Tupelo. The Pacific War was the end of humanity as far as he was concerned. Too many rifle butts. Too much time squatting in a bamboo cage. Too many bodies of men he'd known who'd become carrion alongside jungle roads. Men—mankind—and the animals that prowled the wet highlands. The only distinction was that Hanny retained respect for the tiger that could puncture your chest or the leech that would suck your blood. For mankind, he felt only abysmal sorrow.

Yet Hanny had promised himself that when and if he ever got home he would try to become what he wanted himself to be all along: a good man. A married man who would try to make a family and keep a job. He had a wife. A job still waited. They weren't the ones he wanted, but good men take what's there and make do. And that's all Hanny had wanted to be—a simple, but a good and Godly man. Many of that ilk simply hadn't returned.

But there are some things that don't belong to God or Satan. There are ambiguous places where the heart is king. No-man's-lands. Yeah, a lot like the places he'd been. Those laced with undetonated bombs, burnt places of danger masquerading as havens but dangerous with possibilities. He'd seen men destroyed in such places in jungle ravines. And he had to confess it, he'd never felt so alive. That's what had eventually drawn him to Lisbeth again when he got home. He'd tried not to go. Tried not to watch when he closed his eyes and her dark auburn hair caught the sun. Tried to appease himself with another woman for whom he felt disdain. Tried to listen for a detour from the landmines surrounding the woman in Buena Vista. But all he heard was her radiant laughter... and the tick of excitement. It was dangerous. But a way to live, when as a "good man," Hanny felt himself decaying.

He had seen her every week since his discharge from the hospital at Ft. Benning and Lisbeth had loved him without hesitation. There had been no questions. No recriminations when they met. She had kissed his ruined hand and massaged the muscles of the back crisscrossed with scars. It was as if she always knew he would return. They hadn't spoken of new plans; the old ones were still in place. But for now, they only held each other in the quietness of Buena Vista's woods, walking arm in arm, watching summer algae drift slowly across the little pond, and like children, counting new stars that turned green and red as they rose through the trees. Whatever would happen in their nighttime tears and terrors and in the long moments when one or the other of them left and ventured back into shadows that clung and pulled—they were bound. There were some things of which they would never speak, but they would save their lives together.

Eustus scratched his head and with the other hand stacked and unstacked the little checkers on his side of the table. Hanny was having a hard time paying attention; that was clear. But then so was he.

Always happened around this time of year. The weather—hurricane time. The big blows that took down trees and snapped you off from help. The something rumblin' out there in the Gulf nearly all through the fall. Those storms waited offshore like some army assemblin' for invasion, thought Eustus. Waitin' for the wind to get strong enough to launch its land attack—like it had long ago on a day in late September, when it headed straight for Tilley, Mississippi.

He looked at Hanny, bent from old age, bent from the war, and at himself—a survivor of a night when old Jim Crow had almost killed him—and made a bet that the two of them were in the same place now, feeling the rise of the wind, watching the branches fly across their path, believing they were the only ones in the world to save Lisbeth.

214

"Miss Pitts…, I just come from Bessie's house…, and she says Mr. Rudolf, the overseer is hoppin' mad that the pickers ain't got the cotton all in and that now's comin' a granddaddy of a storm outta Biloxi an' that it's a' headin' directly our way and that no man can go home till the bales tied down, and then he wants some of em' stay and chop down the big branches around the holdin' barn so's they don't crash down on the roof and ruin the bales done harvested inside… an'…."

Angus Tucker's face was wet with sweat. He'd been running from cabin to cabin like a town crier alerting Eustus Pitts' little enclave to what would later be called the *"biggest hurricane of the decade."*

"Y'all better find a place to hide…. That's all I can say. Or go tie youself to a tree…, providin' it holds." Angus ran on to the next cabin where an old deaf woman sat rocking on her porch.

Peony Pitts didn't know much about hurricanes. She was a city girl and she didn't know much about cotton, farms, or the complicated sets of personae she'd had to assume since Eustus had brought her here five years ago. There was the obsequious, smiling sycophant who agreed with every thought enunciated by white lips. There was the hardworking farm wife who boiled her clothes and planted her garden. And there was *"Eustus' schooled-up, Northern wife"* who taught children to read in the enclave's little school and felt responsible for every other member of the poor families who lived in Red Mouth Hollow. She was a chameleon alright—just like the little lizards running on her wood pile that didn't exist up north. In fact, the Peony she was now hadn't existed either. She'd become adaptable—so a hurricane might add just one more color.

She stepped out into the yard, away from the wooden house and trees, and looked down the long rows of cotton that turned the Hollow into a lonely oasis of live oaks and rusty pumps. The wind had been rattling the shingles all night, and she thought she'd heard it shift slightly to a higher pitch as a few drops of rain had begun. But now to the south, the sky was different than she'd ever seen. Shelved with bands of sheared-off clouds, stacked one upon another in malevolent stripes, it looked as if a snowpack were building toward some savage avalanche.

Peony was having trouble standing up now as gusts caught her beneath the arms and seemed to want to lift her high. The sound of wind *in the trees changed again, elevated a decibel or two, or three as she made her way back into the cabin, leaning forward and staggering against the door. There wasn't much to save, but she grabbed the Bible and the diploma that said Eustus was a consecrated pastor and a photo of a black angel she'd found in a magazine. Then she forced the door back open, leapt off the porch, and ran down the line of other small cabins where people dashed back and forth carrying bundles of clothes under one arm and sometimes a child beneath the other.*

And then Eustus appeared. "Come on, Baby! Come on here with me!" He threw his jacket across her shoulders and propelled her, along with three or four children, toward the cold cellar at the back of Old Man Murphy's barn. Half-buried in the earth, the stone building jutted up like a breaching submarine and was just as dank. Packed earth inside kept the temperature chilly even on hot days, but it was the perfect bunker when branches the size of torpedoes would begin to sail overhead.

"Alright, my little honey, I'm gonna put you right here. Here with these blankets and some candles. And lookie here, why Murphy's got himself some cider from last year still coolin'. An' I got the sandwiches you made me early today—so you can have em' now."

"Why are you talkin' like that Eustus? Like they're all for me... and these children? Where you goin'?" She looked around at the covey of wet brown faces, snuggling against her with wide eyes. Eustus was a preacher alright, but this was a hurricane. He had to stay.

"I gotta go out, Baby girl. Storm's comin' on strong an' some people don't even know it's gonna tear things up bad. I gotta go warn 'em. Maybe save' em. I love you all's I can. Don't forget that. All's I can! And I'll be back as soon. We got us a long life ahead. So don't worry none..., none at all!"

The road to Buena Vista had already turned into a frothy stream by the time Eustus got to his car. Flowing so fast it eroded the packed red earth into two foot ruts, huge sections of road had disappeared into small lakes that now lay in the low areas where the route had been. Through the windshield, he could only make out shadows that appeared then dissolved into opaque sheets of grey, while the wind hurled leaves and mud as if it had Eustus in a fight.

In Biloxi, on the Gulf of Mexico, they knew what to do when hurricanes made their yearly slams along the coast and charged north. But way up here, way up here in the fields and forests, there weren't shelters—nor ways to warn. What was a damned 'cane doin' up here anyway? *he thought.*

Eustus figured he'd been half an hour on the road to Buena Vista. He was most of the way there, blindly bucking into holes that were feet under water and making bets he wouldn't hit a fence or be flipped by the increasing wind, when suddenly, there was an earsplitting crack, and above his head the roof of the old coupe gave a metallic groan, then collapsed around him. Ducking, Eustus slammed on the brakes and flung himself into the passenger seat. Above the cacophony of howling wind and pounding rain, he felt his head, then shouted out a benediction when he realized that his skull was still intact, and aside from the roof, the only casualty was the stalled-out engine. Carefully, he crawled out of the car and into the rain, water surging above his ankles. The limb had landed a direct hit, and the steel roof was now folded into the shape of an empty envelope. Then he saw the tree.

Holding onto the fender, Eustus inched forward against the wind. An oak trunk, he guessed four feet in diameter, lay across the road. How could he not have struck it? All he knew was that the branch lying atop his car had probably saved his life. But there were other trees, and they encircled Buena Vista.

The sky was black with clouds now, and the rain seemed to be coming from every direction. The wind's roar was what Eustus had sometimes heard described as dogs from hell. Howling and keening, it screamed at him from somewhere in the canopy as he dragged himself from pine tree to pine tree, holding onto the trunks, and feeling the low roar deep inside.

He'd left the washed-out road, and occasionally, through the moaning trees and blanket of storm, could make out shapes. There was the graveyard to the left. Many of the tombstones, he thought, seemed to be lying flat, including the one that had been ripped out, hurled into his path, and which brought him face-to-face with the fact that "John Able

217

had died in his bed in 1868." Eustus only hoped the same would happen to him—and to those in the house ahead.

At last, he could see the structure. Gertrude's small duplicate was somewhere in the trees behind it. Lisbeth's house had been damaged, he could tell. A pine had snapped off and fallen across the porch. The porch's roof lay beneath it, parts shearing off in the wind. If someone were inside, Eustus would never hear their cries as missiles began to sail through the air, and a new squall of rain shrieked around the house. Just then he saw the car.

And something like a wave of love passed over Eustus. He had never before felt such a sensation. Drenched, his eyes red from the stabbing rain and detritus of the forest, and trembling with a fear he thought battle-scarred soldiers may know, he felt love flood over him. This was Hanford Meyers' car. Hanford Meyers—married into money, a banker now, a hero from the war, a man who had given Eustus back his life— and now he was here. Eustus knew why, and he loved him for it.

Eustus could no longer stand up as he slowly made his way across the open area toward the house—frantically looking when the wind would let him, for signs of Lisbeth or of Hanny. He crawled through the remains of the grape arbor, tearing his clothes on thorns and shards of glass from the windows, and up onto the side of the porch. The storm seemed to have increased in the last minutes, now with a thunderous, unremitting power filled with damnation. And then the house burst apart.

Eustus was lifted into the trees, where in the swirl of branches and chairs and saucers and a beautiful straw hat, he dreamed he was Plato and that he stood on the steps of a snow-white building shaking hands with Jesus—inviting him to a game of horseshoes and noting his skin was black—until the pain racked him awake.

"Eustus! Eustus!" He felt someone shaking his shoulder, a panicky gesture that was sending bursts of fire to his brain. "Christ, Eustus." The rain was enough to choke him, lying face up to the hell going on overhead. Then he heard a man begin to sob. "Oh shit... Oh shit... Eustus." He squinted into the wind to see Hanny kneeling over him. "Oh God.... All gone.... All gone."

Eustus closed his eyes, closed his fists, then flexed his legs, and carefully arched his back. Jesus's visit had gone hazy, and he gingerly pushed himself up onto his good shoulder in the mud. The house was completely missing. Splinters of wood scattered the yard, some of them like spears, piercing trees twenty feet up. The roof lay bashed in half at the end of the drive by the road, and an old wood stove dangled in a pecan tree by its leg. Hanny's car was upside down.

"I'm not dead, Hanny," was all Eustus could think of to say. Hanny lifted his head as if through the roaring wind he couldn't be sure what he'd heard. He stared at the black man, plastered with leaves and dirt and reached down and kissed him.

"Eustus..., we've got to find them. I had them with me..., all huddled up. Had 'em in the damned outbuilding with me.... With me layin' over 'em." He burst into sobs again. "And then they got sucked away.... Right outta my arms. I tried to hold... I tried to hold on...."

Hanny pushed himself up, now oblivious to Eustus, leaning into the wind, walking back toward the broken piers of the house, his head swinging from side to side, hands pulling at debris that could have covered one hundred bodies. Eustus couldn't hear what he was calling, but he thought he knew. He and Hanny were calling the same name.

"Nineteen forty-eight. I don't think any other hurricane ever come up that far north, do you?"

"Nope. That one was the worst ever been seen around Tilley. Had a tornado or two in it, I reckon."

Hanny and Eustus had given up playing checkers. Instead they sat staring toward the orchard that had been seeds when the hurricane swept through.

"You know, I'll always thank you for findin' and tellin' me to come," said Hanny, glancing over at Eustus. Each of them bided his time, taking a sip of tea, and wondering how long grief can remain raw. "You know she wanted to go North and find you, don't you?"

"I heard that," said Eustus, nodding his head and examining his fingertips. "She were different, weren't she...? Brave in a way that you don't see on a given day."

"And you too, old man," smiled Hanny.

"Well, she gave me a great gift. Took a powerful hardship to do it, but she gave me a treasure that will last now my whole life through and that's the one who's servin' us this tea right now." Eustus winked at Gertrude who poured a little more tea in each of their glasses and then disappeared through the screen door.

Hanny watched her slim figure. "Without you bein' there that terrible day and takin' Gertrude back with you, I don't know what would have happened to her. What was she seventeen? Eighteen? The bastard was out to scorch everything off that property one way or another. If she'd been left...."

Eustus rocked silently back and forth. "An' I'm glad I'm the one who done found Lisbeth and could give her over to you." He shifted in his chair, turned and fixed Hanny with his dark blue-ringed eyes. "You know, I did something I probably shouldn't a done that day. It wasn't mine to do..., but... I stayed on behind you when you had her there, holding her head up from under that rafter. She didn't have but a few minutes, I reckon. I'm sorry. I knew I would never see her again, and I just couldn't drag myself on. But I heard her say somethin' that maybe you never knew what it meant... You ever wonder about something like that?"

Hanny turned to Eustus. "Yes.... You heard it? She said it was important, but all these years I was never sure who it was about. You, maybe? I think she loved us both, Eustus."

"No, it wasn't me. Do you remember, she said, 'On my last day, at my last hour, with my last breath, I will breathe all that I am into another one. One who will finish my story..., whatever it may take.' That's what she said."

"Her story was too short," said Hanny, tears spilling along his cheeks.

"It's still being told," said Eustus. "By your daughter. Your daughter, Claire."

Chapter 39

It was late afternoon by the time Hanny parked his car in the spot reserved for Government Officials in front of the Tilley Municipal Police Department. He hadn't gone there immediately after he'd left Eustus. Instead he had spent the last two hours parked in a shady glade alongside an abandoned road, a place no cars would pass and see him. Hanny was exhausted, brain worn out. No emotions left to twist the way his stomach had when Eustus confirmed he had a daughter.

But then, how hadn't he known? Might be that everyone else had. How had he deceived himself enough to invite—he couldn't think the words—his daughter to the Ramada Inn? He thanked God that he had never touched her. His sin had been in his own mind, and he told himself, not with Claire, but with Lisbeth. With Lisbeth's "avatar."

Hanny felt his head spinning, grasping for an axis to align facts and feelings, lies and desires. And in the end, all that he thought was, "How hadn't I known?" And how doesn't she? Hanny had never really thought about Claire's background. Never really connected her to Tilley. She was a banker in Tupelo with a degree from a northern school. She was connected to the Elliston family he knew, but somehow, he'd assumed Charlie was her uncle. Perhaps, a cousin. Claire was never around, never mentioned. But then, neither had Lisbeth been mentioned. Nor had she ever told him of his child. How had he never known? How could he not have seen it?

Hanny pulled a small flask from under the seat, took the last two swigs, and let the liquor evaporate at the back of his throat. He could picture Lisbeth on the swing at Buena Vista, see her full breasts through the plain cotton dress, her soft hips. He wondered if he had touched her abdomen after Claire was begun.

Yet Lisbeth had rarely complained. Not since the day he picked her up outside Charlie's woods. She seemed to have created a narrative that, if clung to tightly enough, could squeeze reality into a tiny footnote. Maybe in the face of despair, Lisbeth had told herself a story and then lived it out as she imagined it. Lived with joy though she was a pariah in town. Lived with poetry even though she'd had to whore to eat. Lived with hope that together she and he would make a normal life—even though she must have thought he'd turned his back on her when she carried his child. How could he never have known?

He wondered if Claire were adept at the same kind of magical living as Lisbeth had been—or the same kind of denial in which he'd made his own life.

It was growing late, but before he drove back to Tupelo, Hanny wanted to do one good deed. Something on this strange afternoon that might help expiate some of his sins. Something that he thought would make his daughter proud of him.

He wouldn't stay long at the Police Headquarters because the collard casserole and sausage jambalaya covering Gertrude's cornbread couldn't last long in a hot car. He thought of taking it inside with him, but it would only lead to questions that were too awkward to answer to a Chief who was known for his "coon-baitin'" ways.

Hanny took a breath and shoved his shirt sleeves up above his elbows as he got out of the car. Even though it wasn't that hot in the newly renovated jail complex, rolled-up sleeves looked confident.

"Jail Complex," of course, was overstating the very simple renovation of Brady's old department store in downtown Tilley. Fluorescent lights had replaced the creamy globe pendant lamps that used to hang over the men's shoe department and ladies' accessories. And sitting in the west half of the 1920's landmark, the prefab steel room with its barred cells and open-view toilets provided an odd contrast to the arched oak-trimmed windows that, despite competition from a bluish glare, still flooded the room with natural light.

"Well, my, oh, my, Grady, I thought you'd be out sendin' a huntin' puppy after a hog today." Hanny marched right past Louella Peters, who'd devoted most of her adult life to looking after Chief Grady Sanders. She gave him an evil look but let him pass. Men who talked dogs had a special bond, and men who wore gold-rimmed glasses like Hanford Meyers didn't always take to women interrupting them.

Grady stretched up from his desk. After the renovation, he'd been excited to have a new office walled off behind a glass enclosure. He'd seen such arrangements on television, but in practice, he felt lonesome inside it and now spent most of his day at a long conference table hunched behind Louella.

"Well Hanny Meyers, what you doin' over here, slummin'?" The men pounded on each other's backs and looked each other in the eyes with broad smiles. If they were dogs, they'd be sniffing each other's behinds.

"Oh, not much, really, Grady. Been out lookin' at some property, checkin' on likely harvest times. Gotta keep an eye on them who took out loans. Gotta know 'bout when they can pay up." Hanny laughed at his burden of looking after deadbeats. Then he added, "Also, I just come over here to visit you 'cause I been overhearin' talk among some folks I know who sit on the High Court...." He let the lie hang in the air for a moment.

"You know, the Mississippi Supremes—the Supreme Court." Grady's look turned from quizzical to the slight squint of caution.

"'Bout what, may I ask? Can't be nothin' to do with us down here in Tilley, I'd reckon."

"Well, yes sir, Grady. It does." Hanny slowly pulled out a wooden chair from the conference table and, glancing toward Louella, dropped his voice. "It's a matter you may want to consider in the privacy of your own shit house." Mississippi slang, but such talk was the code that opened ears. Hanny patted Grady on the shoulder and let his eyes crease with warm camaraderie.

"What's this all about?" Grady was now on high alert. He wanted nothing to do with courts or prosecutors or the goddamned investigators from Oxford. Full of themselves is what they were. Thought they could come in and tell the Tilley Police who to arrest and why and who to let out on bail and for how much.

"Well, it's about this nasty mess with old Charlie," said Hanny. "Seems like there's a lot of protestin' goin' on over in Oxford. Lot of headlines talkin' about Mississippi holdin' a black man without evidence. And the Governor and his Supremes don't much like that kinda talk. You know how they are. Gotta kinda kowtow to anybody who raises his voice." Hanny shook his head at the way the bigwigs were manipulated by the liberal do-gooders.

"Well, what am I supposed to do about it? Let him go? I know we're stretchin' holdin' him, and..., shit.... I already got those citified detectives on my case. But hell, Hanny, he's all we got at the moment." Grady had gotten confessions out of blacks before. It just took time and a special kind of encouragement. It just wasn't the kind of investigation you'd conduct with onlookers.

"Tell you what, Grady, and I only am suggesting this 'cause I don't want to see you starring on some goddamned evening news. What if we put this boy out on bail? A high bail, mind you. But get him out from under you where no Supremes nor anyone else can say you were doin' somethin'... 'Southern' to him. I mean, I just wanna spare you a news truck or somethin' camped out across the street. That'll give you time to come up with some kind of evidence, right? I mean at the moment you ain't got any, am I right?"

Grady looked pained, "No, got none." Then he asked who was prepared to put up a high bail?

"Well, you arrange it with the prosecutors, and I'll stand by you with the bail, Grady." Hanny let his hand linger on the Chief's shoulder, a savior pulling Grady from catastrophe, and Grady nodded in agreement. He'd have Chauncey out by the end of the week.

Chapter 40

Claire hadn't gone into work all the following week. Vacation days had piled up for a couple of years; the work load was under control; and frankly, she thought Starlight could flirt, jiggle, or obfuscate enough to keep the place running for the ten days Claire intended to be gone. With the "personal loan" she had given herself from her retirement savings, she was going to move Buena Vista to conclusion.

Maybe she was losing her mind, or maybe it was already gone. Either way, she wanted to finish what she'd started. She wanted a place she could lay her head down at Buena Vista. Get it done.

Tandy and Sons were in a slow month themselves, they said, and with the lumber already delivered, all that was needed was a hookup to the electric and plumbing, and the contractor could "raise the walls" in a week. They'd already made a good start.

Claire didn't want to go to a hotel. She especially didn't want to go to Doreen's B & B. What had happened there the last time was evidence she would probably land in a loony bin. Or it was something that had really happened—something so beautiful and frightening that she replayed it each evening before she fell asleep. Either way, right now she didn't want to go back to that room, but it didn't mean she wouldn't relive the touch of the unknown hand. Being real wasn't a requisite.

Instead, Claire had hauled her old canvas tent to the clover field in front of the skeletal structure. Pounding the stakes in with the flat of a hammer had cracked a couple of manicured nails, and seeing the polish split, she found herself laughing out loud. Hell, at this point they were so dirty with Buena Vista soil, the polish had turned a deep maroon, and that was just fine.

A swim raft from the dollar store in Tupelo was a decent mattress, and a bathroom's "decorator" lantern with a candle served its purpose after dark. Takeout food from Sully's and a roll of toilet paper were all Claire needed. In fact, as the week went on, each night when she tied her tent flaps shut, snuggled onto the blankets on the raft, snuffed out the lantern, and listened to the barred owl hollering for a mate, she seemed to feel herself reassembling. Maybe it was the chipmunks—she liked to picture them as chipmunks and not rats—dancing along the newly placed rafters or the moths head-banging against her tent, but Claire imagined herself among friends.

She wondered if she shouldn't be a little afraid in the woods after dark. Each day the seated men at Sully's exchanged looks when Claire came in for her takeout, but she couldn't muster the feeling of fear on the property. The sagging, waist-high fence around Buena Vista's perimeter offered a provisional security, and the house that was rising in the clearing emanated a kind of primal protection. As to the less tangible entities, she hoped their vested stakes would keep her safe.

And now this morning, she would share the amazing progress—roughed-in walls, roof, and porch—with someone who knew this place better than she did. Gertrude was coming to visit. Claire wondered if the visits to Eustus' church and Starlight's buoyant hospitality were giving her a certain confidence, a new bravery to face memories that Gertrude's presence at Buena Vista might trigger. Besides, Gertrude was her only living link to her mother.

By eleven AM, Claire had raked the field in front of the house free of magnolia leaves and pulled the metal lawn chairs with their fresh coats of primary color into a circle. Eustus would drive Gertrude to Buena Vista he'd said, and Starlight had insisted on packing a lunch for the two women— "chicken, rice, beans, coleslaw, pumpkin pie," and likely "extras," often in chocolate, when Starlight was in the kitchen.

"Your father just never stops surprisin' me," said Claire, hugging Gertrude and waving good-bye to Eustus as the elderly chauffeur drove away. "That man has more energy than three or four thirty-year-olds."

Claire led the older woman up the lane, taking the basket of food which, by its weight, she guessed would make for dinner as well.

"I got us some lemonade here, Gertrude. You sit down and relax. I'll put this heap of food on the picnic table while you just wriggle your toes in my new clover." Claire bustled around the wooden table, glancing at Gertrude who seemed to be buffeted between pangs of nostalgia and waves of awe as she stared at the structural recreation before her.

"Well, what do you think? You're the authority here, Gertrude. I've got photos and my scraps of memory, but you knew this place better than anybody. Is this the way it looked before? Before what happened…?"

Gertrude was leaning forward, obviously eager to get up on the front porch and walk around the back of the house. "If I didn't know better, I'd think I was dreamin' it back to life, Miss Claire." She sat back and adjusted her ever-present hat.

"Stop, Gertrude. Don't call me that. You never called me that when we lived here." Claire came around and knelt in the grass before her. "There is a new day here at Buena Vista. We are friends now. More than friends. You took such good care of me when I was little. You were the one I think I missed most when Granny Ruta took me away. So don't be afraid," Claire said, standing up. "You just call me Claire, and I'll call you, Gertrude… almost like sisters!" Claire laughed with the obvious ridiculousness of it, but Gertrude looked sharply up, her face now a question mark.

Claire handed her a glass of lemonade and took her by the hand, showing Gertrude the grape arbor and the perimeter of mums she'd planted even before the garden was dug in. "I even got the old sink re-enameled, and though I'm gonna have running water, I found a used hand pump to put by the sink. Do you remember that? I can still feel the icy water that used to come out. Tasted like the way rocks tasted when I was little and used to put my tongue on them!"

Claire was loving the way Gertrude's eyes darted from window to window, measuring the size of the house and the rooms that were finally walled in. But she had a bigger surprise for her.

"Come on out back now, Gertrude. I need your advice." Claire led the way to the grove behind the house. Here a foundation was marked out by stakes and string. "It's where you lived, Gertrude. I know it was here. I can see it in my mind's eye, but I was so little, I can't remember

227

the size or where its own little porch was. There aren't any pictures of it. But if you help me, I'm gonna make it just the same as it was. There was a little lean-to structure too, if I remember...."

Gertrude seemed suddenly tired, stopping and pressing her forehead with a white hankie. "You sure is doin' something, Miss Cl— This is... this is more 'n I thought." Claire saw that Gertrude's breathing was faster and that beads of perspiration had aligned themselves across her nose.

"Well, let's go sit back down. 'Bout time for a bit of lunch. We can look around later."

Gertrude let herself be walked back to the colorful chairs. "You work your way around the property?" she asked. "Out by the pond and up that little hill?" Gertrude kept her eyes on the house, but glanced at Claire.

"Everyplace, Gertrude. I've explored every part of this property, and you wouldn't believe all the old stuff I found on the ground, under bushes, between roots..." Claire was pulling Mason jars of coleslaw out of the hamper.

"Well, I don't wonder..." Gertrude's voice trailed off. "I don't wonder at what got strewn about. Happened on that hurricane day, everything jus' come flyin' and bustin' out like popcorn in an over-fried skillet. Even big things, heavy metal and stones took to flyin'."

Claire handed Gertrude a plate heaped with cold vegetables and warm chicken and stood staring down at the older woman. "It must have been a direct hit when the storm struck." Claire had never talked with anyone about the hurricane. Her grandmother had only told her that she couldn't come home again—that her old life had blown away and never to look back. When you're six, you do as you're told. Now, watching Gertrude's pained expression deepen, Claire decided on another direction.

"I made lists of the artifacts..., the stuff... I found out here," said Claire. "Dishes and pans. The kitchen items in one category, a glass door pull, a dresser handle. And then..., well, lots of other things. Even found what I think was the little cemetery where I must of buried pets. Found the little cross, though, it was pretty well rotted now."

Gertrude had stopped eating. "Say you found a little cemetery?"

"Yes, I did." Claire hesitated for a moment. "And something else over by the pond." Now Claire put her plate aside and turned her chair to face Gertrude's. This was meant to be a social visit, filled with small talk and sweet reminiscence. She didn't want to talk about what she'd found. She only wanted to share ideas for the garden, to scratch down a favorite recipe, to discuss colors to paint the porch. Maybe, maybe a figure on a swing.

"I found a gun..." Claire's throat wanted to close; she wanted to start all over. "But I left it buried in the dirt right where I found it up on that hill." The woman beside her didn't move.

This wasn't why Claire had asked Gertrude here. Why the hell had she mentioned what she'd found on the rise and later its empty hole. And yet, she couldn't go back. Jackson's words, "two elderly black people come to dig somethin' up" had preemptively entered her head like police breaking down a door. All at once, to be asked about the gun seemed the only reason Gertrude was here.

"I just wondered if you'd heard of anybody comin' out here..., lookin' for anything... like a gun, maybe." Claire guessed Gertrude was thinking she'd been led into a pretty, pastoral trap. No, this was not what Claire had wanted at all.

Gertrude said nothing, but her head dropped slowly forward. "Forgive me, Gertrude," Claire said. "I am not accusing anybody of anything. But you have to tell me, did you and Eustus come out here lookin' for somethin'? Somebody saw..., well, people who look like you. An' those two people dug something up from there and took it away. It was right before Charlie Elliston was..., was killed."

Gertrude finally looked up from the plate in her lap, then at the half-finished house and at the string outline of the small house beside it. And then she began to quietly rock in the metal chair.

Claire sat back, listening as the low tones of melody softly rolled from Gertrude's lips. A fulsome hum, a kind of primal vibration with which Claire guessed the leaves and the wind could make a harmony. And then it stopped, and Gertrude looked directly at Claire.

"Child, I'm gonna tell you some stories now. I won't tell them all, but I'll tell you my part. 'Bout why my daddy an' me come up to that hill… and 'bout the little angel buried there that done come home with us."

Claire felt a shift in the light, a shadow passing between herself and Gertrude, the brush against her cheek. If she had reached out her hand, Claire guessed its darkness would be warm.

"About the thing you asked? About a gun that mighta had somethin' to do with a killin'? I can't tell you yet, Miss Claire. My prayers aren't all done on that count." Gertrude's head wandered back and forth, and her eyes closed as if a gospel song's first chords had begun.

"I'm waitin' for my Jesus with answers for me to move; I'm waitin' for my Jesus if sin He shall remove—"

Then suddenly Gertrude stopped, jerked herself upright, and with a righteous power Claire had only seen in pastors who intimidated their flocks with bolts of Holy Spirit, said, "But I tell you this, Sister, no black man nor woman killed that man on his front steps. Though a murderer was murdered, I can testify it was not a black who done that act."

Chapter 41

Hanny Meyers rubbed his hand across his chin, feeling the soft flesh roll under his fingers even as the stubble pricked like a poorly harvested field. He loved it. Loved the fact that he'd cancelled three meetings at the bank the last week. Loved the fact that he wandered his own house in an undershirt without anyone noting that his belly bulged and his armpits stank. Loved a kind of freedom that had crept over him ever since Charlie's murder. And Alma's departure.

Oh, he'd had to field a few calls from Alma's friends inviting her to lunches and a Women's Club fundraiser. Sometimes he hadn't answered the phone at all. But otherwise, his life had taken on a serene quiet.

Certainly, there had been no calls *from* Alma; that was for sure. For sure a blessing, Hanny thought. She'd just left. A fact that didn't bother him. In some odd way, he figured she'd left for good. Hoped it to hell. Yet while she'd made a fool of herself at Charlie's funeral, almost letting the cat out of the bag with her over-the-top nose blowing and all, there'd been something else. Almost from the time news came that Charlie had been killed, Alma had seemed different. Absent, or like she wanted to be. Moving around the house like a paper cutout, like she was already gone. Surely Hanny would know that look—he'd worn it himself for years.

He'd let Rosie know she didn't need to come to clean until he called her, a tangible statement of domestic independence. And then, as if he performed the maneuver every day of the week, Hanny had carefully dumped the dirty dishes he'd piled high in the sink into the trash can outside the door. In their place, he'd substituted a large package of paper plates for use when his new store of TV dinners would run out. Hanny thought he could get used to living alone real fast.

Soon the afternoons he was now spending with Eustus and Gertrude began replacing numbing recitals of fiscal projections and interest rate worries at the bank, and in a way he didn't understand, the old need for the Ramada Inn reveries was diminishing too. Hanny had the feeling that without willing it, he was being drawn back to the real Tilley, to a place where his old life had been interrupted, but that seemed to be waiting for him now. And with it, his mother, his father... and Lisbeth.

Putting his feet up on the ottoman in his study, Hanny gave a long, low belch, sipped at his coffee again, and thought that he just might drop by whatever it was Claire Elliston—yes, his daughter—was building on Buena Vista. One day he would tell her about how she came to be. He didn't know when. He'd come close that day at the church, but he'd run away, hadn't he? Not much of a hero. But then just knowing he had a daughter was probably better than being rejected by one. One day she would know.

Hanny was jarred from his thoughts by the ringing beside him. Hoping it was for Alma and could be dismissed with a casual lie, he picked up the phone.

Grady Sanders pitched his voice deeper than usual if the Chief opened with news and not small talk. And Grady, who tended toward alto when he was excited, this time, spoke in a forced baritone as if he were reading from a television script. Hanny knew Grady was clearly relishing being near the center of a murder investigation that was making headlines across the state and probably had rehearsed in a toilet stall the exact vocal gravitas he was going to convey.

"Good Morning, Hanny. Grady Sanders, here. Just thought we could give you a little update on the turns of events on the Elliston murder case." Hanny thought Grady was a little breathless and decided to keep things slow.

"Well, always interested in what good progress you are makin' over there at headquarters, Grady." Hanny was surprised that the loquacious Grady had abandoned the usual preliminary bullshit. "Yes sir, an' I know

Tilley families always feel safer when you and your boys are leadin' an investigation."

"Well, we finally got us some prints. You know, them prints off the gun...." Grady's voice involuntarily soared toward soprano. "An' you won't believe what they come off of."

Hanny sat up straighter, moved his feet to the floor, and shifted his gaze.

Along his driveway, the leafless trees looked like blackened crones, cackling secrets to each other. He briefly wondered what the trees above Charlie's house had seen. What about the ones at Buena Vista? They'd know who'd been digging on that hill for a gun. Funny, that gun. As if the damned thing had a life of its own. Given to Lisbeth to protect her from Charlie, now the very thing that had finally brought the old man's sorry life to an end.

"Yeah, an it's kinda funny, in its own way." Grady was saying. "Although, to tell the truth, we don't have the connection."

"Well, Grady, how 'bout you tell me. Just take your time and tell me about what you found." The chief's noisy inhalation and expiration made Hanny pull the phone from his ear.

"They come off a man in Oxford. Yeah, guy who says he's a businessman, but guess what his business is, Hanny? He runs a goddamned brothel. But man, this ain't no regular brothel. It's one for ladies. Ladies! Where the women go payin' for the men!" Grady burst into a hacking bray. "They got the sombitch on a morals charge, when two a' the women got into a fracas on the side of the road outside the place." He dropped his voice. "I guess one said she didn't get the servicin' she was anticipatin', and the other one said she was too ugly for any man's dick to get stiff." Grady let loose with an ear-shattering guffaw.

"So what about the prints, Grady?"

"Well, they brought him in, booked the guy, took his prints, a' course, and just now we got the faxed version that gets sent all over to law enforcement. And there they was..., plain as two twins..., a perfect match for the ones we took off a' the weapon that done killed ole Charlie Elliston!"

233

"Well, that is great police work, Grady. I do tell you that," said Hanny. "But what's a 'businessman' over in Oxford got to do with Charlie Elliston?" As soon as he said it, Hanny realized this man could be one of hundreds all over the state who could have some life-threatening bone to pick with Charlie.

"Can't say yet. We will be followin' up immediately, however." He drew the words out as if, with his nod of confidence, a camera would zoom in for a close-up. "Gonna keep the guy over in the Oxford jail for the time bein', till we develop the case from these here prints. Just thought you'd wanna know, Hanny. You bein' interested in that black's situation an' all."

Hanny hung up, poured himself a ten o'clock bourbon, and looked down at the brown lawn, the thatch of dry leaves banked against his fence, the stems of flowers that had seemed so optimistic a few months before, but which today merely poked skeletal limbs skyward in a desiccated last plea.

And then with a humming rumble that, before Hanny could identify it, produced a surge of cortisol that spread faster than the bourbon inside his gut, he saw the nose, the body, and the final fender of Alma's Buick pull into the driveway. Away at the lake house for two months. Thankfully, not a goddamned word the whole time, and now here she was. Shit. And shit, again. It occurred to him he should pack his bag for the Ramada Inn before she saw him.

Hanny downed his drink, poured another, and briefly wondered if the "brothel" news was all over Oxford. She'd be in the thick of the gossip, if it were. He wouldn't ask her. News would get around soon enough. *Always does,* he thought. *Always does.*

Then Hanny walked softly over and locked his study door.

Chapter 42

"Put them big bouquets over by the right side, unless you think there be too much pollen fallen off a' them, and it gonna get all over the Bible." Eustus himself was lugging a heavy wooden chair up onto the altar dais and gesturing with his head to Gertrude.

"You know camellias, Pap, won't be just the pollen, but sure as lighting, by Sunday morning, all them little petals gonna be scattered like pink snow over the white linen. How 'bout I put 'um one on each side a' the altar down on the floor?"

Eustus wiped at his forehead. What happened to October? This was as hot as September, and the damned wind kept rising every afternoon just like midsummer. "Alright, then. That'll be nice to look at too. Nice to look at..." Eustus watched his daughter, for once not wearing her usual brown or black dress or her Sunday white. Instead she had on a sky-blue dress with a lacy white collar.

"Somethin' special happenin' today?" He started down the row of pews, arranging the hymnals and paper fans. "You look like you might be feelin' like somethin' special goin' on."

Gertrude looked up with a palm full of fallen petals in her hand. "No, sir. Nothin' special." She dumped the pink pile in a pail and sat down on the front pew. "Just thinkin' about my visit with Mis—about my visit with Claire, an' it made me feel, I don't know, Pap..., I felt kinda strong."

Eustus worked his way back on the other side of the aisle, running his finger along the backs of pews in a dust check. "How you mean, strong? You already strong for a woman your age."

Gertrude burst out laughing. He knew what she meant. He loved to play. "No, Pap, I knew somethin' Claire didn't know. I have me an understandin' she ain't got. Made me feel like when we was young. When she looked up to me, before times made it that I be havin' to look up to her."

"So you got you an understanding, hmm? You got you a secret?" Gertrude could hear the smile in his voice, but saw him glance at the front door of the church before he sat down in the pew behind her.

Eustus said nothing for a long time, but Gertrude felt him rocking gently back and forth, a sign he was silently calling on the Lord to join in the conversation.

Then, "Sure is good ole Chauncey got himself released outta that there jail cell, ain't it," he said finally. Eustus stared down into his huge hands. "I don't believe there was one of us who thought he did such a thing. Not Starlight. Not me. How about you?"

Gertrude turned to look at her father. He seemed like granite, an outcrop of stone that you could pummel or push, but would always stand. She wasn't sure where the conversation would turn. Wasn't sure how much he really wanted to know. Yet, Eustus had a way.

"Pap, I got me a question for you," she said, redirecting the conversation, but needing to know. "That night..., the night Charlie Elliston got murdered, what you put in the back of our car? I saw you do it. I gotta hear it from you."

Eustus smiled at her, never flinching, but with a sigh said, "I put a shotgun in there, girl. What'd you think? I'm a human being. I am a man. I think a righteous one at that." Eustus shook his head back and forth. "When the devil seizes on a man and lives in him like the man be his servant and the devil his god, somebody gotta stop him. When such a man, in the hands of the devil, tries to kill his own child, tries to murder a man, and smothers a baby, a baby that's his own blood... well, such evil deeds will have a price."

Gertrude gazed at him, shocked he would have had such thoughts, yet amazed at his wisdom and proud of being his.

"But Pap, you didn't use it."

"No..., no..., I did not use it."

"Pap, did you know what you was goin' to say when we rang that bell then? If you weren't gonna shoot ole Charlie. Did you know?"

Eustus let himself smile. "I didn't know I *wasn't* gonna shoot him. But I rang that bell 'cause I wanted to show that son of a bitch what a beautiful granddaughter he had—you. What a prize he done missed out on by not knowin'. I wanted him to see—even if it were a picture—the tiny baby he killed…, the little great-grandson who would a' made any man proud. But not him." Eustus, for the first time Gertrude had ever seen, let tears roll down his cheeks. "I could a' killed him on any day of the week, throughout all these years. But that night, leavin' that photo we dug up and put in that old man's hand was enough. An' that's what I left him with. Willy's picture and the word 'Grandpa' on its back."

Eustus wept silently for a time, then looked up at Gertrude. "Now I have a question for you, too. You didn't come home with me that night…, sayin' you needed to walk around. I understand that. Said you'd have your downtown friend, Irma, bring you home." He waited for Gertrude to answer, but she turned her head away, pulling and kneading at her handkerchief.

"Gertrude," he asked directly. "Where was you before you come home with Chauncey? Where'd he pick you up at? Or did you stay right there at Mr. Charlie Elliston's house…? What'd you see there, girl?"

Gertrude got up and walked over to where a few petals lay on the threadbare carpet.

"I had a meetin' with an angel that night, Pap." Gertrude sat down and stared into a window made of colored shards of glass. "And I believe she led me to safety."

Eustus didn't look surprised. Gertrude turned toward him, and he smiled his understanding of a chance meeting with a spirit on the streets of Tilley.

"Tell me about it" he said. "When your soul stirs you to do it." Eustus settled himself against the pew and resumed his gentle rock.

Gertrude came beside him and sat against the old man, smelling the sweetly sour aroma of his old suit and his old shoes, of the old church and the falling flowers. And she felt safe.

"That night, Pap, after Mr. Charlie come out on the porch and asked you and me what we wanted..., and after we done showed him the picture of little Willie..., he took it, remember? An' he looked at it a long, long time. I wondered what he was thinkin'. If he thought Willie was pretty. If he thought he was seein' Lisbeth in that chil'e. Then that ole man done went back in with a slam of his door. Remember he done that? But he took that little picture too." Gertrude daubed at her neck and chest. Her blue dress was dotted with perspiration.

"After that, I don't know, Pap, I just wanted to be by myself for a little bit. To walk around..., to think why Mr. Charlie would treat his own blood like that. To hold it so hard against a little baby that 'round about, he'd had a hand in makin'.'"

Eustus patted her knee and sat back, quiet and patient; only the ticks of the plastic clock on the sanctuary wall not willing to wait.

Gertrude closed her eyes. "I sat down on that little stump across from Mr. Charlie's house. It pretty hidden from the street, I guess, an' just watched at the house. I could see old Charlie walkin' around inside. Sat himself down by the window and picked up some newspaper, then he threw it down on the floor. I do believe, Pap, I do believe he pulled out Willie's little picture. I think he was studyin' it, like he wanted to really look at that little face..., when, Pap, a car pulled up just in front a' the house." She took a breath and held it for a few moments.

"Then do you know who got out?" She stared straight at Eustus. "It was Miss Alma, Mr. Hanny's wife. Her an' another man, a young one. They left the car a'runnin' and marched up onto that porch like they was bringin' a cake. Pap, I could hear Miss Alma from across the street. Ain't no other houses right close, so I guess she wasn't scared of callin' out like that, but she said, 'Come out here you cheap bast— Pap, she called him a lot of bad names, until the old man came out the door." Gertrude abruptly stopped and looked directly at the wooden cross mounted on the altar. "And that's when the angel came."

"What?" Eustus was plainly hanging on her every word now. "What did Miss Alma and the man do? What was they sayin'?"

"Pap, I don't know any more 'n that. Miss Alma was callin' him cheap, an' a liar, and that he owed her. But then the angel come, took my

238

hand, and told me I needed to come with her. An' I did. She walked me into town, singing a little song along the darkened streets so's I'd feel safe, an' then she left me. An' a little after that come that noise." Gertrude nodded to Eustus. "I know'd what it was... the kind you hear at huntin' season... from back behind me, Pap. Like it come from old Charlie's house, so I know'd she was lookin' after me—like she always did. Not wantin' me to be seein' things I shouldn't."

Eustus' eyes were riveted on her, trying to take in what she was saying. Then he shook his head slightly and smiled at what his daughter had just said. "Oh, 'like in she *always did*'? So you and this angel is acquainted before? I ain't never had the pleasure of seein' one."

"Oh, yes, you have, Pap. Didn't I say it? That angel who carried me away from ole Mr. Charlie's was one you seen all the time long ago. It was Mama, Pap. Lisbeth. Plain as day, she was…, sweet and strong. Had on her yellow dress, the pale one. Watchin' out for them she loves… like in as she always did."

Chapter 43

Gunther Huebsch slowed to a stop beside the woodsy expanse of Buena Vista fronting the road. He didn't immediately turn onto its dirt lane. Instead, he took in the Southern panorama of worn fencing, the knee-deep weeds that heaved in the wind, and a certain kind of quietness, that despite the unsettled weather, always seemed to be whispering secrets.

The sky was dark, and Gunther guessed the rumbling thunder in the distance meant he'd be sorry he hadn't waited a day or two to come. It was warmer than usual, but the air had turned heavy, and a ferocious breeze whipped the barren pecan branches back and forth as if to strip the last tenacious leaf. High in the trees, the foliage seemed hysterical, while lower branches shimmied in occasional bursts then sullenly sagged. Gunther absentmindedly wondered if scientists could somehow color wind according to its velocity and what a beautiful weave of aerial ribbons that would make.

Yet he had heard there was a hurricane off the Louisiana coast. The people in town were saying it had already formed into the widest and potentially most powerful in decades. "A real beaut," they called it. And though he had no experience with these kinds of cyclones, he doubted the storm, if it hit, would be about beauty.

The big gate to Buena Vista was open, which meant that Claire or someone else was on the land. Gunther let his car continue to idle in the middle of the road. He was hesitant, alright, scared, to drive onto her land after so many of Claire's refusals to meet with him. Yet he had some history he needed to set straight.

He sat in his car, moved it backward, then forward again. Maybe if he entered, he'd see a workman or someone on a bulldozer who'd forgotten to latch the gate. Maybe the wind had worked the lock free. No matter, he would stay but a moment he told himself, taking in, perhaps for the last time before he returned to Germany, the place his father had loved—and which a part of himself, he realized, did too. All Claire could do, if she were there, was tell him to leave.

Slowly bouncing along the entrance ruts, Gunther angled the car toward a stand of firs that would give onto the vista of the old ruin. Had Claire planted her arbors? Was the foundation poured? He had learned that the Southern way included not only a gentle meandering at getting to a point but sometimes extended to getting things done as well.

Gunther downshifted to first and eased the old Chevy around the grove of firs and a band of straw-colored grass. Almost immediately, he found himself staring across a tiny lawn at a wooden bungalow that seemed essentially complete. He pulled to a stop and caught his breath. He had no idea so much had changed since he had last been here. Gunther rested his forearms on the steering wheel. This then, would have been what his father had first seen—a charming house and a cottage just like these two structures. Simple, unadorned, and welcoming. The place in which his father's life would be changed.

Gunther got out of the car, only to have the door propel him back against the frame. The wind seemed to be tormenting the trees that now bowed over the cottage's roof. Overhead, the clouds were scrambled and so black the cottage seemed to disappear. But despite the deteriorating weather, Gunther felt the same exhilaration as when Claire had first brought him here. Again, it crossed his mind whether some undiscovered fragment of DNA, a genetic element yet unknown, could be transferred from generation to generation. Why else was his heart pounding and his breathing reduced to gasps? It wasn't just the wind. Nor simply the beauty of the property, or now, the idealized house come to life. There was something more.

All at once, a shaft of orange and yellow streaked across his visual field. Gunther ducked, knocking his head against the car's fender. The air was filled with leaves and airborne pine needles; loose pieces of bark were being lifted from trees, and occasionally a branch was torn loose. But this—this arrow—had been brilliant orange and sunlight yellow.

Gunther carefully stood up, letting his head peek over the top of the old Chevy. There in a tree thirty feet away was the "streak," now whipping back and forth, its cotton tatters impaled on the thorns of vines snaking around the tree. Its fabric was once a cluster of flowers but now only a burst of orange and yellow threads.

Gunther looked around, squinting toward the grove where the house was only a shadow in the unnatural darkness falling over the woods. There was movement on the porch. Coming from the house onto the porch, something moved, and then emerging from a kind of gloaming, there was a woman. Through the wind, he thought he heard her singing.

The woman stood by the door for a moment, the darkness from inside outlining her figure and the fragments of cloth that danced around her legs. She moved slowly, he could see, not bothered by the wind nor the roar that set the trees to a growling rubato. She made her way across the porch to where the swing was tied to its two supports and carefully undid them, letting her weight down onto the loosened swing.

Gunther didn't move. It was as if he were the audience at a play. He may have known the actor, but performers are capable of transforming themselves, taking on different parts, becoming someone else. Gunther's logic told him there could only be one woman on Buena Vista—and yet, nothing about this woman said "Claire."

Her hair had lifted into a kind of Medusan halo, its strands undulating as if each one wished to wrap around her neck, but the woman didn't push them away, because her hands were busy. Gunther saw her fingers working at her throat, then at her waist, and soon she had slipped off the light-colored bodice and pulled its skirt from around her hips. She lay back into the moving swing, a raft onto which she stretched, naked and white, and from which came the faint sound of her voice.

Gunther was perspiring heavily. He wanted to leave. He thought he may be sick. Asthma's triggers can be anything—anything stressful. But he had never seen anything so beautiful. The wind frightened him, and the sight of the woman in the swing paralyzed him. He wanted to see her face. Yet that too made him unable to move. He wanted it to be Claire—and yet he would weep if it were.

The woman had begun to sing more melodically now. Perhaps, with the wind, she was moaning; he couldn't tell. She let her hands run across her breasts and below her stomach, her legs falling open, one foot dragging against the porch's floor. There was a flash of lightning that startled her momentarily, and then she again began to croon, finding pleasure in what she did.

Gunther squatted down beside the car. God knew, something like this was not why he'd come. He had to leave somehow—through the trees—come back for the car. How to explain his car—how to get into town—storm on its way.

"You didn't have to park so far away." Her voice was lowered despite the raging wind. "It's alright, nobody else's here."

Gunther looked up, and she was looking down at him, a shadow of form and billowing hair against the blue-black sky. He could smell her scent; it emanated from her fingertips and made him hard as he knelt in the grass.

"You want it like always, the same way? Or you want it here, here in this here field? The rain's comin' soon. Gonna wash us down I reckon. Make us both wet."

She knelt before him and began to unbutton Gunther's shirt. He wasn't sure she recognized him. No, of course, not. This wasn't Claire. And yet when she leaned in to kiss him, the ridges and swells of her lips were the same, inviting, opening; her breasts freely falling against his chest. He reached his hand to stroke her hip as it turned to thigh and to soft pubis, his breathing suddenly deep and clear.

"We ain't got much time, honey. My little girl's comin' soon. You give me a ten-er, and I make you happy. Been visitin' her grandma at the Big House…, but she comin' back soon. I fixed her some cookies too. But I'll make it up to you next time, hear? You come anytime you want... next time."

Chapter 44

"*Weather patterns have been disrupted across the three-state area of Mississippi, Alabama, and southeastern Louisiana.*"

Hanny leaned down to turn up the radio's volume. "*Late season hurricanes historically have been among the most devastating, and if the one roaring up from the heated Gulf of Mexico continues its march to the northeast, even towns well inland will be heavily impacted.*"

He took a swig of coffee and glanced at the pine forest that bordered both sides of the road. The trees were young enough to bend, but the narrow trunks could take only so much before they would begin to snap. Hanny had seen it before. The not uncommon twisters that often occurred just before or after a late summer storm were responsible for dozens of tornado-belt deaths each year, particularly in rural areas where the fetch the wind traveled before destroying something had allowed the velocity to build. A hurricane added to the mix sent a shudder along his shoulders.

"*Residents should begin taking precautions for the arrival of a major autumn storm system out of Arkansas which, within the last hour, the radar shows converging with whatever Hurricane Ruby will be sending north. Ruby is at present a category four storm, with sustained winds up to 140 mph. It is strengthening....*"

Hanny switched off the radio and pulled into the 7-Eleven a few hundred yards before the entrance to Highway 15 going south. When he opened the car door, he was hit with a wall of moist air. Too heavy to lift itself he thought, much less the whirlwinds of quickie-mart debris that were popping up across the parking lot.

He could see the Tupelo locals rolling carts of bottled water and bags of charcoal to their cars. With their mouths set in the grim lines of people who had procrastinated throughout the summer, they were now seriously focused on gathering supplies for when the storm would knock out their power, and their well pumps go down.

Hanny wanted water too, but for someone he guessed wasn't paying much attention to the weather. He had called the bank looking for Claire, but only found Starlight manning the executive offices. She had been politely protective of Claire's whereabouts, as if Hanny were a magazine salesman or a bill collector, despite her "eternal gratitude to Mr. Meyers for all you a' done for Chauncey."

But in the end, Hanny's flattery, "We are so lucky to have at the bank someone who pays such excellent attention to their personal appearance as you do, Miss Washburn," pried loose the fact that Claire was temporarily camping at Buena Vista. Now he, like the others, would buy up the water and matches. And he would go get his daughter off that land. Away from Buena Vista and whatever kept her obsessed about a place that for him had meant only the termination of his dreams. No, Buena Vista was not a safe place to be during a storm, especially if it was your family.

Chapter 45

Louella Peters had gotten up from her desk and was staring out at the weather. The dirt of downtown Tilley seemed to be blowing away. And that was fine, let the hurricane or big-mother storm blow away all the crap the city's citizens tended to drop as soon as they'd peeled off a candy wrapper or finished a soda. Got no manners, most of 'em. Then she returned to her reception desk to wait for the Chief's coming rant—likely worse than any old' cane, she guessed.

She'd transferred the call to Grady from the FBI office in Jackson and since "hello" had heard the Chief's voice rising with each response. She wondered if his mother had spoiled him too much. He sure knew how to tantrum when things didn't go his way. And the explosion didn't take long.

"Well, shit!" Chief Grady Saunders stood up and kicked the leg of his desk. "Aw, shit!" Louella thought she saw a strong impulse to throw the receiver at his plastic-framed police academy diploma on the wall across the room.

"Whoever done screwed that up? Yeah? Well, I got me some ideas on that...." Grady continued to listen to the voice from the phone, his face alternating between burgundy and what a paint company might call Pissed-off White. "I ain't never heard a' such shitty police work. I have not! An' if it had been left to us, us piddly, poor 'local rednecks,' we would not, you hear me, we would not a' made such a head-fuckin' mistake!"

Grady rammed the receiver back into a cradle that had had its share of near crushings in the past, then stormed past Louella.

"We have reviewed the findings that we recently posted to you…," sang Grady in a prim falsetto. "And we have found that our previous pronouncements need clarification and revision."

He dangled his wrist and swung his hips toward Louella's desk. "We find that the fingerprints of the suspect, Jackson R. Perkins, accused in the murder of Senator Charles Elliston, while in fact are found on the outer tip of the barrel of the revolver, are not, I repeat, *not* found on the cylinder, the grip panels, the trigger guard, nor the trigger of the weapon that killed Senator Elliston."

Grady planted his fists on his hips and after a moment of thought, gave Louella's desk leg what looked like a drop kick. "Oh, the Feds gotta get in on this…, right? The Feds, and the State, and everybody else who ever picked up a gun. An' we here, poor old Muni's, we little police people, we just gotta go out an' tell everybody we got the wrong man. After everybody is feelin' all proud that we can do such fast work, and lookin' like the Tilley Municipal Police is more on top a' shit than anybody a thought…, and now, it looks like *we* just screwed it all the fuck up."

Grady sat down in a waiting room chair and put his head in his hands. "They say the prosecutors ain't gonna press murder charges on this whorehouse mogul… oh… even though he's lived around here from time to time. Oh, no, not enough evidence except that at some time he had his hand on the itsy-bitsy tip of the gun. But now the sons a' bitches say that the prints they tell us they *did* find, don't belong to no one they ever got a record of…, Ever! Son of a bitch!"

Louella got up and came around the desk. She went to the venetian blinds covering the front of the station's office and closed them. Then she went over to Grady, stood directly in front of him, and pulled him against her ample thighs and belly. And as he sometimes did when things were particularly galling, Grady laid his head against her and sobbed in professional frustration.

Chapter 46

Doreen sat erect in the waiting room of the Lafayette County Jail, making sure her back didn't touch the obviously compromised hygiene of the lined-up chairs. The Oxford FBI office housed its suspects in the "new" concrete cubes of a 1963 jail, having bulldozed the Victorian turrets and twirls of the old one. Doreen was sure she would have preferred the old treble mahogany moldings and drafty arched windows to the aqua linoleum and Lysoled hallways of this new rat warren of a facility. But she was not here to decorate she told herself. "Just avert your eyes and think of something porcelain." Then she revised that and decided to think of something damask instead.

Doreen had read the evidence against Jackson in the papers—the fingerprint evidence seemed particularly damning, but she didn't really believe Jackson was capable of the charges he was being held on. He didn't even know Charlie Elliston, if she was right. Whatever mix-up had gotten him here would be resolved soon enough. It was just a matter of getting the facts in order. And in the meantime, well, she was a business woman. As uncomfortable as it might be, she needed to ask Jackson about something that concerned her. How much of their little "ladies' relaxation enterprise" was now known to police? Did the books in Oxford and the books she kept in Tilley have overlapping entries? She felt sure Jackson wouldn't mind helping her stay safe.

"Doreen McCurdy. Are you here to see Prisoner #1475 A?" A voice through two very thick layers of glass called anonymously over a concealed microphone.

Doreen got up and went near the voice and the glass. "I don't have any idea what that means," said Doreen. "I'm here to see someone called Jackson Perkins."

The voice announced for the entire room to hear that Doreen had gotten lucky. "Up until this morning, that prisoner was bein' held on first degree murder charges and just walkin' in and talkin' to him wouldn't a' been possible. But he just got them charges taken off a' him, and you can see him today if you want to."

"Well, I do want to. That's what I came all the way from Tilley to do, isn't it?" Doreen used what she usually referred to as "high-speakin' English" to respond to the gatekeeper. She was in no mood to kowtow to a disembodied voice, after an hour in miserable weather on a highway with drivers all intent on getting somewhere before the storms struck.

"Sign here." The voice sounded chronically ill-tempered.

Doreen was ushered into a closet-like anteroom where the door behind her was clanged shut, and the one ahead remained locked. A woman in trousers came from behind an enclosure and demanded Doreen's purse, which was locked in a box. Then she was asked to permit a pat-down, a shoe search, and a rifling through her hair. The last request she emphatically declined, to which the guard shrugged her shoulders and casually opened the locked door.

Doreen could see other visitors sitting at what appeared to be a lunch counter, all leaning forward staring into TVs. The she realized the animation from the illuminated "screens" was actually made by men in incongruous outfits of green, black, and red stripes—candy colors worn by the black and white inmates of the jail. They were separated from their visitors by more thick glass, albeit with tiny metal grids through which they could talk.

Doreen was ushered to an empty chair, and after several minutes, on the other side of the divide, a tall, thin man was brought through the door by a jailer. Doreen blinked trying to decide if this were the right man. The sun-kissed curls were gone. Now Jackson's head was cropped close enough to display dozens of little moles and old scars. The bulk of his shoulders and chest seemed to have deflated, replaced by the slumped posture of someone who watched too much TV or who perhaps spent too much time deep in thought. Jackson no longer was the beautiful young man with whom she was in business.

"Well, hello there, handsome," she began.

Jackson looked up at her with a mixture of surprise, pleasure, and embarrassment. "I ain't never thought you'd be coming over here to see me, Miss Doreen. That's a long way for you to drive." Even his voice had reverted to some earlier time, she thought—before he owned a nice car, before he'd met Alma or her. Doreen was beginning to wish she hadn't come—or that her reasons for coming had been more Christian.

"Well, of course, I came, Jackson. After all, we did have something goin', didn't we?"

He interrupted her. "Miss Doreen, we don't want to talk about anything like that here. Everybody can hear everything…, and folks is always listenin'. That's how it is this side a' the glass."

"Right," said Doreen, glancing at her visiting neighbors and the open door behind Jackson. "Well, mostly I wanted to see how you're doin', if there's anything I can bring you. See 'bout your frame a' mind, a' course."

Jackson stared at her for a minute then threw his head back and laughed out loud. "My frame of mind is that easy street ain't that easy, Miss Doreen! An' like my mama said a long time ago…, you gotta pick your friends real careful."

"Well, that is true, Jackson. And I guess you are referring to me. Our… relationship, an' how it started an' all, well, I am not too proud of that."

"I'm not talkin' about you, Miss Doreen. Oh, no. You were straight with us from the beginnin'. An' I learned a lot about, well, a lot of things that if I'd a' handled it right, I could a' been a wealthy man. I could a' gotten real big…." Jackson ran his hand across his scalp.

"The other one. The sick one. That's a different story." He looked at Doreen carefully. "You know what the word "corruption" means? It's in the Bible. I looked it up. I been readin' the Bible every minute I can. That word, it's everywhere. An' I think it refers to what happened to me 'cause of her. I done got corrupt for sure."

"Well, I don't know exactly what happened after you and her come over here to Oxford to—" Doreen stopped, frightened that either she would say too much or Jackson was going to say something that would get him, and perhaps her, into even more trouble. Yet he seemed to have forgotten his own advice.

"It was bad. Once we come here, it wasn't just the regular services we was providin'—like the ones from Tilley—but the other ones once she got in charge. Men, women, all them machines she liked, the hollerin' and hurtin', but that ain't why I'm a' gonna go to hell." Jackson dropped his voice and pretended he was examining his fingernails, showing them to her in a pantomime for the jailers' benefit. Instead he whispered, "She got me all wrapped up in something worse."

Doreen sat back. She didn't want to know whatever it was Jackson had stumbled into. Hoped to hell it didn't involve her B & B. Wished to hell she'd never come over to Oxford today, but Jackson wasn't stopping.

'Bout that old man. She hated him, I guess. Said he'd gypped her outta money she'd earned...the hard way. She wanted him gone and didn't care how."

A guard stepped from behind the open door, speaking as if to his second-grade class that they had five minutes more.

Jackson turned his attention and Doreen's to his other hand's nailbed. "She knew I had this old antique of a gun, done dug it up out on Miss Scarlet's, Miss Claire's property. Just an old thing, didn't think it would even work. I was gonna sell it when I had the chance, but she knew I had it. An' she devised that we gonna..., we gonna take care of her ole Charlie."

Doreen put her hand out, worried now that Jackson was on the verge of a confession she didn't want to hear.

"...an' to tell the truth..., as corrupt a sinner as I now know I am..., we almost did. I almost did." Jackson's eyes were filled with tears but so wide now that they wouldn't fall.

Doreen felt shivers along her shoulders, afraid even to glance at the people beside her, sure she would be called to some courtroom to recount everything Jackson seemed intent on divulging.

"We went to where he lived, and she was in a terrible state, Miss Doreen. I ain't never seen nobody so filled with venom as she was that night. I'd wiped off that gun, didn't think there'd be a hint of a print nowhere. An' I put on gloves. She told me all the stuff I needed to do…, an' I just did it." A tear spilled along Jackson's cheek, and he stopped, took a breath and looked back at Doreen.

"Then we parked and went up on his porch. Jesus God! She was crazy…, a crazy woman, yellin' at him to open the door, yellin' at him when he come out on the porch."

Doreen dropped her head and stole a glimpse at the people on either side of her. They were laughing or crying with their inmates, making the most of the minutes they would be recalling for the next week or month. No one seemed to notice the confessional taking place a few feet away.

Jackson lowered his voice to a whisper. "…an' then she screamed at me, 'Shoot the bastard! Shoot the fuckin' cock-sucker!' all kinds a' things like that, but as deep as I was in to doin' what she told me…, I couldn't do it. I swear it, Miss Doreen. I couldn't shoot that ole man."

Jackson gave a kind of rueful laugh, one that seemed to say "and look what my up-standing decision got me." "She tried to take that gun herself, you know. I knew she'd be a' willin', if I weren't gonna do it. But I threw it. Threw it in the bushes somewhere and dragged that crazy woman out to the car where I'd parked it around the corner. Didn't nobody see all that had happened on that front porch under his big, ole light. But then, something that I don't understand happened. I been thinkin' and thinkin', and I can't figure it out. Just after I put her in the car, fixin' to come around and get in and drive us away…, I heard a gun go off. I heard a gun go off right back by ole man Charlie's house. I can't figure it out still."

Doreen sat silent, staring at the young man she'd solicited to help her earn some extra cash for fixing her windows. This boy, a young buck in the woods, a forestry student who could giggle and reel of the names of trees and flowers, who now sat before her in his "ring suit" of black and white stripes.

"I had to try to see what that shot was. Even though she was havin' a fit in the car and yellin' to get out an' all. But I drove back around the block right in front of the ole man's house, and there he was. Flat out on his face, half layin' down the steps a' the porch. Porch light on an' all, just like as if I'd a shot him myself. Just like she'd wanted it to be."

Jackson's round collar was dark with sweat when the jailer came to walk him back to his cell, and there were wet marks on the counter where his arms had been. He didn't say anything to Doreen as he turned to go, only mouthing the words, "Pray for me" before he disappeared into the bowels of the legal system that she guessed would keep digesting him until he was expelled as so much useless debris.

Along with the other visitors, Doreen got up and waited stiffly in the line for exiting. Mothers and wives, elderly fathers, and distracted children shifted from foot to foot, wiping at tears and glancing back at the empty chair where their loved one had sat moments before. Anniversaries, lonesome nights, stifling jobs, boring days, all had been compressed into inane comments about how bad was the food and Aunt Bess's stroke. Doreen couldn't think of what awaited Jackson. Bad food would be a distraction, but Alma's imprint wouldn't go away.

Chapter 47

Alma opened the door of her room and looked down the hallway, listening for a rustle or shuffled foot, a rattling of a newspaper perhaps, or Hanny's clearing his throat after a swallow of bourbon. It was still morning, but that could happen. This morning all she heard were the violent gusts that thrashed branches against the brick walls.

Yet inside, the big house smelled empty, the way still air settles along furniture and baseboards, no warm human organics to stir the dust or the floating motes. Alma was glad. She hadn't seen Hanny since she'd left Oxford and returned to Tupelo. She guessed he came and went somehow. Both of them must have retreated if they heard movement elsewhere in the house.

But she wasn't staying in her room this morning. Despite the weather warnings and prediction of tornados in the area and a hurricane heading north, she felt renewed. As if a page had turned. In fact, despite the weather she was driving down to Tilley to hand over to Doreen private contacts related to their "spa" venture. Over the weeks since Charlie's death and now with the abrupt shutdown of the Oxford "operation," she felt as if an invisible coat had been lifted from her shoulders. The changing of Charlie's will still made her furious, but Alma realized there was another will that she had an interest in. As Millie Sue had said, one closer to home. If she had the wits to wiggle away from an embarrassing business venture with Jackson, she also had the ability to come into a great deal of money right here.

She gazed at herself in the long mirror mounted in the hall. She looked particularly smart, she thought, in a suit that she'd received many compliments on from the women at church. Tailored, crisply beige, she'd attached a costume jewelry pin Charlie had given her to its lapel. She couldn't decide on a hat. Nobody was wearing hats anymore, but she hadn't been to the beauty parlor in the week she'd been back, and the hat could camouflage the lack of maintenance.

With another glance down the hall, Alma opened the door to Hanny's study. His aroma was thick—the mixture of aftershave, cigars, and dried alcohol left in empty glasses. Without wanting to, she stopped and filled her lungs with the fragrance of the man she'd lived in the same house with for over fifty years. She wondered if when either of them were dead, the other would sniff at the other's clothes and feel some emotion. She doubted any sentiment would be pleasant. She took another breath and mentally tried to change the subject.

But surprised, and in spite of herself, Alma felt it. The sensation that when she wasn't careful, began in her head and flooded the rest of her body. Something that came over her when she let herself think of Hanny. No—when she thought of the woman he'd never stop loving. She recognized it well. The kind of heating of her brain, the warm wash of red that she could feel spill across her forehead and down her neck. It was the same vague nausea she had when Charlie had taught her to do things, when he had done them to her. An intoxicating mixture—like soda pop mixed with a dreadful poison—something in the end, to which she'd become addicted and which produced a rage that seemed to emanate both toward and from her.

She had given in to that rage with Charlie, but this time would be different. Alma shook her head and straightened her suit, shifting her girdle at the waist. She deposited the small briefcase she was carrying at the door, crossed the rumpled oriental, and opened the second drawer on the left side of Hanny's desk. She rarely came into this room, and almost never to this side of the old oak antique he'd inherited from his father's defunct newspaper.

Alma looked into the drawer, filled with spools of tape, boxes of paper clips, and random pens and pencils all secured with rubber bands. She shoved them aside, feeling along the joins. Unused packs of 3x5 cards, the pair of scissors that had disappeared from the kitchen. His will was somewhere in here. The old fool never locked his cabinets or his drawers.

She let her eyes wander across the top of the desk. The usual—the same professional clutter that had been here since they moved in. Paperweight plaudits from the bank, a leather cylinder filled with more pens and letter openers, little statuettes and engraved plastic tributes for Hanny's community endeavors. And amidst the photos of Hanny at bankers' conferences and with politicians and investors, was a small photo. Was that something new? Something tucked away, she'd never seen? In an oval frame, as if shyly smiling from behind a picture of an out-of-office mayor, Alma was looking down at a photo of Claire Elliston—her snapshot taken in a leafy field.

Alma slowly withdrew her hand from the drawer. She felt as if she needed to urinate—as if her shriveled uterus had dropped. When was this deposited here? The wave of red passed over her again. Alma knocked aside the other photos as she reached for the small one with the image of a pretty girl with dark hair waving in a spring breeze. Then she sat down heavily in Hanny's chair as a clap of thunder trembled the window panes.

For the first time, Alma let herself picture Hanny and Claire. Not as father and daughter, for she felt sure he'd never known, much less engaged in, the insulting situations she'd accused him of in Charlie's living room.

Did he look at her, watch her, his mind filled with tenderness? What would that have been like? Hanny undressed, erect not with lust or perversion like Charlie, but with an actual physical yearning to share emotion? She pictured Hanny reaching out a loving hand, his face open, his soul visible. What would that have been like, if she had had it all these years? Alma found tears on her cheeks, shocked that she had so desperately wanted anything like that from him, aware that she had never been in the running, that he'd already loved someone else so deeply that he'd traded his soul for the sake of her. Not for Claire. For Lisbeth, of course. Again, Lisbeth.

Alma looked at the picture again. Odd that Claire's photo was in black and white. Alma pulled it closer, looking into the background at the trees and the hint of fence. Then she pulled off the velvet back of the frame and extracted the photograph. It had been cut with scissors from what appeared to be a magazine or a book. She turned it over and realized that on the back, the list of printed names and a corner of another photo marked this as a photo from a yearbook. She flipped it over again and sharply drew in her breath. This wasn't Claire Elliston. Not a recent photo at all. Not anything new. Just the same old knife, turning and turning in duplicate, she thought. Lisbeth. Priceless. The mother and the daughter. So much the same. As if they could be the same. With the same man loving them both.

Alma reached again into the drawer, this time, driving her hand below old receipts, a paid invoice for the new fence, and the folded will. She reached deeply into the recesses of the drawer until she found the gun. Maybe what she'd wanted all along.

It would have been so much better, if she hadn't relied on someone else for Charlie's death. Someone like the kid—Jackson-Who-Thinks-He's-a-Big-Shit! Alma laughed out loud. Everyone would be surprised she knew such words. "Jackson Big Shit! Jackson Big Shit and Hanford Fuck Himself!" She looked down at the photograph of Lisbeth, relishing the redness that each time flooded her.

She recognized the photograph now. It was taken by the snotnose school editor of the junior high party Charlie had held for students on the Big House front lawn. There had been badminton and horse shoes and balloon tosses where everyone got wet. She remembered because she had spent much of the afternoon talking and laughing with Hanny, the tall boy who delivered sundries for his dad. She'd liked him—maybe more than she liked what was going on with Charlie, but then, out of the blue, Charlie had joined the game of balloon toss. Everyone thought it was great fun—the esteemed Mr. Elliston throwing water balloons with the kids. One yellow sphere, Charlie had aimed at Alma; she could see it in his eyes. A look not of fun, but of ownership. When it hit her, the front of her blouse was immediately drenched, its thin cloth transparent and clinging. Charlie had rushed over, apologizing and putting a protective arm around her, walking Alma to the house, holding up a hand that prevented anyone else from coming to her aid. Alma had known what would follow inside the house, and so had Lisbeth, who stood beside

Hanny staring at her father with loathing. Yes, it must have been that day that the photograph was taken. Was that the day Hanny fell in love?

Alma laid the picture on the desk, carefully smoothing its edges. Then she laid the gun beside it. She took off her hat and set it, flowered-side out, on the desk. She was glad Charlie was gone. Glad her father and her mother were too. Looking back, she guessed they'd known. But you prioritize. Choose what's most easy to lose. Alma guessed they'd figured one way or another Charlie would win. Better keep your mouth shut and let the chips—and Alma—fall.

Undoing the top button of her suit jacket, she bent down and took off her shoes, placing them side by side under the desk. She was going to have taken all of the records of the Oxford operation over to Doreen. Doreen would know what to do with them. She was smart in her folksy way, and God knew she needed the money. Maybe Doreen would want to start over somewhere else. Start with the pathetic middle-aged women that Alma guessed would continue to wash up with their love-starved fantasies.

She took off her watch and re-did its latch. Then twisting her wedding ring round and round, forced it over her knuckle, pinching the flesh into a ruddy blue. She laid it inside the curve of her watch. It had never meant anything anyway.

Alma sat back in the chair for a moment, feeling its old leather give, liking its exhalation of years. Then she leaned forward, picked up the gun, and standing, pointed it down at the photograph. A smile wandered across her lips.

"You don't have to kill me, Sugar." Alma heard the taunt in Lisbeth's voice, hating the old name she'd sometimes called Alma.

"Why shouldn't I? Charlie, Hanny…, all I've ever had in my life is a 'second' from you. You always had 'em first. They all loved you first. You, sitting out there, the princess in the wood…. That's what some people called you…, others just called you dog-whore." Alma's voice was dreamy, yet she laughed at the insult she herself had started. "No, it's time you go, Lisbeth. Time you leave me alone…. An' I'll be sendin' your lover—your goddamned soul mate—that what you call each other? I'll be sendin' him right behind."

"No need, now. No need getting all worked up. We're still friends, Alma..., like when we were little. Like when we played. Like when you let me comb your hair..., and we played dress up with each other's pretty clothes."

Alma felt Lisbeth's hands and fingers stroking her arms as she looked up at her from the picture on the desk. Her voice was close by Alma's ear. *"Don't have to be all this upset now. We can be friends again. Let's forget about everything that happened... the old Charlies, the old Hannys..., anybody who come between us two best friends. All you got to do is come over here with me."*

Alma smiled at the photo. "Sounds nice."

"It is nice..., just like swimmin' in a lake for a bit..., and then we start all over..., nice and fresh and new. Lots a' love over here..., all clean, all clean and gentle...."

Alma took a breath, deep and slow. It was peaceful. Clean, gentle... a soft breeze that would always whisper....

Then she pointed the gun at the photo on the desk—and fired. And turning the gun, she did the same into the crisp, beige suit.

Chapter 48

Starlight Washburn had brought her tiny Walkman into the bank. She knew Miss Elliston would not have approved. Definitely would not have condoned the disco beats that were propelling Starlight's shoulders up and down and sending her new Afro curls into a springy reverb. But the bank was empty today. Most people were at home busy cleaning out basement spaces in case a twister approached. Others were cleaning out the shelves in groceries and mini-marts. Starlight was proud she'd decided to stay and keep the bank open. She'd used her executive authority, and it made her feel good.

"Granpap? You alright down there? Well, you go turn your radio on right this minute... an' keep it on! It gonna be bad, I jus' heard. Big tornados sighted just west a' Tilley, 'bout fifty miles, and a top a that there's a hurricane comin' up from the south. Where's Gertrude? All the little ones at school still?"

This was the third time Starlight had called Eustus this afternoon, but the first time he'd picked up. He had a tendency to turn off the radio and put on one of his beloved gospel records, unless he'd found a good religious station.

"No... no, I can't. For sure, I'd be comin' back now, if I could, but I can't close the bank and don't think I'd make it there by the time the weather let loose anyhow. You jus' make sure you stay outta the yard, now. And you take anybody who comes home in the safety of the bathroom, like we do..., ok?" Starlight looked out of the bank's plate glass window and could see that even up here in Tupelo, the sky was a swirling chocolate—loose, angry clouds that were being shredded as soon as they formed.

"One other thing, Granpap. I'm a little worried about Miss Claire. She's down there, you know. Over on Buena Vista…, on that land she's buildin' her house on. I ain't heard from her in a couple a' days. I'm sure she's alright, but you know…. Probably got herself all hunkered down in town somewhere. Anyway, Granpap, I'll call in a little while. Go turn on the radio."

***

Eustus lifted the needle off the record and sat for a moment listening now to the thrash of dry branches against the side of the house. Then he picked up the phone and called Gertrude.

"You hear about the weather? Well, alright then. All the others accounted for an' safe? I think it best you stay put with them two little fellas you sittin' for then. They mom and pa know they okay with you. Them people gotta basement, right? Well, you go down there, if the need come, you hear? Stay there till whatever comin' blows by. Alright…, alright…, I will. An' you too, my girl… my best big girl." He felt his throat tighten. "Gertrude… uh… well, you know I love you, don't ya? My best, my first… You make sure you is safe, now…. Keep a watch out…, keep you safe."

Eustus hung up. He should have told her he loved her again. A branch crashed hard against the house and made him jump. He thought Gertrude knew how he felt, but he should have told her again. Captions. Captions to life that help us remember what the moment meant. Then he got up, found his old rain jacket, and headed out to the Ford, now plastered with small pieces of his roof.

Chapter 49

The inside of the house was different from what Gunther expected. She had taken his hand and led him onto the porch, where, like a dog too long confined, the swing yanked dangerously back and forth. Then she pulled him inside, away from the noise and pelting leaves, and led him to a soft chair in thick green velvet— something of the kind he had seen in his grandparents' house.

In the shadows, she must have put on a pale dress and blotted the rain from her face. Then she knelt before Gunther to help him remove his sodden shirt. This she did silently, watching him as she pulled off his old sleeveless undergarment and handed him a cotton towel.

While the wind snarled against the windows, the woman rose and lit old kerosene lamps—fat glass bowls filled with liquid that wicked into rosy yellow flames. Shadows flickered against vertical wall panels, tiny ridges of wood running from the ceiling to the floor. The architecture wasn't changed a bit, thought Gunther. Nothing modern here. Just the way it must have been then.

"You seem different," she said, watching Gunther. She handed him a glass of amber alcohol, much the same color as the colored kerosene in the lamps, and sat down on the ottoman in front of him.

"And you do as well," he said.

"Well, your talk…, it's not like no one from around here, but it sounds like somebody who used to stay here. Long time ago. Where you from?"

262

Gunther thought he could smell the musty aroma of old wood, of old wall paper that must be in the tiny bedroom whose sagging bed he could just see. Even the patterned linoleum on the floor looked chipped and buckled. He examined the familiar face before him, the dark eyes and auburn hair, the pale skin that the lamp turned sienna. A figure he remembered from a photo, from a bank, and with his fingertips. "From the war," he said. "I come from Germany where there is a war going on."

She looked at him carefully, like a child who is asked a question by a grown-up but doesn't know the answer. "Did you know the other one, then? His name was Dee Dee; my big girl called him that, but I think it was Dee... Dee-ter. Quiet. He was a good man, I think. He talked like you."

"Yes, I knew him very well," said Gunther. He reached out and took both of her hands. "He spoke often of Gertrude."

The woman gasped, her eyes wide in the dark cottage. And then a smile that started with her lips parting and eyes filling with tears ended with a laugh of what Gunther thought was relief. She went on her knees and put her arms around his neck. "Did he know about Willy... his little boy?" She whispered it, her wishing it to be true coming in a burst of warmth against his ear.

"Yes, yes, he did. He never forgot Willy and never, ever Gertrude," said Gunther.

She sat back. Her back to the light, Gunther could only see her dark eyes moving back and forth, as if searching for a pattern in his features. "Do you know me?" he asked.

"You look like I seen you before," she said quietly. Lightning kept the sky alight now, and thunder rumbled constantly among the trees. "Did you come here before... for, you know, for... your fun." She seemed suddenly embarrassed.

"Before I say, tell me," said Gunther. "Did you ever go with Deiter? Did you give him some fun too?"

He might have struck her. She pulled back, and with her jaw set and brow lowered said, "I don't know who you are..., but you ain't got no manners. You ain't like him, who had some. Had him some fine manners, and proper." She got up and poured herself another drink from the glass bottle, setting it down as a clap of thunder cracked overhead.

"Dee-ter..." she said before swallowing. "He belonged to my daughter who loved him. They was like a husband and a wife. I would never a' gone, and he would never a' asked."

Gunther came over to her. "Then you see, when Deiter went away and had another child, another boy..., that boy and your younger daughter—the small one you're waiting to return here now—can't be what you call 'kin'."

She looked up at him as if he had handed her a physics theorem. He said, "Claire and Deiter's second son—his name is Gunther—are not related."

The woman repeated the word again, "Gunther." Turning away, she put down the small jar with the alcohol. He could feel her breathing where his hand touched her back, heaving and filled with tremors. Then she turned and looked at him with wide eyes, letting her hand graze his face, letting it sadly fall.

"A hundred men a' come here. Doin' what they want. Takin' it for the askin' an' a few dollars.... But I know'd only two men with any merit. One of 'em got drove away. An' the other..., he left me... to save me. Save me from the devil."

She slowly smiled at him, tears flowing freely along her cheeks. Then she whispered, "Devil get his due sometimes, don't he, mister."

With a feebly defiant shove, she pushed her hair away from her face, turned, and moved toward the door, pausing a moment with her fingers on its latch. Coming into the lamp light, she turned back toward him and with something resembling a smile said, "Good bye..., Gunther. I think you make three."

All at once a spectacular burst of lightning illuminated the cabin at the same instant that thunder seemed to tear apart the woods. Claire threw open the door and ran out into the pounding rain. She fell once in the muddy moat that had formed around the cabin, then she scrambled to her feet and disappeared into the darkness.

Gunther ran out behind her. "Claire! Claire! Stop! You will be hurt! Come back. Please, come back here!" He felt his feet go from beneath him, and pitching forward, his knees hit branches and dislodged stones. He couldn't see her anymore, couldn't hear above the ear-splitting roar in the trees overhead. All he could do was call for her, using the name he thought she might answer to, "Lisbeth! Come back, Lisbeth!"

Chapter 50

Hanny was amazed he hadn't driven off the road yet. All the way from Tupelo, the streets and highway had been littered with siding, shingles, gutters, clapboard, all impossible to see in the whiteout rain. He thought he'd clipped a car veering its way back onto the pavement, but he wasn't going to stop to find out. Bringing water to Claire wasn't just his objective anymore.

In the driving rain, he'd turned off the highway and headed through downtown Tilley. Here it seemed the top of the courthouse had lost a few hundred pounds of iron fretwork which now peppered its previously manicured lawn. The Piggly Wiggly's metal roof was turned up on one side, and already a few foolhardy employees were trying to stretch a wickedly-whipping tarp across a gaping hole.

The rain pounded from what seemed all sides as Hanny fought to keep the car on the right of the disappearing yellow line, which as he left town and made for the open fields, vanished altogether. Above the hammering rain, he heard sirens, but their sounds shifted constantly. Might be the wind, he guessed. Then somewhere up ahead, as Hanny turned onto the asphalt a few miles from Sully's Grocery Store, he thought he saw an accident—would be right up by Sully's in fact. There were enough flashing red and blue lights for it to be a bad one.

A policeman appeared from the darkness, blurred in the windshield by the torrents of rain, waving for Hanny to stop. The cop leaned in close and yelled, "Can't go farther… the grocery's been hit!"

Hanny rolled down his window, not caring about getting wet. "That you, Grady? What you talkin' about? Been hit? Hit by what?" Like needles, the rain came at his face.

"A tornado! There's a cluster of 'em. Done took out Sully's. I think all it ain't took is the big freezer ... and that's planted out in the lawn!" Hanny looked at him in disbelief. He guessed the Chief would have mentioned if any of the overweight grocery crowd had been hurt, but he wasn't sure. Hanny waved compliance, rolled up his window, and threw the Lincoln into reverse. Then he backed up, and jerking the wheel to the left, floored the car behind Grady and over the front yard of the one house at the intersection. Then he skidded onto the short road toward Buena Vista. "'Can't go farther,' my ass."

"...and in the area around Tilley, Mississippi, devastation continues to mount. Residents report at least four separate tornados have touched down. Telephone lines are out, and radar shows additional funnel clouds forming..., and all this with the forecast of ten inches of rain from Hurricane Ruby."

Hanny switched off the radio for the hundredth time. Better to try to concentrate on the road, hoping the gate to Buena Vista would be unlocked.

He drove like a broken-field runner, dodging branches when he could, using the constant lightning as a spotlight, and feeling the stomach-gripping revulsion of having done it all before. But this time he wouldn't run, he said out loud. "Let her be safe, Jesus, wherever the hell You are, just let her be safe."

The sound is what he first heard. *Gunfire*, he thought. *For Christ's sake, some crazy...* And then, the pellets increased. Thousands of balls, pelting the car like buckshot. The hail quickly became as big as walnuts, mounding on the windshield, stalling the wipers, and making driving impossible. Hanny pulled to a stop, trying to guess where he was. Where was the entrance to Buena Vista?

And through the rampage of hail, he heard another sound—one he couldn't identify at first. Perhaps, in the storm some dairyman's herd had gotten loose, their hooves now pounding toward him. Or was a plane coming down..., the bellowing roar of its jets beginning to shake the car? Then he knew.

Hanny opened the door and threw himself into a culvert beside the road, falling head first into what had become a churning river. Grabbing for anything he could, he wedged himself against the side of an outflow, only his head above the overflowing ditch when it hit.

He thought his eardrums had burst. Hanny squeezed his eyes shut, dirty water driven from above and below spilling into his mouth. His car shuddered a few feet away, and then as if it had been animated by a genie, its tail lifted and, before his eyes, the Lincoln swirled off the road and into the spinning vortex of trees and boards and pieces of lives of people he didn't know.

In the distance, he was sure he heard explosions—trees and light poles snapping or faraway transformers blown to smithereens. He didn't know how long he cowered shoulder-deep in the filthy drain. Minutes? An hour? The roar continued to recede in the rain, the sound of an angry lion growling away a swarm of bees, as the tornado sped east across half-harvested fields. And Hanny realized that the rush of water could kill him just as well as the wind.

He dragged himself across the flooded culvert, half submerged, continually losing his grip on roots that would give in to water, and finally pulled himself onto a slippery bank. Hanny had no idea where he was. Was it evening or still afternoon? The sky overhead was black and roiled, still in biblical disgorge. He looked at where he thought the tree line should be, expecting a suggestion of time, and instead saw the warmth of a flickering light, *As warm as firelight to a lonely traveler,* he thought. And then—

"Oh, my God." Hanny shoved himself up against a splintered oak. He could see it now. Across the field and through the silhouettes of flattened trees, the house at Buena Vista. It was burning brightly.

Chapter 51

From where he had fallen just beyond the porch, Gunther hadn't heard the crash—the shatter of glass on the wooden floor, nor the short whoosh as the kerosene's pool ignited across the floor. The wind had surged through the open door, carrying drapes and table linens, a bottle of whiskey, and the lamps before it, but he smelled the fire. Acrid and oily, the interior of the cabin was almost immediately ablaze with putrid black flames. Even the friendly velvet chair in which he'd just sat was outlined in orange.

Gunther staggered backwards, falling and catching his feet in thick pumpkin vines that waved like anemones in the darkness. Desperate to distance himself from the fire that was already beginning to chew around the windows, he ran toward the woods and the cemetery. He might have called again for Claire, but all he heard was his own weeping as he ran for cover through airborne embers popping from beneath the eaves.

And then a new sound. At first, he thought it was his own voice, a whining like a girl gagged and struggling, or perhaps a siren, police coming to set things right. But all at once, the keening was above him and around him, and the sound burst into an otherworldly roar. With a grinding that Gunther thought came from the gut of hell, the giant oak to his left seemed to erupt with an agonal moan. Lifted sideways, it was wrenched from the earth as a thousand ruptured roots snapped like fireworks. The winds wanted it—to carry it off in the cyclone along with houses and cars, but instead, the tree was left to thunder back into the earth, yards from where it had lived for one hundred years, its hidden parts now obscenely pointed skyward into the rain. Gunther dove beneath its trunk, digging in the mud like an insect for its hole. Maybe through the sacrifice of the tree he could survive.

And all the while the house burned. Generating its own maelstroms, white-yellow at the base, swirling reds roiling higher into the rain, its flaming parts were ripped off piece by piece to become flying missiles that landed in the forest and began tiny fires of their own. Cowering beneath the scabby trunk of the oak, Gunther now heard a tearing, a long slow wail; and leaning from under the tree, he watched the slow-motion levitation of the roof of the house. Burning from below, it was liberated and sent, a flaming discus, high into the trees.

The last thing he saw before the piece of spinning metal struck him was the shadow—a black outline of a woman on the porch—and the sensation of human movement in the field. He opened his mouth to call out, but he was interrupted, and Gunther didn't see anymore. The flaming wreckage of the roof had slammed into the smaller cottage— Gertrude's house—and now, joined, the fire blew into a secondary inferno. Yet, incongruously, of the main house, the tiny porch roof remained. Dismembered from the larger hipped covering and ablaze, it still stood, supporting its swing, a bizarre vestige of the charmed nostalgia Claire had meticulously conjured.

"Get out! Get off a' there!" Hanny ran though the field toward the blazing house that now filled the sky with billowing smoke. "Claire! For Christ's sake…"

Claire had sat down in the swing, her head turned toward the burning interior. Already little embers singed her dress, but she didn't move except to push herself slowly back and forth, an orchestra section spectator to Buena Vista's death.

Hanny half fell onto the porch. The heat from the flames was scorching, the steps immediately blistering his hands. "Get outta here… now! Claire, goddamnit, you're not gonna die here, too. Not like her!"

There was a sound of a siren, then another from somewhere beyond the woods, but all Hanny could hear was the wind-whipped roar of devoured wood and the groan of beams beginning to buckle. He pushed himself to his feet, his shoulders layered with burning embers, lungs aching with fatigue and smoke—and as he stood, so did Claire, slowly turning, and gazing at him for a moment like a visiting apparition, then she turned again and walked back inside the burning house.

Hanny gasped for breath; he couldn't be sure he had seen her move; the yellow heat of the fire was melting his eyes. Yet with everything left in the old man, but one who at last believed himself honorable, he went in after her—just as a father should.

***

"It all over…. It be all over now." Eustus knelt in the rain, running his fingers awkwardly, but gently, up and down Gunther's back. Behind him police radio voices called back and forth with varying levels of urgency, while the blue strobes of two police cars continued to rake back and forth through the woods. They would leave soon, with calls still coming in from dozens of catastrophes along the county's roads and neighborhoods.

A firetruck remained in the yard beside the blackened skeleton of the house; the cottage was nothing more than a charred slurry behind it. Sharing a pack of cigarettes, the firemen hadn't needed to use their precious water tank's contents, but only wearily waited now for the rain to do their work.

"You done a fine job, Doctor," said Eustus, needing to push himself out of the grass, but not sure his legs would let him. "You done everything possible a man can do." Eustus gave up the idea of standing and pushed his back against the oxygen backpack one of the fireman had dropped in the grass. Then, dripping water front and back, he pulled his old homburg low on his forehead and looked at Dr. Huebsch.

"My, my…. It's not every day you see the hand of the Lord. Not every day, such a raisin'. Mmm hmm. The Lord, He here. He be right close in this here pasture. I believe you become his Right Hand, Doctor."

Gunther sat with his arms on his knees, his head hanging between, and a blanket someone had thrown over his shoulders. His face was greasy and black from smoke, his eyes empty with the vacant look of a man just out of battle. One who had seen things he doesn't want to remember. The medics in the ambulance had bandaged his head and his

271

hands, burnt from ripping away the dress's fabric. He hadn't said a word since they took her away.

Slowly, Gunther looked up at Eustus. It was as if a movie had begun to play, frame by frame appearing, the order still not clear.

"Did everybody get out?" he asked. He looked innocent, Eustus thought, like a man who wasn't a participant; as if someone else had controlled events of which Gunther would only learn much later.

"Well, I think everybody who was supposed to..." he said cryptically, still not sure what the doctor was taking in.

"I think there might have been two women," said Gunther. "Two women and a man." He lifted his head toward the smoldering, sizzling ruin, his eyes searching for a recollection.

"Only one woman lived, son," said Eustus gently. He too turned his head toward Buena Vista's remnant, decades spinning backward and forward in his thoughts. Surely Lisbeth was gone..., and the devils who had visited here. He hoped any that had got away and sought somebody else had gotten burnt up too.

"How about the man?" asked Gunther.

"Well, that man is a' revelin' right now. Yes, I believe that I hear, even now, a trumpet soundin' on high for that man." Eustus smiled, leaned forward, and rubbed Gunther's shoulder. "You hear it, son? It is the Glory. The sound of Glory all over heaven this day. Let me tell you somethin'. We ain't all got us a straight path to the Almighty..., but when we makes a promise, when we stands by that promise, even if it costs us dearly, the Lord looks down, and He shouts for joy. He shouts that He got him an angel. An' I tell you, that today, Hanny Meyers be wearin' a halo."

Eustus's head wagged back and forth, his broad smile white neon in the fading embers. "Hanny shoved that girl out the window, Doctor. He couldn't carry her down, an' he couldn't get out himself, but savin' her be just what he wanted to do. Doin' what his "wife"—well, his ought-to-a-been wife—inspired him to do. An' I tell you, he where he wants to be today...."

Gunther heaved a sigh. Some pieces of what happened were coming back, others would fit themselves into place. He pitched himself up and held out his hand for Eustus. "Where did they take Claire?" he asked.

"Up the new hospital between here an' Titus. I still don't know how you breathed her back like that, Doc. She didn't look like she had any life…. I'd not have known there was any."

"I guess you could have said she technically did die, Reverend Pitts." Gunther linked his arm with Eustus' as they walked slowly toward a waiting police car.

"I thought she was dead too. Nothing to suggest she wasn't. And then, even while I was working over her, something changed. Not just that she started to breathe… but, well, I never felt it before. It was like someone else started breathing, someone who was younger and stronger. She was almost breathing life into me." A smile spread across his face. He turned to face Eustus and very politely, then very tenderly, he embraced the old man, nodding together their understanding. Now just the two of them left who had bid good-bye to Lisbeth.

"Maybe when Claire's all healed up, we'll come calling on you, Reverend. We'll see what spring is like. See how the new blossoms bud."

After

The soft music was the perfect touch, she thought, the glue that seemed to be holding the whole thing together—even if it was the strangest reception Doreen McCurdy had ever held at the B & B. But with magnolia buds bursting in the trees, the sky a cerulean hue, and a drowsy dose of April sun, she noted that both the white and the black invitees were finding common comfort in spring's arrival. She watched them sipping sweet tea, eating canapes, and sitting knee to knee, backs straight, gingerly registering that they all lived in the same town and had probably passed each other on the street.

"What a lovely setting you got here, Miss Doreen." Starlight Washburn put a dramatically manicured hand onto one of the wrought iron tables to steady herself. The patio's dome-topped bricks were playing havoc with her stilettos.

"Well, I do thank you for that," said Doreen. Claire had gone over the guest list with her at Doreen's request. "Always know who you're feedin' and what they like" was a hostess mantra she lived by.

"An' I understand there is some congratulatin' due to you, Miss Washburn. Miss Claire told me you've been promoted at the bank?"

Starlight locked her knees so she wouldn't topple and pulled her prim grey suit jacket back with a bracelet-covered wrist. "Well, that is all on account of Miss Claire, herself," said Starlight. Her hair, stretched into a discreet bun atop her head said, "propriety;" the saucy curl bouncing along the ski slope toward her breast said, "It's still me!"

"Because of the accident out there on Buena Vista, Miss Claire just told the board she knew it would be months before she could come back... and so... well, she said that the person who knew the bank the best was me! I done worked with her so long that I guess everybody come to think of me as the assistant. So now, well, glory be... I'm the assistant manager of the bank!"

A dark man wearing an olive-green suit with thin white lines stood up protectively behind Starlight. He was balancing a porcelain saucer filled with tiny edibles and held a demitasse of milky coffee in another hand sporting two large rings.

Doreen offered him a smile. "An' may I present my fiancé, Mr. Chauncey Groves," cooed Starlight. "We gonna be married in August." Her head tilted to one side like a little girl's, shooting Chauncey a glance of sheer devotion.

"Well, that's double congratulations, then..." said Doreen. "An' if y'all think you want a pretty reception, don't you forget about my place right here. You would be more than welcome. I'm right good at such things." Doreen patted Starlight's arm and marveled even as she said the words, that the two races were mixing on her terrace and that what she'd just said was genuinely meant. The times they are a-changin'.

Doreen peeked into the kitchen. Esperanza had most of her family members in there, plating or refilling the bowls of a half dozen salads. Her youngest sons, incongruously decked out like small mariachi singers, migrated among the guests serving finger foods she suspected they'd each tried a few of. All under control, she thought, unlike so much of what had happened the last year. Still this new normal was one she thought she was going to like.

"Doreen..., Doreen...." She turned, looking over the elegant floral headdresses of white women in pale colors and black women wearing blues, yellows and reds. *It's an arbor of softly burbling doves*, she thought, with the occasional squawk of amusement rising through the trees.

Gunther stood up and came toward her. He took her hand, and in a move Doreen doubted was one he performed in Germany, he bent at the waist and kissed her fingertips. She guessed he'd realized women went crazy for that continental stuff over here, and that out of courtesy or pity, he occasionally tossed them a European move.

275

"A beautiful reception in a wonderful setting, Doreen. You have outdone yourself, I assure you." Gunther had lost all of the weight he'd put on by dining at her place twice a week last year. She also knew he'd spent much time driving back and forth from Tilley to Atlanta where Claire had been recovering.

"Have you seen Reverend Pitts, Doreen? When does the ceremony start?"

Doreen laid a hand on his arm. "Now stay calm, Doctor. Everything is organized and you are not to worry. We leave for the church in half an hour. And Reverend Eustus Pitts? He likely is the one around who all them ladies is clustered. The Reverend does have charisma, an' that's all I got to say."

Doreen smiled as she looked out over the bobbing hats on the ladies and the men in suits attempting to eat dainty salads with delicate silver forks. Occasions like this were likely the only times even businessmen from Tupelo were forced to eat canapes and call it a meal. Still, it was good publicity. Doreen's newly printed business cards were in everybody's pockets, and Esperanza's oldest boy had tucked a paper menu behind the windshield wipers of every car: *"Delicacies by Doreen: Catered French and Southern Cuisine for Every Occasion."* Hell, you had to stay flexible. When one business goes down the tubes, start another. Even so, Doreen had to laugh. A good half dozen of the primly-coiffed women in white gloves and stockings had been her clients in the earlier incarnation.

In a way, she considered this reception a gift. From Mr. Hanford B. Meyers and from Claire. Because Hanny was known and respected all over central Mississippi, many of his colleagues and old friends had come down for this, his second funeral. The official good-bye had taken place months ago in Tupelo, but Claire had been unable to attend. Now, as his only surviving relative—as he had stipulated in his will—she had called on Eustus to hold a second memorial service.

Doreen led Gunther over to the group ringing Eustus, where both white and black guests were listening raptly to what seemed to be a homily or a parable delivered from a hill. They were alternately laughing and shaking their heads, and Doreen heard one white elder from the Lutheran Church mutter, "Praise Jesus" as he lifted his hand skyward.

Catching each other's eye, apparently the old preacher and Gunther exchanged a kind of code, for quickly Eustus brought his message to a finale with a charming joke that left each of his listeners wishing their own pastors were half as mesmerizing. Then Eustus signaled to Gertrude who stood waiting for him on the B & B steps.

"We'll be right along," said Gunther, giving Gertrude a little hug. "I will bring your sister."

***

The last chords of the piano faded as the mourners filed from the sanctuary of Tilley's Zion Top Baptist Church. Keeping the service short, Eustus blessed the remains sitting before him and blessed the congregation, thanking them for keeping the memory of the departed in their hearts. In his black gown, he stood quietly at the pulpit, without going into touching moments from the past, nor calling upon others to stand and testify as to how their lives had been changed by the deceased. Those things were private. More so because they touched him and those he loved.

And then they filed out, Eustus leading the congregation, making his way slowly down the church steps and around its corner to the back plot—the little cemetery where a hundred souls had been laid to rest. Floene lay here; Willie Mae Johnson; Isaiah Trumble; Hattie Buford; Old Sam, who seemed to have had no last name; Sarah, Eustus' own mother—and little Wilhelm Pitts. Most laid to rest in the church grounds before the "coloreds" of Tilley had even had half a town cemetery. But not all.

Now there was a newly opened grave. Next to it, a small lectern had been placed, and beside it under a little tent, were chairs. Gertrude sat in one. Gunther in another. And beside him, was Claire's wheelchair.

Gunther kept his hand stretched over hers. Once or twice he adjusted the light blanket that lay over her damaged legs. Mostly, Claire remained impassive, the tight scars along the right side of her face seeming to freeze it in place. But now and again when Gunther slipped an arm around her shoulders, she would turn to him, and her left side would light up with tenderness. The outward signs of beauty had been replaced with something else, something unconstrained by face or figure. Claire was openly and proudly in love; a woman come into her own with no ambivalence left.

"...And when the Lord looked upon the land, He saw in doubles. Doubles of cows, doubles of fish. He saw in pairs. Pairs of birds, pairs of dogs, pairs of people. But unlike the beasts of His Kingdom, He gave unto these creatures called people a special ingredient, a special glue that binds 'em. And not one thing can pull these people apart. Oh, the earthly life tries to do it. It presents these people with war, with arguin', with greediness, and... and in the end, with death. But them who's got the glue ingredient called Love, is not gonna part from one another... not ever... not never... not by way of the Devil... nor by way of his sin." Eustus' voice was filled with tears, but he continued.

"There once was a pairing. A fine pairing it was. Made in Heaven with God's own seal. It had in it a Mama and a Pap, and one day there come a little brown baby. All made in Heaven, mind you... not a' this here earth. But that don't make no never mind. Heaven-made is all that counts. An' then that Pap was forced away, an' another Pap, a godly man, come to help that there grievin' wife. But mind you, those first blessed bonds didn't get broke. Well, this new godly man an' her got blessed by the Lord as well. A new pairing did get formed... an' a beautiful little baby come. An' those bonds too, of a sorrowful woman and an honorable man... they last too... they last... into Death... and beyond it." Eustus gripped the lectern and lowered his head. When he lifted it, his voice was strong.

"An' that is why, Hanford Meyers and Lisbeth Elliston is gonna lie together. They be married in Heaven, so why not let 'em lie together on this here earth. Let 'em sleep side by side, in holy dirt right here 'long side this humble little church. Let 'em be safe among folks they cared for an' saved and who cared for them."

And with that, Lisbeth's coffin was lowered into the grave, and near where her heart would be, Eustus placed Hanny's urn of ashes. "The two people who meant most to me, 'cept one." said Eustus.

Then he slowly turned to Claire and to Gertrude, handing them each a pinch of dirt, saying, "Now girls, go say good-bye to your mother and to a man who loved you. Lisbeth is free now. You set her free, and she done let you go." Eustus' eyes lingered on each of them.

"Elliston women. Elliston women…" He slowly shook his head. "I been proud to know each one a' you. Some a' you got scars on their body, yes…, an' some a' had scars 'round their heart. But scars heal, don't they? And scars fade away to pale little memories. So go sprinkle that dirt, girls, and plant you a new life. It time for your own stories to start beginnin' and to bloom."

About the Author

Marina Brown was born in Indianapolis. She has written for newspapers and magazines for the last twenty years: *St. Petersburg Times, Tallahassee Democrat, Florida Design, Dance Magazine, Tallahassee Magazine*, and *Sailing Magazine* among them. She is the recipient of numerous writing awards, including First Places in the Porter Fleming Short Story Contest, Second Place in the Lorian Hemingway Contest for Short Stories, First Place in the Red Hills Poetry Contest, and the 2013 Florida Authors and Publishers Gold Medal Award in Adult Fiction for her debut novel, *Land Without Mirrors*.

Marina is a former ballet dancer, a sailor, figurative watercolorist, and cellist. She lives in Tallahassee, Florida.